Also by Alba de Cespedes

NEVER TURN BACK

THE SECRET

THE BEST OF HUSBANDS

REMORSE

LA
BAMBOLONA

by Alba de Cespedes

Translated from the Italian by
ISABEL QUIGLEY

Simon and Schuster • New York

First Printing

SBN 671-20377-0
Library of Congress Catalog Card Number: 76-101869
Designed by Mike Shenon
Manufactured in the United States of America
By American Book–Stratford Press, Inc.

LA BAMBOLONA

Giulio was not used to finding himself in the street at that time of day. He had figured that the meeting would be over at about eight; instead the builder had accepted his terms immediately, and by seven he was free, with the check in his wallet. As a rule he spent the whole afternoon at the office, and the light from his desk lamp kept him from noticing that in Rome at the end of May darkness fell very late. Now he realized that he had been wrong in sending his secretary home earlier than usual to make up for the evenings he had kept her working late. Since he had been sure that he would be arguing with Amati for a good while, and would not be going back, he had left his assistant exact instructions, being afraid, as usual, that something might happen while he was away.

Nothing ever happened. Angeletti was scrupulously careful. "He's no marvel, but I can trust him," Giulio said to himself and, to avoid the temptation of going back to the office, started walking along Via Po. It used to be an elegant street, and now it's just the main road of a lower-middle, white-collar district. The neon lights were dazzling and the showy window of a boutique stood beside that of a delicatessen, full of dried cod. It was Friday: a day of abstinence. Some people still bother about such things, he thought. Friday, the twenty-seventh: the people crowding the pavements on that mild spring evening looked satisfied. Thanks to his unexpected freedom, to the season—and to the check handed over a little earlier—Giulio felt positively euphoric. He lingered at the gay, glittering shop windows, as if it were just before Christmas or Epiphany, and nearly bought a sports jacket. He almost went into a grocer's to buy provisions that, since he lived alone and never dined at home in the evening, and for lunch had just a green salad and cheese, would have been useless. Finally he gave up the idea of shopping and went into a bar for an espresso.

There, the gaiety continued among the brightly colored boxes of chocolates and mass-produced china pots with gaudy bows on top. Giulio drank his coffee, wondering: "What shall I do?" He would not be picking Sylvia up before nine o'clock; every evening she went to the hairdresser, and stayed until about that time. He did not feel like going home; an already summery languor had come over him. He felt as if he were in one of those small provincial towns he sometimes went to on business, where, in the evening, he could enjoy the films that women never wanted to see. When their affair was over, Marité had told him: "I've had to sit through over fifty westerns to end up like this." He bought cigarettes, then went to the telephone, hoping to find out that something had happened at the office, and to tell Angeletti, who had always been opposed to this business: "I've already finished and I've got the check in my pocket."

8

The telephone was being used; from a kind of shelter made out of a pile of cracker boxes poked a large dark head. Giulio walked up and down impatiently, cursing the Romans' lack of consideration in chatting for hours on a public telephone, then went round the wall of boxes to glare at the speaker. But the girl turned slowly to the wall, avoiding his eye, and continued talking.

Not very young, Giulio thought. The fullness of her hips was out of proportion to her middling height and slim waist, and the tight-skirted dress accentuated her round buttocks in an unbecoming way. The girl went on imperturbably, although another man went up to her trying to make her realize the urgency of his claim. "Oh no," Giulio said to himself. "When she's finished, I'm next!" But he felt calmer: in fact, as he gazed at the soft flesh outlined by the pale fabric, his irritation vanished.

Uncomfortable in her patent-leather shoes, the girl let the weight of her body fall first on one foot, then on the other; and the way she moved her hips gave Giulio a sexual pang. A third customer complained to the cashier, who said loudly: "Hey, miss . . ." with no result. People were now making remarks: "It's a disgrace, they ought to have time checks, what does she think she's doing, you'd think she was talking at home." Still facing the wall, the girl kept agreeing with the invisible speaker on the other end, nodding over and over again but in a way that spared her hairdo. A little later she hung up calmly—as if she had no idea of the fuss going on around her—and turned.

She was very young: her face was round, her forehead hidden under a heavy lock of black hair, and her bosom was large and tremulous under the high-necked dress. She had a childish air that contrasted with her figure, and large, staring, doll-like eyes. For a moment she frowned and stared at him as if she was aware of the insolence of his expression and his thoughts. Then she went proudly to the door and walked out, turning right.

"Maybe she stayed on the telephone out of spite," Giulio said to himself as he followed her from a short distance. "To provoke me." She was walking ahead without turning: her tight skirt and over-high heels prevented her hurrying.

Outside a shop window she stopped and, taking a small plump foot out of its shoe, started rubbing it against the other leg. Giulio had come up so close to her that he could hear her breathing, or perhaps it was just her breasts rising under the dress that gave him this impression. He wanted to say something, but what? They were outside a butcher's shop window, in which cuts of beef were displayed on a marble slab. What could he say, facing that red meat, with its waxy fat, and the blood clotted in the enamel basin? Could he say: "Do you like meat, signorina?" He tried to smile, imagining an approach like that, but could not. "Do you like meat?" he repeated to himself. Meanwhile she had begun walking again and he was following her.

"She's seen me following: that's what matters." At least that was what he had thought when, as a boy, he had followed women in the streets. He had not done it since. Even in those days anything he planned to say seemed silly, the kind of thing to make a woman laugh in his face. Sometimes, hesitating over what to say, he would follow an unknown woman to the end of some outlying district, and just as he was nervously going to speak out—or at least thought he was—the woman would vanish through a doorway and that would be that. It was wartime, there was no transportation, so he had to walk home and got in very late. His mother would be waiting for him, in tears. "They must have caught him," she kept saying to her husband. "They've caught him, I can feel it." One evening he came back exhausted, having walked right through the cardboard soles of his shoes; to avoid being scolded he told them that the Germans had actually picked him up and had kept him for over two hours. His father laid a hand on his arm and said: "It's my fault." He answered: "What's it got to do with you?" "It has got something to do with me," said his father, sighing. "But one day you'll realize I was right." Their old manservant dried Giulio's feet; they fed him things it was then quite impossible to buy, which they had stored for special occasions, and put him to bed with a hot water bottle.

But at his age it was absurd for his heart to beat faster because he was following a woman. "In any case, this is a perfectly ordinary girl. . . . Why don't I approach her? What am I scared of?" He remembered a blonde in those early days who, tired of hearing herself followed, stopped suddenly and said: "Well, come on, talk!" He had nearly tripped over her: "I'm sorry, I'm sorry," he had stammered, and dashed away, with a scarlet face. Some evenings, though, things went well: he managed to get through the doorway behind the woman. The first time he had made love, at fifteen, it had been with one of those unknown women, between one floor and the next, on a half-lit staircase.

In the twilight the girl's dress turned pale, as that of the first woman he had possessed had done in the light of the torch painted blue because of the blackout. He no longer knew whether he was following the memory or this plump, rather common girl. Yet in the shadowy stretches between the street-lamps, he felt that there was an understanding between that body and his; that, through her obstinate indifference, she was in fact drawing him on. Suddenly he caught up with her and asked quickly: "Excuse me, may I walk with you?"

The girl stared at him without answering. Her mouth was large and fleshy; her skin, milky white. With a grimace, she turned her back on him and continued walking.

So they reached the traffic lights of Via Nomentana, the girl ahead and Giulio behind her. Soon she'll arrive and go into a doorway, he thought. The lights changed to green and they crossed. Giulio, seeing the girl stumble as she stepped on the pavement, tried to help her. But she wrenched her arm rudely away and said: "Mind your own business, will you? Get away from me!" A voice like her hips, like the knees that showed below the short skirt.

Undeterred, indeed desiring her more and more, he followed her into a small tree-lined street, between low modest houses. There was a scent of oleander. ("How many years since I smelled it? The real smell of summer.") When he saw the girl going up to a small gate he stopped in front of her firmly: "Signorina, listen . . ."

"Get away from me, I said!" she interrupted, glaring at his effort to take hold of her wrist. "Stop it, or I'll call the police!"

From the half-open gate, Giulio stood gazing at the small building beyond a graveled garden, into which the girl had disappeared. A short flight of steps outside, vaguely meant to be decorative, led to the door she had unlocked and then slammed angrily.

Ignoring her hostility, Giulio went into the garden. Maybe she lives alone, maybe she's waiting for the man she was talking to on the telephone, he thought. At the side of the building, the small door opened on to a poorly lit staircase. "If anyone goes by they'll think I'm a burglar. I'll say I don't feel well and came in for a rest." He really did feel unwell, confused by the desire that pinned him there against the low garden wall, which bristled with climbing roses. "Sylvia must have called me up at home several times by now." It was past nine. He decided to stay a few minutes longer before rushing to Via Po to get his car and go to her, without changing.

A woman came in with a small child who jumped on the gravel with his feet together, counting: "One, two, three . . ." The woman scolded him feebly: "Calm down . . ." They passed without seeing him. He breathed again. But he was wondering if the girl might have left the door on the latch, if she might be expecting him: he could have sworn that a gleam of light was coming out from the slightly open door. Perhaps it was the glow from the streetlamp, filtering in through the trees: all the same, he had to find out. "I'll pretend I'm looking for someone, any name will do . . . Angeletti, that's fine." He also thought: "Don't do it, you'll only get into trouble," but the ordinariness of the house seemed to guarantee mildness and submissiveness. He imagined Sylvia ready to go out, nervously dialing his number, her bracelets jingling. "Never mind," he said to himself, resigned to the inertia that had made him follow the girl when he left the bar, afraid he would not distinguish her in the crowd, afraid he would lose sight of her before he found out who she was and where she lived.

When he was on the landing, in the open, he saw that the door was shut: on one side of it was a brass plate with ornate engraving on it: *Accountant Rosario Scarapecchia.*

Her father, he thought, or else her brother. He thought also, her husband, but such heavy flesh in so young a girl clearly suggested virginity, even more than the surprise in her huge black eyes. So did her way of walking, painfully, legs together. "I'll ring, and if she opens the door I'll make her make a date with me. Otherwise I'll ask for the accountant, and get into the house somehow with some excuse. Then I'll say it's a mistake, a namesake. . . . With such a surname?" he wondered, but he had already pressed the bell.

A small thin woman in a long, flowered, cotton housecoat and a sweater came to open it; her grayish hair was in a roll round her head. She wore the kind of crescent spectacles that are only for close work. When she saw him she poked her head forward a little and looked up at him over the top of her glasses. "Who do you want?" she asked.

Behind her, the large living room was empty, the television off. Presumably there was no one else at home, except the girl.

"Mr. Scarapecchia?"

"He's not here," the woman answered, and seeing him hesitate, she explained: "He's not back yet, try later . . ."

Politely but firmly Giulio said: "I'd rather wait."

"Are you from the co-op?" she asked him suspiciously: "If you are, they already bothered my husband about it, yesterday evening."

Unwillingly she let him in, indicated a cane armchair, and went back into the kitchen, out of which came an appetizing smell. Giulio heard her mutter: "There's a man who wants to see Papa."

Giulio looked around, searching for an excuse to see the girl again. He noticed a divan, covered in shiny light-blue material and protected by a plastic cover, which contrasted with the rest of the furniture—if this conglomeration of shabby, useful objects could be called furniture. Maybe the girl slept there, close to the front door, and Scarapecchia was a permissive parent; maybe he was the sort whose daughter was a source of income. But this idea implied no moral judgment; it was not in Giulio's nature ever to condemn what might be to his own advantage.

On one of the walls hung a number of photographs, conspicuous among them that of a dark young man in an army uniform: maybe a member of the family lost in the Russian snows or the African desert, and now a symbol of the family's military glory. Since the mistress of the house gave him time to do so, Giulio would have liked to continue looking around, and find a portrait that might be that of the unknown accountant, who might be a civil servant or else bookkeeper in a private firm; but his eyes kept straying back to the divan.

The kitchen door opened and again only the mother came in. She had taken off her glasses and was twirling them in her hand, in a submissive gesture.

"I'm sorry, the buses are crowded at this hour and the traffic's heavy. . . . He leaves at eight, but sometimes stops to look at television in a bar in Piazza Buenos Aires. They have the second channel there." Then she went on: "If you're from the co-op, you really must understand that my husband's got nothing to do with it."

Giulio hastened to say he knew nothing about the co-op, that he had come for quite another reason.

"Can you tell me what it's about? After all, my husband has no secrets from me."

"I assure you it's not bad news. On the contrary," said Giulio. He was no longer thinking of the girl; he sincerely wanted to reassure this little woman who smelled of cooking.

She sighed with relief. "Ivana," she called loudly. "That's my daughter," she explained smiling and called again: "Ivana!"

The girl peeped in, waiting for an order, a job to do, so that she could disappear again.

"Come in," said her mother, reassuring her. "It really seems this gentleman's not from the co-op . . ."

Ivana had put on a childish pink-and-white-checked smock that made her figure seem even more provocative. She came forward reluctantly, avoiding Giulio's eyes.

"In fact, it looks as if he's brought good news," the woman went on. Disappointed by her daughter's silence she added: "Haven't you got anything to say?"

"It's probably an unimportant bit of news. It depends on how you look at it," said Giulio with a suitably modest smile, tinged with melancholy.

"Is it something about money?" asked the mother, and when he said no, she said, "Ah," as if disappointed.

Giulio turned to the girl, hoping to discover what she did with herself. "And does this young lady have a job?"

"She's seventeen. Everyone thinks she's older because she's very well developed. She gets that from my mother-in-law," her mother explained. "She's taking a course in shorthand and typing, four hours a day. She's just come home. I'm afraid there are too many shorthand typists already. Do you think she'll manage to get ahead?"

"I have no doubt she will," said Giulio meaningfully. "If she wants to . . ."

In spite of the desire that dazed him, a twinge of caution warned him not to go too far; he realized he was slithering down a slope, and would reach the bottom, but there he would find Ivana's body: he would be able to touch it.

"What do you want from my father?" the girl asked him. "What do you want to say to him?" The intensity of her gaze, which was hard and forbidding, made her seem slightly cross-eyed.

She was afraid. Giulio had no idea of what, nor did he want to know; so long as she didn't tell her mother that he had followed her to pull a fast one on her, and was now trying to pull a fast one on her mother.

"Excuse me but that's my business," he replied.

At that moment they heard the lock click and Ivana's mother said, "Here he is," as a short, thick-set man came in, carrying a bulky package under his arm. "Rosario, here's a gentleman waiting to see you," she said. "He's not from the co-op," she added, seeing him pause. "It's got nothing to do with that. In fact, he says he's come about something nice." Then she called her daughter and they left Giulio alone with him.

Giulio had risen and was smiling, carefully relaxed. He wanted to look at Ivana once more, but Scarapecchia, having put down the package, came over quickly and introduced himself.

"Scarapecchia. At your service."

Scared by the bald little man who was staring at him with lively round eyes, Giulio dared not give a false name, as he had meant to do. "Broggini," he said, holding out his hand, which Scarapecchia shook cautiously: "I'm a lawyer."

Scarapecchia pointed to the armchair: "Please sit down. I'd rather stand. Go ahead."

Under the peremptory gaze of Scarapecchia, who naturally was determined to discover why he was in the house, Giulio began uncertainly: "As I told the signora . . . that is, I really didn't tell her anything, but actually . . . what I have come about is a survey."

"A survey?" Scarapecchia disliked the word and turned frowningly to the kitchen, as if his wife had allowed him to fall into a trap.

"Exactly: a newspaper survey. A referendum, let's say." Pleased with this helpful idea, Giulio went on: "We're collecting information for a weekly review . . ."

"Will you kindly tell me whether you're a lawyer or a journalist," Scarapecchia interrupted coldly.

"Well, in the group I represent, which is finding out about opinions . . ."

"I have no opinions. And if I had I wouldn't tell you about them. Besides, I don't like either lawyers or journalists," said Scarapecchia. The gesture with which he buttoned his jacket over his stomach was a dismissal.

All hope of seeing Ivana again that evening seemed lost, and if he was thrown out he would never have a chance of seeing her in the future.

The thought made Giulio get up resolutely and go over to Scarapecchia. "I'd rather tell you the truth," he said. "The survey, or referendum, the inquiry—that was all an excuse."

"Don't worry, I realized that," replied Scarapecchia with a small spiteful laugh. "What is it, then?"

"It's about your daughter."

"My daughter?" repeated Scarapecchia glowering. "How does my daughter come into it?"

"I've come to ask your permission to visit her. You'll think me old-fashioned . . . it's true: I don't agree with present-day customs, in these matters."

"But where did you meet my daughter? Adelina!"

"It's in no way your wife's fault."

"I should hope so! But I'm sure she's listening at the door. This way at least she can sit down."

Signora Adelina came in at once, apologizing to her husband: "When he said he wasn't from the co-op I felt so relieved I didn't worry about anything else. But I didn't leave Ivana for a minute, I swear. I was here, she was there," and she indicated the chairs. "I never moved."

Scarapecchia shut her up and turned to Giulio: "I repeat: where and when did you meet Ivana?"

"I haven't met her. I saw her in the street, I followed her for quite a way, and in the end I asked if I could walk along with her."

"So you think my daughter's the sort of girl to pick up in the street?"

"Young people . . ." said signora Adelina soothingly.

"No," answered Giulio. "Certainly not. In fact she didn't answer me. She didn't even look at me: she went on walking, coldly, and I followed."

"She was wearing her light blue dress, wasn't she?" said signora Adelina.

"I never noticed her dress. What struck me was her candid expression, her ingenuous eyes, which you don't find in girls nowadays. When we got here I spoke to her again, and again she snubbed me. Maybe you won't believe me, but I wasn't sorry: maybe that was why I stayed. I was—how can I put it?—I was under a spell. There are women who—to speak frankly—you try it out on and then, if there's nothing doing, forget about: there's plenty more of them. But with her, I just couldn't get away. I didn't even know who she was. . . . I read the name on the door when I'd already rung the bell."

"Tell me the truth: you hoped to find her alone."

"Rosario, why do you insinuate such a thing?" said his wife reproachfully.

"Perhaps," Giulio admitted. "All right, I'll admit it. But when I saw the signora I could have said, 'Sorry, wrong door,' and tomorrow I could have waited for your daughter in the street or sent her a note. Instead, I behaved openly."

"What about the inquiry, the survey, then?" said Scarapecchia.

Giulio spread out his arms and confessed: "Shyness."

Ivana's mother looked kindly at him. "I knew at once that he hadn't come here with any wrong ideas."

Her silly tone annoyed him. "I didn't know what my own ideas were. To be quite honest, I still don't know. But I feel this meeting wasn't just any meeting. And so," he concluded persuasively, "I'd like to come and call on signorina Ivana, if you'd allow it—not every day, but at least sometimes. I'm not asking to take her out, because I don't know what your customs are."

"I was born at Catanzaro," said the accountant. "And besides, I know what men are like. So you can imagine whether . . . What did you say your name was?"

"Broggini, Giulio Broggini." He took out his wallet. "I'm sorry, I haven't got a card."

"It doesn't matter," said Ivana's mother, smiling, "among nice people."

Scarapecchia went on. "What is your profession?"

"I work in the office of a lawyer called Angeletti."

"You're a bachelor, aren't you?" signora Adelina asked shyly. "Do you live with your family?"

"I have no family," Giulio sighed and saw her gazing at him in stern surprise when he said: "I'm an orphan."

After a respectful silence Scarapecchia went on: "So you live alone."

"Well, yes. I mean, my boss allows me to live in the office." He was not going to give Scarapecchia his address, because he hoped to meet Ivana secretly; in any case, his home address was not in the telephone book. "Rents are high, and anyone who wants to save . . . I haven't even got a car," he added, thinking this would reassure them further. "Now I've told you everything. It's your turn."

Scarapecchia waited for a moment, puzzled; then he called, "Ivana!"

Giulio turned to the door: not only was he going to see her again, but her father had called her in specially on his account.

The girl came in looking down, embarrassed. Her strong firm body made it impossible for her to move casually.

"Ivana, this gentleman has confessed that he followed you in the street, and I've nothing but praise for the way you behaved," her father said in a rather solemn tone. "Mr. Broggini," and he indicated Giulio, to introduce him, "has now explained things and asked me to allow him to come and see you occasionally."

"Why?"

"Because, if you've got nothing against it, he'd like to court you."

Without answering, Ivana looked sidelong at Giulio.

"It's not the kind of word that's used nowadays," said Scarapecchia. "But it means that—"

"That you'll get to know each other, talk to each other," his wife broke in. "And what will be, will be. What's wrong with that?"

Ivana shrugged. "As far as I'm concerned, he can come," she said indifferently.

Next morning Giulio sent her flowers, a modest bunch that would suit his avowed situation in life: seven delicate tea roses. He waited for her to call and thank him: nothing. After forty-eight hours, afraid that Ivana was not going to see him again, he decided to telephone himself. Her mother welcomed him gaily, saying Ivana had loved the flowers and had carefully changed the water in the vase herself, every day, and even before he could hint for an invitation, she suggested: "Why not come and pay us a visit? Ivana gets home from her course about seven."

He went there the same way as he had gone on the first evening, leaving his car outside Amati's office. Walking along Via Po, he imagined a light dress and a body with heavy curves, guiding him like a comet. He saw the bar and the butcher's shop window, and in the street where Ivana lived the smell of grass and damp earth from the small gardens sharpened his impatience and his desire for her—so much so that when he knocked at the front door he felt sure her mother would take him straight into a bedroom where, ready and welcoming, lay Ivana.

Instead, she was not at home; but to make up for it, signora Adelina said that when her husband left the office he would be going to his usual bar to watch television, so that Giulio could stay longer if he wanted to. Then, glancing at the clock, she said Ivana disliked this course of hers: "Of course, you'll realize that with those hands . . . Didn't you notice them? It's a sacrilege to spoil hands like that on a typewriter. I don't let her do a thing in the house, just make her bed, that's all."

When Ivana got home, after eight, Giulio was on edge with waiting, all the more so since her mother, by talking about Ivana, had made him more and more eager. When she saw him she merely said, "Ah," as if there was an agreement between them that forced her to put up with him; then, with slow heavy steps, she left the room.

"She's gone to freshen up," explained signora Adelina, who then put two chairs next to each other and went and sat down on her own.

Soon Ivana reappeared, in the checked smock. "Here I am," she seemed to be saying. "Now what do you want, what must I do?" Her scared yet stubborn expression made it clear that she was still an adolescent, in fact almost a child who had grown up too quickly. The smock seemed tighter than it had the first evening, as if those two days had matured her body even further.

"Sit down, you must be tired," Giulio said and made room for her on the chairs set down in the middle of the room; there was not even a table beside them to lay his cigarettes on. "Do you mind if I use *tu* in talking to you?" Ivana shrugged. "Forgive me, it came quite naturally." There was a silence. "What did you do today at school?"

"The usual. She dictates and we write."

"And what does she dictate?"

"Who knows? Once I'm outside I never remember a thing."

"That means you'll make a good shorthand typist: like a machine," said Giulio. "Like a machine. Not remembering anything. That's fine."

Surprised by his enthusiasm, Ivana turned to look at him, and he realized she was not stupid. She knew when he spoke so appreciatively he was not thinking of her work.

"What beautiful hands," he remarked, taking one of them delicately. She let him hold it, let him touch it as she would have let a manicurist or a doctor do. Actually it was not so much that Ivana's hands were beautiful as that they were strongly sexual— at once childish and experienced, white, rather large and full, with pointed nails, perfectly cared for and varnished, a faint mother-of-pearl pink, standing in the fleshy row of fingers like almonds in their shells. Another remarkable thing about them was the coolness of the skin, even at that time of year, which was already hot. So Giulio delightedly held her hand in his and, caressing it and kissing it, tried to make Ivana realize the ardor of his feelings.

Even later, every time he came to see her, this was the best way of communicating with her. Ivana was not only taciturn, she was uninterested in everything; in fact she seemed to consider life as something to be wary of, not to have views on. It was not easy to hold a proper conversation with her, particularly because she often answered Giulio's questions with gestures: she would raise her head very slightly to say no, shrug with one shoulder if she wanted to express doubt or indifference, and nod by poking her neck slightly forward, thus giving her agreement an air of resignation.

In spite of this rather unencouraging attitude, he asked her questions, in order to find out what she did. One evening he asked: "Do you like dancing?" She looked up and answered no.

"Why?" said Giulio.

"Papa says that boys take advantage of us. And anyway, you've got to have the right sort of figure for the dances they do nowadays."

"Do you like reading?"

Ivana frowned, as if to say: "What do you mean?" She spent her evenings watching television, but had no favorite program: "I watch whatever's on." She rarely went to the cinema because her father didn't let her go without her mother, who was always tired.

"But we'll go sometime," signora Adelina promised. "When there's a film about the ancient Romans we'll ask Mr. Broggini to take us. I love the ancient Romans."

Ivana's mother was no help, as he had hoped she would be. True, she was always some distance away, with her back to them, but there was always the danger that she might turn around; and when she left them alone she came back so quickly that, unless he had flung himself brutally on Ivana, which would have been a mistake, Giulio never got anywhere, having no time to get started.

Yet he now went to Via Delle Alpi every evening. During the day, in order to free himself from a desire that was becoming an obsession, he told himself he wouldn't go; but shortly before six he would start to long to see her, become angry with Angeletti and his secretary, and finally send them away shouting: "That's enough! That's all I can stand!" Then he would pick up the telephone and call signora Adelina: "May I come?"

During his visits, which ended when Scarapecchia got home, Giulio sat beside Ivana as if he were in the parlor of a boarding school, or, more accurately, in the parlor of one of those cheap brothels he had gone to as a boy, where he waited before going upstairs with the girl he had chosen. But now he had to content himself with imagining what he would do to the body he glimpsed through the dresses that gradually became lighter, as the summer advanced. Ivana seemed unaware of his glances and his disturbance; but if, after peering to see what her mother was doing, he tried to put an arm around her shoulders or to raise the hand which he had casually laid on his knee a little higher, she pushed him away with a gesture, as if swatting a fly.

Every evening signora Adelina went away three times. The first time—when she was making coffee—was the least useful, because he had to again become familiar with Ivana after twenty-four hours' absence. Later she went away to prepare the supper, but she might come in suddenly to get something, as happened sometimes. The best time was the last of the three, when at exactly eight o'clock the telephone rang and she went to answer it, saying: "It's Raffaele."

It was obvious that signora Adelina had more confidence in her brother-in-law than she had in her husband: she often mentioned him, and seemed to care a great deal about his opinion and to be frightened of his reactions. They talked on the telephone for a very long time, and during these conversations Ivana was nervous and often turned toward the hall, where her mother was talking softly.

One evening the doorbell rang three times, in the agreed signal. Signora Adelina went out on to the landing, holding the door behind her, and came in again with a basket full of early fruit and vegetables and large fresh eggs, which Uncle Raffaele had sent from his farm. Ivana said: "Bring it here, let's have a look," and smiled unexpectedly. Giulio noticed a certain vulgarity in her smile. All the same, when Ivana showed her lower-middle-class tastes or used expressions that showed her lack of education, the power she had over him was in no way diminished. Even her obvious greed did not upset him. In fact he often took her boxes of sweets. She would open them at once, choose eagerly, and when he asked, "Do you like it?" nod with her mouth full.

Her laconic manner suited her frowning expression and her obvious indifference toward everything and everyone. Giulio had not yet discovered whether she was indifferent to their meetings, or disliked them, or whether her disdainful behavior was not a kind of flirtatiousness, much appreciated in southern Italy, as her mother maintained: according to her, even the fact of arriving late was a ruse to make herself more desired.

"Do you like the sea?" Giulio asked her. "Would you like to go to Ostia or Fregene?"

At last Ivana nodded. "But I'd have to buy a bathing suit. I've seen a blue one, with lace on it."

"If you tell me where, I'll go and buy it for you."

Ivana indicated with her chin that she would have to ask her mother's permission, and her mother refused. "Some clothes can't be accepted as presents from a man. It's not done."

Ivana, who had been shaken out of it for a moment, went back into her apathy. She knew nothing about the things that interested her contemporaries—records, films, comic strips, gossip about actors or princesses. All she cared about was food, first of all, and secondly her appearance.

"You're never gay, you never laugh," Giulio told her. "Anyone would think you didn't want to see me."

"I'm here, aren't I," she retorted impatiently.

"But do you think of me sometimes? For instance, would you like to have me near you in bed?"

"In bed I'm always hot," said Ivana. He remembered that a few evenings earlier her mother had confided in him: "She's not a bit artful yet, like women are. She always sleeps naked, just imagine."

Although he had decided to continue with his plan, Giulio felt uneasy; his nerves seemed to creak, as if the whole structure of his personality were about to collapse. Although he seemed calm, the smallest difficulty in the office, a traffic jam, or any other trifle was enough to make him explode with disproportionate rage.

What annoyed him most was the tact and silence of those he worked with. At first Angeletti had said, "Are you going out again today? Where to?" and had pointed out that he ought to meet a particular client himself. Giulio always answered evasively and with such unusual churlishness that no one now dared to ask him anything. Astonishment and small smiles had given way to respectful tact, and although he had always said that he wished to remain a bachelor, everyone must have thought now that he was on the verge of forty he had grown tired of love affairs and was settling down to marriage.

It was not only the evening visit that took him out. Often, while waiting for an important client, or shortly before a meeting, he would say, "I'm going for a short walk to clear my head," and stay away for several hours.

He would start walking slowly, like a man who had come to Rome from elsewhere and wanted to enjoy the city. He would look at the red, sun-warmed housefronts, and sit down at some café table, without even buying a newspaper. "There's nothing but bad news in them: murder, fraud, theft, blackmail, accusations of financial skulduggery which threaten to ruin all sorts of useful people—until somebody sensible shuts them up—or else gloomy forecasts of atomic war. If a war breaks out, that'll be the end of us all, of course; so we may as well be fatalists and carry on calmly. Life's still good, he said to himself. He would have a barley water, tamarind with fruit, or a cassata, the sort of old-fashioned things he hadn't tasted in years because, in his set, they would have been dismissed as provincial. Unchecked, he could at last give way to the images his imagination suggested, images that were obsessive but imprecise and transient, as in dreams; he no longer had to think secretly of Ivana and her body, pretending to listen to someone sitting on the other side of his desk, pretending to be interested in his problems, playing a wearisome, irritating double role.

During these outings he bought small presents for her. He went from one shop window to another, hesitating over what to choose; she never mentioned a single wish or whim. Indeed, when Giulio held out the package she took it without enthusiasm. Like a goddess she accepted the offerings that were her due, and which mortals had to pay.

While he was buying these presents he was seized by an excitement that abated only when he had left the shop, squeezing a rustling tissue-paper parcel in his hands. He would hide it in the car before going up to the office again, and always find he was back too late: the client had left, the meeting was over. Not that his office was far from Piazza di Spagna or Via Condotti, where he could have found the smartest shops in Rome; but he felt that what Ivana would like best could be found only in Via Po.

He would pause outside jewelers' windows as well, but stopped himself from going in; even though it might have brought him more quickly to his goal, he was not going to let the Scarapecchias know his real financial position, by doing something out of character for the part he was playing. Besides, he was not sure that he didn't prefer this slow advance to a quick victory; waiting multiplied the delights that would finally be his.

Ivana, as if suspicious of him, refused to tell him how she spent her time; and in spite of his skill Giulio had not yet managed to find out where she went for her lessons in shorthand and typing. Finally, one evening, taking advantage of her mother's absence, he asked her.

"If you tell me where your school is, I'll come and pick you up tomorrow, in a taxi. That way you won't have to bother with the bus and we can be together a little longer."

Ivana raised her chin, which meant no.

"Why not?"

"Because Papa's made me promise never to tell you where I go and to see you only when Mama's there."

"But it's quite harmless. We'd come straight home. You could get out here at the corner and come in and after ten minutes I could turn up."

Ivana shook her head. "He made me swear."

"Promises like that don't count when you're in love. In fact it would be nice to have a little secret between us."

But Ivana was not to be moved. "Anyway, Papa would find out somehow. He finds out every single thing I do. I can't even go and have an ice cream with another girl. I'm sure he has me watched to see if I'm behaving."

Giulio laughed. "That would need a proper organization. It would be terribly expensive."

"It doesn't cost a thing," she replied. "It's Uncle who arranges it." And, raising her chin to indicate the photograph of the man in uniform, she said: "He's a very big noise at the Home Office."

The figure of Uncle Raffaele dominated not only the living room wall but the entire life of the Scarapecchia family. Often, after the evening telephone call, signora Adelina mentioned the instructions she had received and followed scrupulously. "Raffaele said that if the co-op people come I must open the door," she said one evening. "I'm to tell them my husband's away and I know nothing."

Giulio might have asked for explanations about this mysterious co-op which had been mentioned on his very first visit, and should have reminded signora Adelina that he was a lawyer should she ever need help. But he was reluctant to mix his real personality with the one he had assumed, and to have any further connection with the Scarapecchia family. In them, for the first time, he was discovering the monstrous strength that a family represented and unleashed; he realized that the financial security of his own family, and the culture, mutual respect and intellectual freedom it involved, which his father had impressed on their whole family life, were a much frailer link than the economic insecurity of Ivana's family, and with it their struggle against exploitation and hunger, and their moral standards based on suspicion. Seeing how important the family considered Uncle Raffaele, he was surprised never to find him at the house during his visits, which now were more or less official.

"Uncle never comes to see us," Ivana told him.

"But does he know that you love me?"

"Who said I love you?" she answered haughtily.

In fact, he had no proof of this, nor did he want any because, although hypocritically he translated feelings that had a totally different origin into the language of love, he was sure that Ivana had realized, from his expression and overtures, what kind of attachment he felt, and that she too was playing a part.

One evening, when he was sitting beside Ivana, they heard a sharp ring at the door. Her mother, who was busy going over bills, rose quickly and gestured to them to follow her in silence; then she hid them in a cubbyhole filled with trunks, suitcases and junk. "Don't put on the light," she murmured, shutting the door. A feeble gleam came through a small window covered with blue blackout paper, a hangover from the war. "The co-op people?" Giulio asked softly. Ivana made a vague gesture.

The bell rang a second time, more insistently. They heard signora Adelina going across to open the door, muttering: "What's the hurry . . ." Then some gay music from the television cut out the conversation she was presumably carrying on with the visitors.

Giulio was not complaining: he could now stand close to Ivana in the tiny room. He made a move to kiss her but she drew away and covered her mouth with her hands. "Not that," she said. Reassured by the music, which continued, he made another attempt, which Ivana rejected violently, turing to the wall. The fear of ruining the opportunity he had longed for so much made him lose his head: he let his hands run over her body, caressing it, touching it with delight, all the more since he could no longer see Ivana's sulky face, only her back and the prominent round buttocks that had first attracted him. He pressed her to him, put his arms clumsily round her, patted her breasts, and Ivana, while in no way encouraging him, did not try to defend herself or struggle to get away, as she had done shortly before. Giulio began lifting the back of her skirt and might have done anything if, with the television suddenly silent, he had not heard signora Adelina's footsteps, and then the click of the door opening. This brought him quickly back to reality and to the appalling prospect that Ivana would talk and he, looking distraught, would be unable to deny her charges.

But Ivana went and sat down again without a word. Her mother flopped into the armchair, crushed. "It was them," she said. "I was scared stiff. I thought: Rosario will be back at that very moment. Then I prayed to St. Anthony, I promised him quantities of candles, and two minutes later they left. It's a miracle . . . But there's no point in telling your father, do you understand? My legs are still shaking."

"I'll go and make you some coffee," Ivana said calmly.

Her mother was now apologizing: "I'm sorry. What must you think?" Giulio sincerely and ardently begged her to treat him as she had done already, with trust. "Thank you," she said. "My husband is the victim of a great injustice . . ." At this point the door opened and Scarapecchia came in.

"Where's Ivana?" he asked before taking his key out of the door. "Isn't she back?"

Just then Ivana appeared, holding the tray. When she saw her father she hesitated, then went over to her mother and held out the cups, saying: "There's sugar already in it."

"Coffee at this hour?" Scarapecchia asked suspiciously.

Signora Adelina gulped down her coffee in a couple of mouthfuls; then she ran her hand over her lips and explained humbly: "I didn't want to tell you, Rosario, but I felt faint. My head was going round. We were so scared, weren't we?" she asked Giulio, who nodded, pleased to enter into the game. "But you mustn't worry. You've got enough to worry about, poor soul. . . . Well, it's quite natural, I'm on my feet all day, up and down, up and down. . . . I'm tired. I must get a bit of fresh air and distraction." Then, turning to the pair of them she added: "Tomorrow we'll go to the pictures."

Next day Giulio turned up earlier than usual: the chance of being with Ivana again, in the dark, made him feverishly excited. In the office, while the others were talking, he had done nothing but relive the previous day's scene and imagine the one that awaited him.

Signora Adelina was ready, dressed in black, her thin hair piled back and flattened into a net. "Ivana isn't ready yet," she said. "In any case I'd rather be alone with you a minute, because I've got something to tell you." (Remembering what had happened, Giulio turned pale. "This is it," he thought.) "This evening I've just got to go to church," she went on, "because of those candles I promised St. Anthony yesterday, and I want to go to the service. So I won't be able to come to the picture. But I don't want to make you two miss it. So go along and enjoy yourselves, and at the end of the film I'll meet you. It's the first time I've left Ivana alone with a man," she said, and added: "If my husband knew, he'd throw me out of the house. You can't imagine what a daughter means to a Calabrian! It will be a secret between us, but you must give me your word that . . ."

"I give you my word," Giulio interrupted. (It was clear: before allowing him the freedom he longed for, signora Adelina had wanted to know him, had wanted to be sure he was a man who could be trusted, who would not be a girl's downfall.) With an impulse of gratitude he seized her hand, raised it to his lips and said: "Word of honor."

"I knew there was no need of it," said signora Adelina. "But you're in love with Ivana, that's obvious, and it's dangerous to leave straw by the fire. But you can be sure that if you broke your word Ivana would tell me. She tells me everything."

Until the previous day Giulio had been sure of this; but what had happened in the storeroom proved that Ivana was his accomplice and that it would not be very long before she agreed to meet him in secret.

Ivana had dressed with particular care for her outing. She was wearing a chiffon dress, with flowers on a flesh-colored background, sleeveless, but high-necked; and through the thin material it was possible to see her shoulders and the beginning of her bosom. On her breasts, among the colored petals, he could just see two round, purplish circles. ("Lovely. Maddeningly lovely.") Wearing the heavy French scent he had given her, Ivana was nervously swinging her long pale leather gloves, another present from him.

"Come on, don't stand there gaping," signora Adelina said, smiling. "You'll have the rest of your life to look at her and enjoy her. . . . Put on your sweater," she told her daughter, "and I'll go and get my handbag."

When they were alone Giulio could not hold out: he went

over to Ivana—gazing into her eyes, which were staring at him—and with his fingers squeezed the dark circles to make sure they were not a mirage aroused by his desire. He had acted so quickly that Ivana could not refuse; but her face contracted into a grimace. Immediately afterward her mother came in again. "Come on, let's go," she said, looking at the clock. "I've chosen the Riviera, which is near the church."

Outside, in the still bright light of sunset, Ivana's outfit looked so flashy that Giulio was glad he was going to a surburban cinema where it was unlikely he would meet friends or acquaintances. "I haven't got a car," he said apologetically. "We'll take a taxi."

They were walking down the steps when the gate squeaked and Scarapecchia came hurrying across the garden.

"We're going to the movies," signora Adelina told him. "If you want to eat, I've left everything ready."

But Scarapecchia's face promised nothing pleasant. "Come into the house," he told them and, when his wife protested: "Get inside, I told you!" When he had shut the door he said: "You two may as well take off those clothes because we're having no more movies. Mr. Broggini and I are going to have a talk." And the moment they were alone he started: "Mr. Broggini, you turned up in this house in a way I can only call strange. In spite of that, I've always trusted you . . ."

"Well?" said Giulio arrogantly.

"Don't interrupt me!" Scarapecchia burst out. Then, with studied calm, he continued: "As I was saying, I've trusted you, admitted you to my house without checking on you in any way, as I had a perfect right to before letting you see Ivana. And now I've discovered that many of the things you told me about yourself were inaccurate or actually false! I'm a trustful man and that's been the ruin of me. Even recently, in this co-op business, which it would take a long time to explain . . . Luckily my brother's not like me. Today he called me at the office and he said: 'Listen, that boyfriend of Ivana's, Giulio Broggini, did he tell you he was an orphan? Well, he's got a fine pair of parents, alive and kicking in Milan, Via Spiga 16,' " said Scarapecchia, as he took a sheet of paper out of his pocket. "And they have a villa on Lake Maggiore as well. He says he hasn't got a car, but there's a black Ferrari sports car, number plate Rome A239964, licensed in his name.

"That's not all," he went on. "You said you were working for a lawyer who let you live in his office, didn't you? Whereas," he read, "it seems that *you* are the employer of the lawyer Andrea Angeletti, as well as of Marina Boschi, stenographer, Tilde Frapistoni, ditto, Nerio Palazzi, office boy, and of Diodato Marietti, manservant, notorious pervert, who works for you at home: a luxurious five-room penthouse at 41 Via Fracassini." He laid down the sheet of paper. "Is all this true, or not?"

"It is true. I can't say why I deceived you . . . maybe to avoid involving my parents in a decision they would very likely disapprove of, and which, at my age, I can take without their agreement."

"Maybe," said Scarapecchia. "And I must admit you've behaved as you should toward my daughter. Otherwise, if you'd tried to see her alone, say, I would have found out. 'He certainly seems a nice young man,' I told my brother—not that you're all that young. 'I wonder why he was trying to hoodwink me!' He said: 'You fool! Don't you realize that by saying his career wasn't successful and his financial position was modest he made it seem impossible to set up a home, and so he could put off getting married indefinitely?' "

Giulio looked hurt. He had quite sincerely forgot that he had told lies for these very reasons, and because, if he had to pay for having Ivana, he wanted to pay as little as possible. The way Scarapecchia now turned on him seemed insulting—when a poor man turned on him it always seemed insulting—and he defended himself dramatically.

36

"I've made a mistake, I admit it. But out of love. Yes," he went on, when Scarapecchia looked skeptical, "the way I behaved could be called silly and shameful. I pretended to be someone else, a man who had nothing, who had nothing to offer, because I wanted to be loved for myself alone. I was afraid that my economic advantages and elegibility might influence a choice that I wanted to be completely unbiased."

"So you think my daughter capable of such feelings?" said Scarapecchia angrily. "That she'd marry for material advantages?" Giulio protested, but he went on indignantly: "A girl like that, who's never had to go without a thing! Who's had everything my modest income could afford! My daughter will never marry except for love, and you may as well know it. Besides, let me tell you, she's not entirely without expectations: this flat will be hers one day, and this district keeps going up in value. Then my brother Raffaele today confirmed that as he's a bachelor he means to make her his heir, and leave her everything he owns, both in the Agro Romano and in Catanzaro. If this is what you thought about my daughter, you can stay away from us, from now on. Better break off a connection which you consider, quite mistakenly, is a case of your condescending to improve the lot of Ivana and our family!" Out of all this, Giulio merely understood that he was not to see Ivana again.

"But I never thought this," he said. "Truly I didn't."

"You did, considering . . ."

Giulio broke in, looking pale: "All right, I behaved thoughtlessly, I admit it, in spite of my feelings and my intentions. I beg you to accept my apologies. My humble apologies," he added, seeing Scarapecchia shake his head.

"It's not a matter of apologies. If you're dead set on it—right, I'll accept them. As for the rest—that is, as for your seeing Ivana again," Scarapecchia said, leaving Giulio in suspense, "let me think. I'll talk to my brother about it. Then I'll let you know my decision." With this, he led him to the door.

"When?" asked Giulio, his throat dry.

"Soon, I hope. In any case, don't be impatient. Better suffer for a few days than for a lifetime, especially when there's someone else involved too, don't you agree? I'll call you up myself," Scarapecchia promised, holding out his hand and dismissing him.

From the gate, Giulio turned to look at the small white house and steps, and then walked slowly away; he felt lost, as if he had no home and knew no one, in that city where he had lived for twenty years. The whole world seemed to have cast him out. "Serves you right," he said to himself. "You always go too far. Someone who'd teach you a lesson was bound to turn up someday."

The trouble lay in his own character, he thought. Whatever he undertook, he never considered whether his motives were right, but simply trusted in his own ability to carry it through. Sometimes he knew he was not up to a job entrusted to him, but by following his own instinct and depending on his ability to improvise, he always managed it. So, after climbing up and up, he was now earning a great deal in his profession, and was also known as a man who had remarkable success with women. Success in both these fields was due mostly to his appearance, which made people like him, but partly to the arrogance that allowed him to face every new problem as if it were already solved. And in the end, his qualities—but even more his faults—did solve all problems: that is, his natural gift for compromise and for adapting himself immediately to the views of those around him.

When they had last met, his father had told him, reproachfully: "For years you've been carrying on like this, never stopping to think." And he had answered, laughing: "This isn't an age of thinkers, it's an age of technicians."

But this time it was the technician who had gone wrong. He had made a childish plan, certain that he would manage to carry it through as usual, inventing ploys that would confuse his opponent as he went along, and would at the same time give him the thrill of taking risks. In fact, he had always depended on his own coldness and impassibility, and had failed to foresee that this time he himself would become involved. He had always lied to women, and here, for less important reasons than usual, he had been shown up, and by a ridiculous opponent, which made it worse—by Scarapecchia, of all people. "When he calls to tell me his decision—a favorable one, since it was favorable when he thought me much poorer than I am—I'll tell him I've been thinking it over as well, and that I'm sure he was right. Better to break off the relationship, and my regards to his wife and daughter."

He hung up, imagining this conversation, trying not to notice the overwhelming bitterness he felt, and the bruised, unpleasant feeling all over his body, as if he had been beaten. "By Scarapecchia," he kept repeating, although he knew it was not Scarapecchia who had defeated him, but Uncle Raffaele.

What right had this unknown policeman to pry into his life, to throw up to him the harmless lies which he had told almost without meaning to in the embarrassment of presenting himself to Ivana's father? His anger grew as he thought of the robust southerner's heavy features in the enlargement of a passport photograph—the low forehead, the wavy hair—and the way he smugly watched over Giulio's labored courtship of Ivana, safe behind glass, as he was safe behind the walls of the Ministry. "Let him go back to snooping on other people's private affairs," he thought. From that building, which so perfectly expressed all the bad taste of fascism, a dark gleaming eye was following him wherever he went.

"My brother, being a bachelor, intends to make her his heir." Scarapecchia's words came back to him, making him suddenly suspect that Uncle Raffaele might have an eye on Ivana himself. Maybe he was waiting for her to mature further before marrying her, thus keeping such an appetizing morsel in the family. With his presents of fruit and fresh eggs he was tending her, fattening her, to gobble her up on her wedding day, plump and fertile. Maybe Ivana had been talking to him that evening in the bar; he was the speaker Giulio had carelessly failed to inquire about. "All right, I lied," he replied to Scarapecchia's accusations. "But what about your daughter? Who was she telephoning that evening, from a bar? You've been checking up on me: right, perfectly right and proper. But what do I know about Ivana's life? What do I know about her family?"

This imaginary revenge did not succeed in calming him or in soothing his humiliation. He felt that the eye in the Viminale was following not merely his actions, but his thoughts, and that his arbitrary suspicion of Ivana was another reason why he should be kept away from her. The Scarapecchias were shrewd, prudent people, by the look of things; in a rough and ready way they were astute. Their weakness lay in their fear of being caught out, and in the ferocity with which they defended whatever helped them to survive—not least, the modest capital represented by Ivana's virginity.

He was walking toward his car. The streets were empty. Through the open windows he could hear an indistinct monologue; at that hour everyone was listening to the same voices and looking at the same images on television, everyone was reaching out toward a single ideal: welfare-love, detergent-love, vacuum-cleaner-love. Rome's a wretched ctiy, he thought, a big bureaucratic town, unplanned yet state-controlled, dominated by the clergy, the police, and the Pope's Swiss guard. A conceited city in which the lowest of cashiers thinks himself fit to hold forth about anything and everything, and to parade principles and prejudices no one gives a damn about anywhere else, simply because there are a few triumphal arches still crumbling about the place, and even more because of those endless statues of Caesars and emperors. He had no better opinion of his father's prejudices and principles: living on unearned income, his father could well afford to defend Negroes and Jews, illegitimates and illiterates, could afford to be faithful to his early days as an academic antifascist who had spoken out against the anti-Jewish laws. Guests of his parents at dinner could often chalk up a half-century of imprisonment between them, men who, under fascism, had hoped to change the course of history through their own intransigence. And now these same men deluded themselves that they were warning the world with their manifestos and meetings and half-secret publications, while the world—loyal to its own, completely opposite interests, both before and after—respected them and took no notice. To himself: "What runs the world is ideas like Scarapecchia's, and the power of the police."

As he passed a gate Giulio smelled the sharp scent of honeysuckle. Apart from everything else, Scarapecchia and his notions had ruined his summer. At that time of year, during trips to the sea and long evenings full of walks and streets and fountains, he always started up a new love affair that lasted until autumn, when—because he spent his leisure in a different way, because life was no longer out of doors but back in hospitable well-heated houses—another woman meant another relationship, at once pleasanter and more useful. Women who like the theatre, music and painting usually ruin a holiday, he thought. In winter he liked women a few years older than himself and houses where there was good food and drink, women who dressed in a way that made them noticed wherever he took them. Vaguely intellectual and deeply misunderstood, these women were all separated from their husbands, but because of the divorce laws—which, fortunately, stood up to the attacks of his father and his father's friends—were chained eternally to these ex-husbands. Understanding, motherly women, who waited forever, believed his lies, spoiled him with their kindness, and gave him presents—books and records at first, working up gradually to gold cigarette lighters, cuff links, abstract paintings, exotic objects chosen lovingly during some trip abroad, returning from which, at a change of season, they found themselves jilted. In Giulio's home every ashtray and lamp bore a name, like the trees in a cemetery—names of delightful mistresses to whom he was still linked by a devoted tenderness, which helped them to get over the bitterness of his desertion.

He stopped at a lighted shop window displaying women's underwear. In the middle stood a figure with black glass eyes in a thin, lace-trimmed white nightdress; on the silky black wig lay a spray of orange blossoms, and another was held in the hand stretched out toward the customer.

"My doll, my big doll," Giulio moaned, his desire flaring again. "Oh, how I want my big doll." He saw Ivana still, her body veiled and protected by a wedding dress. "I want her. At once. I'll even marry her; then, when I've had enough, I'll leave her."

At home, he looked for Diodato. Since Giulio always dined out, Diodato also went out every evening and came in very late. He was, as Scarapecchia had said, a homosexual; Giulio knew this perfectly well. In fact he maintained that queers made the best manservants; they could wash and iron and even sew. Besides, his own success with women protected him from suspicion and even from the possibility of Diodato's interest, since it meant that he considered Giulio insensitive and coarse, incapable of the delicate, secret relationships whose delights and whose sufferings he himself experienced.

Like many other homosexuals, Diodato was an unhappy lover, the victim of young rascals who were greedy and demanding, unfaithful and mean; sometimes he could not hide his tears, which he put down to family troubles. Giulio, who valued his tact, consoled him.

But that evening Diodato's absence made him fly into a rage. "Scarapecchia must have been trying to get me. My number's not in the book but his brother's sure to have it." He was sorry he had not given it to Ivana, who might have called without telling her parents and arranged to meet him. On the other hand, he doubted whether she would have done anything against their wishes.

He waited well into the night. Diodato was still not back. Next morning Giulio scolded him: "Why did you go out last night without my permission? In the future you'll stay in the house until further orders and be sure to make a note of every telephone call."

Outside, the glorious weather and dazzling sky put him in a good humor. He was no longer grieved over Ivana, and this was not merely because he did not usually see her at that time of day; it was because he no longer cared about her at all. He felt full of enthusiasm again, ready to work, to meet people, to act—in short, freed from a nightmare.

In the light of day Scarapecchia's uncompromising attitude seemed providential. He could not have continued to neglect his work and his clients: it was nonsense. On other mornings he had felt guilty as he entered his office, imagining rumors, gossip and speculation behind his back; in order to avoid the questions which in fact were no longer asked, or perhaps to justify his colleagues' silence, he had made himself appear irritable. Now he regretted his unkindness to the servant who had served him well for three years. Diodato had been crushed by the cruel order that deprived him of these fine, promising summer nights. "I'll call him up and tell him to go out whenever he likes."

He had lowered the car top: the wind swished against the windshield, the wheels slid easily along the road, and he felt restored. His state of mind the previous evening showed nervous exhaustion. "I really must see a doctor. I'll go and ask Ugo for a tonic. I haven't been to the gym or the river, and I've been smoking too much." Driving in the open air now made his breathing easier. He checked the dials on the dashboard: petrol, oil, fine, perfect.

When he arrived at the office he glanced at the headlines, then called the switchboard girl: "Today or tomorrow a Mr. Scara-pecchia will call. Take a note of the name . . . no, not *petta,* signorina: *pecchia,*" and he spelled it out, irritated that she should stumble over this (admittedly rather peculiar) name. "When he rings up put him straight through to me, even if I'm at a meeting and even if I've given orders not to be disturbed."

While he was giving these orders he saw Angeletti peering around the door and, with an expansive gesture, invited him in. "Come in, come along in, Andrea . . ." Behind Angeletti, Giulio's secretary came in, timidly. "Good morning, signorina Boschi, come in. . . . Will you open the window, please. . . . That's it. Thanks." The others obeyed, smiling, as if they had feared for his health, but now found him well again. All he needed was fresh air.

Angeletti, taking advantage of his good mood, had laid a bulging file on the desk. "I must talk to you about a few things we're involved in. That's if you want to, of course."

"Of course I want to! But we'd better take things in order. Let's look at these first," said Giulio, laying a hand on the papers. "Meanwhile, signorina, would you please send for coffee?" When his secretary had left the room he said awkwardly: "Listen, Andrea . . . maybe it hasn't been easy to understand me lately. The fact is . . ." he meant to tell him how exhausted he had been, but Angeletti immediately began protesting.

"Of course not, I understand perfectly," he said, and left him to look at the papers.

Giulio began reading carefully. He realized that since the end of May he had not been consulted for anything, even the most important or the most difficult cases. Yet he could find nothing to object to in the way things had been dealt with. On the other hand, examining them coldly and with detachment, he found them quite uninteresting. "What a dreary job," he thought. In spite of what he had felt at first, he now had no wish to work: there was no mental alertness to correspond to the enthusiasm with which he had talked and to his outward liveliness. The words he read made no impression on his mind. There seemed an obstacle, a wall, between him and the work—the wall of the house in Via Delle Alpi, which cut out not just the sight of Ivana but the expectation—the hope, at least—of something exciting, something new.

It was eleven o'clock. No sign of Scarapecchia yet. Every time the telephone rang Giulio's heart seemed to stop, as if the blood had suddenly stopped flowing; but each time it was merely a client or a colleague. Once again he told himself that he would consult a doctor about these odd palpitations.

He sent for Angeletti. "That's enough for today," he said, closing the file which Angeletti took away without a word. His secretary came in with pad and pencil to catch up with the mail, but he sent her away as well. As she was leaving the room, he stared at her legs: they were not particularly good legs, but yet they disturbed him. "Maybe I'm in this state just because I haven't made love for three weeks," he thought. "Being near Ivana, being worked up but getting nowhere, has exhausted me."

The thought cheered him up. He had always disapproved of people who wasted their time brooding over the fate of the world instead of enjoying life, asking themselves questions that no one could properly answer. These people were dissatisfied, physically unbalanced, and so unable to enjoy a healthy sexual life. As a boy he had been almost ashamed of his sociable and well-adjusted disposition: most of his friends found relations with their parents, teachers and girls a problem and, torn between their instincts and their principles, could not make contact with other people. But he had no difficulty in communicating with anyone; and when, on rare occasions, he failed to establish contact, he preferred to give up rather than exhaust himself in probing for a reason. He boasted that he had never been deceived because, without meaning to, he was always the first to deceive, by letting others think his cozy indifference was friendship or love. Daria had told him: "Your optimism allows you to put up with everything and everyone. You never choose. You take whatever comes." To stop her, he had replied gallantly that this time something good had come to him. Obviously Daria disagreed: a few days later she jilted him.

Giulio had thought he suffered over it. He wanted to feel pain as a new experience, an experience he had a right to. What had actually happened had baffled him. He was always the first to break off an affair, and had perfected the technique of dismissal so that he now knew how to do it tactfully, very gradually. Like a jet that starts slowing well in advance, to make a smooth landing, after which, like the good aircraft it is, it'll fly off somewhere else. Incredibly, Daria had made him make a forced landing. Why? Giulio hadn't asked. He never asked. "The secret of my optimism, Daria dear, lies in not trying to understand other people. A lot of people analyze the behavior of those around them so much that they pare them down to the bones." Sylvia, for instance. He had never talked about Sylvia to Daria: he was sure that she would dislike her. (No woman likes the one who takes her place, even three years later.) The previous evening, though, he had been on the point of telephoning Sylvia, but had been dissuaded by the necessity to explain his disappearance.

Since he first met Ivana he had only been to see Sylvia on a few evenings at about half past nine, that is, when Scarapecchia's return obliged him to be free. He took her out to dinner, and then said goodbye at the street door, pleading a headache or the need to get up very early. Later he had invented excuses not to see her—his parents' arrival in Rome, a dinner to celebrate a colleague's teaching degree, trouble with the car. Then, when Sylvia began to be suspicious, he vanished.

"It would be a nuisance if she no longer wanted to see me," he thought: resorting to professionals depressed him, and starting up a new affair took time.

In the past, the risk of being discovered by the mistress he was leaving had increased the pleasure of his new one. This time, though, it was another kind of relationship; Ivana hadn't given him more than the shyest schoolgirl had when he was an adolescent. Yet he couldn't bear the company of any other woman.

"Well then, is it love?" he wondered. "Can I posssibly love a girl who hasn't my education or my ways, a girl I'd be ashamed to show myself in public with, a girl I not only wouldn't dare to introduce as my fiancée, but would be ashamed of even as an acquaintance? It can't be love." But very soon he began wondering again: "What are the signs of love? What is it like?"

Daria had been sure that he mistook the wish to go to bed for love and that, quite apart from this, he had never known real sensual passion. "You make love gaily," she told him. Giulio had laughed and asked why love should not be gay. "I don't know why," she had answered, puzzled. "Maybe because it's a mystery." When he replied that this was nonsense, that there was nothing mysterious about it, it was all a matter of skin, Daria shook her head: "It seems to be, but it isn't. Besides, when you've loved someone, it takes years before he becomes a friend; and even then he never really becomes one. Whereas you're your ex-mistresses' best friend."

Her attitude irritated him, and showed him that she had never loved him: she thought him a "mistake," which a few weeks' intimacy had shown up. "There's something monstrous about you, below the surface: it might be anything, from something that hurt you long ago to rancor, to the killer's instinct. Or else nothing, emptiness," she told him, two days before the end. Perhaps this was why she seemed to have no regrets about him. His other mistresses would all have been ready to take him back, but, to him, they had lost the magic of newness, the only thing that made him curious about them. They were all alike, all having in common the idleness that made them available at any hour, and the melancholy of having being abandoned. So they accepted whatever he did, admired him, flattered him, took over his opinions. Daria had her own: in fact, her whole way of life was one he had never come across elsewhere. "Everything should be altered in your life," she had told him cheerfully, adding, without much conviction: "Or perhaps in mine."

She was a lawyer too; they had been at the university together. She earned much less than Giulio, and her reputation in professional circles was very different from his. After their break she had met a man with whom she was happy: Giulio had guessed it from her new gaiety, from the success of her work. Besides, she had become much prettier. This annoyed him, like the gay way she welcomed him, which seemed somehow to suggest she was grateful to him, since, if he had not disappointed her, and thus impelled her to break off with him, she might never have met her present lover. Giulio didn't know who he was; but his presence in Daria's life had always upset him, making him suppose she was constantly comparing him with another man. This unfavorable comparison he imagined was now joined by Uncle Raffaele's opinion of him, by the eyes that watched and judged him, night and day. "What right does he have, anyway?" Giulio thought. "The pair of them can go to hell!"

Meanwhile, almost without meaning to, he was dialing Daria's number. (The tone was always the same between them: joking, brotherly.) After the first question he asked her: "What are you doing? Are you free for lunch? Today, seeing the sun, I said to myself: call Daria and take her out. If not, I don't know when we'll find time to meet." But Daria was leaving for Mexico that evening and had all kinds of things to do. "Don't be difficult," he said, insistently. "Always tied up, always working. What's the point of living, then? Finish things off and come on out. Nothing'll happen. You just think you're too important."

She laughed. "You're right, I'm a fool. But only because I'm not clever like you and can't believe I'm important. You'll see, one day I'll manage to. But let's arrange something for when I get back. How about the twentieth, would that do? Wait, I'll put it down in my diary. Monday the twentieth: Giulio. Big letters, to cover the whole page. Will you ring me? . . . Right." She was in a hurry, he could hear voices around her. "So long, then."

"Listen, Daria . . . I'm sorry, but I've got to see you today. Just for a few minutes."

After a pause, she said reproachfully: "You should have told me straight away. Let me think. . . . Maybe the best thing would be for you to come now. Or else . . . look: come to my house this evening about nine. The plane leaves at eleven. We'll have an hour."

Giulio offered to take her to the airport. She declined. ("Obviously she's going with someone.") "Till nine, then."

When he had put down the receiver he realized he had done something silly. "What shall I say? I've got nothing to tell her. I'll invent some story and she'll think I've wasted her time. She'll think: another hour to add to the two months I wasted three years ago."

Instead, he went to Sylvia's at nine. He had telephoned her, saying simply: "It's me. I'll come this evening at the usual time. Right?" Sylvia, who had replied with her deliberately vague "Hallo!" had hesitated. "This evening? Well, actually I've got a date, but I'll see if I can get out of it. If I don't ring you right away it means it's all right." She hadn't rung.

That evening Giulio dressed slowly, rediscovering the pleasant habit of changing for dinner, of having a shower before putting on a clean shirt, a dark well-pressed suit. As he knotted his tie at the mirror he thought with satisfaction that what he had said to Daria when he put off their appointment was true.

He had rung her in the afternoon. "I needn't bother you when you're leaving. I've settled it." "Bother me? . . . What nonsense! Or rather: you're sure you've settled it? I'm afraid you've just regretted having let yourself go. That would be silly. We all need a hand to pull us out of the pit, at times." He had made a joke of it: "There's no pit, honestly. I've a rather complicated nullity case on my hands, and wanted your opinion." Daria replied: "When will you lose the habit of telling lies?" "Really that's all it was. I don't lie to you. I never have," he said emphatically, and added: "Till the twentieth, then. Have a good trip: Mexico, Acapulco and so on . . . Lucky thing."

The lie itself had partially restored him. He was now convinced that he ought really to talk to Daria, who specialized in the annulment of marriages. "I might marry Ivana. A marriage that was merely religious, because of my parents' opposition, taking all the precautions beforehand to make it null and void. That is, the usual letter sent to a friend on the eve of the wedding, in which one of the pair desperately admits to being pushed into it, forced by a wicked mother, a shameful pregnancy, a father's debts: an old-style sob story, arranged by an ecclesiastical lawyer." The grotesqueness of such a stratagem put him into a good mood.

When he looked in the mirror he noticed a bulge at his stomach. Sometimes, in the evening, when he left Ivana, an irresistible hunger sent him to a nearby restaurant well-known for its Neapolitan food. There he had meals of spaghetti and fried things: food he had always avoided in order to keep slim and because he thought that rich, spicy, overflavored dishes showed a vulgar taste. In the past he had looked scornfully at the smoking plates piled with pasta served by the waiters to fat customers whose choice implied both a lack of control and a lowly social position. He, on the other hand, rose from the table feeling lightweight, and proud of his own restraint. But when he left the pizzeria Posillipo, which was always trilling with mandolins, he felt heavy with food and fuddled with wine (appalling, like all Neapolitan wines). One evening when he left it he went to the cinema and dropped off to sleep. He now avoided places where his friends were to be found; and, possibly in order to draw nearer to Ivana, took on the tastes of her home, which at mealtimes smelled strongly of tomato, marjoram and garlic.

Pleased to have finished with this unsuitable episode, he went to the door. And seeing Diodato's melancholy face as he came with him, he remembered the veto he had imposed on him that morning and said: "Look, Diodato, if you want to go out this evening, go ahead."

"Thank you," said Diodato stiffly. "I've already put off the appointment I had with a friend."

"I'm sorry. Last night I was expecting an important telephone call. That's why I scolded you."

"You were quite right; and, as things have happened this way, I'd rather stay in. Actually it's better."

"Maybe it's better for me as well. Yes, it really is," Giulio thought as he arrived outside the apartment house in which Sylvia lived, a luxurious glass building with huge windows that sent out no smells. "Not even the smell of honeysuckle," he remarked, crossing the lawn beside the entrance. Water flowed softly in the fountain, a sort of tiled swimming pool with an abstract sculpture in the middle: two grainy blocks of plaster twisted in and out of each other like rings. The first evening that they had gone back together Sylvia had told him, in her slightly ironical tone, that it was called *Man and Woman*. Close by he saw Sylvia's car, a small green MG ("appallingly parked, as usual") and could not repress a wave of tenderness.

The jerk of the elevator when it stopped. The door with the carriage lamp. The chiming doorbell. Sylvia opened it herself: sometime ago she had given up having a maid live in. ("It's one of the tiresome ways women nowadays pay for their freedom to see anyone they want, day and night, without being watched," she used to say.) She was holding the telephone on a very long

54

cord that allowed her to carry it about the apartment while she talked.

"I'm talking to Bianca," she told him, and then said to her friend: "Hallo . . . Go ahead it's Giulio."

He thought he noticed a hint of triumph in her voice. Sylvia never confided in other women: avoiding this complicity was another thing women managed to do today. So Bianca could not know for certain that he had recently vanished. But finding Sylvia always free and ready to go out, she must have suspected that everything was over, that Sylvia had been jilted at the beginning of the summer holiday, just when it would be hard to find anyone to go away with. In fact, in order to show that her visitor was one she was quite used to, Sylvia put down the telephone and made him a sign to go into the sitting room.

Alone in that room, which he had not seen for nearly a month—after he had spent the entire winter there, evening after evening—Giulio looked around like a prodigal son who realized how stupid he had been and at the same time all the dangers he had been through. "Of course. It's clearly the first sign of old age." He thought of old bachelors who ended their lives with the servant girl. Ivana no longer appeared to him even desirable. "How could I have thought of marrying her?" He could not even remember her clearly, now. A slowly growing awareness, or some providential mental censorship, had wiped her and her home and family clean out of his memory. All that stayed in his mind was Uncle Raffaele, enlarged in black and white. "You were right: I was joking. It wasn't very hard to realize that. Marry her, if you really want to. She'd make a fine wife for a police chief." He concluded that man must have a tendency toward renunciation and defeat, a longing for death, which he first submitted to in marriage and which, from time to time, laid traps for him in every sphere of his activity.

The pleasure of finding himself in that room again was increased by the certainty that, yet again, he had thwarted the threat of danger. It was very hot, because of the heavy curtains, and the emerald green wall-to-wall carpet throughout the apartment. ("I always go around barefoot, which gives me a feeling I'm walking in a field," Sylvia had told him. She told everyone.)

He went over to the antique cradle, which had been made into a bar, and poured himself a whisky, pleased that Sylvia was taking a long time over her telephone call. It allowed him to become familiar with each object there again: the pear-shaped ice bucket, the bottle opener with a horse's head. He ate one of the biscuits stuffed with cheese which she ordered from London. "A pleasant house. A very pleasant house," he said to himself, seeing Sylvia come over to him, holding the telephone base in one hand and the receiver held by her cheek against her shoulder, as a violinist holds a violin, to offer him cigarettes, his favorites. As she did so she said to her friend: "It's an idea. But we'll talk to Giulio about it. He's very good at these things." She laughed, flinging back her head, and tossing the long, straight blonde hair that took her to the hairdresser's for several hours every day. ("At the hairdresser's, I can rest. I don't know what I'm resting from, because I don't do a thing, yet I'm always tired.") Giulio watched her as she put down the telephone—slimmer than ever, living on lettuce, carrots, cucumber and other raw vegetables— and, afraid she might reproach him, he wanted to say: "Everything's so good like this, Sylvia, don't ask me questions, please, don't spoil everything," but she gave him a reassuring smile. After wandering about a bit, looking for an ashtray, she sat down opposite Giulio, tucking her very long legs up on to the sofa.

"Well? Pleased to be here?" she asked him, lighting a cigarette.

"You know that, don't you?" he said. He could always tell when Sylvia's voice held a trap of some sort, but that evening he was determined not to argue. She must have thought she had lost him for good and was delighted to have him back, just when she had lost hope.

"You're the one who should know you're much better here than anywhere else."

"I've always known it," Giulio answered sincerely. "But you can't imagine how important it is for me to realize it once again."

Sylvia didn't gloat over her victory by asking for further details. They had dinner out of doors: the restaurant terrace looked out over the city, from which glittering lights rose to brighten the night sky. Sylvia was too gay and lively to be quite spontaneous, as she told him about the endless unimportant things that had happened to her, the shopping she had done, the friends she had seen. There was no need to look around for things to talk about: she talked, and as she did so moved her long thin hands, clinking the bracelets on which dangled animal heads, each one of which he knew. When he heard her munching away at the lettuce leaves which she bit into like biscuits, he said: "You don't know how glad I am to see you again, Sylvia."

He agreed that it would be an excellent idea to hire a boat and wander about the Greek islands, as Bianca suggested: "Sooner or later you've got to see Greece, don't you agree?" Sylvia said: "Apparently there aren't many vegetables, just tomatoes, but they're huge. And fish. According to an article I read recently, if you want to live long you should eat raw fish, like the Japanese. That's fine for me. I loathe meat: I always have a feeling that a pair of beseeching eyes is gazing up at me from my steak. Have you ever thought you're living off corpses?"

He thought that Sylvia would look fine on board, wearing slacks. Sylvia, narrow-hipped, her small bosom free in a shirt that was open to the waist. Summer and winter, she was perfect. Intelligent, too, since she realized it would be a mistake to dramatize things, and made no snide remarks about male behavior. After long sessions with a psychoanalyst—concerning the tiresome business of getting to sleep, which she never managed to do before six in the morning—she was sure that she had found the secret of dealing with anyone she met. She would suddenly ask some odd and usually indiscreet question; then, with an ambiguous smile, say: "That's it, that's it exactly," as if the reply confirmed her own diagnosis.

"Do you know that queers like me?" she now remarked.

"You're a bit crazy," Giulio said, amused, and they got up to dance.

"Honestly, I excite them," she insisted.

"Not only queers," said Giulio, realizing that his sufferings over the past few days were merely a longing to make love. ("That's it, that's it exactly," he said to himself delightedly.) Soon afterward, when they were swaying on the dance floor, pressed tightly together and not moving a step, he said: "Shall we go?"

When he left her it was dawn. The large windows on the staircase were already lightening, while outside the red sky was reflected in the fountain, and the water around the two rings, man and woman, seemed tinged with blood.

As a rule, Giulio stayed at Sylvia's until morning: his perfectly balanced nervous system allowed him to sleep anywhere. In the morning he enjoyed having a shower among the green plants, blue parrots and glass jars in the bathroom Sylvia had decorated in the latest fashion. At that hour the birds were singing and everything around him seemed to beckon him on to a pleasant day. On the dressing table was a bunch of artificial flowers, pink and mauve, like the towels and curtains; another stood on the small Chinese chest containing the endless sleeping pills Sylvia took. "Fun, aren't they?" she said, turning a heap of small pills over in the palm of her hand; they were all sorts of colors or else silver, like those used to decorate wedding cakes.

The streets were empty, the shutters down. Giulio was starting up the engine when a small white car, parked behind his, revved up and shot away. "Someone going to work. All workmen have cars these days," he thought.

His stomach felt empty. The night before he had eaten practically nothing, out of consideration for Sylvia's lettuce. He would have liked to eat, but where? Although it was already light, it was only half-past four. The summer air reminded him of the cruise to Greece. "Holidays are obligatory nowadays, they aren't any fun," he thought: you had to write and telephone and get busy over them. He couldn't even find a bar open. "All the same, there must be some of them for truck drivers or bus drivers on duty." The thought of appearing in such a place wearing a dark suit, and heaven knows what sort of a face and eyes to match, made him feel uncomfortable. Men who used to spend all night roistering and then, wearing evening dress, go and have coffee outside the city gates, belonged to a class that could impose its own hours, its own customs, even its own disorder on others. "We're neither one thing nor the other."

He opened the door of his apartment cautiously, trying not to make a noise. The rooms were depressing in the pale light. Hunger sent him into the kitchen, but in the refrigerator he found only a flabby mozzarella. He took a packet of spaghetti from the pantry, filled a saucepan with water, put it on the stove and, while he waited for it to boil, flung himself down onto a chair.

What had happened to his life? He felt it had been abruptly interrupted, actually snapped into two, on the day he met Ivana, after his talk with Amati. He couldn't put the two pieces together, or fill the space that had formed between the pieces, these past few weeks. "People should never stop," Amati had said.

"Never turn to look at others, never let them speak. Above all, never stay alone. Take my tip: even while you're working, send for one of your colleagues, or your secretary. As a last resort, your wife . . . And never write letters: always dictate them. Otherwise, at some point, your thoughts go off on a tangent, take forbidden routes, stop where parking's not allowed. . . . Thought is the greatest enemy of action—of success."

The water took a long time to boil. And yet, Giulio reflected, it wasn't the first time a journey or a business matter, or, more often, a love affair, had distracted him. On his return from a journey, or at the end of a love affair, all he had to do to involve himself in the old way of life was make a few telephone calls and see a few people. But now, although he pretended he could do so, in fact he could not. Admittedly he had been delighted to see Sylvia again, to return to a well-furnished house—in other words, to be back in the world he was used to and liked—but after making love he had collapsed into suffering.

From the bathroom he had heard the faulty tap hissing, the sound of the glass stopper Sylvia always dropped when she opened her cologne bottle, bouncing on the tiles; the swish of the brush as she gave her hair its ten-minute evening treatment, as the women's magazines advised. On other occasions, while he was waiting, he had to struggle against sleep and take care that the cigarette didn't fall from his hand and burn the bedclothes. But last night, although not at all wide awake, he gazed at the framed dried flowers, at the music box with an ape on the top of it, playing the flute, at the lumps of quartz, the shells, the ex-votos and other expensive oddities Sylvia bought at antique shops in order to give herself a whimsical image. What was it all for? So-called good taste no longer expressed a personal choice, or aesthetic standards: it was a dreary, expensive obligation, offering nothing in exchange but the right to belong to a certain society. A dreary one, at that, Giulio thought. Then Sylvia came in, naked, shaking her hair to fling it back over her eyes. Giulio bounded up athletically and, standing up straight, belly well tucked in, went across to the bathroom.

But as soon as he had shut the door he felt his muscles suddenly slacken. He turned on the tap to let the water gush out and make her think he was washing energetically, and dropped onto the stool in front of the dressing table. He had already seen his toothbrush, which was green, the green bottle of lavender water, the soap and towels (also green) for his use. Everything showed that for the moment Sylvia was determined not to notice the vacant eyes that contradicted the smiles he had been so lavish with, and which had become increasingly difficult to give her. In bed, unable to pretend so easily, he had let her take the lead: after all, she was an experienced woman who had no wish to be possessed passively. "How long is it since you made love?" she asked him. "Since the last time with you," he replied. Sylvia laughed. Although it was unlike her, she said nothing more.

Their armistice was confirmed by these toilet articles, taken out of the cupboard where they had been awaiting his return (or another man's coming). Articles *pour un homme,* for a man, decorated with galloping horses, whips, gray toppers, boots and tartans, all the usual symbols of virility. Feminine fragility, on the other hand, was represented by pink opaline, bunches of violets, and the bottles full of colored powders that embellished Sylvia's bathroom as they had done those of Betty and Marité. Virility and femininity were now nothing more than cunningly manipulated commercial symbols. His green toothbrush poked out from a glass with *His* written on it, as it was on the towels, to make the sex of those who slept and lived together quite plain, a sex made to seem dubious by the very need for such labeling. Giulio felt quite unlike the man in the pink coat and tall hat riding a thoroughbred on the talcum-powder box; fatter than before, and short-winded, he plumped down on the dressing table pouffe that should have been *Hers* and fingered the delicate powder puffs, the colored wads of cotton-wool, the lipstick brushes; and where Sylvia in fact feverishly opened small bottles of pills, silver, blue, pink or mauve: their names, suggesting serenity, tranquility and forgetfulness, were mingled with those of creams guaranteeing eternal youth.

When he went back into the bedroom Sylvia was already going through the solemn ritual gestures of bedtime. She had put on her black glasses to set the alarm clock: "Will eight o'clock do?" she asked. She was naked: her small pointed breasts, slightly swollen at the tips, made her look like a wild animal. But the large round black glasses on her tiny face gave her the air of an insect. "I ought to lose two or three pounds, I know," she said, seeing him watching her. "Troubles make you put on weight. But you seem to have had a little trouble yourself. You've taken on a bit of tummy." She spoke carelessly, because for the moment—thanks to whatever sleeping pill she had just taken—nothing mattered. "I'm getting old," Giulio answered. "But there's a sort of relief in letting go, in giving way to the flesh; it's a conquest." Sylvia laughed, moving away to pick up her cigarettes. Her body, uniformly sunburned, showed that she went about naked, or almost naked, even on the beach.

"Eight o'clock, then." she said, setting the alarm. But Giulio was beginning to get dressed. "No thanks. I've got to go. I can't turn up at the office in a dark suit at nine in the morning." Sylvia found it hard to sound good-humored. "You could say you were going to a wedding later in the day." "Don't you think that would take a clean shirt, at least?" Giulio retorted. And, as he said it, there was another cold, glassy laugh. The large dark glasses prevented him seeing Sylvia's bewildered expression as she took him to the door, a little later; barefoot on the green carpet, as if walking in a field.

From the kitchen window Giulio now saw a few lights being switched on in the building opposite. People were waking reluctantly, as electric light clashed with the morning brightness, and returned with an effort to their dreary everyday life. For the first time Giulio felt the pain to which everyone else was subject. He saw Ivana sitting beside him, her hands in her lap, her staring eyes—an object that was complete, enclosed within itself, an object it was impossible to seize hold of.

The water had begun to boil. "Must put a bit of fuel in the engine," he thought as he put in the spaghetti. Now he had to wait again. He went to the window: people were going out of the street doors, looking chilly, although the day promised to be hot and the sun was already gilding the balconies. "I've always been a stranger to others and to life, cut out, excluded," he thought. But the sight of the day seemed to him unbearable.

There was no butter in the refrigerator. There was a whole packet on the breakfast tray yesterday morning, and thinking that Diodato must have gone to bed early, he went along to his room to wake him. He knocked quietly, then more loudly. No answer. He called: "Diodato . . ." Finally he opened the door.

The bedroom was empty, the bed still made. Through the open window came the frantic song of the sparrows waking in the plane tree below. The room was impregnated with a sickly smell: scattered about the floor he saw the fragments of a bottle of scent which Diodato must have dropped in his hurry to leave. On the chest of drawers, among holy pictures and statues of saints, was the photograph of a sharp-faced, curly-headed youngster, his mouth large and creased-looking, heavy-lipped.

Obviously Diodato had been unable to hold out. Well, so he hadn't really thought it was "better that way." The night had gradually worn down his conviction. Giulio felt all the defenses he had been building up during the past few hours crumbling about him. Suddenly and violently, Ivana's image returned. He saw her walking ahead of him as she had that first evening—her body revealed by the streetlamps or the headlamps of a car—and realized that he had merely been pretending to have forgotten her.

The sound of the boiling water recalled him to the kitchen.

Clumsily he drained the pasta: the steam burned his hand, dampened his face. Then he took the cruet of oil, emptied it over the spaghetti, and began eating greedily. The unsalted pasta tasted of nothing but hot oil; it was disgusting, but he gobbled it up with a kind of cheap delight.

Diodato suddenly appeared in the doorway, wearing light trousers and sandals, as if he had been at the sea. His neck was chalk-white in the open-necked shirt, where the collar usually covered it.

"Oh, sir," he said, embarrassed. "I had a telephone call and had to go out and meet my nephew, who was coming from Terni."

"The one in the photograph?"

"What photograph? . . . Oh. Yes, that's him." He kept twirling the housekeys around in his fingers, then went on humbly: "I'm glad to find you up, sir, because I had a bit of trouble just now. Nothing important," he hurried on, "but you know what the police are like . . . dreadfully suspicious. I was walking about in the San Giovanni district—you know, where that avenue runs along the wall—when they stopped us. I'd seen a small white car coming along behind us, very slowly, but I hadn't worried. All the same, I knew the police have grown cunning lately—they don't go around in police cars these days, but in Fiat 600's. They asked us for our papers and wanted to know what we were doing there at that hour. I thought I was lost. Then—forgive me, sir, but I said the young man was an electrician and that I'd come to fetch him on your account. If I'd said he was my nephew, they wouldn't have believed me, seeing his name isn't Marietti, like mine. But this way they let me go. But they wanted this phone number and the one at your office. I've taken advantage of you, I know, but I've been in your service for three years now and I think I've always been loyal and honest . . ."

Giulio nodded, his stomach heaving. He thought of the white

600 which had started up and left as he was leaving Sylvia's house: obviously Uncle Raffaele was having him followed. Next day he would tell his brother that "that fellow Giulio Broggini" had spent the night with a certain Sylvia Lowell, divorcée, where, according to the porter, he often spent the night.

"I don't feel well," he said. "It must be this filthy pasta. I forgot the salt. The oil's got a disgusting flavor; it must be refined." Overcome with nausea he got up to go to the bathroom, but was too late and rushed over to the sink.

"There, there," murmured Diodato, holding his forehead. "If I'd stayed at home I'd have prepared the pasta for you. . . . It's all my fault."

Each time he heaved and vomited, Giulio took a breath and said: "I'm sorry. Leave me now. I'm sorry."

But Diodato kept protesting: "What an idea! I wouldn't dream of it. You just do what you like and free yourself of it all. You'll feel better once you're free of it," he said, noticing how Giulio stared disgustedly at the curdled filth in the sink. "Don't look, sir. You mustn't ever look."

He supported Giulio into his bedroom and helped him undress. "What a horrible night," he kept muttering. He closed the shutters carefully and prepared the bed, saying, "There . . . now, that's ready." When Giulio was in bed he brought him hot lemon juice, held the glass to his lips, then tucked him in. Giulio accepted it all, bothered only by the smell of musk that came from Diodato's bald head. Diodato stared at him pityingly, as if he recognized his own sickness in Giulio, a sickness he had now resigned himself to accepting.

Next morning Giulio arrived at the office at eleven. Scarapecchia had not telephoned, the girl on the switchboard told him. Giulio was now quite sure that, having heard of his visit to Sylvia, Scarapecchia had made up his mind not to let him see Ivana again. ("I was there, I admit, but you must remember that although I'm in love I'm still a man—a young man. And the very fact that I respect Ivana means that I'm forced to seek sexual satisfaction elsewhere.") In his mind he was replying to Uncle Raffaele's accusations, and hoping he would say nothing to his brother, especially because, after a hasty marriage and an equally hasty divorce from an American, Sylvia was free and some people were saying that Giulio would finally marry her. ("I've got to get ready to duck them, when he makes his accusations.")

Giulio sent for his assistant and told him that as he had to write an important memorandum, he hadn't a moment to spare: so he must see to things, and not disturb him over anything.

"Suppose Mr. Scarapecchia calls," said Angeletti. Giulio stared suspiciously at him. "You said to put him right through. Do you want me to talk to him? What's it all about?"

"I see you check on my personal telephone calls. Not satisfied with taking advantage of my being away so as to take over the office, you now find out what orders I've been giving the staff. I'm not going to put up with this sort of thing, from you or anyone else. Understand?" said Giulio, thumping his fist on the desk.

"What are you talking about?" said Angeletti, sitting down and putting his hand on Giulio's closed fist in a friendly way. "Why do you imagine things I couldn't possibly do? I'm doing nothing but what I've always done, ever since I've been in your office. As for your private life, when have I ever interfered with it? You're overwhelmed, you look so odd. . . . Look, I'm your friend. Tell me if I can help in any way."

Exhausted, Giulio hid his face in his hands. In the darkness, under his shut lids, Ivana's white, never-smiling face appeared before him. His condition, as always, depended on his desire to get what he wanted—and this time, on the fear of not getting it.

"There's nothing wrong, I'm just tired," he said, recovering. "If Scarapecchia calls I'll talk to him myself."

When Angeletti had gone he took a sheet of his best engraved stationery out of a drawer and began: "Dear Mr. Scarapecchia, Nearly forty-eight hours have passed since the painful moment in which I had to leave your house, and I have not yet received the answer you promised me. This length of time is not long to a father who needs to reflect, but to a man in love it is an eternity. I know I have made many mistakes, yet the separation from Ivana and the uncertainty of this waiting are too severe a punishment. I hope you will be generous enough to forget what has happened so far; in the future I will be able to dissipate fully the suspicions unfortunately aroused in your mind and in your brother's about my intentions toward Ivana, suspicions based on appearances, not on what is substantially true. A month ago, on May 27 precisely, I asked you to allow me to visit your daughter. Today I ask for her hand."

Delighted with this cunning move, Giulio lay back in his armchair, pervaded by an unexpected happiness. Thus a woman, yielding to the lover she has tenaciously resisted, allows herself to be overwhelmed by a sense of delicious guilt. Giulio, too, at last felt at one with life. Nothing else counted—not his past, not the career he had pursued so tenaciously the success of which showed in everything around him—colleagues, pictures, furniture, the books in his office. He saw Ivana standing where the dummy had stood in the brightly lit shop window; her hand, once it wore a wedding ring, *could not* push his away like a tiresome horsefly. He owned that body: he could run his hands over it, touch it, and no one could contest his right to do so.

". . . I ask for her hand," he reread, and continued: "The wedding day, which I should like to settle in October—this will give me time to turn my bachelor's home into something fitting for a bride—will be on the date you decide. Please reflect that on your answer depends the happiness of my whole life and, I am sure, of Ivana's as well."

He finished off the letter and sent for the office boy to deliver it at once.

"Take a taxi, that'll be quicker," he said.

"Is there an answer?"

"No, leave it and come back."

But as soon as the office boy had left, even before he had gone through the front door, Giulio began waiting for an answer. In his mind he followed the messenger, spurring him on: he watched him light a cigarette, fiddle with the envelope, drop it, lose it. It was one o'clock. Scarapecchia today should leave his office at two; even if everything went smoothly, it would be a couple of hours before he read the letter.

The telephone rang. Giulio picked up the receiver and asked disagreeably: "Who is it?"

A very distant voice replied: "Scarapecchia."

This caught him by surprise. He had forgotten that he had said this one telephone call was to be put through to him; in fact, he was no longer hoping to receive it.

"Well, sir, I'm here at the Ministry with my brother. We have reflected, considered all the pros and cons and . . ."

"Just a minute," Giulio broke in quickly. "Don't say a thing, don't say any more."

There was silence on the other end. Perhaps, Giulio imagined, Uncle Raffaele had glanced across at him: he was sure to be listening to his brother's conversation, with his habitually suspicious air.

"Listen," Giulio said. "I've written a long letter. My office boy left with it about five minutes ago."

"And what do you say in it?"

"I said that . . ." Faced with the coldness which Scarapecchia's distant voice had acquired, Giulio made up his mind: "No, you'd better read it. Before making any decision or giving me a reply, you really must read it. Please."

"Well, if you're really set on that. I'll talk to you when I've read it, then," said Scarapecchia, and hung up after a quick, "Goodbye, then."

Giulio gasped, as if he had just escaped disaster. Then he realized that Scarapecchia had said nothing: he himself had been in such a hurry that he had stopped him from talking, instead of letting him speak first, as he usually did. That letter was a mistake. Worse, it was idiotic. Very likely Scarapecchia had no intention of refusing to let him see Ivana or of putting a rope around his neck by fixing the actual day of the wedding, as he had done, like a fool. "Southerners are used to long engagements," he thought. "Mothers take ages preparing the bride's things . . ." But anyway, even though he had fixed a date, he could always put it off with the excuse that he was moving or that he was waiting for his parents' approval, which—perhaps because of the inheritance—Scarapecchia seemed particularly anxious for him to have. Meantime he would have a chance to establish a satisfactory intimacy with Ivana; and even if he did not achieve what he would later—since she was a minor—have to pay for with marriage, he would soothe his longing for her.

The telephone call from Scarapecchia had removed his fears, meanwhile. He was sure that both he and Uncle Raffaele would finally give way. The constant presence of this invisible uncle watching him was irritating; Giulio had crawled to the fellow, and perhaps the very speed with which he had acted—a clear sign of insecurity or guilt—would make Uncle Raffaele more suspicious than ever. The thought of this made Giulio more irritated with himself; particularly because, now that the telephone call had restored his peace of mind, he was gradually being persuaded that he had overestimated the importance of a quite insignificant policeman; possibly because of what had happened to Diodato last night, the same night that he had stayed with Sylvia. Since then the invisible Uncle Raffaele had been limiting his freedom. He imagined him sitting at a big black desk covered with switches and telephones, watching him and following him from there, with a special electronic eye that registered his movements on a panel, on which he was merely an antlike glimmer.

He went over to the window, hoping to see the office boy return. There on the street, in a white 600, were two darkly dressed men. When he left the house that morning he had noticed a similar car, with two similar-looking men in it, at the front door of his own house. Another had stopped abruptly behind his car, when he braked suddenly at some traffic lights. Now that he was sure he was being followed, he felt equally sure that his telephone calls were being bugged as well, that the spy system used by the police in fascist times was still in use.

When he saw the office boy return, Giulio went down to meet him at the door.

"Who opened the door to you there, a girl?" he asked.

"No. A short chap in striped pajamas."

"What happened then?"

"I said: 'Are you Mr. Scarapecchia?'" said the office boy. "And he said: 'I am.' He took the letter, made me a sign to wait outside, and shut the door again. After about five minutes he opened up again and gave me this," and the office boy took a dark blue envelope out of his pocket.

When he was alone Giulio hesitated before opening the envelope, on which his name was childishly written, in clumsy capitals. Perhaps, in spite of her father's agreement, she had refused him. Perhaps it was a first love letter.

But there were only a few words: *"Papa says you can come this evening after supper. Yours, Ivana."*

Though longing to see Ivana again, Giulio arrived at ten o'clock. The Scarapecchias had supper late, and people of their sort disliked being caught at the table, since they all behaved very informally as soon as they got home. Giulio had actually had the shutters closed in his face once when he had happened to glance through the ground floor windows as he left Ivana's, walking slowly to the car he had deliberately parked at a distance.

That evening he parked noisily outside the gate, as if to guarantee his present and future sincerity. And instead of feeling uneasy over his previous lies, he felt rather magnanimous for now agreeing to be truthful—or, at least, for pretending to be so.

Scarapecchia opened the door. "Come in," he said. "First of all, let's have a talk."

Giulio seemed at ease, though he was irritated by the obstacles put in his way before he could see Ivana again. Why all this drama? he wondered, feeling that the playacting was not so much amusing as tedious.

"Well, my dear Mr. Broggini, the very fact that I've asked you to come this evening shows that I've decided to trust you." (Giulio could hardly fail to be pleased with that "dear.") "Besides, who hasn't played pranks at one time or other?" Giulio nodded, his smile half cordial and half servile. ("Yes, my dear Scarapecchia, dear, dearest Scarapecchia, you're quite right to decide it this way, perfectly right and proper.") "Indeed, from now on I consider you officially engaged," Scarapecchia continued. "I've got nothing against a wedding in October, but you'd better talk to her mother about that. As you know, it's the women who settle these things." He laughed, and Giulio laughed as well, although he felt Scarapecchia was growing vulgar; he had the same way of laughing as Ivana, which Giulio disliked so much. "Now, the pair of us have got to talk about what you can guarantee my daughter. I'm talking about the material side of things this time."

"I'm perfectly prepared to answer," said Giulio, flinging out his arms. "But don't you know everything about me already? Your brother," he said, turning to the photograph of Raffaele, "knows everything: past, present, friendships, way of life . . ."

"That's true. But I must admit that, when it's a personal matter, I don't trust any official arm, not even the police's. I'd like to hear the facts from you yourself."

("He wants to know how much," Giulio thought. And as always, he sized up the life of the man before him before mentioning a figure, a figure that was in no way based on just or objective principles, but on his adversary's economic position, on the urgency of his demands.)

"I can tell you exactly what I pay taxes on . . ."

"Oh, come on," Scarapecchia broke in. "What have taxes got

to do with your real professional earnings? You can't think I'm so simple as to believe . . ."

"Agreed. But it'll give you something to go on. Besides, on the day of our marriage or even before, in fact definitely before, I can give you a certain amount . . ."

"Why's that? I'm not selling you my daughter."

"I expressed myself badly," Giulio hastened to explain, knowing Scarapecchia's touchiness. "What I meant was, after the marriage you could settle it on Ivana."

Scarapecchia shook his head. "I don't agree. Women always fritter money away. They spend it on clothes, beauty products, rubbish like that."

"The best solution," said Giulio, leaning forward in his chair, "is for me to give it to you right away. It'll be a guarantee of my commitment to Ivana. You can use it as you like, get some profit out of it."

"Is that what's done among people like you?" Scarapecchia asked hesitantly.

Giulio seized on the suggestion. "Yes. It's . . . how can I put it? . . . it's a way of showing one respects the shrewdness and integrity of one's future father-in-law."

"Thank you. That flatters me, I'm really delighted." ("We're beginning to understand each other," Giulio thought, with a sigh of relief.)

"Thank you," said Scarapecchia again. "But, you see, I've my work, my business . . . which hasn't always gone so well—like that of the co-op to which I've given so much of my life, only to get . . . well, let's forget it, this is hardly the time for regrets and recriminations . . . *I gave as good as I got*," he said emphatically. "Well, as I was saying . . . why this money? If anything, it's the bride who should bring a dowry, but Ivana's an only child and all I have will be hers one day—a day I hope's a long way off, because although I'm a believer I think it's always risky to leave what you know for what you don't. Above all when what you don't know, if I can call it that," he said, glancing heavenward, "doesn't seem to offer much hope to a good Christian, now that everyone seems so much at home up there in their space ships. Well," he sighed, "let's forget philosophy, or who knows where it'll end . . . A sum of money, I was saying, is always an awkward business. I'd sooner it stayed in your hands. Or rather—do you know who I'd like to settle it on?"

("On your brother," Giulio thought. "A variation on the usual system of bribes." Uncle Raffaele would retort: "No. A suitable payment for the information I've provided, for the part I've allowed him to play in our house.")

"Rosario," signora Adelina interrupted, coming into the room, "What shall we do, shall we drink it right away?" She turned delightedly to Giulio and said, "Good evening," then went on: "This business of the spumante has made me so nervous. All I keep doing is opening and shutting the ice box."

"Fine, fine," said Scarapecchia, shaking his head. "If spumante isn't really cold . . ."

He went into the kitchen and his wife took the opportunity of speaking quietly to Giulio: "Happy, now? I knew it would all go right in the end. Ivana's pleased too. She's not the sort to show it, but she's spent an hour in her bedroom, getting ready . . ." and she made a mimicking movement, as if making up her eyelashes.

"I thought Ivana slept here," said Giulio, indicating the divan.

"Well, it belongs to her—it's nice, isn't it?—but she doesn't sleep on it, she never has. She'd seen it in a shop window and liked it so much that one day her father said: 'Would you like me to buy it for you?' And he did. It'll be her wedding bed," she went on, in a knowing way. Then, overcome with emotion: "Please remember, she's still a child. She's frightened. She's very frightened of the act itself."

Giulio reassured her, and even went so far as to stroke her

arm: a frail bone inside the sleeve of her sweater. That contact, and even more his own hypocrisy, made him feel a sudden revulsion—toward himself and toward everything around him. ("I've made a mistake," he would write and tell Scarapecchia. "Besides, as you told me yourself, it's better to break things off early rather than late . . . " and then he would simply vanish.)

"Ssh," said signora Adelina, indicating the tapping of heels on the passage tiles. "Here she is. You'll see how pretty she is," and she blew her nose and moved away.

Ivana stood in the doorway, embarrassed at her party clothes: her shoulders were bare, and the very tight bodice showed a great deal of her bosom. Giulio was stunned. He had not seen her for three days and had even thought of never seeing her again, had even supposed that it was merely pride that had made him pit himself against her father and uncle—a cockfight. But Ivana had only to show herself for everything to crumble. ("I don't care about anything else, nothing else can give me this . . . this . . .") He could not have said what it was.

Ivana was staring enigmatically at him. "You're back," she said.

("She's understood. She's understood everything and she agrees, but she hates me.") Shyly he asked her: "Are you pleased to see me?"

"Who'd force me to, if I wasn't? I'd have said no."

Scarapecchia had come back, carrying the bottle of spumante wrapped in a napkin. "Let's open it!" he said gaily, urging Ivana forward. "Go on, go on . . . You can give your fiance a kiss tonight, you know." He smiled and encouraged Giulio to come forward as well, then busied himself discreetly at the table, with his wife.

Giulio went over to Ivana, who was coming toward him hesitantly because her heels were as usual too high; they were both obeying something that was quite outside their conscious feelings. Giulio approached and took her in his arms. As he kissed her, Ivana's eyes stayed wide open, and her thick-lipped mouth stayed closed.

The cork popped, and shook Giulio out of his trance: "Come over! Or it'll all be spoiled," called Ivana's mother, while her husband quickly filled up the glasses.

"First to the happy couple!" he cried, and the toasts and good wishes and clinking of glasses began; and then their excitement suddenly died, and they raised their glasses to their lips and drank in silence. "Ah," said Scarapecchia, as if slaking his thirst after some hard running; then he noticed a fifth glass that stood empty and asked: "Who's that for?"

"Raffaele promised to come," said signora Adelina. "But then he called . . . I didn't put away the glass because it seemed unfriendly, somehow."

"Yes, of course," sighed Scarapecchia. "In his position, my brother's never free. Do you know that while we're peacefully sleeping he's often awake, and quite willingly?" He ran his finger over the glass on the tray. "In large cities there's an ugly atmosphere at night. But there are those who look after us, praise be, and as long as there's good order everything's all right. If there wasn't, what on earth would happen? People say we don't give a damn for the police here in Italy, don't they? We ourselves think we're not the sort of people to accept restrictions and put up with any discipline. But actually the more undisciplined people are, the more power the police have. That's exactly it. And do you know what? The strength of the police doesn't lie in the number of men, or the way they're equipped, or even in their weapons. Their strength lies in people's consciences. Or rather in their bad consciences. And, in fact, something does happen . . . now I'll explain," and he pulled a chair up to the sofa where Giulio was sitting with Ivana.

"Oh, do let them alone, Rosario! Today of all days, when they want to talk to each other."

"They'll have all their lives to talk," said Scarapecchia, shrugging.

"Do you imagine he doesn't know all about that sort of thing? As a lawyer, he's always having to deal with delinquents and criminals . . ."

"You might at least remember that your future son-in-law's not a criminal lawyer," said Scarapecchia.

"I always thought he was a lawyer," said signora Adelina, mortified.

"Yes, of course he's a lawyer. It's just that he doesn't deal with criminals, only with civil law."

"Oh well, how could I know that. . . . Does that mean he's a notary?"

"Keep quiet, Mama," said Ivana, without turning around.

"No, it means he deals with people who commit crimes in a civil way!" Scarapecchia laughed, delighted with his own wit: "That's true, isn't it?" Then he spread his first finger and thumb across his forehead: "Adelina's always interrupting me. What were we talking about? Ah, yes, that as a rule it's as if the police didn't exist. Take this evening, for instance—who's bothering about the police in this house? But suppose one of us was a criminal. Suppose that when you came here you meant to commit a crime . . . then in everyone you passed you'd have seen a policeman. Your imagination would have multiplied the entire police force. Although there really aren't many of them, you'd have seen a policeman wherever you went—in plain clothes, of course, as most of them are."

"Oh really? Do they wear plain clothes?" said Giulio. "All this is extremely interesting. Tell me, now, is it true that the police don't use those proper police cars any more—the ones they call panthers, with a little blue light on the roof? I've been told they go round in any sort of car: a Giulia, or even a Fiat 600. I've heard they often use a 600 to go around without being noticed."

"A 600? Certainly. Sometimes when I go to the Viminale I see them all coming back together. They look like white mice. Whereas they're the ones that catch the mice," said Scarapecchia shaking his head. "A mouse they've been secretly playing with for weeks, for months, before they get their claws into him. Because, you see, the great thing about them is that they know how to be patient. As a rule, they know."

"Know what?"

"Well, they know beforehand who their customers are going to be. They know them, even if they've got no police record. They keep an eye on them, certain that someday . . ."

"Oh, really, I think you're exaggerating," said Giulio.

"I only wish I was! Unfortunately I've had plenty of proof of it."

"You see, being close to Raffaele . . ." explained his wife.

"Yes, of course. You see, from his desk my brother seems able to read into people's consciences. And when he's perfectly sure a man can't get away, and that sooner or later he'll have to bring him in . . . he's sorry for it, truly. It's like the good Lord when there's a soul that just can't be saved."

"And what about free will. Where do you put that?" said Giulio, smiling.

"There isn't any. It doesn't exist. No one's free because no one's innocent. We're all up to something, in some way or other, even if we're perfectly all right on paper. My brother says he could have anyone arrested; but the cleverness of the police lies in *not* doing that. In fact, its power is based on the general guiltiness of people, that's what it consists of. That's why they pretend not to see or notice anything. Admittedly they sometimes get bored with hanging around and, instead of waiting, they provoke the right moment, just to hurry things up."

Giulio wondered if Scarapecchia was trying to warn him that Uncle Raffaele had guessed his intentions, and at the same time let him realize that he himself would be quite ready to let him off—after pocketing the sum they had mentioned—but that his brother, with his police force and his mania for good order, was not the sort of person to play tricks with. Perhaps he was also trying to put him on his guard against the chances he would be offered, and which he must be careful not to take. ("Everything's been calculated, foreseen. Even Ivana's dress, with its excessively low neck, may have been one of her uncle's ideas. He may even have paid for it. As a way of making me corrupt a minor, a crime I'd have to pay for with marriage. It's your choice, he'd tell me: marry her or pay up.")

In the past, when one of his mistresses mentioned a permanent tie, Giulio had at once said that he was not the marrying kind: he would die a bachelor, in the arms of an old housekeeper. If the woman pressed it he hurried off, quickly and cruelly. But that evening, while they drank the spumante, he had actually felt moved. "Because I know it's all a fake. Everything, except my longing to get this girl to bed, whatever happens. Whatever I have to pay," he thought, forgetting his own meanness. Indeed, the thought of paying gave him a sense of relief. The deal with Amati meant he could fully afford such a luxury; besides which, it meant that he was now in the confidence of a group that had its hands on every big building job in town. "I always worried over marrying other women because it was always a possibility. Here it's all a farce." He realized that persuading Ivana to yield was going to be difficult; but he trusted in her lethargic nature, in the apathy with which she accepted everything imposed on her. "You mustn't see him," and she did not; "Kiss him," and she did.

Later Scarapecchia excused himself: he had to join some friends at the café to talk business. He kissed Ivana and said: "You really are a pretty fiancée. And for the moment, you're still all mine."

They all went to see him off on the stairs. "You can breathe out here," Giulio remarked. "The air's a bit fresher."

"You stay out here where it's cool while I straighten up the kitchen," said Ivana's mother. "In any case, all the neighbors know; they asked me when we'd be having the wedding. And anyway, with this moon it's just like day."

The landing, high above the garden, made a kind of pulpit fringed by the dark tangle of a climbing plant. Ivana went over to the railing, with a detached, dreamy air.

"Why do you wear lipstick?" Giulio asked her. "I can't kiss you, if you do."

"Why not? Didn't you kiss me before?"

"Yes, but . . ."

"Well then?" said Ivana, and looked over the rail, lifting up her face and shutting her eyes happily, as if sunbathing. When she did this the top of the dress, which was stiffened with whalebone, shifted and Giulio caught a glimpse of her large white breasts, with their dark tips, turgid as olives. Giulio glanced quickly up at the house front to make sure no one was watching from above, and then, quite naturally, as if he wanted to admire the material of the dress, he put two fingers between it and her breast.

"Put down your hands," Ivana said.

"Even now, when we're engaged?"

"Put down your hands," she repeated, motionless, eyes shut, face turned to the moon. She did not notice, or pretended not to notice, the way he was staring at her breasts. ("Round, full, already drooping a little, like those of a mature woman.") She opened her eyes again, with a sigh. "Is it yours?" she asked, jerking her chin at the car parked by the gate. When he told her it was, she said: "I like red cars."

"Oh, all right," said Giulio. He smiled, but felt indignant at Ivana's casualness at the sight of a car that had cost several million lire. "I'll give you a red one, a tiny one all to yourself. Can you drive?"

"I've tried two or three times, in Uncle's car. He said I shouldn't get a license, I'm too nervous."

While they were talking Giulio had delicately managed to lower one side of the dress, exposing one of her breasts. Ivana made no objection and this encouraged him to defy her uncle.

"It's absurd the way you all depend on what this famous uncle says and decides."

"How can you possibly tell? You don't know him."

"All right. But, to you at least, what I think ought to carry more weight. Tell him: I'm taking driving lessons because that's what my fiancée wants me to do," said Giulio. Then, thinking it might be a good opportunity, he added: "Besides, I'll teach you to drive myself."

Ivana straightened herself, without answering; with a jerk of her shoulder, she put the breast back inside her dress.

"Well?" said Giulio. "Aren't you going to say anything?"

She turned just as much as was necessary to give him a side-long glance. "Do you know why Uncle didn't come this evening? It's not true that he's busy. He's always busy, but when he wants to he can get away. He didn't come because he doesn't agree."

"Doesn't agree about what?"

"About you. He doesn't approve of you."

"Ah," said Giulio, thin-lipped and sarcastic. "And why, may I ask?" Ivana's only answer was to go back into the sitting room. Her mother was pouring what was left from the bottle of spumante. "There was still a tiny bit," she said apologetically, and raised the glass toward them. "Here's to you!"

"I want to know the reason," said Giulio insistently.

"The reason for what?" asked signora Adelina.

"Nothing, it's our business," Ivana told her; and to Giulio she said: "Excuse me, I'm going to bed. The spumante's given me a headache."

"I'll bet! Why, she hasn't even had supper!" exclaimed her

mother, and was immediately silenced by a threatening glare from Ivana. "What's wrong with that? Of course, it's all the excitement."

"Well, till tomorrow then," said Ivana. "Good night," and with a slightly ironical air she held her lips out to Giulio. Then, as she went to her bedroom she said, without turning: "Wipe your mouth, Giulio, it's all red."

He slammed the gate, slammed the car door and shot away with a roar, mentally composing the letter he meant to write as soon as he got home. " 'Dear' . . . no, why 'dear'? Let him go to hell. 'Sir, perhaps my character does not suit your daughter's, or else we lack the natural attraction which . . . However that may be, I am now quite convinced that Ivana does not love me . . . that Ivana does not return the feeling which . . . Therefore I think it my duty . . . I think it is right, therefore . . .' " He was glad to be jilting her now that her father had consented, now that she had let him pull down her dress. Signora Adelina would sigh: "If I'd known, I wouldn't have bought the spumante." He felt a little touched by the heroic way she pretended they lived a middle-class life—

symbolized by the pompous way her husband spoke, hiding his coarse ideas and rough accent—while her defenseless face and frightened eyes showed wretchedness and dismay.

Whereas Ivana was merely ridiculous, greedy and gross. A provincial girl, thirty years out of date. What longing for degradation could have made him actually consider marrying her? "My wife," he thought, laughing at himself.

(In the middle of the darkish street, beyond the windshield, he saw Uncle Raffaele: his squat, short-necked figure, his fleshy shoulders. He accelerated to catch up with him, but the man moved off at the same speed as the car. Then Giulio ran through the great dusty passages of the Viminale, knocking on doors and hearing, "Come in," spoken in Uncle Raffaele's accent; he carried on till he reached the desk where he sat, clumsily preening himself: "Look, will you satisfy my curiosity? Why aren't you pleased, why don't you approve? I'm engaged, I've been drinking toasts . . . drinking toasts in that foul sweet spumante that's ruining my stomach. What else do you want? Come on, tell me.")

He was driving too fast, deliberately. "If only they'd stop me, I'd really blow up. In any case I'd get the better of that 600." In the driving mirror he saw a white one following him and suddenly braked. "If it's Uncle Raffaele I'll knock his block off." It was a little old man who only just managed to swerve and then leaned out of the window and yelled: "Cuckold!"

Maybe the old man was right. Uncle Raffaele must be in love with his niece. "Maybe he's threatening to take no more interest in the family, or in that mysterious business of the co-op; maybe he's blackmailing her because of me and she's scared." Then he wondered suspiciously whether Ivana was in league with him, and this strengthened his decision to write to Scarapecchia. (Again he ran through the passages of the Viminale, bursting into rooms without knocking, this time: "I see what you've got in mind: Broggini marries her, Broggini pays, and then Uncle enjoys her, that's it, isn't it?" But Uncle Raffaele calmly replied: "Oh, come off it, when have you really thought of marrying her? All you want to do is take her home and do filthy things to her. Go on and write that letter, then. Write it here, if you like," and he held out a pen. "Shall I dictate it to you?")

He went back along Via Quattro Fontane, feeling depressed. For a while he had wandered around the Viminale—with his engine in low gear, to annoy them—but two policemen popped out from somewhere, and came forward to watch his maneuvers and maybe stop him. "I'm a fool. What do I care about this famous uncle? Let him enjoy her. Let him. Let's both of us enjoy her. I like her and this evening I've had proof that I can get what I want from her, so long as I don't ask her to participate or even notice what I'm doing. All that tact, all that patience, all that amusing background I invented, all those chocolates and presents and carefully chosen words—all lost on the eve of victory." He saw Ivana leaning over the parapet, with her naked white breast in the curve of the armpit, and no longer felt anything. "I'm over it, thank heaven." Instead he felt an absurd longing for that room over the garden, for the scent of wet grass and oleander that came in through the window. Bewilderment, sudden fear, and at the same time a spurt of rebellion at the idea of losing everything, as if someone was plotting to take away a kingdom he had won through some clever maneuver; a throne on which he felt a security he had never known before, where he was the boss and could relax and feel at ease, served by two humble, silent women who took off his jacket and bent down to unlace his shoes; after which one of them vanished ("See how pretty she is? I'm leaving!") and Ivana continued to serve him, making practiced, loving movements over his body, while taking no part at all in them, either with looks or with words. "What does the rest of it matter? Let her go to bed with anyone she likes, so long as she lets me touch her, so long as she stands still." But fury returned and blinded him. It was not jealousy, it was more a longing to make some violent gesture that would smash the silence and impassibility of Ivana and her uncle. "They've agreed, they need me, they need the marriage in order to be free." The passage again, the door again, he opened it and went straight over to the policeman who was sitting behind his heavy desk. "There's no need to introduce myself, is there? I presume you know me, after the reports from your spies, the photographs, the card indexing, the way my phone's been bugged. Maybe there's a microphone in the chair signora Adelina puts out for me every day. . . . Well, here I am in person, since you haven't the courage to show yourself. I've come to tell you you're a coward." A crowd of policemen surrounded him and dragged him away by the arms, while he kept saying: "Coward, filthy coward!" In real life, he would never even have got inside. "Who are you? Where are you going? Documents. Reason for visit? Personal reasons. Fill in the form. Indicate your wishes exactly. Put down the truth or you'll be detained." He wrote it, and then they arrested him for outraging decency, for pornography. "But didn't you want to know the truth? All I asked was to talk to Dr. Raffaele Scarapecchia." He's not here, he's off-duty. Nothing doing. Talk to his secretary. "But if I meet him I'll pretend to be drunk, or rather to be ill all of a sudden, and then I'll get hold of him. I'd be unlikely to meet him round here: he's the sort of person who belongs near the Esquiline, who never goes far from the Ministry, and always stays in the shadows." The best thing was to telephone Ivana and make her talk. "I'll call her now, from somewhere—from a café. 'She's asleep,' her mother will say. 'Wake her up, get her up at once,' I'll say. She'll come without hurrying, like a queen. And I'll say abruptly: 'Who were you talking to that evening in the bar? Who were you talking to, you whore?' "

He had stopped in Via Veneto, among innumerable other cars, in a traffic jam. Occasionally there was a bump, a tinny crash: angry faces behind the panes, threatening fists through the windows, then the closely pressed column would start up again and crawl a couple of yards forward. Everyone, at that hour, was going home from the movies. He saw a friend entering a nightclub with two tall girls, and thought of going in later and joining them for a drink. He looked for somewhere to park. The attendant said: "No space, sir!" In the side streets, cars were squashed together on either side. He refused to admit he couldn't find a space, couldn't telephone, couldn't discover anything, that he had to stay tied to that wheel of black plastic. Foaming with rage, he wanted to drive at a shop window and smash it. But he was surrounded by other cars that stopped him from committing the violent action that would have soothed him. He had to control himself, live in a civilized way, we're a civilized people, all you need do to see that is look around you. A couple in the car in front of him, another couple in the driving mirror: two still heads close to each other as they were in the movies, or in front of television, or in church on a Sunday morning. Man and woman, silent, patient, bound to each other, in fact intertwined like the two plaster rings in the fountain outside Sylvia's.

At last the convoy of cars moved out of Via Veneto. Joining his friend with the two girls probably meant ending up at his own home: whisky, records, "What, going already? Stay, have something to eat, let's go and see what there is in the kitchen"; eating and then—with the dirty plates in front of them, and the ashtrays full of olive pits, salami skin, bread crumbs and cigarette stubs—lingering on through inertia, while time went by and the night became tattered and torn, showing the sinister glow of morning among the last kindly corners of darkness. Or else he would end up in bed with one of the two girls and then: "Will you go first, yes thanks, run along then, if you really don't mind I'll go now, cigarette? Nice, you've been nice, you've been nice too, really sweet, let's meet again, let's fix a date, let's have supper, let's call, give me your number, where shall we write it?"—looking for a piece of paper, a pencil—we should wear our numbers printed on ourselves somewhere, like criminals in police photographs, or tattooed on our chest—that's even better, "What do you think? Good idea, you're a scream, you make love so gaily," gaily my eye, now I'll have to take her home, up to the very top of one of those damned hills—Monte Mario, Monte Verde, Monte Sacro—first right, then left, left again, "Here we are, no, further on, the next gate . . . Here we are . . . oh, it's nice here"—thinking: wouldn't be seen dead—"Yes, it's nice, there's a bit of garden at the back, you've been sweet to bring me back," a kiss, " *'Bye,*" crossing the garden of the block like long-legged birds flapping their wings, have to wait while they open the door, while they go in, then a wave to say " *'Bye*" again, then it's over. Next day, say hullo: endless hullos on the telephone, from Monte Mario to Trastevere, from Monte Verde to Parioli, "Just saying hullo, it was lovely yesterday, just lovely, sleep well? You're a real man," oh, come off it! "You are, honestly, you make a girl feel protected," bells ringing, endlessly calling, calling insistently in furnished rooms, by unmade divans, just to say, "Hi, what are you doing today?" the voice of loneliness itself, of emptiness, of nothingness, calling for help.

In Via Veneto, among the men sitting at the café tables, or placidly crossing the street, with their hands in their pockets, he kept thinking he recognized Uncle Raffaele. "The fact is that we're dominated by the dark southern type, with shiny black eyes, and olive skin, full of fatty secretions. God knows why Nordic people find us so fascinating."

He moved away disgustedly from the fine old street, which had once been flanked by large leafy plane trees, and now, with its closely packed vertical neon signs, looked like a street in Hong Kong or some other Eastern port.

Beside Via Pinciana, the pines of Villa Borghese made a shady roof. Years ago he sometimes went for walks under these pines, with women who wore flat-heeled shoes. Now, he was incapable of walking a single step: if he wanted to go a hundred yards he took the car. "I no longer feel like it. I no longer want any-thing." The fact was that he had never really wanted anything, but had gone on without a pause, never stopping to wonder what was the object of his energy—as if the energy itself were his only motive.

When they last met, his father had said to him: "You've been like this for years, never seeing what's happening around you in the world . . . without a plan." Giulio had told him he was wrong: his plan was to live well and make money. "You've never been without money," his father had answered, and he had said: "That's true. But I want a lot. Because, unlike you, I think the world belongs to the man who's got most." "What world? What do you mean by the world?" His father's familiar soph-isms. He had replied that there was only one world that mattered and that his father failed to understand it because he was out of touch with the present. "Out of touch or untouchable?" An-other long-winded speech. "Forget it. Let's stick to our own plan," Giulio had told him.

But now he was afraid of growing to be like some of his worried, neurotic friends. He had always felt perfectly in touch. He didn't even bother to define the meaning of the word: he kept using it as he kept using others—alienation, cosmic suffer-ing—which Sylvia's friends used in a knowing way, although they were now current even in the daily papers. His father was on the editorial board of *Orsa Minore*, a monthly review Giulio laughingly called "the malcontents' charter." He flicked through his complimentary copy, whirling the pages like wind-mill sails: it always put him in a bad temper, and he handed it to the office boy for the waiting room table. One of his clients had once said to him: "I was glad to see you subscribe to *Orsa Minore*. In fact, I've been wondering if you're any relation of Elpidio Broggini." When he heard that Giulio was his son, he had looked at him with new respect and said: "I'm glad, I'm so glad."

The house smelled stuffy, the rooms looked desolate. Before, thanks to his long nightly chats on the telephone, he hadn't noticed that he lived alone. Now he let the telephone ring without a flicker of curiosity, scarcely glanced at the mail, put letters aside without opening them and tore up invitations to the social gatherings he had always been to, feeling that, professionally, he could not fail to visit his more important clients, to meet people and be seen himself. In the hall, the calendar on which he wrote down these appointments, and which he paused every evening to consult, had stopped at May 27.

He began pulling off the pages, one by one, weighing the days that had gone by. Since meeting Ivana, he had done nothing. "And I didn't before that, either," he thought disconsolately, but he realized he was not being objective. "I'll soon be thinking I've done nothing in my whole life." He was still tearing off the calendar pages, and on June 20 he stopped, feeling puzzled, and certain that he had forgotten an appointment on that day. It must have been an important one, too. "I'll check at the office tomorrow. I've forgotten everything, dropped everything, because of this absurd sex business, and Uncle Raffaele doesn't agree, doesn't approve."

Once again he felt shaken with rage. "Tomorrow I'll go to the Viminale and see him myself. No, I won't put myself out that much—I'll telephone. I might even call him at home, at night, to catch him off guard. Anyway, according to Scarapecchia, he keeps a sharp eye on us all. Checks on us even while we're asleep."

He picked up the telephone book and started looking through the letter S: there were several Scarapecchias, but no Raffaele. "He must be ex-directory, like me: I might have known it." But Raffaele Scarapecchia knew Giulio's number and listened to his conversations, always hidden, always invisible. Maybe he had found out where he lived through signora Adelina.

The telephone rang in his study, making him start. He thought it must be Sylvia—or some other woman on the alienation jag—and decided not to answer. But it went on ringing. "It must be Uncle Raffaele calling to see if I'm at home." He ran into the study. In the darkness he failed to find the light switch on the desk and tripped over the electric and telephone wires, until at last he found the instrument, cursing to himself. "Hello," he said. No use, he had picked the receiver up the wrong way round. He turned it. "Hello . . ." The speaker had already hung up. He angrily banged the telephone several times. Whoever had suddenly dragged him out of his solitude, whoever was looking for him, making him exist, for whatever reason, had vanished. He stayed listening to the telephone ringing at the exchange, shrilly and regularly, like a telegraphic signal in code, the very language of space, of the unknown universe around him. For a long time he listened and at last hung up and dropped into the armchair close by him, not even switching on the light.

From the window he could see the dark outline of the Olympic Village, glinting with lights, like a cemetery. Alone in the silence of the empty house, the thought of death came to him for the first time, and he was filled with a sense of rest and peace. The days still left to him—a great many, since he was only thirty-nine—seemed interminable, superfluous, with nothing at the end of them but a dark landscape where silence and gloom were symbols of forgetfulness, of nothingness, into which those who already lay there had disappeared. "There's always a reason for thoughts like these; they're premonitions." Uncle Raffaele, who forbade him to possess Ivana, seemed the incarnation of something more serious, something that threatened his life. He put his hand to his forehead: it was frozen. "I must call Ugo tomorrow and get him to send me to the hospital for a checkup." He wanted a drink of whisky but an absurd fear of the dark—or rather, of his presence in the darkness—stopped him from moving. "This loneliness, these gloomy, unlived-in rooms . . ."

The telephone rang again, and he grabbed the receiver desperately, as if salvation might unexpectedly come to him from it.

It was his mother in Milan. "How are you, Mama? Did you call me a while ago?"

"I've called you so many times . . . yesterday and today. I was worried. . . . Have you seen Papa?"

"When?"

"That's it, I don't know. I just can't find him. . . . He should have been back from Mexico the day before yesterday."

"From Mexico?" Giulio repeated. ("That's the date I forgot: Daria on the twentieth.")

"Didn't he telephone you a couple of weeks ago, when he went through Rome? How extraordinary! He promised he'd ring you from the airport. He went to Mexico for one of his congresses. Didn't you get my letter?"

"What letter? When?"

"Giulio, what's the matter? You sound strange."

"No . . . you see, I was asleep."

"Ah," said his mother. "I'm sorry. . . . So you didn't get it?"

"I don't know, I don't think I did."

"Heavens, don't you even know that?"

"If it came this evening I'll find it tomorrow in the office. . . . How are you, Mama?"

"How about you, are you all right? This evening I couldn't get hold of you, of either of you. I was afraid there might have been an accident, the plane . . . you keep reading about disasters in the papers, riots, earthquakes, floods . . . I kept dialing you and hearing the bell ringing in emptiness."

"But what's the matter? Your voice sounds—"

"You know, when I haven't got Papa . . . the days are endless, I don't feel like doing anything. In any case, I wouldn't know what to do . . . old age is very dreary, you know. And here, it's stiflingly hot. . . . Listen, see if you can find Papa, tomorrow. Then send me a telegram, will you? Do you understand?"

"Right. Is there anything else?"

"No, what else could there be? Absolutely nothing. Anything new with you?"

"New?" ("Now I'll say: 'I'm getting married.' ") "What sort of new?"

"Well, I don't know, just in general . . ."

"No, nothing." ("She'd ask me: 'Who is she? What's her name?' 'Her surname's Scarapecchia.' ") "No, nothing new at all, Mama."

"Well, goodbye then. I'm sorry I woke you up. Go to sleep now, won't you? Sleep well."

"Yes, thank you, don't worry. Good night."

"Good night, darling."

Her voice lingered plaintively in his ears. These days, when he thought of his mother, he had a feeling she was already dead. Since he had moved to Rome, that is, for the past fifteen years, they met only at Christmas and for a few days at their country house on the lake at Easter or in September. She was a keen collector: first she had collected porcelain birds, then rosaries, and recently clocks. The house was full of clocks that had stopped at all hours: bronze clocks, enamel clocks, *bisquit* clocks, upheld by half-naked women or in the midst of pastoral scenes. Giulio happened to be in Milan when a huge dark wooden pendulum clock had arrived at the house: two men had had to carry it up on their backs because it was taller than the ceiling of the elevator. It looked like a tall stretched-out person, its hands stopped at a quarter-past nine, like broken arms. "I find it a bit sad, Mama," Giulio said. "Why sad?" she objected. "It's going, can't you hear?" It was, in fact, going, making a dully jerky sound like an old heart beating. She would have liked it to go into her husband's study, but he refused, saying the noise would interfere with his work.

Giulio was a child when his mother started collecting china. She said if a collection was to be worth anything, you must choose a single subject, and she began buying birds in marvelous colors: parrots standing on bars, herons with wings outspread, and all sorts of singing nightingales in valuable golden cages. She would wind them all up at once, in the morning—her bedroom was an aviary—and if her husband or the maid came in to talk to her she would say, laughing: "I can't hear a thing, not a thing!" When she gave up praying, she began collecting rosaries to keep at least an external air of devoutness. They were hung on the walls of her bedroom—the birds had been moved to her boudoir—rosaries of garnet, amethyst, and pearl jumbled up with others made of great carved wooden beads from Portugal,

97

filigree rosaries from Toledo and others that women friends brought her from famous shrines, unpretentious ones made of metal or glass.

Giulio never knew what to talk to her about: he would ask for news of someone she knew, but now she often answered: "Why, didn't you hear? She's dead. I don't like to think of it, it makes me feel quite ill." This meant she now refused to take a last look at the bodies of her friends, but still went to their funerals. In the evening, at supper, she would linger over descriptions of the hearse: "A lovely coffin, with ornate bronze handles. I touched it to say goodbye to the poor soul: it was fine, smooth, expensive wood. Mahogany, I think." So they never really talked and Giulio had been surprised when she mentioned her letter, because neither of them liked writing. She used to say that when you wrote things you always ended thinking melancholy thoughts. "You write to me, Giulio, you're young. It's different for young people." He would promise and then put it off and forget. "The fact is, I've got nothing to say to her any longer. I've got nothing to say to anyone now." But did talking, did communicating, really matter at all? He had talked a great deal, in his time, yet of all the words he had said and heard nothing was left. His memories were never aroused by words, only by sensations.

This seemed to him reassuring. "I must tell Papa that, when I see him again. Tomorrow, maybe." He would have to telephone him, have to go to his hotel and see him. The thought of taking any step alarmed him. He would rather be alone. "To think I've inherited the virus of thought," he said to himself. "Now, near forty, it's turning up to poison me."

With an effort he rose to pick up the whisky bottle and fill a glass: he needed something to keep him going. He was unable to follow any train of thought for any length of time unless it had an immediate, practical object: without this object his ideas became confused, they scattered and gave way to images, glimpses of erotic scenes, the same as he had had in his adolescence. And those faceless female forms now all had Ivana's face. He saw the girl going up the darkening staircase of a poor building; he followed her; she hurried, pulling her sweater tightly around her shoulders; she tried to run, but was clumsy, and handicapped, too, by her thick cork soles. This meant he could reach her, could almost attack her, pressing her against the wall. He didn't kiss her; he pulled down the straps of her flowered cotton dress. Ivana spoke to him using the formal *"lei"*: "What are you doing?" she panted. "Are you mad?" At last the top of her dress dropped to her waist, leaving her breasts exposed, large and white, bluishly white. He gazed at them as if seeing a girl naked for the first time. His gaze dismayed Ivana even more. "No," she begged, although he was doing nothing: "I'm scared. No, no . . ." To protect herself, she turned her face to the wall. Magically, the dress vanished, and her broad, powerful back, all that full rounded flesh, was offered to him naked. He no longer saw her imploring eyes, only the neck that was surprisingly slender under the black hair that was parted on it. "I must take her by surprise, I must squeeze her, I must hold my arms tightly round her waist, I must put my hand on her mouth to stop her screaming." He had to act quickly because he could hear a heavy step coming up the stairs. She struggled to free herself, and finally managed it; then quickly she pulled up the straps of her dress and tidied herself, and, as she turned, she glanced at him with an expression he had never seen in Ivana's eyes: sweet, almost maternal. Then she continued calmly up the stairs again and he went down whistling, and met no one.

He went into his bedroom to look for his mother's letter and took the bottle with him. He had no idea how he could have failed to open the letter: he remembered getting it and putting it down somewhere to read when he had time for it; then he had forgotten it. It was not on the chest of drawers in a heap of unopened letters. He gulped down some whisky and told himself he must find it; and while he was undressing, to feel more relaxed, he saw himself in the mirror: loose tie, scruffy shirt, untidy hair. He decided to put off the search. At ten—that is, in just over four hours—he had to see Arthur Lasky. He was always slightly worried about his English, and when he was tired he spoke worse than usual. "I shouldn't have drunk anything tonight." Meantime he was still rummaging in a drawer; he took out a photograph of his mother with the black lips, cropped boyish hair, and knowing look that women had in 1925. "You'd been born a month before that," she had told him when she gave it to him. Born for what?

He put the bottle on the bedside table. "To meet Ivana Scarapecchia," he said to himself, laughing, and got into bed. The coolness of the sheets failed to soothe him. "Don't keep on about it, Papa; there's nothing in the world but money and sex. Proper or improper, who cares. What's more, I'd say, what's more . . ." Instead of the usual images that led to sleep, he saw Amati sitting at the desk where he had once dictated orders. "Right, I understand: all I have to do is sign. I'll sign, then. Let me have your pen." Reluctantly, Giulio had handed his pen over. "You really must, you know. Tomorrow might be too late." Amati, without answering, had signed a check in Giulio's name as well. Then he had flopped down on the table, resting his head there, showing its yellowish, sweaty skin. Giulio looked at Amati's heavy body, his hands spattered with brown stains, a lump of decaying flesh. As he gave him back the pen, like an empty syringe, Amati murmured: "Thanks. Really, it's a liberation."

The office boys, the porter, all waited in silence; and when they saw Giulio pass, they watched him bitterly. The air was sweet outside, full of shrill swallows that swooped about between Via Po and Villa Borghese. "A marvelous city, the only place to enjoy life, and to eat," Lasky had told him on the telephone. "I never felt so young since I was born." "Born for what?" Giulio wanted to ask him. "As far as I'm concerned, to meet Ivana Scarapecchia."

Why laugh at it, anyway? No other object seemed to him so desirable. A woman's navel is the center of the universe: force her, tie her, if she doesn't want you. "Emancipation my eye: the whip, dear Papa, that's more like it. You're standing up for principles that simply don't exist. You're obsessed with the French Revolution, with the Rights of Man." His father would reply: "Right, then. What do you suggest?"

Put out the light: on the black background of his shut lids appeared another image that often came back to him at night during telephone conversations with Sylvia, or with Betty, or any of the many others. In the darkness, first of all, he saw only their faces, or else a corner of their houses. Then something he had never yet defined exactly—the lumpish idiocy of Betty's fine eyes, Marité's spiteful air, Sylvia's desperate air of relaxation, or else a word, an accent—made them vanish. White and sumptuous, glowing from every pore of her tiny body, Manet's *Olympia* stared at him with a mischievous expression on her dwarfish face, as in the coffee-table art books. Beside her, in the darkness, instead of her black accomplice with the bunch of flowers, he saw the dark head of Uncle Raffaele. "Another race to segregate. To suppress, in fact. Got to think up the perfect crime. A massacre. A bomb at the Viminale . . . I really am drunk," he concluded. "Actually, money's quite enough. You can buy anything, or rather, everything's for sale." His father and his father's fine friends, who thought it immoral to pay, would never really accomplish anything. And anyway, why was it immoral? Receiving money gave the flesh itself profound pleasure: it is the flesh's destiny to be corrupted. At the thought of the money piled up, the shares bought abroad, of all he would own when his now elderly parents were dead, Giulio was filled with a glow of virility that sent him to sleep, while Ivana struggled nakedly in the shadows of the old staircase.

He woke with an iron band around his head, woolly-mouthed, his eyes fighting the light that poured into his bedroom. The curtains were drawn, the window open; so Diodato must have been in to waken him. Beside his bed was a small cup of coffee, cold and foul, and the tray with the newspaper and the mail. The alarm clock said 10:30, but it had stopped.

Diodato had let him sleep on, though he knew he had to be at the office for an appointment before ten o'clock. He would have liked to call him and scold him; yet, still dazed with sleep as he was, he felt in no state to exercise his authority. He felt he was surrounded by enemies: Uncle Raffaele, Angeletti (who obviously didn't give a damn whether he was there or not), even Diodato. Someone, he suspected—and the image of Uncle

Raffaele flashed through his mind—had come into his room, and surprised him in a state of animal unconsciousness. But as soon as he was under the shower he felt his long sleep had refreshed him. The water, first hot and then cold, got his circulation going again. He was in good shape and ready to face his problems much more vigorously. "So it's war you want, is it? Right, that's fine, I accept. But remember that whether you agree or not I'm Ivana's fiancé. That means that the law—the *good order* you think so important—is on my side," and, blowing out his chest, he rubbed it vigorously with a horsehair glove. He couldn't see why he had felt guilty the previous day; at his age it was natural to want a woman and try to get her to bed. In no time at all this abstinence would really bring him to some sort of nervous disorder. Everyone would now be put in his place: Diodato, Angeletti, Uncle Raffaele. Besides, he wanted to make love. "And not with a prostitute, with your niece."

Outside the bathroom door he heard Diodato muttering something he failed to catch, because of the running water. He turned off the tap and asked irritably: "What is it?"

"It's two o'clock, I wanted to know if I should get lunch."

"And I'd like to know why you didn't wake me at the usual time," Giulio shouted through the door.

"But how could I, sir? I came in two or three times, I opened the window, I brought coffee . . . No response from you, so . . ."

"So you thought there was nothing for you to do?" said Giulio, coming out in his dressing gown.

"What do you mean, sir? I even telephoned the office and told Mr. Angeletti: 'I'm sorry,' I said, 'I can't wake the master up.' "

"And who authorized you to do that? It's incredible! I can't sleep on for a couple of hours without everyone being told. Why not put out a news bulletin? That would be simpler."

"I'm sorry, sir, it was because of that important appointment. Then Mr. Angeletti told me he'd see to it himself."

"As if that was the same thing," said Giulio. He had begun shaving and irritation made his hand shake. Put them in their place, my eye: he'd kick them in the pants.

"Get out of my sight," he ordered. "Vanish."

Diodato stood quite still and seemed to want to say something further; at last he sighed, and bustled off in his housewifely way.

At the table he served Giulio with an apologetic air. ("They're beginning to see I'm not to be trifled with. I put up with things as long as it suits me, and then, when they least expect it, I remind everyone that I'm the one in charge.") Diodato had acted reasonably, indeed conscientiously; all the same, he must stick to his guns, if he wanted to be respected— especially when he was wrong.

"I'm sorry, sir . . ."

"All right, all right. Now leave me alone, there's nothing else I need."

"I meant I'm sorry because something's happened." Giulio looked up questioningly. "This morning, while you were asleep, a police sergeant came."

"Oh! And what did he want?"

"I don't know. I said: 'My master's left,' and he said it wasn't true because the car was still in the garage."

"I'm being watched, then," said Giulio, pleased.

"He must have been told by the porter, who's a spy. I told him it wasn't my fault, that when you were asleep I had orders to say you were out."

"Quite right. And then?"

"He glanced at me in that suspicious, southern way—Sicilian, he must have been—and said: 'I'll be back.' "

"Well, when he comes back we'll know what he wants," said Giulio. "Thanks. Now run along."

Diodato made no move: "Sir, I'm afraid . . ."

"Afraid of a policeman?" Giulio broke in, smiling. "Anyway, it has nothing to do with you."

"He must have come because of me. I told you—didn't I?—that they stopped me in Piazza San Giovanni, just by the wall. Don't you remember, sir? The night when you felt so sick. I was with my nephew when we were stopped, and I took the liberty of giving your name."

"Oh, yes . . . I remember vaguely. I don't think it's anything to do with that. Anyway, what's your nephew's name?"

"Sergio . . . Sergio Picuti. Do you think they'll send for him?"

"That depends. What's his job?"

"He's an electrician, but he hasn't got a permanent job. He's looking for one. That's why we met. I told him you might be able to fit him in somewhere . . . and that's why, unfortunately, I gave your name. If they should ask . . ."

"Don't worry. They'd have come the next day. Two days later, at most. Anyway, if I'm not at home when this sergeant comes again, tell him to make an appointment to see me."

"Yes, sir. Thank you. Thank you very much." Diodato went hesitantly into the kitchen. "Please forgive me again, sir. I wanted to tell you that, in any case, my nephew's of age."

Giulio reassured him almost affectionately. When he awoke he had been furious, spoiling for a row; but the sergeant's visit had changed his mood. He now felt ironical, magnanimous.

He lit a cigarette, went over to his open study window, and sat down; he drank his coffee in small sips, his legs crossed casually. The house that at night seemed unwelcoming, even hostile, was now obviously pleasant and comfortable, and he felt like a man who, in the middle of a serious illness, realizes his temperature has gone down.

"I'm sorry. I really do regret it because it was flattering to feel I was fighting a terrible enemy. So I'm disappointed to hear about your mistake from Diodato. Your great clumsy mistake.

I'm all the more surprised because only yesterday evening your brother Rosario told me that patience was one of your special qualities, as well as one of the methods most widely used in what we might call your activities. But you're a southerner. Southerners have a generous, impulsive nature that often leads them into mistakes. I'm the son of a Lombard father and a Ligurian mother—solid, greedy, unimaginative people."

He was facing the armchair in front of him, an armchair with a stiff, high back, and fluted wooden arms that ended in a whorl, like convulsively clenched hands, which gradually became distorted, monstrously human, as in a metaphysical painting.

"I feel it's my duty to confess that I wasn't far off making a fearful mistake myself. Don't worry," he went on, staring boldly at his indifferent listener. "So far you've played your part beautifully, in fact I nearly made a jealous scene with Ivana over you. You'd have heard of it through signora Adelina, and I'd have put myself in a very weak position. But my strength lies in not worrying about your reasons for being interested in Ivana. In believing—or pretending to believe—that they're just proper family feelings. This gives me the advantage now, and will give you the advantage someday, later on. And even if you've already had her, I don't care. Virginity doesn't matter to me. In fact, just between ourselves, I feel it's a rather vulgar business, a sort of butchery."

It was perfectly true that the vision of Ivana carnally united with Uncle Raffaele didn't make him jealous. Judging from the photograph, Uncle Raffaele was no Adonis, and the years could not have improved his clumsy frame. Besides, Giulio couldn't imagine him except in uniform, and this made their copulation seem somehow grotesque.

He had now got a hold on himself, and decided to make a definite plan of action. First of all he must tell his secretary that he would not be going into the office, even in the afternoon. He cared nothing for the remarks this umpteenth absence would arouse among his colleagues; in fact the thought of them amused him. He finished dressing calmly and at last decided to press his professional advantages.

If he could not get others to work, and lightheartedly enjoy his freedom for hours, even days, where was the famous technical ability everyone said he had? Thinking himself irreplaceable was an excuse he had inherited from his father, who still wrote all his letters by hand and went out to post them himself. Giulio had always had someone ("a slave," he used to call him) who licked the glue on his stamps; but for years he had always been present, always available.

On the other hand, what would he do outside the office? Every evening he gave over to women. And bed took the least part of them: the rest was often spent in bars, restaurants and night-clubs. With Ivana, it was not one of his usual love affairs, in which he took part anonymously, disguised as an extra in a documentary, but also a fight with an invisible competitor, waiting in ambush everywhere, and between his own longing for complete license and the so-called morality that appeared, in equally damaging ways, in the Scarapecchias' opportunism and in the feeling for justice that ruled his father's life.

He knotted his tie at the mirror, pleased with his own image and even with what had so far bothered him: the outline of his face, which was losing its clean-cut lines, the hint of baldness. ("Thank heaven I don't look like a martyr, I'm not a walking reproach," he said to himself, remembering the melancholy asceticism of his father's face.)

He thought how, even in this whole affair, it was all a matter of strategy. As usual, he would win—and with no moral involvement, seeking only his own selfish pleasure. "What's stopped Uncle Raffaele from hanging on, and completing his plan, is jealousy. Passion removes the coldness needed for success. During the last few days I lost because I'd been surprised by an unexpected technique and I didn't know how to deal with it. Now I won't find it hard to seize my chance," he concluded, ready to go out.

Diodato heard his footsteps in the hall and ran to the door.

"I can't find your briefcase, sir," he said. "I wonder where you can possibly have left it . . ."

"It doesn't matter. I don't need it. I'm on holiday today!"

"At last," said Diodato approvingly. "I've always said to myself, what a pity to waste your youth. If I could only go back . . ."

"What would you do? Tell me."

"First of all, instead of suffering, I'd make others suffer."

"Fine! But what for?"

"People always suffer for the same reason, sir. They say people suffer because they're worried about the future, because they're scared of war, of the atomic bomb. But these are political inventions," he said, shaking his head. "People think crimes are due to hunger, or vice. They talk and write such rubbish. . . ."

"And what do you think they're due to?"

"Well, sir, I think people suffer from lack of warmth. You're young, so you can't make comparisons. But for the last few years, the earth seems to have frozen."

"You're a philosopher, Diodato," said Giulio, slapping him on the back.

"Maybe," said Diodato, with a sad smile. "That reminds me, sir. That package which came a few days ago . . . I thought it was shirts or clothes, so I took the liberty of opening it. If it's a present I'll wrap it up nicely myself. Or else we would put it on an armchair, or on your bed. It's so lovely . . ."

"What is?"

"The doll," said Diodato.

"Oh, the doll . . . of course, the doll . . ." Giulio repeated, puzzled. "Do whatever you like with it. It was a present, actually. A present for . . . for the daughter of a client of mine who afterwards went away."

"I can send it on, if you like."

"What an idea, they're in America! I don't even know the address . . . the porter's got a little girl, hasn't he?" Diodato nodded. "That's fine, give it to the porter's child, then."

Via Delle Alpi was still steeped in sunshine when Giulio arrived there, earlier than usual. He felt he was going back to a small town on the Adriatic where he had spent the holidays as a boy, which, in his memory, had taken on the magic of a place in which he had been happy. Was it Ivana or was it the street that gave him this impression of serenity? His own home was not far away, and Parioli was just as green, just as high; yet when he went out he was agitated by a competitive instinct, by a wish to do better than anyone else—if only at the wheel of his car—which gradually was soothed until the mere sight of the little houses in Via Delle Alpi dispelled it altogether.

In the gardens the flowers looked sweet and homely. In the cement boxes that adorned the Parioli balconies they lost their naturalness, as they did in his parents' country house. Suddenly he remembered that he had failed to call the hotel to find out if his father had arrived, had failed even to leave a message for him at the office, and nobody knew where he was. His friends thought Giulio had vanished because of a love affair he could not openly admit to. But he had always avoided married women who forced him into tiresome secret meetings, at a time when he should have been working, and vanished when he most needed company—in the evenings, on Sundays and during the holidays.

No one could have imagined that every day he fled to this small, modest-looking house. But as he entered the sitting room —always cool behind the bluish-green shutters—Giulio felt real contentment; he felt sheltered from all that was tedious, threatening or disagreeable. Its furniture, reduced to essentials—and frankly in bad taste—made him think what he had so carefully chosen for his own home, where he never found the same tranquility, superfluous and pretentious.

Signora Adelina was in her dressing gown. She seemed not so much surprised as worried to see him at that time of day. He explained that as he had happened to be in the district he had come straight there, even though Ivana was not yet home. "In any case, I'm used to waiting for her," he said smiling. "But you go ahead with what you've got to do. In the meantime I'll rest.
. . . It's terribly sultry today. If you'll allow me to, I'll take off my jacket."

She gushed round him and put his jacket on the back of a chair; then she said, "I'll go and tidy up," and left.

Giulio looked at his gray jacket, set on the chair as if it were on a hanger: signora Adelina had taken it from him with a care—indeed, a respect—that no one had ever shown toward his clothes. "I feel at home, here." He told himself that so far no one had really taken trouble over him, although Diadato took great care of him, and the old servants in Milan or in the country put themselves out to wait on him. But whenever he went home he had a feeling that he was taking over from someone else, that he had to imitate his own way of speaking, his character, even his smallest habits so that no one would notice he had taken over.

After a while signora Adelina brought him coffee: "I've just made it. Smell how good it is!" she said, stirring it with the spoon.

"Do you know you spoil me, signora Adelina?"

She was flattered, but refused to accept this: "Oh nonsense! You're used to comfort . . ."

"Comfort's very little compared with what you're offered kindly—dare I say, affectionately? May I say this, or am I wrong?"

"Do you think I'm not fond of my daughter's future husband?"

"I know, I know . . . In fact I doubt whether Ivana's as fond of me as you are."

"Lovers never feel they're loved enough!" she said mischievously.

"That's true. But sometimes I feel that Ivana's fonder of her Uncle Raffaele than she is of me."

"It's natural for her to be fond of her godfather."

"Of course. But while we're talking about this, I must tell you I'm sorry not to have met him yet."

"You'll have a chance . . ."

"Look, signora Adelina," Giulio said, pulling his chair up to hers. "May I speak to you confidentially, between ourselves?"

"Of course. But remember I'm very shockable."

"There's nothing to shock you. It's this: Ivana told me that Uncle Raffaele is against our engagement. I wondered why. She said: 'He doesn't approve.' Nothing else. But I'd like to know why, particularly because Ivana cares a great deal about her uncle's opinion. So I decided to go to the Ministry and ask him myself."

"For heavens sake don't do that!" signora Adelina said quickly.

"Why not?"

"Raffaele's in a very delicate position there. He doesn't want to bring personal matters into the office."

"I see. Then I'll go to his home. Where does he live?"

"Outside Rome, in Castelli. But if I had to tell you where, I couldn't. He's a mysterious man, you see, because of his work. It would be a great mistake to insist on seeing him. After all, what do you care what Raffaele thinks? We're Ivana's parents and we've given our consent. Ivana's pleased, although she's got a proud nature. . . . As for the rest, leave it to me. Don't you trust me?"

"Of course I do. But to be quite frank, I'm proud myself and I can't bear this unjustified hostility."

"It's obvious you're not used to southerners," said signora Adelina good-naturedly. "They're suspicious of everyone. Marriages are arranged between families, sometimes when the youngsters are still children. Families know each other, they know every single thing there is to know about each other . . . whereas this engagement has taken place without your parents knowing. I don't mind. We women think: are they in love? Yes, they are, and that's enough. In any case when it's all settled, when a baby's born, even the most stubborn parents finally give way."

"My parents aren't against it; they just don't know about it. I prefer to keep quiet about it because they too have some silly prejudices . . . you could call them regional ones."

"That's quite natural," said signora Adelina in a concilatory tone. "But try and get Raffaele to see it! To him Ivana's more than a princess and she's got to be kept in cotton wool. He doesn't want us to let her out alone, she must never see men. . . . He's jealous."

"Ah, he's jealous," Giulio repeated, hoping to reach the nub of the matter. "But how on earth is he jealous of Ivana?"

"Southerners are like that. We women are worth absolutely nothing to them. Yet everything in their lives depends on the honor of their women. You two may have met in the street, but the other evening—when he called to say he couldn't come—Raffaele said to me: 'Remember that you're responsible.' " She went on, more softly: "I've got a feeling the Scarapecchias had some sort of trouble with a northerner. I don't know anything exactly: secrets like these are carried to the grave by men in the south. But I think your engagement reminds him of something he wants to forget. Have you ever heard of crimes of honor? Everyone keeps quiet and then, one fine day . . . Of course, this has nothing at all to do with you, I don't even know how I got around to talking about such a thing. But take my advice and leave Raffaele alone."

"He's a good-looking man," Giulio said, indicating the portrait.

"Not bad."

"Of course, the years go by . . . What's he like now, has he aged a lot?"

She glanced at the portrait. "No. He's stayed more or less the same."

Signora Adelina was obviously afraid of her brother-in-law, although she boasted that she could make him do whatever she liked. The doorbell was a constant cause of apprehension, and Giulio wondered if it was merely "because of the co-op men," as she said, or whether she was expecting Uncle Raffaele to appear unannounced. That evening, when Ivana came home, she said at once: "Don't switch on the light. That way it'll look at if there's no one at home."

Giulio had learned to be patient. When Ivana came home from school she went to change before she came to sit beside him. Conversation was only a way of keeping her mother, in the kitchen, from noticing their long silences. In fact, for two hours or more all he did was try and touch her. To him, the engagement meant trying and waiting for the right opportunity. However things went, he was never bored.

The fact that Ivana seemed to have no sexual desires did not dissuade him from trying. Indeed, the submission he could foresee, the docility with which, out of duty, she would submit to anything she disliked, promised to make exciting a ceremony which, until now, he had taken part in fairly unenthusiastically, considering it merely less boring than others. The ingenuousness of her behavior and conversation confirmed that very likely she was afraid of "the physical act," as signora Adelina had told him confidentially, but was not going to refuse to submit to it.

"Ivana, do you know what I told your mother this afternoon? I told her I was surer of her affection than of yours."

"Why?" answered Ivana, without interest.

"She always tries to please me, when I ask her anything, and you don't."

"That's a fine comparison! It's not at all the same."

"With you, even if you give me a cup of coffee, you look suspicious while you're doing it."

"Because even when I bring you coffee or a glass of water, you're thinking of certain things."

Giulio laughed. "It's natural to think of them, when you're in love. In fact, if you always behaved the way you did the other evening, I'd think you didn't love me in the least."

("But I did get something. My victory's all the greater, since Ivana's in love with you; she'll marry you when I leave her. All the same, today there's something urging her toward me. It's not a matter of money-grabbing—because although I earn a good deal, you're a wealthy landowner—but maybe a case of the wrong she's doing in betraying you and her own feelings at the same time.")

His hand could now swoop down the neck of her dress and

creep along inside her bra, while he used his other hand to stop her trying to stop him. They were sitting by the open window; wholly absorbed in the chance of repeating what he had done and attempting other movements as risky, Giulio realized with dismay that darkness was falling and his time was running out.

"Well, do you like what I'm doing?" Ivana raised her head with a grimace. "Then what will you do when we're married?"

"Once you're married you've got to do it."

"And suppose you don't like it even then?"

"Like it or not, that's marriage."

Anyway, Giulio was not asking to be loved: so long as she would stand him, that was enough. With other women it was a matter of an exchange of love, at least on the surface, or else of tender friendship, or profound interest, or curiosity. Whereas now his subtlest enjoyment came from imposing on Ivana something she disliked, and from the idea of scheming under the very eyes of Uncle Raffaele, who stared at him from the portrait, of planning a betrayal he might suspect, but could in no way prove. ("Above all, when you call I can make progress in the familiarity you'd like to prevent.") Indeed, as soon as she heard the telephone ring, Ivana shot up, scared; and as she was paralyzed with fear, Giulio could the more easily take advantage of her.

Perhaps she behaved like that merely to stop him from putting into action what he had threatened. "Do you know what I'm going to do one of these days? I'm going to snatch the phone from your mother and say: 'Hullo, I'm Ivana's fiancé. I should like to know what you've got against me, why you don't approve of me, why you don't think me worthy to meet you.'" (And he might have added: "Why, instead of turning up yourself, do you send your men round to my home in that cowardly way?")

Ivana answered calmly: "If he doesn't want to talk to you he won't. He'll hang up and that'll be that."

Once again, instead of backing him, she was justifying her uncle's behavior. Giulio told himself that signora Adelina was right: southerners were a Mafia, a tribe to flee from and avoid at all costs, or else to study, like an anthropologist. Now, as he went about, he often noticed he was being followed by a white Fiat 600; another empty one was parked almost permanently at the gate of his home: to avoid being recognized, the police must have been mingling with people round about.

Next morning, in the office, he heard that the sergeant had turned up there, as well, but toward evening, when he was at Ivana's. Uncle Raffaele, knowing his habits, chose the hours when he was out to send his man. What was he trying to do? Scare him? Remind him of his existence? Or simply poke into his home and office? Besides, the sergeant always managed to get away without leaving any trace of himself.

"Didn't anyone think of asking what he wanted?" Giulio protested furiously. "Didn't anyone ask him his name, or tell him to come back?"

"You're quite right, sir, it's my fault," said his secretary. "But you never tell these people to come back. In fact, you hope they won't."

"As far as I'm concerned, they can come whenever they like," he retorted coldly.

These visits, this constant, invisible check on him, were a nightmare. So, in spite of what he meant to do, when he saw Ivana in the afternoon he couldn't stop himself. "Look," he said, "I've always been open with you and I want to go on being so."

"What's up?"

"It's that you're not being fair to me, as far as your uncle's concerned."

Ivana opened her eyes wide with fright, making him think he had hit on the truth. "Why? What have you found out?"

"Can you really tell me the truth if I tell you everything?"

117

"Of course."

"I've heard that Uncle Raffaele's your lover."

Ivana burst out laughing. "I wonder who told you that nonsense."

"Name the sin, but not the sinner. Is it true or not? Why don't you answer?"

"It's not worth wasting breath on it."

"So it isn't true, then? Could you swear?"

"I swear," answered Ivana, still laughing. "But you believed it."

"No, but you must understand . . ."

"All I understand is that you think I'm capable of doing certain things with my uncle."

"Your uncle's a man like any other."

"But we're blood relations. And anyway, you may as well know that I just haven't got these desires—either for my uncle or for any other man."

"And yet . . ." said Giulio, slyly.

"What?" she said, frowning.

"And yet, when I saw you that first time, in the bar, who were you calling? If it was an innocent conversation, you could have called from home."

"Oh really? And who do you think I was talking to?"

"Well, to a man, that was obvious."

"Yes, I was talking to a man."

"You see . . ." he said, pleased.

"What's there to see? Men aren't all like you, with just one thing on the brain."

"Don't trust that: everyone's got it on the brain," said Giulio laughing. "Those who don't talk about it think about it even more than anyone else. Anyway, may I know who this highly . . . disinterested man was?"

She turned to look at him defiantly. "Uncle," she replied.

When he had confirmed, in an indirect way, what he had long ago guessed—that Uncle Raffaele was her ideal man —Ivana gave no further explanations. The ironical remarks he had teased her with were useless. Scarapecchia turned up soon afterward and Giulio was forced to leave without gaining any advantage from the accusations he had made. From the wall, Uncle Raffaele's dark, shining eyes glowed victoriously.

"There are two sides to it," Giulio said to himself. "Either I love her, in which case it's quite right that her past life should interest me and make me suffer; or else I just intend getting her into bed, in which case the more brazen and clever she is at lying the better pleased I should be, because someday I'll get my own back. And as I'm quite sure that love just doesn't come into it, it seems pretty silly to care about her lies."

So the next day he sent her a big basket of flowers. He didn't want to find Ivana in a mood that would prevent all intimacy; and he hoped that the flowers would make an impression on her.

As soon as he came in he realized she had not been indifferent to his sumptuous present.

"You shouldn't have bothered. Thank you," she said pleasantly. "All the same, you mustn't think that flowers can make me forget your lack of trust. If we go on like this, we'll be doing badly."

"Don't you see I'm jealous? Being a southerner yourself, you ought to understand it."

"I understand and I don't like it. Anyway, how does the south come into it? Things are quite clear between us, aren't they?" she said, staring into his eyes. Though not knowing exactly what she meant, Giulio nodded. ("She hates me. She hates me but she can't send me away: that's what really matters.") "So," Ivana went on, "I can't see why you're making such a fuss. You may as well know I dislike complications and suspicions. They make me tired." ("Oriental women, made to lie down and nothing more.") "If you think I suit you as I am, that's fine. Otherwise . . ."

"As far as I'm concerned you're fine. I've made a mistake and I've asked you to forgive me," he said, indicating the basket of flowers that smirked on the sideboard. (The flowers were decorated with tufts of asparagus and tied with a blue ribbon like those worn across soldiers' chests on ceremonial occasions.) "On the other hand," he went on, in spite of himself, "don't you think I have a right to know who you were telephoning that evening? I remember thinking: 'She's talking secretly.' It was the first thing that struck me. I hadn't even seen your face. You had your back to me."

"Right, I'll tell you what I was talking about," she said, as if making a concession. "We were talking about this business of the co-op. Papa had felt ill during the night and had taken some drops. . . . I couldn't talk about it at home."

"You might have told me right away. We could have avoided all this fuss."

"It's easy to trust people when there's no reason to be suspicious. You ought to trust them even if things don't seem quite clear."

"You're quite right," he said. "And now let's drop it: come over here." He put his hand on the chair beside him, but Ivana did not obey. "Besides, your uncle doesn't trust me. When you see him you should persuade him that he was wrong."

"I haven't seen him," she said, sitting down. As she did so, her skirt rose and showed a flash of white flesh above her stocking.

"Oh, come on . . . Haven't you seen him since we met?"

Ivana's only answer was to get up and go across to the door that led to the hall. She walked leaning forward a little, as if she could hardly support her own body and all that it provoked: men's looks in the street, Giulio's hands, these scenes. Then, when the door was open, she called authoritatively: "Mama."

Her mother shouted from the kitchen: "I'm busy."

"Drop everything and come."

Signora Adelina hurried in, wiping her hands on her apron. "What's happened? What's up?"

"Is it true, or isn't it, that I haven't seen Uncle for a long time?" Ivana asked her seriously.

"Of course!" said her mother, raising her hand as if to say it was an incalculable time. ("They're lying," Giulio thought. "There's no doubt about that.")

"Did you hear?" Ivana asked him, with satisfaction. Then she turned to her mother again, indicating Giulio as if he were an object: "You try and make him see. He's stifling me with his jealousy."

"Now you're exaggerating. All I wanted to know was why your uncle doesn't approve."

"Do you really want to know?" Ivana burst out exasperatedly. "Well, because according to him you've got no intention of marrying me."

"Oh, fine! And what makes him think that?"

"He says you haven't spoken to your parents, or to the people in your office. In fact, when you call from here you say: 'I've been held up,' you never say: 'I'm with my fiancée.' And then . . . Tell him," she said to her mother. "You tell him."

"It's just as she says. For the reasons she gave."

"No, it's not just for these reasons. Go on. Tell the truth."

"Now look at the trouble you've got me into," muttered Ivana's mother unhappily.

"Go on, speak frankly, please," said Giulio, seeing she was all on edge.

"Well . . ." said signora Adelina, and then broke in on herself to get things straight: "Of course, I'm only saying what Raffaele said. I've got nothing to do with it, none of us have."

"All right," said Giulio. And then, as his recent life flashed before him, and he tried to think what Uncle Raffaele could pin on him, he urged her on: "Well then?"

"Well, Raffaele says: 'Not even an engagement ring.' He says: 'Even a beggar has some sort of ring, something that says "Look, this girl's mine." ' . . . Actually, one of our neighbors looked at her hand when she met her and was very surprised to find she wasn't wearing one."

"That's quite right," said Giulio, impressed. "Uncle Raffaele's right. Maybe you won't believe me, but I just never thought of it. And if we hadn't talked about it today . . ."

"Do you think I don't know what men are like, at my age!" signora Adelina said kindly. "Just think, on our wedding day, when we were at the altar and Rosario put his finger in his waistcoat pocket to get out the wedding ring . . . nothing. He'd forgotten it, left it at home. It was Raffaele who went to fetch it."

Giulio was nodding his head. "Of course, I should have thought of it. But that's easily put right. Tomorrow. Just give me time to find something she'll like. Tell me, in fact," he said to Ivana, "what sort of ring would you like?"

Ivana did not reply. She had gone over to the sideboard, had put her hand into the basket, and was now patting the earth in the vases to see if it was damp. Then, still without a word, she picked up a jug and went into the kitchen.

"Good girl," said her mother. "Those flowers need plenty of water, otherwise they fade. And that would be a pity."

"Tell me, signora Adelina" said Giulio confidingly. "What sort of ring would Ivana like?"

"These are things the families see to, especially in the south, as I told you. As for Ivana . . ." and her mother looked tenderly at the door through which she had gone out. "Haven't you realized what she's like, don't you know her yet? She doesn't even think of it. More than anything, she likes flowers."

All the same, when he left Giulio realized that again Uncle Raffaele had got the better of him. "Now the ring," he had said. And Guilio had meekly agreed. The thought filled him with anger. "It isn't you who arranged it: it was I who decided I'd pay, right from the start." Leaning lightly against the hard back of the fake Renaissance armchair behind his desk, Uncle Raffaele smiled odiously. "Let's see how much," he said.

Next day Giulio looked in the shop windows, wondering how much this ring or that one might be worth. He had begun with the jewelers who had shops in the side streets off Via Condotti, instead of going to the more famous jewelers, those whose famous name on the case you paid for, apart from the value of the stones.

It was early afternoon. In the morning he had been unable to avoid going to court for a case. He had spoken reluctantly and without conviction—because the man concerned was someone he thought unimportant—but all had gone well, because Angeletti had made a cast-iron case of it. "Andrea does his very best even for people who send you a chicken at the end of the year, instead of paying your account," he said to himself as he left the court. Then he went to the hotel where his father generally stayed. There he was surprised when the doorman recognized him and said: "Your father's just left. He went off toward Via Boncompagni. If you hurry you'll catch him." Giulio had no wish to hurry: the sun was scorching and he was already hot. "Thanks, I'll leave him a note," he replied. But the porter was quite definite: "He hasn't been here," he said. "Of course I'm sure. Do you think I don't know our own guests? . . . No, not today or yesterday. . . . There's no need for me to check. Ask at the reception desk, if you like," he said absently, and turned to someone else. The clerk at the reception desk confirmed that Professor Broggini was not there: he had not been in touch with them, and he was not expected. The doorman, a bright, sunburned lad, interrupted: "I saw him, though. It must have been ten minutes ago. He turned into Via Boncompagni. . . . Why, do you think I mistook someone else for him? No. I know him well. I saw him yesterday, really I did . . ." The porter denied this peremptorily and the manager upheld him; the boy was sent back to his place. An albino clerk took Giulio to the door and said, with a stupid smile: "It must be a touch of the sun." Outside, the doorman's face was red and his eyes were flashing furiously. "Take no notice of him, sir. It was him all right. I saw him!" Giulio would have liked to question him, but the boy was running after an empty taxi, whistling. Finally Giulio was persuaded that he must have been mistaken. What reason could his father have for hiding?

He thought, "A woman," and seemed to hear his father answer: "Why, Giulio, what an idea!" Certainly Elpidio Broggini would never have bribed the hotel staff. "I wonder if he's always been faithful to Mama? Maybe on some of his trips he's gone off the rails a bit. Or else done it sometimes for health reasons. But can he still be doing it, at his age?" He had telephoned his mother and to quiet her fears told her that the end of the congress in Mexico had been postponed. "I read it in the paper." "What paper? I take them all . . ." "Where can I have read it? . . . Wait. In the *Observer*, maybe, or *The Times*." His mother did not read English.

After lunch he gave up the idea of a siesta and went out into the scorching city: he wanted to take the ring to Ivana that same evening, thus hoping to overcome the final obstacle to her complete submission ("I must hurry, time's going by.") But the shops were still shut: the jewels glittered through the mesh of the lowered metal shutters. The sounds that came from the artisan's workshops—a tapping hammer, a plane swishing back and forth —echoed in the empty street.

In other years, at that time, he had been at the sea. He saw himself in his open car on the highway, beside a woman with a headscarf knotted under her chin, then on the beach where they met friends who had boats and transistors, and played with beach balls. He would return to Rome about five, and go to the office with a kind of swagger his sunburn gave him; his clients were generally pale and worried and his appearance reassured them. All this seemed very remote to him now. Anyway, things were going very well. Better than ever, in fact. To excuse him, Angeletti said he was busy at important meetings, or abroad; and the difficulty of seeing him, and getting an appointment with him, increased his prestige. "You're very grand these days," a client had said to him that very day. "Rome isn't enough for you." It was true that for some time now he had felt he was walking in the streets of a city hidden in the womb of the one he had lived in for so many years. "When have I ever found myself in Via Bocca di Leone at four in the afternoon?"

He had stopped absently beside a mesh shutter when it suddenly clanged up and a dark youngish man asked politely: "Were you waiting for me? I'm so sorry. I went to the bank and put off opening up."

Giulio felt shy, as if he had been caught out. "I'm sorry. I was just looking . . ."

"What were you looking at? Please come in." Giulio went in, thinking that, here or elsewhere, it was much the same thing. "If you'd be so good as to tell me what you're interested in," said the jeweler, opening the window from the inside.

"That ring there on the right, with the pearl . . . or else the one with the blue stone."

"Ah, now those are two very different jewels," said the man, laying a piece of leather out on the glass counter. His delicate, precise movements were like those of a doctor or a dentist, in fact, of a man who wants to avoid alarming his patient in any way.

In the bluish lamplight the rings, stuck into open containers, took on new splendor: the stones glittered in the man's cautious fingers, as he sat opposite him. Giulio felt very cool in that pleasant shop, shelterd from the sun. The jeweler stayed outside the circle of light, and his voice came across persuasively.

"I don't want to be indiscreet, but I've got a very large stock and in order to save you time could I know how much . . . ?" the man asked, leaving his question tactfully in the air.

"I don't know exactly," said Giulio. "It depends."

"I see, I see," said the man quickly. Then picked up one of the two holders: "This is a cultured pearl, mounted with very pure diamonds in a very effective way. It's really surprising," he said with a knowing laugh. "Whereas the other's an Oriental sapphire, simple—naked, in fact—but valuable. The pearl's nine hundred thousand lire. The sapphire—" he paused respectfully and in the darkness his eyes stared into Giulio's—"three and a half million."

"That's a big difference."

"That's why I took the liberty of asking you . . . A jeweler's like a confessor. Better than a confessor, as he gives you no penance. So, in order to advise you, may I ask if it's a present . . . how can I put it? If it's a case of something really important . . ."

"Not really," said Giulio.

The man gave a sigh of relief and turned back the sleeves of his jacket a little, as if he was only now getting down to work: "I thought not," he said.

"Tell me why," said Giulio, slightly annoyed.

"I'm the son and grandson of jewelers. Our work is handed down, it's a family tradition, like that of a lawyer . . . or of a policeman," he said with a smile that to Giulio seemed ambiguous. "So we've got what you might call an atavistic instinct that allows us to guess the customer's wishes. We create them, in that we draw them out so that he himself can discover what they are. In your case it was very easy. For instance, I knew right away that it wasn't an engagement ring."

"Indeed? How?"

"Well, it's hard to explain. . . . Partly because you looked at the jewels rather furtively, as if you were buying secretly. . . . Then there's the time of day. Because this kind of shopping . . . the sort you might call official . . . is always done by men who bring along a woman to advise them—their mother, or a relation. And then because they always go for a diamond. Small, perhaps, but they rarely choose a colored stone."

"Why is that?" Giulio asked, curiously.

"Because sapphires, rubies and emeralds—stones that are sometimes more expensive than diamonds—are, let's say, easy to imitate. Relatively easy . . . Other colored stones can deceive even an expert's eye. Besides, they're not really false: they are made up from chips—the throw-outs from fine stones that have been cut. In fact, sometimes . . . Look."

From a side drawer he took a strip of white satin and showed Giulio a ring on which a large red stone glittered between two bluish diamonds.

"All precious: the setting is platinum; the diamonds were cut in Amsterdam—there's no one here who could do the rectangular cut in this way—the stone was cut in Amsterdam as well. As for the color: a perfect *sang de pigeon*. Perfect in appearance," said the jeweler with a meaningful look. "But how many people can distinguish the appearance from the substance, nowadays? Not just in stones, either . . . This would make a royal gift and the price . . . a million eight hundred." He read a tiny label tied to the ring, made a quick calculation with his lips and then, sure of making an impression, said quickly: "Oh well, a million and seven." And he added more softly: "A royal gift for—to be blunt—someone we don't want to get too much involved with."

"I'm afraid your guesswork's at fault," said Giulio coldly. "In fact it's an engagement ring I want." (Beyond the counter the man raised his eyes and stared at him.) "I said it wasn't to be too important because I can't get involved in anything too expensive."

The man took it calmly. "It means I was wrong this time." Then, seeing Giulio examining the pearl ring: "No. A pearl isn't right for an engagement. They say pearls bring tears. Here are some rings that would suit your case." On the doeskin he laid several rings with small diamonds. "Two million and five," he said, "two million and eight . . . three million and three: that's a bargain, a very striking stone because it's so big, but cut in an old-fashioned way, from an old mine." Then he shut the case containing the ruby: "So we can put this one away."

"Just a minute," said Giulio, dropping a ring he had been examining without enthusiasm.

"Of course. Please . . ." the jeweler said anxiously. With a single movement he pushed away all the other boxes and pressed the catch of the white one. In the middle of the diamonds that surrounded it, the false ruby glittered.

When he had left the shop Giulio had no time to go else-where: he had to rush to the office because Arthur Lasky was coming at six. The jeweler had told him: "Think it over. You can think about it until this time tomorrow. Later I can't guarantee that you'll find it. I have a colleague coming from the provinces to buy a good many articles, and I'm sure he won't let this one slip. But, until five o'clock, think it over."

Giulio was sure the provincial buyer was one of those excuses he himself made when he wanted to press for a decision. "Until tomorrow evening," he had told Amati. "I can't wait any longer." Amati knew perfectly well that he was bluffing; but the weaker man is always afraid that this one time it may be the truth.

Now, Giulio also suspected that in spite of the cleverness he was credited with, he had always been at the mercy of anyone who dealt cunningly with him. He had to admit that he liked the jeweler, in spite of all that was cheap and phony in his voice and accent, and that the man seemed to be assuring him of his complicity in the web he was weaving round the Scarapecchias: he was an ally in his defiance of Uncle Raffaele. And yet among all the stones in his shop, he had urged him to fall in love with what meant danger, since Uncle Raffaele, without any trouble to himself, could send one of his underlings to value the jewel.

("Well then? Do you suppose that if Ivana had become engaged to someone from her own social level she'd ever have been given such a valuable ring? You'll say: to make up, she'd have had a husband. That's true. That's perfectly true. But all sorts of prejudices can be got over nowadays: the man who marries her will have it afterward. As for the—what shall we call it? . . . the compensation, let's say: don't you think a million and a half is enough?" "One million five hundred and it's a deal," he meant to propose to the jeweler. "Now, my dear sir, let's not exaggerate. Think that I'm paying this amount because I *like* paying it: you can find better for far less, or even free, I assure you." "Why not say so, then?" Uncle Raffaele retorted. "Why the deceit?")

He would be upset to be caught cheating. But the jeweler, being an experienced man, had foreseen everything. "In cases like this, you must say it's a piece of family jewelery, one that reminds you of someone who's died—mother or godmother or someone—to whom you were very much attached. So, if the bride's relations realize that the stone isn't exactly genuine, what can they do? How can they mention its wretched material value, when it represents a whole patrimony of feeling? And if they haven't got the delicacy to keep quiet, the fiancé can always pretend he's surprised—heavens, he can be scornful—and say that the stone (which, word of honor, he knew nothing about) must have been replaced by a relation—also dead, of course—an uncle who went to any extreme to get money for gambling, roulette or horses. Then the bride cheers him up and the others tell him it's the thought that counts—the proof of love. All the more," he explained, "since the diamonds are real—Amsterdam and all that—in fact the whole thing's real except for the stone."

But it was the stone itself that fascinated him. *Sang de pigeon.* "It seems that pigeon's blood has the same vermilion color, with a touch of blue in it, the same glow," the jeweler had told him. ("Why pigeon's blood, then? Dove's blood would be better. A drop of blood on a dove's white feathers.") Then he had asked: "And what about the size?" Giulio had hesitated: "A fairly large, full hand. I think it would do as it is." The man winked: "Better not risk having the ring taken to another jeweler to make it the right size." He held out a bunch of metal rings. "Tomorrow, when you come and give me your answer, you can bring these back. In any case you'll need the measurements, even if you decide on another ring."

But he knew Giulio would choose that one: an understanding in his eye, a certain familiarity as he saw him out of the shop, proved it. So it was obviously not an engagement and Giulio had lied. "What shows it? What clue?" he wondered, seeing himself reflected fleetingly in the shop windows as he went to his office.

The Scarapecchias, though, seemed reassured. Ivana carefully tried out the metal rings: number 13 fitted. Her mother, afraid that Giulio would forget the number, tied a ribbon around the brass ring. Uncle Raffaele's eyes seemed to have softened. And Scarapecchia, coming home with a big watermelon, insisted on Giulio staying to supper.

"Stay and take pot luck," said signora Adelina. "Another time I'll do something special."

"Mussels, that's what you must do for him. Or else a ragout. The sort you used to make me to stop me going out in the evening," Scarapecchia suggested slyly. "She's a great cook,

Adelina," he added squeezing the bony bundle to him with a movement that suggested the memory of her as a young, desirable bride.

She pushed him away: "Rosario!"

"Well, it's just the family, isn't it?" said her husband, slapping her on the bottom. "Hurry into the kitchen, now. Mr. Broggini's probably starving."

Giulio hesitated. "I'd like to know if Ivana wants me to stay."

Ivana, busily varnishing her nails, had said nothing. "What nonsense," she said, without raising her head. "You always ask me such a lot of silly questions."

Her father laughed. "Come on, then!"

Giulio laughed too, and gave way. "Right then, I accept."

Signora Adelina's cooking was even better than he had been told. In it Giulio rediscovered flavors he had known in childhood and lost over the years. The evening was sultry and not a breath of air came through the open window. Giulio had taken off his jacket; he now always took it off as soon as he came in. Ivana put it on the back of a chair, settling it and dusting it here and there with a sort of professional competence. When they were ready to sit down at the table he made to put it on again, but Scarapecchia stopped him: "No, look, I'm taking mine off as well. You've got to be comfortable when you eat," he said, holding his jacket out to Ivana, who put it on another chair beside Giulio's. Every movement she made was noticeable because of her way of moving, of moving her hands. Giulio longed to feel those hands caress him calmly, so sure of what they were doing that they could do it casually. (Generations of women who obey without a word, who don't think, don't judge, don't comment. Many generations of women-slaves, of women-in-bed, are needed to give a girl who's still innocent, still a virgin, such sensual intelligence.)

Once she was sitting down, Ivana concentrated on the plate in front of her: her arms sprawled across the table, the cutlery on the side of her plate, completely unaware of her manners. She chewed slowly, savoring every mouthful, undisturbed by Giulio's unusual presence and by the attention she felt fixed upon her.

"Come and sit down with us," Giulio said to signora Adelina, who was running back and forth between table and kitchen.

Scarapecchia, mouth full, gave him a look that meant he was not to worry; then he explained: "She's used to it."

When she had brought an appetizing stew with peppers and potatoes to the table, signora Adelina sat down on the edge of her chair, as if temporarily, peering into the others' faces to see their reaction to the dish. Giulio was made to serve himself first, then Scarapecchia served himself, then Ivana; and finally her mother, having taken the dish, tried to give Giulio another piece of meat because she said he had made a poor choice.

"You let her do it," said Scarapecchia. "Women never eat: they feed themselves with watching us eat. Don't think that this one does," he added, indicating Ivana. "It's just that she's young."

The telephone rang: Ivana went straight over to answer. Her mother got up too and turned on the television.

"What do you think you're doing?" asked Scarapecchia. "You know I can't stand noise while I'm eating."

"I thought you'd like it," she said apologetically. "And then we need a little music this evening, a bit of gaiety. Do you know Mr. Broggini took the measurement for the ring?"

"That's fine," said Scarapecchia carelessly. "But it's no reason for spoiling our dinner. You've got to pay attention to what you're eating: you've got to concentrate to appreciate the flavor of the sauce and herbs and spices . . ." and when his wife said, mortified, that there was nothing else, that she had only had time to prepare a little zabaglione, he turned to Giulio. "You'll see how delicious it is," he promised him. "My Adelina nabbed me through the stomach, as they say. And when you get down to it, there are only two good things in life: eating and women."

At the end of the meal—with the scented flavor of the zabaglione still on his lips, watching Ivana coming and going as she cleared the table—Giulio thought that Scarapecchia was right.

"At home in the south, after supper, the women do their work and the men have discussions," Scarapecchia went on. "Women don't like discussions: all they care about is facts. Besides, what's the use of discussion? What's the use of talking politics nowadays? I've told everyone in my office: 'Look,' I said, 'if things go on like this I'll leave my voting paper blank at the next election.'"

"Why?" asked Giulio.

"I'm not anticlerical. On the contrary, I'm a believer. I just can't stomach these semi-priests. But there's no other choice: we're between the devil and the deep blue sea. And if only it was deep and blue! But they've adulterated that, like everything else. I say there was one good thing, only one, that was ever any good in Italy." He broke in on himself to shout: "Adelina, bring a little wine for Mr. Broggini!"

Giulio had already drunk a good deal. But he enjoyed lingering at the table: at his home, when he was growing up, in the society he was used to, good manners made people rise straight after the meal, as if everyone felt disgusted with the act which, out of pure necessity, they had just taken part in. Besides, he felt that cordial relations had been established with Scarapecchia, although his way of addressing Giulio as Mr. Broggini kept him slightly at a distance. He could—in fact, he should—have said, "Call me Giulio," but he preferred to remain a little remote and professional.

"Well, as I was saying, we had one good thing in Italy. Something that no one, not even our enemies, could deny us: and that was pasta. He—He whom you can't even mention nowadays," said Scarapecchia, emphasizing his words: "He knew perfectly well that . . . but you're too young, you can't possibly remember the battle of the harvest. . . . He used to take part in the harvest himself, you'd see him in the papers looking fine and sunburned, standing on the threshing machine or bending over his scythe among the tall ears of corn. He took it quite seriously and at the end of the day, collected his pay like any day-laborer. Then in the evening, in the barn, he'd take the peasant girls round the waist and dance with them . . . and more! He was a man. He really was," sighed Scarapecchia. "Not like those creeps we've got nowadays. When he was working in Palazzo Venezia there was always a woman waiting for him in the next room. He'd had a secret communicating door made, it seems, and between one talk and the next, between one minister and the next, he'd say 'Excuse me a minute,' open the door and bingo!—he'd leave them lying breathless. There were women there from every country, and they all said he had such magnetic eyes: he'd look at you and you couldn't resist." Scarapecchia blew his nose and went on: "The dictatorship had its faults, there's no denying, and it's natural and right for every country to work for democracy . . ." He looked up, to see how Giulio took this.

"There's no denying that," Giulio said.

"Just so, democracy's democracy. Although, as far as that's concerned, you've got to make distinctions, starting with the character of the people you're dealing with. Take Italy, now, I'm wondering where it'll end."

"We're all wondering" said Giulio. (For the moment all he was wondering was: "What's Ivana doing? Why doesn't she come back?")

"What we need is an iron hand, to get things in order. A man, but that means the sort of man Italians need. We're not England or Sweden. Here a man doesn't . . ." he made an obviously pointed gesture: "You follow me?"

"Of course!"

"That's the whole problem. If, instead of having all these discussions and round-table conferences and investigations and so on, they'd only come to me I'd explain it to them at once: a man who doesn't show he's a man, in every sense of the word, won't ever get respect from the Italians. These men nowadays, whether they're on the right or the left, whether they're for one sort of morality or another . . ." He waved his spread thumb and index finger. "Hopeless. And pasta's done for as well. Instead of using corn they put horses hooves, umbrella handles, plastic and god knows what inside us, and pickle away the money they get for it. And then they preach to other people and tell them to tighten their belts and save. . . . As far as I'm concerned, I've given up the rest. You've seen poor Adelina, haven't you? When she comes to bed at night she's so tired that she seems at her last gasp—but I'm not going to give up food. Anyone who touches mine had better look out! Everything's bought and sold under the counter these days. Degrees, jobs, votes . . . men, in fact. But they're the only ones who've got a right to buy. What happened to me wouldn't have happened under the old regime."

Giulio realized that Scarapecchia was urging him to say: "What happened?" But he had no wish to hear it, just as he had no wish to be called by his Christian name.

"Listen," Scarapecchia continued, pouring out a little more wine for him. "I may have been wrong, I admit it, but what's really hurt me is the unfairness of it all. When you know the way it went . . ."

He broke in because Ivana was calling, "Mama," in her usual drawling yet peremptory tone. She went over to Giulio. "Look what I've done," she said, holding out a napkin folded in the shape of a duckling. "It's yours. I'll leave it for next time. So you can't say I'm not glad you're staying."

"Very nice," said her father, annoyed at the interruption. "Now, let's finish what we were talking about."

"Rosario!" his wife called from the kitchen.

"Oh, hell . . . What is it?"

"Now there's a surprise!"

"What surprise? Who?"

Giulio thought: "Uncle Raffaele." He sat up straight and ran his hand over his hair.

"The watermelon!" said signora Adelina, coming in smiling, weighed down by the vast fruit on a dish.

They continued chatting till midnight. Then Giulio left and Ivana went as far as the gate with him. It had been a really lovely evening, he had told signora Adelina, squeezing the hand she always held out to him in the unsophisticated way of someone unused to visitors. "You mustn't thank me, you know this is your house," she answered, tremendously flattered. Giulio said: "If only it was!" and Scarapecchia laughed: "Lawyers really are first-rate liars, aren't they. This house is a mousehole: in summer the garden looks nice, but in winter it makes the house as damp as a cellar. I don't think you'd swap it for your luxurious penthouse." Giulio said he would do so willingly. "Then you need your head examined," said Scarapecchia, laying a hand affectionately on Giulio's shoulder. He then started taking off his braces and cuff links, making it clear that he wanted to go to bed. "Ivana can take Mr. Broggini to the gate this evening, can't she, Rosario?" his wife asked. Scarapecchia agreed, but Giulio heard him say softly afterward: "If Ivana stays too long, go and see what they're up to and bring her in."

In spite of its practical disadvantages Giulio was excited by the suspiciousness that always surrounded him; indeed by the certainty that he wouldn't need more than a minute to do with Ivana what a man and a woman who like each other and are left alone together must do. The casualness with which other mothers handed over their daughters—for an evening, for a trip to the sea, even for a weekend—gaily seeing them off with: "So long, children, enjoy yourselves!" was no more than hypocrisy, an excuse to wash their hands of what was happening, to let bogus trust take the place of responsibility, for now that girls did everything, they could hardly delude themselves that their daughters were the only girls who didn't.

"Put on your sweater. It doesn't look right to go out of doors with bare shoulders. And don't go into the street, you know quite well why. I'll be down myself in a few minutes," said signora Adelina jokingly, taking them to the door. There she added softly: "You can stay a bit longer if you like. Papa was dropping with sleep and I'm sure he's already gone off, because he's drunk quite a bit."

Ivana went downstairs in the cautious way she always did when she was wearing her best clothes. ("The way some women I saw in the street as a boy used to walk: in a silk dress and hat, and with plenty of pearls. They were going out 'to call,' but mostly they must have been calling on a man.") The moon had gone down and the small garden was blue and shadowy. After the sunny day the oleander put out a warm scent. "How wonderful. If only this evening could go on forever."

Ivana had stopped at the bottom of the stairs as if to say: "Now what?" Giulio, disconcerted by their unusual solitude, took her arm and slowly led her under the stairs that went up to the flat. He told himself that if signora Adelina let him linger in the garden with Ivana at this hour, it meant she could hardly fail to know that he would do "certain things," since they never talked, when they had a chance; and if her mother came in from the kitchen, Ivana uneasily tidied her dress and Giulio's face was scarlet. "I should have asked her: 'Tell me frankly, what may I do? Everything?' " The uncertainty froze him, or rather, the unexpected freedom. In fact, he felt none of the desire he had on other evenings, when he wore himself out in waiting and took advantage at every minute. "Let's stop here," he said. "Then when your mother looks out, she won't see us." Ivana obeyed without protest, which meant she agreed; yet, while Giulio was staring enchantedly at her, she yawned, showing a set of perfect teeth.

"Are you sleepy?"

"I'm always sleepy, I told you. If it was up to me I'd sleep all day."

"When we're married I'll go to the office and you can sleep till one o'clock. We'll go to bed early in the evening, but you'll have to stay awake as long as I want to, or even wake up in the middle of the night or at dawn."

"You just try. Mama says even the bells ringing don't wake me."

"Do you think I won't be able to?" Giulio asked her, meaningfully.

"I don't know. We'll see," said Ivana, pulling off a bit of honeysuckle to sniff. Under the arch of the staircase, the honeysuckle grew so thickly that it formed a green niche around them.

"You're lovely like this," said Giulio. "All you need is a pedestal to make you look like a statue. But statues are naked." Softly, he went on: "Pull down your dress. I want to see you." She looked at him as if he had gone mad. "I won't touch you, I swear. Let me see you."

"Yes, and then Mama'll come along and she'll show you!"

"Don't you realize your mother left us alone on purpose? We're engaged now and she, as an experienced woman, knows that engaged couples have to get to know each other. Why do you think they've kept such a close watch on you until now? But now that I'm giving you the ring . . ."

"Are you really giving it to me?"

"I've promised it, haven't I?" said Giulio. He nearly added: "A ruby: a family jewel my grandmother left me in her will. A *sang de pigeon* ruby." But he was not going to commit himself: considered coldly, it seemed too expensive. Maybe the jeweler had something cheaper that would be just as effective. "Do you think I've forgotten the size? Thirteen," he said, clinking the bunch of rings in his pocket. "Do you like this noise?" He felt he was being slightly vulgar; but this way of treating her like a pretty animal was just what would remove the suspicion he had felt since he was alone with her in the garden, that he was trying to get close to Ivana, and indeed to other women, just because there was nothing else to do. "Take off your clothes," he urged her. "Do you think it's fair for me to marry you without even knowing what you're like?"

"I'm all right. For today's fashions I'm rather fat, though," said Ivana, running a hand over her bosom as if to smooth it out, and then over her stomach: "I ought to eat less, but how can I?" she went on, as if talking to herself. "I do so enjoy it."

"And don't you enjoy this?" said Giulio, pressing her to him with sudden fury. "Don't you like being kissed and touched?"

She drew away, as if she were hot. "Oh dear . . . Now we're off again. You've messed up my hair."

"I want you as you are, you mustn't get any thinner. In fact you must eat a lot, so as to get even fatter: you'll eat chocolates, creamy cake . . ."

"I prefer highly flavored dishes," said Ivana.

"I prefer you, most of all," said Giulio with conviction. He laughed.

"But why?" Ivana asked him seriously. "I'd really like to know why." She had asked him as if she were talking, not of themselves, but of a couple they both knew. Between the pair of them, though, there seemed to be no friendship. Giulio was silent, looking at the gravel as if he were walking on his own a long way from there, wondering just why he awas infatuated, just why he was driven so obstinately—so inexorably, without any choice—toward this girl, whom he knew nothing about, who seemed to him strange and remote and not even desirable—yet necessary.

"I don't know," he answered. "Maybe because I'm in love with you." As he said this he looked up: Ivana drew back toward the staircase with her short steps—longing to escape, and at the same time afraid to—as if it had suddenly flashed on her that she was in the hands of a criminal and that she might make a movement he disliked, and be lost. With surprising mildness she let him take her in his arms and kiss her neck and her shoulders; while she murmured breathlessly: "What are you doing? Are you mad?"

Giulio stopped suddenly, wondering why and when Ivana had said these words to him, in the same slightly hoarse tone of voice. He even wondered whether he had met her before. "Impossible: she's twenty-three years younger than me, she's a child." He could not remember precisely; all he knew precisely was that he must get what he wanted, must force her to obey. "Then I'll vanish, they won't see me again. I'll try and get everything and then it'll pass, I'll calm down," he thought, holding her close with one arm, while his other hand went under her skirt. Ivana made no protest. "Either she agrees or I'll force her to agree, so long as she doesn't start screaming. But a few moments were enough to make him see the reason for this total passivity: from thighs to breast Ivana was squeezed into a corset tighter than a bathing suit. No inch of skin was free of it, and the elastic web was so thick that no warmth, even, could come through it. She was a statue. A kind of monstrous power was released by that perfectly groomed head, by the round face, the rather bewildered eyes, the sumptuous shoulders—where the healthy texture of the skin was hidden under the inimitable bloom of youth—by that stone body, solemn and full and untouchable.

"What have you done? Why have you put on this armor?" he asked angrily.

"It wasn't me, it was Mama," said Ivana. "Do you think she'd have left us alone for so long at night if I hadn't been wearing it? She said 'From now on you'll wear a corset. That way I shan't worry and you'll have nothing to fear.'"

Next day Giulio went to the jeweler's a few minutes before five: he wanted to make the man fear the deal had fallen through, so that he would accept the price Giulio intended to offer him: one million five hundred, not a penny more. And, in fact, he saw him jump up with a smile of relief.

"I was waiting for you," he said, holding out his hand and then a chair; and then he went behind the counter, on which the doeskin was already spread. "Coffee?" he suggested, dialing a telephone number. "I was afraid, seeing you were late. For you," he added. "But luckily that colleague of mine telephoned a short time ago—I'd only just finished speaking when you came in—to say he was held up by a customer and would come before I shut up shop . . . this line's always busy," he muttered, hanging up.

He took the white satin case from the drawer and held it out to Giulio saying: "I've had it cleaned because here, passing from hand to hand . . ."

The ring looked even more luxurious than it had the previous day. The jeweler was right: it was a royal present. Giulio imagined Ivana's hand in his, the ruby contrasting with the whiteness of her skin, and his mouth was full of saliva. He swallowed.

"I repeat: not just a layman, but even one of us—I, myself— seeing it on the finger like this . . ." said the jeweler, slipping the ring on as far as the first joint of his ring finger, stretching out his arm and raising his hand, waving the fingers to make the stone shine more brightly. "Now, what do you say?" On that male hand with its hairy wrist the jewel looked so vulgar that it was almost obscene.

The jeweler removed the ring and rang the café. While he was waiting for an answer he asked: "And what about the size?"

"Thirteen."

"Thirteen?" The man repeated, with satisfaction. "A very good number. I'm Neapolitan and I believe in these things. Thirteen. The devil." He winked. "Everything will go well." And then, into the telephone: "Dante? Send me two espressos. . . . Good ones, mind. Do you know who's speaking? . . . Right away, now!" He put down the receiver, smiling and looking pleased. "Everyone knows me here. Just ask for Peppino. My father served the flower of the aristocracy and only the other day—I never give names, but seeing it's you—Prince Corsetti came in for something . . . very delicate and told me: 'You're like your father, Peppino, you can be trusted.'" He put the ruby back in the box and switched on the lamp "Look at this!"

Giulio took the box and considered the ring in silence. "Come and get the ring at my home," he would tell her. There was a relationship between that big red ring and Ivana—they tempted him, together. Ivana came into the flat and then into his bedroom, sat down beside him on the edge of the bed, he opened the box, put the ring on her finger and as he did so pushed her down, be quiet, what are you afraid of? Be quiet, kissed her on the mouth, kissed her endlessly to keep her still and as he did so . . .

The waiter from the café came in with a tray. "Put it down here," said the jeweler. The man waited. "Charge it to me."

"He said that . . ."

"I haven't time now. Don't you see I've got a customer? Tell Dante to charge it," he said in a nervous, strangled voice quite unlike the one in which he had spoken of Prince Corsetti. Then, turning to Giulio, he said persuasively: "Even the box is new, the white has got to be fresh. These boxes are a terrible price now-adays, but it doesn't matter. The great thing is to please the customer. It's splendid, isn't it?" he said, indicating the ring with his chin and holding out the coffee.

"It's very beautiful," said Giulio. He gulped the coffee. "But what I really came to say was that a remade stone . . . No. It won't do, in my case."

"Oh, really? Well, it doesn't matter. Let's see something else. . . . Something more . . . important, as we were saying yes-terday," said the jeweler. He was smiling nervously as he took the velvet tray with the diamond rings on it out of the drawer.

Giulio made a gesture to stop him. "Thank you. But this morning I saw a stone somewhere else, a diamond of remarkable size and absolutely pure, so I bought it."

"It's all settled, then? In fact, you're already fixed up?" said the jeweler and swallowed when Giulio confirmed it, still trying to smile: "Pity. A pity because I'd have liked to show you some-thing that I've just got in and that . . ." He bent down to rummage in the bottom drawer of the counter.

"Too late, I'm sorry," said Giulio, getting up.

"Another time, perhaps," said the jeweler, getting up after him, wearily. "And, forgive me—maybe I'm being indiscreet—but might I know where? I know everyone and I might be able to tell you *how* you've bought it." His cunning, suspicious expression grew slightly more confident.

"Willingly," said Giulio, and named the most important jeweler in Rome. "At Bulgheroni's."

"Ah, in that case," the jeweler hung his head deferentially, then said, in a maliciously pitying tone, ". . . in that case, apart from the stone, maybe more than the stone, you've naturally paid for a whole . . ."

"Naturally," said Giulio coldly, and went to the door. Then he turned round suddenly: "Ah, excuse me, I was forgetting . . ." He took the bunch of brass rings out of his pocket, and they fell, sounding like small change, into the jeweler's outstretched hand.

He went out into the small paved road, then turned into Via Condotti. With relief he found himself on the pavement of that street of elegant shops, feeling he had got free of a slimy snare. But he couldn't help asking himself, with a kind of bewilderment: "What shall I do now? Ivana's expecting the ring."

At the end of the street, on the steps of Trinità dei Monti, a great many tourists were sitting, exhaustedly—women with swollen, dusty, sandaled feet, shirt-sleeved men with cameras slung round their necks. It was very hot: several foreigners were bathing their feet in the water of the Barcaccia and arguing with a policeman. "That's a fine thing to do. Where do they think they are—in the colonies?" The city he had recently felt such distaste for, now seemed like his own domain, something to be defended. A group of long-haired youngsters came decisively down the steps, to back the tourists up against the police. Giulio looked at them with manly disgust. "Take these to the barber: clean them up, then take them to the police station." Suddenly the image of Uncle Raffaele came into his mind, extinguishing his high spirits. "Lies again, eh? It's lies and blustering all the way," he was saying to him, looking at him as the jeweler had done when he refused to believe Giulio had bought the ring at

Bulgheroni's. "And what's odd about that?" Giulio answered. "What right have you to talk about lies?" He passed the shop where he bought his shirts: the man standing in the doorway greeted him with a deferential, "Good evening, sir," and he answered with an amiable distant gesture. "Why do you call it blustering? After all. I'm one of the best-known professional men in Rome . . ." he thought, skirting the building in which Bulgheroni's had their windows. "In fact, it's perfectly natural," he said to himself as he went up the steps that led to the shop entrance.

The door opened at once from inside and he found himself in a marble-lined hall. For a moment he hesitated, embarrassed. Behind a counter a tall, fair young man stood quite still, waiting for him, and bowed his head slightly when Giulio was standing opposite him.

"I'd like to see a ring," said Giulio, and when the man stared at him, waiting for more details, he went on: "A diamond. A solitaire."

The other man ("loathsome, an S.S. face") took him in with a half-bored, half-indifferent glance. "Might I know how expensive?"

"Fairly expensive," said Giulio, sitting down and casually taking out his cigarettes.

The ring would not be ready for another week: it had to be set, and it was just as well he knew the size already. It was a tiresome delay; Giulio had been aiming at a particular target in making this gift, and he was in a hurry to achieve it. The salesman refused to budge, though: the work could not be done in a few hours at the standard his firm required; besides, it was a stone that must be treated by specialists. All Giulio could do was choose another ring or buy elsewhere, he concluded coldly.

All the time Giulio was there the young salesman had kept up the same attitude. He watched Giulio suspiciously, as if doubting his capacity to pay; and Giulio had even wondered if he was another ally of Uncle Raffaele's, who must certainly have been in touch with the Neapolitan jeweler over that business of the ruby. So long as he was dealing with false stones, stones made up from rejects, it was all very well; but faced with a really valuable jewel, where was the pompous complacency he had shown in order to mortify a poor shopkeeper? Or perhaps the Bulgheroni salesman, being experienced in his job, realized that Giulio had come into the shop merely out of defiance.

Yet Giulio kept reassuring himself: he was not as weak as he felt in that rather banklike shop. Until now he had liked women to spend money on him, and his clients to accept his very high fees. In other words, he had been up for sale. (Everything can be bought, Scarapecchia had said: in fact that business with Amati wasn't too clear. On the other hand, Amati had lost. Don't save a drowning man, he'll drag you down with him.)

But he had found a new pleasure in competing with the taciturn youth who picked the stones up with pincers and laid them delicately before him on a piece of black velvet, without wasting a word in praise of them. Unset, and wholly without artifice, the bare stones glittered and almost winked as the light flashed upon their facets. At first Gulio asked: "How much?" for each jewel. Then he merely raised his eyes and the young man murmured a number, "Three," "Eight," "Five," trying to see his customer's reaction before showing him another stone. Giulio felt he was engaged in a trial of strength with someone who was trying to test his power. ("Let's see, let's see how much.") But already the image of Uncle Raffaele and even that of Ivana, were receding: the stones he was looking at no longer seemed like gifts—or merchandise—but like a means of competing with himself, with his own power—his economic power, and the power he needed to assert his freedom to buy even a woman, if he wanted her. At the jeweler's in Via Bocca di Leone he was a secret buyer; the very fact that he had chosen that shop showed he felt guilty. Women are paid, women can be paid for, he thought in the intervals which the salesman wisely left between one stone and the next. But he must not be ashamed, as he had been ashamed as a boy, because of his father's warnings about respecting the personality of others. "Weaklings are ashamed. To weaklings it's really an abusive action, based on a superiority that's only financial, which lets them swap their roles for the time being. To the strong it's a right that's derived from their own power. You can buy whatever is for sale: people are goods, like any other. Only not everyone can buy them."

He on this side, the salesman on the other side of the counter. In the silence, between the marble walls of that great, silent, unadorned shop, the young man would take a stone and display it enticingly. Then he would remove it and cautiously put a larger one before him. ("Let's try again, then: can he resist this one? Maybe with a little effort even this one? Let him rest, let him catch his breath.") He would leave the stone on the velvet in front of Giulio. ("Too much, is it? I see. Well, we can at least get this far. Can he hold out? Is he breathing easily again? Good.") Giulio, meantime, was sweating coldly.

Thus he found himself faced with a remarkable stone. A stone that was square cut, and glittered less than the others, a form in which innumerable other forms, small and identical, were repeated in perfect geometrical patterns. The round stones were more pleasant to look at: they glittered and the smallest of their facets flashed with all the colors of the rainbow. Whereas here was calculated precision, abstract value, and in the cold purity of its straight lines, it held a blue glow. It would not be possessed, it gave nothing in return, except the certainty of its perfection. "Ten," said the salesman, in the same dull tone.

Giulio felt the blood rush to his head. Ten million: the amount he had had from Amati after a year of work, of efforts, of uncertainties. Ten million for ten minutes—or rather, for the hope of ten minutes.

While he tried to recall himself to reason he saw Fausto Gottardi coming in. "I'm here to get a little thing, a birthday present. It's ready, isn't it, Cesare?" he asked the salesman. Obviously he was quite at home. "And what about you?" Then, pulling himself up: "I'm sorry, maybe I'm being tactless." "No, why?" Giulio said, pleased to be able to answer casually. "A diamond."

Gottardi stared at him with comical severity: "A wedding on the way?" And, seeing Giulio make a grimace of horror, Gottardi sighed with relief. "Oh, that's fine. Marriages make me feel terribly glum. But, of course, the years go by, and you're now at an age when a man starts spending money on women. It's a pleasure, you'll see, an even greater pleasure than bed. Luckily they don't know it," he added laughing. "Let's meet, don't disappear. I've got something important I'd like to talk to you about, which you might fix up for me. Let's go out together, one evening. Or rather, come to my place: first we'll talk and then we'll organize a game of poker—you do play, don't you?—something rather special. You haven't got a bad heart by any chance, you're a gambler, aren't you? Bring anyone you like along, of course: a woman with a new jewel wants to show it off like a new dress."

Giulio imagined Ivana arriving at Gottardi's house in her pink net dress. If Gottardi met her he would never dream that such a diamond could have been meant for her. He went about with elongated, angelic-looking women, cover girls or models who betrayed him without trying too hard to hide it. Anyway, it never worried him. Presumably what he wanted was the pleasure of contemplating their beauty, of owning them as if they were jewels, of weighing his own dark, rough, knotty strength against a value that was absolutely pure. Giulio realized that the same pleasure could be found in a woman's flesh. But she would have to be reduced to an object by being bought.

"May I?" asked Gottardi, indicating the square stone lying on the piece of velvet. "Of course," said Giulio and moved aside, but Gottardi said: "No, I like looking at stones this way." He took it and, holding up his hand, laid it in the palm, just where the lifelines and the lines of luck and brain met, among the bumps that rose at the roots of the fingers. "They say there's no give-and-take with objects but that's not true," he said. "There is, oh yes, there is." Then, in another tone he continued: "A fine stone. Small, but beautiful. You're a newcomer, you can still keep a check on yourself. But for a newcomer it's not bad, is it, Cesare?" The young man allowed himself a faint smile. Thin, blond, very pale, almost incorporeal, he should have vanished, and not have so embarrassingly intervened in the dialogue, or fight, developing between a man and an abstract geometrical form in which the man wished to acknowledge himself. Softly he asked: "This one, then?" Giulio had collected all his defenses, had told himself it was madness, and yet as he did so he answered: "Yes."

Outside the sun was still shining. Giulio frowned, as if he had emerged from underground: yet inside the shop the great lamps had poured a daylight glow over all the marble. In the doorway he stopped for a minute to light a cigarette so that everyone could see him coming out of the shop. "Well," he thought, looking toward Via Bocca di Leone.

He went along Via Condotti and paused in Piazza di Spagna. The police had been beaten in their argument with the tourists. "Nothing works in this country any longer. Scarapecchia's right: we need a man." He had a weird feeling that he had grown in height: he felt taller than the houses, like Gulliver, with people walking between his legs. ("What was it you wanted, a ring? Well, here it is. All fixed. Now stop bothering me, will you? And remember that although you may run the police, I can plead with the minister.") Who was the Minister of the Interior? No matter: whoever he was, he could reach him. At a certain level everyone inevitably finds himself bound to everyone else, forming a sort of enormous tree: once you have climbed onto a branch of it you can easily jump on to all the others. A few telephone calls, and after a couple of hours someone rings up to tell you that *it's been arranged,* thank you, I'll do the same for you, but you always paid for it in the end. Having settled this business of the ring, he must get a move on. It was absurd to spend hours and hours with a girl in order to touch one of her breasts in secret. (Desire rose again, irresistibly violent.) Then there would be another difficult moment to get over, in order to get away. The letter he had always meant to fall back on ("My character doesn't suit," etc.) was no longer enough. The best solution would be for Ivana herself to break things off. He would have to speak plainly to her. "Listen: do you know how much I've spent?" At the thought of it he felt dizzy. At first, when he was examining the stone, he meant to say, "I'll think it over," and then, away. Instead he had been overcome by the stone, and then Gottardi had turned up and he had let himself be conquered by his usual inferiority complex. Thank heaven they needed a week to have it set. "The moment I get back to the office I'll call and say: 'Look, I'm sorry but I've got to cancel the whole thing because . . .' What excuse can I make? 'The person I meant to give it to . . .' The salesman will think, 'She's jilted him,' but I'll say: 'She's dead.' "

The mistake had been to ask if he could take the stone away for a couple of hours. He wanted to show it to Ivana, in order to get a move on. (What exactly he meant by that he couldn't have said.) The salesman had replied that the lady could come into the shop to see it, it would be much simpler. "She's someone who can't be compromised," said Giulio, and the young man nodded respectfully. "I see," he said. "But she won't have to give her name, and we can arrange a way of . . ." Here Giulio broke in haughtily: "Hasn't it occurred to you that it might be someone very well known?" The man was silent. Then he said: "Of course, if you paid for it right away . . ." ("Why not? In a shop like this I can always return the stone and get back my check.") He signed, as if it was nothing very important. The salesman hesitated, with the check in his hand, then, looking up slightly to check the clock on the opposite wall, he asked if Giulio wouldn't rather take the stone next day. "Why? Because the bank's already shut? Do you think I may have given you a bad check?" "Just a moment, please," said the salesman, and vanished behind a velvet curtain.

Giulio was left alone. The clock was ticking dully, like his mother's pendulum clock. "They say it's a bad sign to hear a pendulum clock ticking in the silence." He realized that once again he was being weighed in the balance: on the one hand was a tall man with a check for ten million, on the other a stone as big as the nail of his little finger.

The doorman stood by the door and stared at him, as if it were his duty to watch him. He might have been a policeman they had put into uniform. Or rather, he definitely was. Giulio imagined discussions going on softly behind the curtain, maybe telephone calls to Gottardi or to someone important at the bank. Although he had nothing to fear, he was so nervous that he stubbed out a cigarette he had just lit and lit another. The doorman must have noticed, because he stared harder at him. At last the salesman came in again with a black satin box containing the stone, and started wrapping it in tissue paper. "Everything all right? Can I have it?" Giulio asked ironically. The salesman handed it over with a small bow: "It is yours." "There you are," Giulio's glance said to the disguised policeman, who respectfully opened the door for him.

"Whatever happens, I've got until nine tomorrow morning: the trouble is that the shop opens at the same time as the bank.

Just now, I've got to find a telephone, as soon as possible," he said to himself, and went into a café where there was a telephone booth.

"Hello . . . Good evening, signora Adelina. It's Giulio. I've got to see Ivana right away, because of the ring. I'd like the address of her school, so that I can go and fetch her there and take her to the jeweler's."

"The address of the school? Are you joking? Rosario has made me swear not to give it to you, and I don't want to go to hell. Let's do this: tomorrow Ivana can skip her lesson and we'll go to this jeweler's. There, if you like, you can go in and I'll wait outside."

("Take it or leave it," thought Giulio. "If they make a fuss they won't see me again.")

"Oh come, signora Adelina!" he said arrogantly. "Do you really think that today, when I'm going to buy something worth—forgive me, I don't like to mention it, but it's really a lot of money—that today of all days you think I'll be thinking of *that?*"

"As far as I'm concerned," said signora Adelina. "I trust you completely and you know it. But heaven help us if Raffaele ever found out . . . Have you got the ring?"

"Of course I have." (He nearly said: "I've got it in my pocket.") "The jeweler wants to measure her finger himself, because afterward he can't make it any smaller."

"Oh, is that all? Don't worry: if it's too big we can put a little wire round the inside, it doesn't matter."

"Signora Adelina, you must be joking! A bit of wire round a ring that cost ten million!"

Silence on the other end. Then: "Let me think."

The first hesitation. The first time she had considered the possibility of leaving them alone. ("I'll get her into the car, lock the door . . .")

"Well then? . . . Hello!"

"Hello, hello . . . Look, I can't give you the address. But I can call Ivana and tell her to be in Piazza dell'Esedra at seven o'clock, in front of that church—what's it called?—where there's a monsignor who preaches and who's so popular with aristocratic ladies."

"Santa Maria degli Angeli?"

"Yes—that's it. But if you should happen to meet Rosario—who's going to watch television this evening—I don't know anything, you just met by chance."

"Right."

"Listen . . . Be good, won't you?"

"Don't worry. Thank you."

He looked at his watch—half an hour till his appointment. He touched the inner pocket of his jacket, where the box was. When she had heard him say ten million, signora Adelina had been quite breathless. He must get things straight with Ivana. "You know perfectly well that marriage is absolutely out: we've got nothing in common, and you don't even bother to hide your dislike of me." And yet, occasionally, some dark enchantment made her stand still and look out of the window while he was unbuttoning her blouse; and even in that stillness there was agreement. "As for your future, you needn't worry. I'm not a child and I'll not leave you as I found you."

But was this really true? He couldn't tell. He must be dexterous. He remembered the way the salesman had offered him the stones, drawing him on where he wanted him, discreet, inexorable. Perhaps at some point Ivana would no longer have the strength to defend herself: he was counting on her suddenly giving way, and on his own swiftness. At that moment the man is so excited that he realizes nothing, but the woman, if she feels pain, struggles and screams. The thought of her screaming paralyzed him. His apartment had the thin walls of a modern building. Then Ivana wouldn't come again, there would be trouble with her family, her uncle, she was a minor, the law would be on to him; in other words, ten million for ten minutes of butchery, and maybe several years in prison.

He had been waiting for the past half-hour in Piazza dell'-Esedra. The days were shortening: he was hot, but wasn't going to put down the top of his car, because if Ivana was to be home at her usual hour there wasn't time to take her to his flat: he must find some isolated place, toward Acqua Acetoza, maybe. It was years since he'd had these problems; the women he knew received him at home. There was no need to trap them suddenly and then leave them: they said yes or no, in fact they always said yes, unless they were unwell. Where, then? Villa Borghese was full of police, mounted or on foot. He thought of the whole city: Rome suddenly seemed to him a tangle of streets and traffic lights and concrete blocks, where there was no quiet corner with a bit of green and a few trees. "It's the priests who destroy any greenery there is: they're thrifty and buy up bits of land or get it at auctions, to save people's morals; they burn up trees and woods, push the countryside out along the dazzling highways, until it's too far for sinners without a roof over their heads, for secret lovers in a hurry."

On the fountain in the middle of the piazza the naked bodies of the bronze naiads, gleaming with water, gave an illusion of coolness; one, riding on a swan, was making it bow its head.

The women who went by were not dressed like those in Via Condotti: they had merely shortened their skirts and showed bony, unpleasant knees. They walked fast, with the stubborn pride of all women who have a horrible knowledge of life, and who, the moment they finished making love, were sure to say: "My God, what's the time? I must run."

Seven twenty. Ivana was always late, but this time Giulio was afraid she might not come. Her mother was naïve, whereas she had an animal's instinct, she could scent things, and she foresaw deception in a completely physical way, as cats foretell rain. To reassure himself Giulio patted the box in the inner pocket of his jacket. He thought that perhaps Ivana cared nothing about jewels, as her mother had said. She had not bothered to find out what sort of ring it was, nor did she seem anxious to receive it. "The Roman proletariat's usual regal indifference, which is really an incapacity for emotion or sentiment."

A traffic policeman appeared at the window: "You can't park here."

"Who says so?"

"I say so and I'm giving you a ticket."

"I'm sorry, but wait a little. I'm expecting someone."

"Well, I'll be back in a few minutes. See that I don't find you here."

At that moment Giulio saw Ivana in the distance. She came forward, screwing up her eyes to gaze about her, scared of the traffic. She looked quite unlike the insect-women who shot surely and speedily among the cars; more like the plump naiads. Giulio watched her anxiously while she was crossing the piazza, as if she were the last example of a dying species and must be preserved. "She's fatter and she's not wearing the corset," he thought, noticing the opulence of her thighs and the slightly protuberant belly.

"Be careful," he said to her. "You must always be careful when you're crossing."

She looked at him, controlling her anger. "I wonder if you've gone mad."

"Why? In this traffic . . ."

"I mean, are you mad to make this date with me? How often have I told you we can't be seen in the street. And here of all places, just by the Ministry."

"If it's the place you're worried about, your mother chose it. And as for the rest, don't you think you're exaggerating? What would happen if we did meet him? I'd say hello, good evening. In fact it would be better. Else we'll go on like this even . . ." he was about to say "even when we're married," but he had

162

already talked enough nonsense and the subject was becoming dangerous. "If we can't even go to the jeweler's together to choose the ring . . . Obviously he's a maniac."

"I don't say he isn't. But we must be careful. Where is this jeweler's? I'm not getting into your car. We'll walk."

"We'll get there when it's shut and anyway it's a long way away. Come on, get in," he said, raising his voice. "Be a good girl and get in, otherwise . . ."

"Otherwise," said Ivana.

"Otherwise I'll give you a ticket," said the traffic policeman over her shoulder.

"What business is it of yours? How dare you?" Ivana burst out furiously.

Giulio tried to take advantage of this: "We're just going. Come on, hop in."

"Get in, miss, you'll save him a thousand lire," the policeman said pleasantly.

"I'll get in when I want to. And you shut up, if you don't want to lose your job. A phone call from me could ruin you. Do you know who I am? I'm Dr. Scarapecchia's niece."

The man was thunderstruck. "Sorry," he stammered, "I didn't know. But I was nice, wasn't I?" he said to Giulio. "I said: 'I'll be back later.' "

Ivana looked him scornfully up and down and got into the car. Giulio started up, shouted, "Don't worry, she's joking," to the policeman, and shot away. He didn't turn to look at Ivana but, feeling her hostility, drove dangerously to scare her. Piazza Porta Pia, Via Nomentana: "Where shall I take her, where?"

"What, are we going home?" she asked. "Aren't we going to the jeweler's?"

Giulio realized he was not far from Via Delle Alpi and swerved on screeching tires into Viale Regina Margherita.

"Will you tell me where this jeweler's is?"

"No."

"I see. Let me out."

"Jump out if you like, but I'm not stopping."

Where, he kept wondering. After Piazza Ungheria he chose two or three streets at random, but greenery and peace were always behind walls or bars. Everywhere there were lights, people, shops. "I've got to find somewhere, anywhere." Time was short and he felt as if he were carrying a corpse in his car, without any idea how to get rid of it. He drove toward the river, where the lights grew fewer between large patches of darkness.

"I knew it," she said. "I told Mama I didn't believe this tale of the jeweler's, but she insisted . . ."

Giulio stopped abruptly in a wide lonely road; on the right was a row of parked cars.

"Get me away from here," she said. "Or else I'll walk home."

"It'd do you good."

"What have I done? Tell me. You told me to come and I came. I keep to the bargain, but you don't."

"Instead of being glad you're alone with me . . ."

"If I wanted to be, I'd have been alone with you before this. Get going, or I'll get out."

He tried to calm her down. Besides, it was a horrible place. The couples had parked in a line, one behind the other, for protection against thugs who might attack them. But the double row of small red lights, the white tin boxes in which they were all doing the same thing, made it seem humiliatingly like some [communal erotic rite, in which needs were aroused and satisfied in exactly the same way.]

"All right. I will. But I'm going to stop somewhere else. I made an appointment to talk to you."

Ivana stared at him, doubtfully. Her short tight skirt showed a good deal of her legs above the knee; and her ready-made dress showed part of her breasts. She didn't bother to conceal herself: fear made her appear a fat, backward child. Giulio suspected that some illness had retarded her mental development. ("I can't stop here, or over there, too many people there, and further on there's a restaurant.") He went on down the hill and finally stopped where a drive led up to a house that looked uninhabited. On the other side, the grass sloped down to the Tiber. Giulio switched off the engine and they could hear the croaking of frogs.

"Why have you stopped?"

"I want to talk to you."

"That's just an excuse, I know what you want. Look, couldn't you wait? Papa's decided on October. You've only got to wait another couple of months. Can't you manage it?"

Giulio laid his forehead on his hand and shut his eyes. Two months: they would pass in a flash, without his getting anywhere. "What an idea I had, that evening," he said to himself, thinking back to the moment in which he had knocked at the Scarapecchias' door.

"Of course I can. But you don't know men. Some men wouldn't behave like this: they'd trap you." ("I must find a way of getting her out of the car. There's no one around. I'll say, 'Let's sit here' and roll her over on the grass. If she screams I'll hit her, I'll make her do what I want and then I'll be off, I'll escape. But where?") He himself was the corpse he couldn't get rid of. What would happen in two months' time? Or even earlier, when her father said: "Now we'll put out the banns." He drummed his fingers on the steering wheel, wondering whether to use force instead of relying on diplomacy. There was never any time, anyway: soon he would have to go home. But signora Adelina had said that her husband would be staying out to watch television; and if they came home punctually and properly she might think, "What a fool"!

"Listen, Ivana, I want to tell the truth. Marriage, here, lasts a lifetime. I saw you in the street, I followed you, I spoke to your father even before I'd met you, because, quite obviously, I was attracted to you at once. Marriage, to me, doesn't mean a family and children: you can have children if you like, but I don't give a damn. I became engaged to you because I was attracted to you. Otherwise I'd have stayed a bachelor. In other words, I'm marrying a girl I want to enjoy myself with in bed. Do you follow me?"

She nodded. "Go on."

"Don't you even want to talk, now?"

"Yes, but I'm scared here and I want to go home because it's late."

"Wait. I'm behaving myself."

"You're behaving because I want you to."

"That's true. I'm no moralist and if you wanted to jump the gun I'd do it. But you said no and I agreed. Sometimes, though, I have a feeling that when I come near you or touch you you feel a sort of horror. Now what I wonder is this: if, when we're married, you find you don't like making love, then what am I to do? That's why it would be best to try it out a bit, and see whether, gradually, you could come round to it. You know I'm a gentleman, that I'll respect you as I've always done. I mean that I'll leave you as a virgin until our wedding day; but if, before that, you tell me you don't like it, if you feel repulsion—either on my account or because of the lovemaking—then we'd better give up the idea of marriage and go our separate ways."

"But a man doesn't get married just for that."

"Well, I am."

"So, what is it you want?"

"Well, I'd like to lead you gently along to accept all that people do in marriage. Get you used to it, prepare you, if you like—a bit today and a bit more tomorrow—so that afterward everything will be easy and natural."

"But can't we do that after we're married?"

"I won't have the patience to wait. That night, as I'll have a right to it, I'll consummate the marriage."

166

"I see. You feel we're not all right as we are, we're not doing enough."

"It's too little. It's nothing. You just have no idea of all the things a wife has to do to please a man! We should meet outside occasionally, perhaps at my home, where you can be quite free, where we'll be alone and have all the time we need. We can begin and then very slowly, a little at a time, go forward. And when you say no, I'll stop."

"And would I have to do anything?"

"If you like. Would you like to?"

"No. No, I don't think so."

But for the first time Giulio felt that she would. She had drawn back against the door and was looking at him with dismay. ("Lovely, lovely," he thought longingly. "But I must keep a hold on myself because she really is ingenuous. Or I'll ruin everything.") He felt his veins were bursting.

"If you don't want to, do nothing. You're in charge, do you understand?" She nodded and continued to stare at him: "But at least you must keep still. Will you?"

"Sometimes, when you touch my breasts, I'm bored. You go on for hours. Don't you get bored too?"

"No. Never. But you must let me see what you're like. At a distance, if you want to. I won't come near you, I won't touch you."

"In other words, I'm to pose prettily."

Giulio laughed. "Well then, what do you say? Do you accept?"

"Listen, I'm not saying yes or no. I'll think it over. This time, as you've spoken frankly, I'll be frank myself."

"But if you say no, remember that—however much it costs me—I've decided to break it off. Do you realize that?"

"Yes, I do. You're the one who doesn't realize anything. You say: come to my home. Suppose I don't want to come. What about Uncle? If we get away with it this evening, it'll be a miracle. If he were to find me in the car, on a lonely country road . . ."

"You'd tell him: I'm with my fiancé who wanted to find a nice romantic spot to give me the ring."

"Yes, and he'd ask: where is the ring?"

"Here it is," said Giulio, taking the box out of his pocket. "Actually it's not the ring, it's the stone, that's why we had to go to the jeweler's. They need a week to set it. Would you like to see it?"

She nodded, without enthusiasm. Giulio unwrapped the package slowly, as people do with children, to prolong the waiting. As he did so he thought that Ivana was really unusual. Other girls made any excuse to get a ride in his Ferrari: she hadn't wanted to get in and hadn't even glanced at it. She wasn't curious about the ring. She wasn't merely uninterested, she seemed to know nothing about the values which everyone, not just girls her own age, considered. Perhaps bad luck had sent him to the one girl who really was disinterested and chaste, to the one family that really was respectable.

"Come here," he said. "Come closer."

He opened the box. The stone, lying on its black satin, looked like an ordinary piece of glass.

"What is it?"

"A diamond, a solitaire."

Ivana took the box, looked at the stone and then, turning to Giulio, asked: "Is it a good one?"

"It certainly is, it's extremely good," he replied, laughing. "If you knew what it cost!" He didn't mention the price because that would have been crude and, besides, he was afraid he might have been cheated. Perhaps, behind the curtain, they had changed it for another.

"Did you buy it from someone you know?"

"It's from Bulgheroni's," said Giulio smugly. But even that name meant nothing. "Give me your hand." She held it out, slightly arched and half open, like that of a ballet dancer. "Your hand is really beautiful!" He bunched the fingers together and laid the stone between the middle and the fourth finger. "Wait," he said, lighting the lamp on the dashboard. It was a blue light that made her hand even whiter and the stone flash amazingly. "What do you think?" When she bent forward to examine the diamond, Ivana showed her breasts, and Giulio, carried away by an ancient, uncontrollable impulse, flung himself upon her, kissed her, pressed her to him.

"Mind! The stone!"

He drew away, frozen. It had dropped, never to be found again. Vanished. "Oh, my God," Ivana murmured, distressed. "Oh God, God . . ." They had to get out of the car. "Mind, mind, in case it's on your skirt!" "No, it dropped in the car, I'm certain." They took a flashlight that was used for looking into the engine, and in its beam Giulio searched everywhere. Nothing. His throat was dry. At last, beside the gear lever, something gleamed for a second. "Here it is! It had practically dropped into the gear box. We'd have searched for hours."

"That reminds me, what is the time?" said Ivana, running her hand over her forehead. "We must go."

"Wait, let me get my breath a moment. Another scare like that . . ."

"Do you know what? I said, 'Dear St. Anthony,' the way Mama does, and we got the stone back."

He took her hand and kissed it: "Forgive me," he said. Actually he was asking her forgiveness for having suspected that she had taken the stone and hidden it in her bosom, in her stockings, somewhere. ("I'll make her undress here on the grass: she's got to give it back, whatever happens.") "Come, we'll go for a little walk. In any case, your father's watching television this evening."

It was a beautiful evening. Beyond the road the moon had risen and was lightening the grass that sloped gently down to the glittering water. Giulio took her arm. "An engaged couple out for a quiet walk," he thought; but he felt a rending melancholy, sharpened by the frogs' gloomy chorus. ("I'm in a blind alley. And nothing can save me.") Here and there there rose clumps of reeds, like tall spears. "Come, we'll go down a bit nearer the bank." Perverse feelings were rising up in him, clouding his mind. ("I'll take her behind the reeds, I'll undress her. If she screams there's no one about. I'll take her and afterward—what on earth shall I do afterward? I'll throw her in the river and get away.") It was the only way to free himself from his obsession. As they walked he ran his hands over her hips, her buttocks.

"I can't walk on the grass in high heels."

"Come," he insisted, pulling her by the hand. "If you can't walk I'll carry you." He made to take her in his arms; she was warm, fleshy, firm: "Come on, don't make such a fuss."

"No, no, I'm not coming," Ivana kept saying. Giulio held her tightly round the waist and dragged her along by force. "What are you doing? Where are you taking me? No, no . . ." she said, struggling. "No!" and with a hard shove she managed to get free. She moved quickly away from him, hesitating on the damp grass, and stood looking at him, breathless, her eyes squinting slightly, emptily.

"I wasn't going to do anything. Why are you so scared?"

"Because I'm small," she said.

Then she tidied her dress and hair, and resumed the haughty air he was used to.

"Come on," said Giulio. "Let's go home."

Coming slowly down from the bend in the road, coming noiselessly, as if its engine were switched off, was a white Fiat 600.

"My God . . ." murmured Ivana, raising her hand to her mouth.

"Be quiet," Giulio told her, thinking how crazy he was to have gone down there with that jewel in his pocket.

The car came on, very slowly and silently. A few steps away from them it stopped: the door opened at once and a policeman jumped out. Giulio squeezed Ivana's arm as they walked along. He was ready to say: "What do you want? What are you looking for? We're not doing anything wrong, we're just out for a walk." But as the policeman passed him, he touched his hat politely and walked on down the road leading to the empty house. The car's engine was switched on, and it moved away at once.

In a few minutes the pair of them were back among lights and people. "It was just a coincidence," Giulio reassured Ivana. "A fellow who lives down there and got his girlfriend to bring him home. Rome's full of cops, after all!" But Ivana was not persuaded. She shook her head, insisting that it must have been one of Uncle Raffaele's cars and that everything would have been reported to him already.

"Suppose it was? You can tell him about the ring."

"You still haven't realized what he's like. He doesn't trust the whole business, and he won't trust it right up to the very last day. Right up to the altar. I think Aunt Giovanna even had a ring."

"What happened, then?"

"I don't know. I was a child. But I do remember my aunt's stomach. She stayed in her room, crying all day. Crying and hating the heat, and fanning herself with a newspaper. In those days I thought babies were cut out of the woman's stomach. I thought she was crying because she was scared of being cut."

"And what about him?"

"He came from Bergamo. He was never seen again. Uncle Raffaele searched everywhere for him. I believe he's in Brazil. He'll have to die there, though, because he can't come back again. Uncle said that whenever he came back he'd operate on him the way his sister was operated on, a caesarian. That's when they cut the woman's stomach, the way I thought. The baby came out, but she never came out of the operating room. She was a lovely plump girl, like me and like my grandmother."

As she told this story she had become excited, her teeth biting at a strip of skin beside the nail of her little finger. They had reached Via Delle Alpi, in the meantime. "And now, what are we going to say?"

"Don't worry. I'll do the talking. Remember, we met in the street."

It was an effort for Giulio to drive, because his head was spinning slightly. "When am I going to ring Ugo . . . Something must be wrong with me and I don't want to have it confirmed." Outside the house he switched off the engine with relief. "Nice work, eh?" he said, slapping a hand on the steering wheel as if it were a horse's neck.

"Yes," said Ivana. "Too bad it's not red."

It was past nine but they hoped Scarapecchia would still be out. Signora Adelina's face, though, told Giulio he was back.

"Just look who I'm bringing back home!" said Giulio loudly. "I saw her here in the street, drove alongside the pavement and then said: 'Can I give you a lift, signorina?' She turned on me like a fury. And then . . ."

Signora Adelina broke in with a gesture. "Don't explain. Papa's feeling ill. He came home looking half-dead and had to take some of his drops." She moved away, flinging a sweater over her shoulders as if to hide under it.

Giulio turned to Ivana with a conventional expression. "Aren't you good at telling lies," she said, staring at him.

Later Scarapecchia came into the sitting room. He felt better. "Forgive me for looking like this, I'm not going to stand on ceremony." He was wearing pajama trousers and a long-sleeved sweater. "That's the nice thing about home, you can do what you like."

His wife and daughter arranged the cushions behind his back, while he directed operations: "Higher . . . no, no, further down now . . . That's fine, good." He looked pale. "What's a man, though?" he said to Giulio. "Just a few drops and a poor old crock like me's as right as rain. I say this sometimes to a priest I know: how can you judge a man's behavior if all it needs is some chemical combination to change him? With these drugs they have nowadays, a tiny pill can turn him into an angel or a devil. And what about the chemicals in food, and all the filth we breathe in the air, where does that go? Myself, I think it produces a kind of precipitation in the blood—as in a retort—and our will, our seriousness, our character is all done with . . . It's terrible, though. You're perfectly well, chatting and watching television . . . Suddenly, you're bathed in cold sweat. You say: it's nothing, it'll pass, it's the heat, you put up with it, put up with it, and then feel a hand squeezing your throat and chest and you think: it's all over and done with. How you change, in that moment! I'd like to tell some people—some of those smug bastards that take it out on a poor guy—I'd like to tell them they should have their blood pumped faster, so as to feel their heart squeezed like that."

"It must be the sirocco," said Giulio. "My head was spinning, a while ago."

"No," said signora Adelina. "It's those men from the co-op. He met them in the café."

"She's right. When I saw them the blood rushed to my head. . . . Besides, I'm terribly tired. It's been a ghastly year. As a rule I spend a week in the summer at Montecompatri, where a friend of mine's had a small house built. The air's so wonderful, there. . . ."

"Do you know what he ought to do?" said signora Adelina. "Ask for leave, pack his bags, forget everything and go off to Montecompatri. I could go with him, we could go together and take things easy."

"Wouldn't that be nice. . . . But they'll never let me go until . . ."

173

"Giulio, show Papa the diamond," said Ivana. "It's the diamond that's going to be set in the ring," she explained to her parents.

"With pleasure. I'd forgotten it."

"Give it to me, I want to enjoy it quietly." Signora Adelina went and sat down behind her husband, to see it for herself.

Scarapecchia opened the box and looked at the stone. He took it in his hand and twirled it round: "It's beautiful. Not that I know anything about these things, but it must be very fine, if as Adelina tells me, it's worth . . ."

"Ten million," said Giulio.

Scarapecchia looked at him with the suspicious air he had had the first evening. Giulio realized it was not so much because of the ring's value as because, given his own lack of experience, he suspected Guilio was pulling his leg.

"Ten million, did you say?"

"It's a very special stone," Giulio answered calmly. "The square cutting is terribly expensive, and look at its wateriness. . . . It looks blue." Scarapecchia looked, obviously saw nothing, and stared at Giulio again. "They need a week to set it because it must be touched only by experts." He continued to talk about stones, using the Neapolitan jeweler's expressions—cut, water, weight, Amsterdam, etc. "I wanted Ivana to see it this evening, so I had to pay at once. . . . Look." He took the checkbook out of his pocket and showed Scarapecchia the stub.

Scarappechia put on his glasses and read: "Bulgheroni, ten . . . What a lot of noughts!" he remarked smiling, and counted them: "Ten million." He was shaken by that amount, which until now had merely been a figure in the firm's accounts and on the books, and which he had never imagined having at home, lying on the table like a pebble. "Well, well," he said. And then severely, to his daughter: "Do you hear that, Ivana? And what did you say to your fiancé? Did you thank him, at least?"

Ivana seemed quite unimpressed. Presumably she knew the

value of the stone: her mother must have told her when she called her about the appointment.

"Now she certainly can't go out alone," said Scarapecchia, "wearing all that capital on her finger . . ."

"Oh no, that's absurd!" said Giulio, foreseeing complications.

"But suppose it's stolen or lost?" said Scarapecchia. "It's an heirloom. A whole lifetime's work wouldn't . . ."

He was getting excited and his wife intervened: "You must keep calm, Rosario. I called the insurance doctor and he said: 'No, I can't come this evening but I'll certainly come tomorrow. Keep him in bed in the meantime.' And you've not only got up but you're talking and talking . . ."

"It's good for me. We southerners need to talk. We're a people of philosophers, of lawyers. What would philosophers and lawyers do if they didn't talk? And those of us from Magna Grecia are descended from Socrates, from the school of Athens . . ."

"Oh, Rosario would have been educated," sighed signora Adelina.

"What do you mean, *would have been?*" protested Scarapecchia. "A man either is or isn't educated, and I'm not. They started me off on the wrong road because I had to earn my living, a dead end in which I've only learned a little quite recently, at my expense. Too late! We always learn too late . . . So this evening, when I found myself collapsing, I thought: it's over."

"It's a nervous disorder," said Giulio. "You mustn't worry.

"I'm not worried. The last act is part of the show. It's just that, if I have to go, I'd like to see Ivana settled. We've gone through so much for her."

"Like all parents," said signora Adelina.

"What's that? . . . Yes, of course. And knowing she's in the hands of a decent young fellow is a great satisfaction. In fact, I must take this chance of apologizing to you for being so harsh at the beginning."

"What are you talking about! Let's not say another word about it."

"Don't get worked up, Papa, drop it," said Ivana, trying to cut the strip of skin that hurt her.

"But I want to talk about it, especially as I may not see him again. I want to make him realize that when a man lives the way I do, when life's as precarious as mine is, he's always got to be on the alert. Because the poor aren't merely poor. As if that wasn't enough, everyone tries to take advantage of them because they're poor. Well, that's enough for today. But one evening, as soon as I'm feeling better, we must have a little talk about this wedding, settle where and when, so that if I've got to go—which I'm not exactly looking forward to—at least I may see you happy and go without worries."

In spite of all his talk his complexion was not reassuring, and before Guilio left he collapsed again. "A healthy, strapping man who'd eat three plates of pasta and beans of an evening and then sleep like a baby—it took those wretches to bring him down to this," said signora Adelina. Giulio offered to fetch a doctor but she said: "No, thank you. The insurance doctor will come to-morrow, but if his hour has come, as I pray to God it hasn't, then no doctor can put it off."

All this trouble confused Giulio's plans even further. He was sorry for Scarapecchia, whom he thought a good fellow: but his efforts to hurry up the wedding arrangements were alarming. "Admittedly, people say things like that in times of crisis." Whenever his mother felt ill she telephoned Giulio and reproached him for not having given her a grandchild. "I'll never live to see one," she would say, growing maudlin; then, when she was well again, she never mentioned it—particularly because, as everyone knew, she detested children.

Next evening, Scarapecchia was no better. Giulio found him in bed and through the gaping sweater saw his hairy chest rising and falling painfully, like an old man's. He was fifty-seven, yet he looked older than Giulio's father.

"Ivana's the child of our old age, as they say, although we weren't really old," he said the following day. He was in bed, but much livelier and wanting to chat. "I was about forty and Adelina just over thirty. By then we were almost resigned to being childless. There'd been several hopes, but she couldn't carry them. She was mortified that she couldn't give me this joy, because of what people said, among other things. Finally, one day . . ."

"It was Padre Pio," signora Adelina broke in.

"What do you mean, Padre Pio? It was me, wasn't it?"

She shook her head. "It was him, with his hand. You weren't there, you know nothing about it. A crowd of us women had set off, and lots of them had brought their children. It was in spring. At dawn we went to Mass, which he said. The birds, the trees with their new leaves, the hills covered in broom, all those gay children, and I felt like a cold, dry stick. When he came over to us, I was ashamed to speak to him. Then I got up my courage and went up to him, and looked at him—how beautiful he was, with that fine beard!—and I said: 'A child.' No one said a word. He put his hand on my stomach, like this," she took Giulio's hand and laid it on her belly, "and said to me: 'Those who despair of the Lord think they are empty even when they are full.' I didn't understand: even in the Gospel, when Jesus speaks, I can never understand. But actually . . ."

"She was full!" cried Scarapecchia. "And I'd been the one who filled her!"

"What a vulgar lot you men are," said his wife. "You always have to spoil the poetry of things."

Giulio laughed, with Scarapecchia. What he liked about this house was the very fact that one could let go, that one could unrestrainedly exercise a right that didn't have to be put off each day but was enjoyed through the simple fact of having been born a man. It was an old-fashioned household. Old-fashioned in the sense his own had never been; or perhaps it had been, in the days before he knew it, when his grandparents were alive, and his great-grandfather, Pinin; but from the stories he had heard, this great-grandfather sounded like a dry man, urbane and gay in the arrogant way they had in Piedmont. Besides, they had always been rich, and the rich are always slightly above ground-level and can look out on wider horizons; whereas the Scarapecchias could see no further than their noses, which meant just themselves and the small amount of space they occupied.

"Ah, you don't know yet what it means to see your own woman gradually swelling up and growing enormous, and being able to say: that's what I did. We'll talk about it again," Scarapecchia said slyly. "I've no doubt there's plenty of satisfaction in making a scientific discovery—Marconi and the telegraph, those Curies, that polio man. But these are imagined joys. On paper. It's a matter of calculations, numbers, proofs, or else germs to be wiped out. Creating's different. And creation's there, right there growing in your wife's belly. Women are stupid, or else they wouldn't be women. . . . They wear those loose dresses and smocks and shroud themselves with all sorts of veils and things, not realizing that they've never been so beautiful. When Adelina undressed I'd be in ecstasy watching that round belly of hers, as tight as a drum. Oh, Mr. Broggini, the trouble is that today men aren't men any longer; they haven't the courage to say these things or maybe—poor guys—they no longer feel them. I'm afraid that's really it. Nowadays they let their hair grow, have you seen them? Now if He was still about. . . . First, they'd never have thought of growing it; second: He'd have sent them to Ponza for a haircut. He understood all about these things, that's why He ran the population battle, and gave prizes to mothers of large families. . . . People said it was because of colonial expansion. Nonsense. Propaganda nonsense. He did it to make men feel virile—in their work, in sport, in war. Tell me, did you ever hear of alienation, when He was around? Did people buy drugs and sleeping pills and tranquilizers? It was He who suffered the exhaustion of modern life for us, we didn't have to think of a thing. 'Don't talk to the pilot,' they told us. All we had to see to was giving him more men, and the minute they came out of their mother's wombs he put them into uniform. Because, among other things, he realized the importance of uniform."

"To tell you the truth, I don't like uniforms," said Giulio. "I've always been antimilitaristic."

"Good for you! But do you think we can go on like this? Boys nowadays—and I see plenty because there's a nightclub near here where they dance in the evening—do you suppose they don't want uniforms? Long hair, boots, leather jackets, all the stuff they sell and call by those stupid names, op, pop, gear, are only substitutes for black shirts, brown shirts, red shirts and Alpini plumes, because a young man without a uniform is nothing. Now, because of birth control and the rights of women, they've been unmanned. They make love because they won't make war and give their girls pills to avoid having babies. In the old days, women took pills to make more milk: Adelina may be thin, but she had a couple of fountains of it that even wetted her dress. My opinion is that we're paying for the crime of killing Him— and hanging Him up on a hook, in Piazzale Loreto, like a stuck pig. He was a man everyone abroad envied us! They used to say: That's the sort of man we need. In a hundred years, when history's put on trial, we'll have to pay for Piazzale Loreto. Yes, make no mistake about it, we'll have to pay dearly. It'll be your children, and your children's children, but someone'll have to pay for it. I'll be manuring the ground, thank God, because I wouldn't like to be here."

Talking politics bored Giulio. To women, he repeated what he had heard his father say, and so, at least at first, they thought him left-wing. In fact he was neither left- nor right-wing: he was a man who worked, a technician; but as everyone was wrong, on both sides, he preferred to be with those who, though wrong, at least made money. Scarapecchia had sense. But Giulio had heard his father too often not to put forward the objections on which antifascism was based: the racial laws, the Axis pact, the war.

"I don't deny it," said Scarapecchia. "He made mistakes. He wouldn't have been a man if He hadn't. Or rather, He made a single mistake, the war. He slipped on a banana skin," he said, biting his finger. "On the other hand, how could He fail to? It wasn't so much because of the Germans . . . You know that we're mentally independent and we've always managed to get out of alliances that have grown uncomfortable. But, let's face it, seeing Germany gobble up a dirty great bone like France in just a few days, as if it'd been a cracker, well, even I—and I'm a prudent man—even I'd have said: 'I'm diving in.' Anyway, He dived and it didn't work out. If it had, why now . . . I don't know where He'd be, by now. And how about the King, poor little squirt, whatever did he do wrong? There he sat with his money, and it was all fine, He said, 'Sign, your majesty,' and he signed. On the other hand, he owed him something, you know. Like it or not, he was the Emperor. The Emperor, no less. And who've we put in the Emperor's place? First of all, a lawyer—an honest man who died in an iron bedstead. All very well, but you might think: 'If he ends up in an iron bedstead, after running the country, what about us, where will we end up?' Then a professor, a distinguished scientist, respectable as well, but crippled. Now, you've got to keep up appearances. What's a young lieutenant going to say when he sees a cripple take the salute? Oh come, come! Young lieutenants don't think, though, thank God. Did you hear him when he said: *Italians beyond the sea, listen* . . . Zacconi. That's who he sounded like, Zacconi, he sent shivers down your spine. And since when does Italy take on England and the United States?"

"But the war was lost from the start," Giulio said.

"I repeat, He was wrong. Let's say it was imprudent. They should have made him see his mistakes. He'd have learned his lesson and become less impulsive. Instead, He's underground and we're in the muck. And what about prestige, where's the country's prestige? If nothing else, the stamps. That profile . . . It looked as if we'd gone back to the Roman Empire."

"Papa's nostalgic. I know all this by heart. When I was small he always took me to the gate of Villa Torlonia on Sundays: 'This is where he was,' he used to tell me. 'This is where he came out.'"

"It doesn't matter to you," sighed Scarapecchia. "In those days they sent the soldiers off to Africa at night. They made them march to the station and always managed to take them along Via Nomentana. When they passed that fine white house where He was sleeping, they all turned to look at it, and then they left singing."

"Where were you, during the war?"

"Well, I was . . . partly because of Adelina, who never stopped having miscarriages. . . . The fact is, they simply made me stay here in the hospital at Celio, in the quartermaster's department."

"Oh, and wasn't he clever during the war, my darling Rosario," said signora Adelina, looking tenderly at him. "We had everything. When the war was over we still had coffee, sugar and cheese . . .

"I was champing at the bit, believe me. And my poor brother died."

"Your brother?" said Giulio, surprised.

"Nicola," said signora Adelina.

"What do you mean, Nicola?" shouted her husband.

"Nino, Nino," she said soothingly. "He liked us to call him Nino. He couldn't stand the name he'd been given. Wasn't he furious when we slipped up, too! Can't you see I'm sorry?

Nino," she repeated to her husband, gently stressing the dead man's name. "He was a fine man! Nino was very handsome, wasn't he, Rosario? That lovely black hair, and those eyes . . . Ivana's eyes."

Giulio asked how he died.

"Well, at home. He died at home, several years later but of an illness he'd caught in Africa, a kind of dysentery. The amoeba, you know. Poor Nino."

Scarapecchia's head drooped. "A tragedy. It was a tragedy."

"Mama, change the subject," said Ivana, "or he'll be feeling bad again."

Ivana cared for her father patiently, but didn't seem worried about him. Perhaps this was her way of showing her affection—bringing him a glass of water, taking a jacket and settling it on a chair. Giulio was now leaving later and later each night, because in his own home he now felt as constrained as he did at his parents'. That evening, before leaving, he told Ivana that he hoped to have the ring a day earlier than he had foreseen. "But you haven't given me that reply yet."

"Don't you trust me? Are you afraid of losing the money for your ring?"

"Of course not. What do you think? Besides, if we break the engagement you'll have to give it back to me."

"Really? And who told you that?"

"You've got to give it back, it's the law." He laughed and took her in his arms. "Let's stop talking nonsense. Have you been thinking about me? Have you been thinking about your reply?"

"Oh yes, I have, I have," she replied absently, but seemed disappointed.

For some days Giulio had had a feeling that he was not being so closely watched; and thinking back to the policeman's sudden appearance that evening by the river, he thought it must, in fact, have been a coincidence. Yet Scarapecchia had said that they knew their victims in advance and that when the time came they provoked the crime that would ruin them. Perhaps they wanted to give him the illusion of being free, in order to catch him when he made his first secret appointment with Ivana.

But would there ever be an appointment? For some time, he had been living in a completely novel state of chastity; but he was not prepared to put up with it much longer. Within a couple of days he would ask Ivana for an answer; she would probably ask him to let her postpone it, and in the meantime, the ring would be ready. Since meeting Ivana Giulio had done nothing but dream, and perhaps this was what really mattered. He wondered if he had missed the best in love and in sex, since every time he visited a woman he felt full of exaltation and of joy, yet at dawn, when he left, he was steeped in a coldness that lasted throughout the day. "It's your fault, Daria," he said, as he put his key into the lock.

What did Daria have to do with it? There was no connection between her and the idea he was brooding over. All the same, he would have liked to go to her office and beat her up: he had felt exactly the same impulse when he first met her. She had come toward him, in the short gown that showed her legs, and apart from her legs there was nothing special about her, only a confidence in her walk, and in her way of looking about her. Then one day he had heard her pleading. Indeed—he could now admit it—he had gone deliberately to hear her. "She's very good," he had said. "She's right, we'll never become friends." This meant he'd loved her. No, never. He'd always found her unbearable. She always wanted to talk, but not casually, about anything that happened to come up. She never fitted in with his plans: she had her own work, her own travels and responsibilities. In bed he preferred her to other women because, apart from a beautiful body, she had a brain. Yet he could not control a kind of bitterness he felt toward her. "If she hadn't jilted me I'd have jilted her a few days later. She just saved me the trouble." He had come to Rome to be free of his father's moralizing, and it was more than he could stand to find it all over again in a woman. "Why did you choose Rome?" his father had asked him. They had been there for several years and their memories of it were bitter. Those were the years in which his father might have been arrested at any moment, leaving them on their own. Whatever happened they kept saying: "We've got to stick it out, time's on our side, and the way things are bound to go." One day his father came home with one of his eyebrows cut open, and said he had fallen off his bicycle. Afterward he told Giulio: "I was attacked, but I didn't want to frighten your mother. You're a man, now. If I don't come back one evening, if I disappear, go straight to the Viminale and see what they've got to tell you."

Giulio unhooked the telephone to avoid talking to his mother. He was now quite certain that his father was in Rome; that afternoon he had telephoned *Orsa Minore,* asking if Professor Broggini had returned from Mexico. They had told him that his father had not left at all: at the last minute he had given up the idea. Then Giulio said: "It's his son speaking. I've been worried because we haven't heard from him for some days. My mother's worried . . ." "Don't worry, he's sent his articles quite regularly, as you must have seen." (Giulio never saw them.) "But from where?" "From where? Let me think . . . From Rome, I think . . . Yes, from Rome. In fact, now I come to think of it, he called the other day. Call the Excelsior. I'm sure you'll find him there." Giulio had telephoned and his father was not there. So he had to search for him. His mother's telephone calls were painful. Giulio kept telling her: "He's probably gone on to some other congress, after Mexico." "But he'd have written to tell me. As a rule he writes to me every day." "He must have been in some place where it was hard to post letters." "Oh, my God, where?" "I don't know, Vietnam, China . . ." "Now you're making me even more alarmed. He will come back, won't he?" Giulio said, laughing: "If you think you're going to free yourself of your husband, I don't think you'll manage it. Of course he'll be back." Actually he was not at all sure, but he hated to think of it.

He was tired, he felt his usual irritating uneasiness. The apartment was quite airless, airless and without Diodato who—unlike Giulio—became like a butterfly crazily in love on summer nights. He had just bought himself a Vespa. "It's so useful," he said. "I'm not very good with it yet so I get my nephew to come along. We've made some lovely trips out to the Castelli. Oh, how beautiful the Castelli are at this time of year, sir!" Whereas Giulio had enjoyed none of the summer. Unless he settled things with Ivana he would set off for a cruise to the East, and write to Scarapecchia from Japan or from India. It was the only thing to do. Above all, on a cruise he would meet all kinds of women on their own, foreigners longing for distant parts, for nights on the Bosporus, longing, really, to find a man. After he had made the break he need expect no trouble but the yearly Christmas greetings. He would answer with a Portuguese word: *saudade,* nostalgia. *Saudade* for all the lovers who had left him nothing, no regrets, no irritation, none of the rancor that had made him want Daria to crash in the plane that was taking her to Mexico.

A suspicion suddenly flashed on him. His father and Daria were to have left for Mexico at the same time; and now his father was not to be found and neither was she. He had tried to find her—to apologize for having forgotten their date—and had been told she was on holiday for a few days. Perhaps the people at *Orsa Minore* had orders to say that Broggini was in Rome, while the articles were coming in from Mexico, from which neither he nor Daria would return. In Mexico his father could get a divorce and remarry. "That would be the last straw: Mama would land on me, collections and all!" Yet this must be just what had happened: Daria's lover, the unknown man he suffered from being compared with . . . No, it was too funny. That his father should give gaiety and joy to a woman of thirty who had become tired of *him*—oh come, it was grotesque! "You really must tell me how Papa makes love, Daria: it would be terribly funny. Maybe he's rather a dirty old man . . . Anyway, it can't ever have been much fun with Mama."

He felt his suspicions were confirmed when he remembered having found *Orsa Minore* at Daria's home. "Dreary, isn't it, this review of my father's?" he had said. "Dreary?" she cried, up in arms at once. "Why, it's the only one worth reading!" "Clearly we don't like the same sort of thing," Giulio had answered. All he read were legal publications. Or rather, he subscribed to them and they all ended up in Andrea's room, where Andrea made notes in the margin and said: "Look Giulio, you really ought to see an article I've marked for you." "Oh, fine, thanks, thanks very much, put it there." The copy would lie about on his desk for weeks, reminding him that he ought to read it; then he would suddenly call the office boy and tell him to file it with the others.

In other words, he was trailing about in empty space. But it's not really trailing about in space because one fine day, like Scarapecchia, you feel a cold sweat, a heart attack, or else a small, insignificant but lasting pain. You go to the doctor and he tells you it's nothing, a small cyst, let's have an X-ray; and after seeing the plates he confirms that luckily it's nothing, but it's always best to have it out, just a small operation whenever you like, there's no hurry, right, you say when. How about tomorrow? You understand, but pretend you don't because you're ashamed of your fear, of the death that is still remote for other people because they don't know when it's coming, but for you it's come like a thunderbolt out of the clear blue sky, just as you're about to set off on a cruise to the East, what a bore. The operation goes well, you cheer up, go out, start living again, decide to enjoy the little time that's left and besides, it may not be *that*, everyone assures you it isn't, you've heard the same things said even when it was, but if it wasn't how could they persuade you that it really wasn't? Cobalt was used in lots of other cures and even to avoid complications, the doctor explains, he gives you all sorts of explanations, and you believe them, although you know they aren't true, but irrationally hoping they are; you're surrounded by care and courtesy, even from those you've never liked, who now come up to you kindly, and put their heads slightly on one side and say how are you, I'm so glad to see you. A plebiscite: relations, childhood friends, ex-service friends, even professional colleagues show they can be loyal to you. But you start wondering if the enmity they used to show when they feared you isn't preferable to this kindliness and—when you're forced into bed again—those visits that try to fill the emptiness already opening out between you and your work and women and nature, between you and life, which is nothing but a patch of sky with a few branches framed in the window, because you're gradually weakening: those who come and see you say it's convalescence, you're better, you're well now, you've got a good color and bright eyes, be patient a bit longer and soon you'll be fine, you'll see. In fact you're very well, everyone says so, they say he's fine, he looks asleep, at last he's not suffering, he's smiling a small ironic smile as if saying: I've done with it, and it's your turn now; then they look at the clock. Are they there? Have they come? Someone looks out of the window, yes, they're here. And in they come, dressed in black: the friends look at your cold indifference once more, stroke your hand, goodbye, goodbye, then "they" shut you up tactfully, they're always very tactful; and at last you leave the house triumphantly on their shoulders, while a woman's voice cries: gently, go gently, do go gently! A nonreligious funeral's a great bore; ideas are all very fine but, for convenience these days, you've got to do these things like everyone else, and if you don't go to church you haven't any idea where to go; besides, you've got to find someone who'll say a few words and friends are all away or out of town, there's such a general exodus you'd think it was a public holiday, though they're *appalled, regretful, over-*

whelmed, present in spirit, remembering, regretting, weeping,
from the prostitute's bed from which they dictate the telegram
or on the point of going out to dinner at a restaurant where they
make the most fantastic pasta, especially the *bucatini;* then a
colleague lets himself be persuaded, though not without protesting: this is the third this month, it's a bit much! At least tell me
something about him, I hardly knew him; but when it comes to
the point he does it with dignity and even brings out the ladies'
black handkerchiefs. After the few words the friends put their
hats on again, sighing: so that's over, are you going to the
Verano? are you crazy, in this heat? or else in this cold, and only
a few stragglers take you to the grave, which is already dug: out
in front is signora Peppina who gave you those injections, looking like a close relation, you sway and bump and slip and practically slide off the ropes, damn him, what a weight he is, at last
you squeak down into the grave and evening falls over the
cemetery, over the city where you still existed yesterday and
today you're just a small empty space that removes all solidity
from the name you bore. A stroke of the pen cuts it out everywhere; at last you vanish from telephone books, Christmas card
lists, police files, rowing club membership, even tax registers, in a
few minutes all your things are swept away, thanks to signora
Peppina, the injections woman who's got thirteen grandchildren,
the furniture's moved out, and the house stands empty. Nothing
left of you but a few photographs, a few images in the memory
of women who have loved you, fleeting images that suddenly
appear as they are walking in the street, or arrive at the beach, at
the most unlikely moments, in fact: they see you laughing in a
boat again, or saying goodbye at the door of their house, at
dawn, Giulio, they think, and their heart seems to tighten,
Giulio, and that's all, apart from a name in the home office files,
nothing else to say you were once alive.

He unbuttoned his collar. "It's your fault, Daria." What was
her fault? The way he was feeling? He touched his belly, ran his

hand under his armpit, afraid he might find a plague-sore, the way they did in I Promessi Sposi. "I must go and see Ugo, right away, even if I've got to see him in the hospital early tomorrow morning." The university clinics are terribly depressing: what is this fear, what do you feel? I can't say anything exactly, a constant tiredness, you must have made love too often, on the contrary, too little then, come over here, undress, undress and lie down, keep still: in a moment you're miles from him, poking, prodding, solemn, frowningly examining you, it must be his white coat, but how different he looks from the way he does at the rowing club, very odd with those tubes in his ears, listen, Ugo, whatever it is I want to know the truth; Ugo doesn't hear, doesn't want to hear, now I can't communicate with him either, Ugo, listen, keep quiet, don't breathe, hold your breath, now breathe, and at last he takes the stethoscope out of his ears: "I wish I knew why you come wasting my time this morning."

Giulio sat with his legs dangling from the couch. "Everything in order?"

"Perfect. Come on, get dressed. I've got sick people waiting."

He had hoped Ugo would find something: a virus he could blame for his dizziness, the slothful drive that was urging him toward Ivana.

Ugo went up to him, drying his hands: "Listen, take my advice: get married and have a couple of kids."

"That's the advice people give to hysterical girls," said Giulio, smiling without meaning to. "I'm not the marrying kind."

"No one is. Even the need to have children is a cliché. Children are important, not for the reasons people give you, but because they make such a row, they create so many problems, they're so expensive, that they stop you from thinking about anything else."

"You can spend a lot on women, as well."

"You can, but you're spending it on your own pleasure. When

you spend it on your family and home, you don't feel any pleasure, you just pay and that's that."

"If only that was all . . . I earn a lot."

"So do I," said Ugo. "Cigarette? . . . But the more you earn
the more women spend. The kids grow, the house grows. . . .
Do you know why old bachelors get married? Because they're
ashamed of enjoying so many privileges."

"That's all very fine," said Giulio, dressing. "But you might
actually marry because you like a woman, because she attracts
you."

"Well, as a rule the women that really attract us aren't those
we can marry. Now me—I like those birds who stand on street
corners saying: 'Coming, love?' But would you marry one of
them? Trouble is, I never have time to stop."

"I think that a man gets married at a certain point and brings
a child into the world because he wants to relieve himself," said
Giulio.

"Nonsense! You lawyers don't understand a thing. A child's
the final spurt before you give up. Your last hope of creating
something, of escaping from the mass, from a society you don't
fit into, and which, from that day onward, you can't escape. It's
over. You've got to accept all that's destroying you. But if it
should change . . . Tell me, what would you do without your
car, say? You look after it, coddle it, open the hood every second
minute, pretending you're checking the engine. You love your
car. What would you do if women weren't free, the way they
are? A fine old balls-up that'd be, wouldn't it? And then," Ugo
concluded, "if you, with your perfect nervous system, with your
sociableness, don't get married . . . To me, marriage has been a
punishment . . . a way of punishing myself . . ." While he
talked, he was taking Giulio to the door.

"So I'm all right? I don't have to do anything?"

"Have a good meal at the club and a swim, you lucky dog,"
he said, patting him affectionately on the shoulder. "It's Satur-

day today. At one o'clock I'm off to join the family. At Riccione, for heaven's sake!"

Outside, in the dark waiting room, there were a good many people: shabby women in black, men with great hollow eyes. When they saw him come out, two of them sprang up and rushed to the consulting room door, dazzled by the light.

("If you want anyone to take you seriously you've got to look like that, or else have *that* wrong with you. Doctors just don't realize that a man can look as healthy as I do and yet be quite near death, to suicide . . . What on earth am I talking about?")

He scolded himself as he went to his office. "I've never thought of suicide, and I never will. Especially not through desire for a woman or fear of a cop." He had always managed to deal with people, to stop them from grumbling and going on about law and justice, right and wrong. Abruptly he would take out his check book and ask: "How much?" This was what he must do now.

"Right then," he would say. "Ten million for the girl and I'll enjoy her until October. Freely, though: when I arrive you go out, go to a restaurant, go anywhere you like. Or else I'll pay rent for this flat, and you can go away for a couple of months, to Montecompatri, say. And how much do you need for the co-op?" (Families like the Scarapecchias blanched at the thought of repaying 300,000.) "Shall we say a million?" At the sight of the check, Scarapecchia would be nonplussed, like the salesman at Bulgheroni's. "What is it, don't you trust me? Do you want it in cash?" "No, it's perfectly all right by me. Thank you," Scarapecchia would say, "you've been very generous, the country needs men like you. We'd be quite prepared to leave you the house, and go off to Montecompatri, but . . ." He shook his head and returned the check. "But what?" "My brother." The Viminale again, halls sweltering in the sunshine, large windows, policemen's footsteps following him, and himself hurrying ahead, reaching the door, slipping in, going over to the desk;

Uncle Raffaele waiting for him, thinking he'd come without being sent for to sit down in front of him as if he were hangman, pawnbroker, judge; Giulio looking up, waiting to hear the price, but Uncle Raffaele still silent, lolling back in his armchair, not batting an eyelash, not losing his composure. "How much?" he asked at last, in a strangled voice, and Uncle Raffaele replied: "Everything."

He went into his office, wiping off the sweat: "Whew, it's hot."

"So it should be, sir, in August. It's the first today," said the office boy, indicating the calendar.

"Is it?" said Giulio, surprised. "Any phone calls?"

"None," said the switchboard girl. "Oh, I'm sorry, I forgot. Ettore."

"Ettore? Who's he?"

"I don't know, that's all he said."

"I've told you a thousand times to ask the caller's name and number."

"You're quite right, sir, I'm sorry. But it was the voice of someone . . . how can I put it? . . . it sounded like a workman, so I thought you must know him."

"Signorina Boschi," he said to his secretary, who came up to him. "If this Ettore rings up again, be sure and find out who he is."

"Certainly. . . . Oh sir, the police sergeant's here. I gave him the newspapers and sent up coffee. I was so afraid he'd go before you arrived."

"Oh, fine," said Giulio, going into his office. "When I ring, send him in."

He went straight to the washbasin adjoining his office and looked at himself in the mirror—hot, red-faced, his hair rumpled. He talked to himself as if he had Uncle Raffaele before him. "Now let's see what sort of excuse you'll make. Let's see which comes out on top: my improvisation or your experience, the experience of generations of policemen brought up in the brutality of the Viminale." ("That word, Viminale, was a nightmare, an obsession," his mother used to say.) "And suppose I bashed your face in? Suppose I cut open one of your eyebrows? But you never go out alone: you're escorted by a fleet of white 600's."

He was cool and tidy again when he sat down at his desk; breathing easily, only faintly irritated by the buzz of the air conditioning. He rang the bell, then picked up a letter, and pretended to read it: his heartbeats fluttered the sheet of paper.

"May I come in?" A tall, thin man entered, a man who wore his uniform with a certain style. He came over to the desk, cap in hand, and clicked his heels: "Sergeant de Simone."

"Do sit down," said Giulio, indicating a chair. ("Well-shaved, short hair, pleasant-looking: they've sent me the choicest one they can find.")

"I must apologize, sir, if . . ."

Giulio broke in: "You've been before." The sergeant agreed. "To my home, too, I believe . . ."

"No, that was Sergeant Mascolo, who's on holiday in Naples."

"Are you from Naples?"

"No, from Catanzaro."

"Ah yes," said Giulio. ("A local chap he can trust.") "Go ahead."

"Well, then, I must apologize for insisting on talking to you personally. It's a delicate matter. I thought you yourself would prefer not to have it discussed with a third party."

"I myself? Why?"

"It's a subject you might call confidential. The task of the police isn't just to look into misdeeds already done, but to foresee them. We keep an eye on suspected persons and so implicitly protect those who might be their victims. Maybe I'm being long-winded but . . ."

"Well, then?"

"Of course, I'm relying on your discretion. This visit is on my own initiative . . ."

"Will you please explain yourself?" said Giulio.

"I'm sorry. It's about someone who's close to you: your servant, Diodato Marietti." ("It's an excuse; he might have found a less silly one.") "Maybe you don't know that Marietti is . . ."

"I know perfectly well. Go on."

"We've had to get information about him and about his habits . . ." ("A good excuse to follow me," Giulio said to himself.) "So we've discovered that he goes about in a very unsavory set. Especially with a fellow called Sergio Picuti, who lives at 25 Via Della Spada d'Orlando, by trade an electrician, but actually following no trade except the one you can imagine."

"He's Diodato's nephew, I believe."

"Oh yes, and a good many other people's nephew as well," said the sergeant, smiling. "But according to his papers, he's nobody's nephew. He lives with his sister, Luigina Picuti, known as Lulu, which is a more suitable name for the profession she practices—manicurist, let's call it. From all this you can imagine what poor Marietti's tumbled into."

"I understand. But I'm not responsible for my servant's private life, nor am I interested in it."

"I've come to tell you that Marietti uses your name. When he was surprised talking to Picuti on June . . . twenty-seventh, he said he was there because of you."

"Oh, yes. I remember telling him to go for this electrician, who I knew was his nephew, to mend something that had gone wrong."

"He couldn't possibly have repaired it, he's a pervert who . . ."

"I don't see why perversion should stop him from being a good electrician."

"Let me explain," the sergeant said patiently. "These people aren't electricians or perverts. They're people who profit from the abnormality of others to get money, to steal. Your servant . . ."

"Is extremely honest. He's worked for me for three years."

"In spite of that he's got to the end of the small savings he had left, he's sold a small house of his mother's, in his hometown. You'll say: that's none of my business. But when Marietti has nothing left, it's fatally sure then, whatever his own feelings are, and even though he may weep—because he cries very easily— he'll have to commit some crime against you. He'll take first one thing and then another . . . and at last, when he's been pressed and blackmailed, he'll be reduced to every sort of baseness. . . . People will do anything, when all they respond to is sex."

"I never make generalizations and I trust Diodato," said Giulio. "Is there anything else?"

"Do you know that Marietti has recently bought a Vespa? Can he afford it?"

"Why not? I pay him seventy thousand a month . . ."

196

"Which he gives to Picuti the minute he gets it. Where does he get all the money he spends?"

"I wouldn't know."

"Are you quite sure you haven't noticed anything missing? Are you sure Picuti or any of the others haven't been in your apartment while you've been out? I think it would be prudent to dismiss him."

("To get one of them into my home . . .") "Thank you. Our points of view differ, professionally: you've got to seek out the guilty, I've got to defend them."

"At your own expense?"

"Maybe."

"Allow me to press you, sir. Why risk all this? These abnormal people may be as good as you please, but there comes a time when they get desperate. Good on the surface, basically good, but between the base and the surface there's—how can I put it? A gap. And you must remember his age, as well. Marietti's forty-five." Giulio had thought him older. "The typical age. The climacteric, if you'll forgive me saying so. At that age the flesh is greedy, but so are these youngsters, these Picutis. Do you follow me, sir?"

"Thank you. For the moment I'll carry on as I'm doing. Later, we'll see." He looked at his watch: "I'm sorry but . . ." The man leaped up. Giulio shook hands across the desk, and then picked up some papers. As De Simone was leaving he called after him: "Sergeant!" The man came politely back to the desk. "I've just thought: remember me to Dr. Scarapecchia." The sergeant hesitated. "Don't you know him?"

"Who doesn't? But considering my rank and my position I haven't . . . I haven't the honor of knowing him personally, still less of seeing him."

"Oh, I see," said Giulio, pretending to take a note. "He's my fiancée's uncle."

"Congratulations. He's very well known at Catanzaro.

197

Wealthy," he added. "No one knows how much land he owns, around there. Maybe he doesn't know himself. . . . My warmest congratulations."

When the sergeant had left, Giulio was in such a state of tension that when the telephone rang he started. "Hello!"

"Is that Mr. Broggini?"

"Who's speaking?"

"It's Ettore. You know me, sir. It's something very delicate and personal."

("A young voice, a Roman accent. It must be Picuti: what can Diodato have tangled me up in?")

"This is Mr. Broggini speaking. What is your name, please?"

"Is it really you, sir? I'm Ettore from the Excelsior, you know, the one who calls the cabs. Look sir, I've got that address. 84 Via Sardegna. Do write it down."

"What address?"

"Your father's address. He comes occasionally to pick up his mail. I followed him, and then went after him. See what barefaced, hypocritical liars they are, sir?"

"Fine, Ettore. That's splendid. I won't forget you."

"Oh, that has nothing to do with it. I didn't do it for that. It's because they said I'd got sunstroke. Goodbye, sir."

Giulio sat staring at the address: 84 Via Sardegna. A rented flat where he could see Daria discreetly. Or else another woman. In any case, it must be an experienced woman. "People will do anything, when all they respond to is sex," the sergeant had said. And what do they expect us to respond to? Dr. Scarapecchia?

There was a scent of grass and summer in the garden. Giulio pushed Ivana against the side of the door that opened onto the stairs. He put his hand inside the neck of her dress, touching her breathlessly with his hands. He felt no desire to possess her: touching her was enough.

"What happened then? Will you stop it! Tell me about the policeman," she said, pushing him away. "What did he want?"

"Nothing, it was an excuse. He wanted me to dismiss Diodato because he goes around with . . . with some electricians," Giulio said, thinking Ivana would know nothing about homosexuality. "Darling, lovely one, come here . . . Where are you going?"

"Didn't you hear Mama? If we go where she can't see us she'll make us go straight back indoors. And so every now and then we've got to go back to her." She went over to the staircase that led up to their flat. "Let's sit down here, on the steps. Be good . . . It's still light enough to see each other. And talking of light, what has that sergeant got against these electricians?"

"Well, they're not really electricians. It's just an excuse to get them into people's houses and steal."

"Are they a gang?"

"Yes," he said smiling. "An international gang."

"That's clever, you know, it's a good idea. I've been reading all sorts of strips lately and electricians never come into them. But," she went on, "that sergeant must be one of them . . ."

"Uncle Raffaele's gang?" Giulio broke in laughing.

"You never understand about these things. Gangs are illegal. Uncle Raffaele's is an organization."

"You're right, I understand nothing, these days. Today I was longing to see you . . . And yet I really should have gone to see someone else, a professor from Milan. I should have gone to his house, it was very urgent. But I thought: it's Sunday, Ivana won't be at school, why should we lose all these happy hours? And so I came dashing over."

He had gone to Via Sardegna feeling he was being indiscreet, and hoping to meet his father accidentally. "Why, Papa, are you here? When did you arrive? I tried to find you at the Excelsior several times." His joy certainly came from relief at knowing where his father was. As a child he had been present when his father was arrested. He had come back from school with his satchel under his arm and, in the hall, had found two gentlemen who were not really gentlemen but were not workmen either: they were people he had never met before. Instinctively he had felt he must tread very carefully with them. These men were opening and shutting drawers and then they started leafing through the books on the shelves, putting them back in place without even looking at what was written in them. His father appeared wearing his overcoat and carrying a suitcase, and said: "I'm ready, let's go." When he noticed Giulio he hesitated a moment, then called him over and said: "Giulio, I've got to go because they've come to arrest me." He must have looked at his father as if asking what he had done, because his father said: "I haven't done anything wrong. On the contrary, I want to stop wrong being done in our country and to all Italians, including you. But we obviously don't agree on what's wrong." Then he hugged Giulio and said: "Work hard and be good; and now, go and keep Mama company." Giulio had followed him to the door; there, suddenly dismayed, he asked: "Papa, when are you coming back?" and nearly burst into tears; his father hugged him again and said: "Soon, you'll see. Very soon." "Tomorrow?" His father nodded, not promising—something, some sudden difficulty, a cough, stopped him speaking—and nodded again, looking at Giulio as he went off down the stairs.

But he had vanished. And in this way Giulio had realized that his whole childhood had been dominated by the fear that his father would vanish, that he would become—as he became later, when he was in prison—someone who is, who exists, but who cannot be reached. Indeed someone you might even forget, playing and laughing as if nothing was wrong; but a glance from his mother was enough to remind him, to reproach him for his gay, expansive character and his longing for fun. Two days before the trial she came into his room and found him dressed up as a clown with some of his friends, wearing a costume roughly put together from whatever he had found around the house. The other boys were his audience, laughing their heads off at his jokes and grimaces, but getting up at once to greet her when she came into the room. She didn't deign to glance at them, but merely stared at Giulio in his disguise, his face streaked with chalk and charcoal. "You're completely irresponsible," she told him, "irresponsible and . . ." Without finishing the sentence, she left the room. Giulio dashed into the bathroom to wash his face and as he did so completed her sentence: "A fool. Irresponsible and a fool." All the same, he couldn't see what he had done wrong; his nature was quite unmetaphysical, and so the concept of right and wrong—and of every other strict and, to his way of thinking, inhuman distinction—was something quite alien to his life. He had never had any feeling of guilt. But to his mother, there had been a short period of religious mania, necessary, perhaps—as Giulio was later to realize—to allow her to bear her husband's absence with dignity, since she was beautiful and still young. Indeed, when he was freed again, she abandoned her religious practices just as she gave up wearing mourning dress.

Recently—that is, since his father had vanished again—it was not so much a sense of duty or regret at his absence that was making Giulio search for him so much as the vague fear that his absence would again become a void that swallowed up everything that was good in life.

He had appeared rather shyly at the house in Via Sardegna. It was a small house that must have been built for a financially comfortable client by an architect who had combined what was called the Florentine style with the tail-end of art nouveau. Women swathed in long veils and squatting griffins were painted on the front. The high narrow windows must have made the rooms dark, and the tiny garden was overcrowded with trees. He had hesitated before going in, scared that his father might say: "What are you butting in for, why have you come?" A glance at the house was enough to show that he would not have chosen it for normal life.

In the hall, the walls were painted in lozenge shapes, the gothic windows had leaded lights, and there was a small iron gate that could not cut out the smell of onions that seeped through from the portress's room. The portress looked so hostile that Giulio pretended he had come to the wrong house, and went out into the street again. Maybe his father wasn't registered as a tenant; maybe he was some woman's guest. He could hardly ask the portress for information: he must decide to go in or else—ignoring what Ettore had told him—go to the police.

As he looked up at the front of the house, he saw the opalescent sky between the dark branches of the cedars of Lebanon. It wasn't hot: a pleasant breeze lifted the climbing plants that dropped from the balconies like bunting. It was one of those days in which the summer was at its best. Tomorrow it might rain. If Giulio stayed there any longer, and in particular if he had found his father, he would have gone to Ivana's much later or not at all. An uncontrollable longing to see her again persuaded him to do nothing, to leave his "vanished" father for at least one more day. He even went so far as to say: to hell with Ettore.

He almost tiptoed away, fearing that—now, when he had made his decision—his father might come out and surprise him. It was Sunday and it was August; the streets were empty. He reached Via Delle Alpi in no time and leaped up the steps, two at a time. Ivana came to open the door. When she saw him she was so disconcerted that he suspected she was expecting her uncle. But she said: "I thought you were the vegetable man."

Her father was better; after lunch he went back to bed, meaning to sleep through the afternoon. "Poor soul," sighed his wife. "We're already in August. Just another month and it'll be October."

Giulio would have liked to settle the business himself—so long as it wasn't too expensive—in order to get a hold on the Scarapecchias; but he was disturbed by Ivana, whom he had surprised wearing more informal clothes than usual. She was wearing one of those modern dresses with a yoke and a very short, wide, flounced skirt that flared out into a bell shape as she walked. Her hair, which she usually wore in a complicated way, was held quite simply with a hairpin.

"Papa doesn't like me wearing this dress. He says it doesn't suit me. But he doesn't understand what girls wear nowadays.

What do you think of it?" Ivana asked him before they went down into the garden. She was like a little girl who had put on a maternity dress as a joke; dressed like that, she looked her age. Besides, Giulio thought, it was loose and would allow him to maneuver. What excitement, what joy: it was worth having spent all that money, worth all the other troubles in life.

"You're right: it suits you beautifully. To me, it's just one more torment. Don't you see what a state you get me into? I forget everything . . ."

"I wonder how things go in your office, if you forget everything . . ."

"They're all right. I've got a very good assistant: one of those up-to-the-minute, intelligent, terribly dreary young men. I have to force myself to like him. Serious, hardworking: an ant." ("The sort of man who already belongs to the insect world.") "I think it's silly to rest when you're old and don't know what to do. I want to be free now, to be with you. Right?" She stuck out her chin, as if to say: "If you want it that way." "So I thought I'd hand more over to Angeletti. Of course, I'd have to reward him for it: I'd have his name printed beside mine on our letterhead and give him a share in the profits instead of a monthly salary. I've got lots of gorgeous plans, but they all depend on what you tell me."

"Well, I'm nearer saying yes than no."

"Oh, darling! Give me a kiss, then." She raised her head in a way that meant: certainly not. "Well, this *is* a good start! Would you believe it, I still haven't managed to kiss you? Can you tell me why you actually let me touch you, but not your mouth?"

"It's one of the things we'll do later," she said, not losing her composure. "If I had to tell you why it's easier to let you touch me, I couldn't. Maybe it's because the other parts of my body are farther away. Go ahead, laugh, but that's the way it is: they're far away. Can you compare a mouth with a foot?"

204

"But other girls let you kiss them quite easily."

"Why should I be like other girls? I've never been like other girls. When I was ten the others were all little girls; I was already a woman. They didn't want me to play with them and I felt like a big rag doll because, being fat, I wasn't very active."

"Tell me, now, when are you coming to me?"

"I haven't said yes, yet. Don't torment me like this, or I'll say no and that'll be the end of it."

Giulio, raising a piece of her skirt which fell on to the step she was sitting on, was caressing her knee. "Listen," she said, "if you try going any higher up I'll throw you out. Before I decide, I want to see whether you respect agreements. Stop it. I don't like making a spectacle of myself in front of the neighbors."

"They're all on holiday. The house is empty."

"That's what you say. But there's signora Cesira, who's the great gossip of the building. They call her the Trumpeter, in fact. She's always in because she's got arthritis. She can't do a thing and spends all her time at the window or behind the shutters, watching what people are up to."

Giulio had never longed so much for darkness; but at least another couple of hours would have to pass. "And then Papa'll get up and we'll have supper. . . . I was so happy! Have a heart! You're made of stone, you know."

Ivana seemed struck by this and gazed more kindly at him.

"We'll go up now and get the wash Mama hung out in the sun this morning. I nearly forgot. I'll go and get the key for the terrace." She went a couple of steps, then turned and murmured: "Meantime, look around and see if there's anyone about."

"What sort of anyone?"

"I don't like this business of the police visit you had. I don't like the sound of those electricians, somehow."

Giulio went around the garden. The melancholy of the hour was in contrast with his state of mind: for this reason, perhaps, it affected him painfully. Or perhaps the shrill cries of the swallows took him back to his adolescence, when he used to tell his parents he was going to be coached by a schoolteacher and instead went chasing after girls.

Through the railings he saw his car and it no longer made him feel proud, as Ugo had said it did: his passion for cars now seemed something very remote, something he had long ago grown out of. He was glad that the people he had once gone around with had forgotten him: at first, out of habit, they had tried to get in touch, but soon they had wearied of it and the summer had scattered them. From the quiet garden where he now found himself, the evenings he had spent with them, their trips to the sea, their ambitions, which he had shared, seemed absurd. This garden had similarly quiet gardens on three sides of it, and the walls of these small unpretentious houses gave more shelter than those of grander buildings.

The small house his father was hiding in came into his mind. Very likely Ettore had mistaken someone for him, and his father had really vanished, landing from an airplane in a country to which his ever disillusioned enthusiasm had called him. This seemed likelier than meetings with Daria or some other woman in a house that in the past must have been an elegant brothel.

His father had never taken much notice of women. Giulio was certain that men who persisted so ridiculously in trying to put morality into politics were not the kind who enjoyed the pleasures of life: morality was a scourge they hoped to impose on others, to punish them for what they could never have themselves. This meant that some men would kill their sister's seducer not so much to avenge their affronted honor as because they couldn't bear another man to enjoy what they unconsciously felt was their right—and to enjoy it without even paying for it with marriage. This was why Uncle Raffaele, once his sister had escaped him, kept so close a watch over his niece.

Having all the women they wanted, Giulio said to himself, men nowadays frittered away their erotic impulses. To feel their force, a man had to center these impulses on a single woman, and to pour out on her the virility he also needed in the struggle to make money, the violence used to get it from some, to defend it against others. "Lots of people think the appeal of money is less noble than the appeal of love—in fact, that money in connection with love is immoral. Lots of people, and particularly my father." Luckily he had none of these built-in prejudices himself: he realized that if he had no money, very likely Ivana would never have accepted him. But without money he himself would have been different. He would not have had the manners, the clothes or the way of life he had, still less the confidence to enter the Scarapecchia household and lie, quite certain that he would get away with it.

Ivana was away some time. At last Giulio saw her coming downstairs, her face slightly forward because of the full skirt that prevented her seeing the steps. She was holding her hands up—as people do when clicking their fingers—and playing with a couple of keys tied to a piece of string. In some mysterious way, she understood the value of gestures and of clothes, which in love are like the ceremonial of some rite.

"Your father's quite right to stop you going out in that dress," said Giulio, moving toward her. "When women take off their clothes, they show their bones. But under this bell of a dress, you make one imagine such gorgeous, maddening flesh."

"Your mother can't have had enough to eat," Ivana answered, laughing. "She must have been poor, like me. All you think about is flesh, meat. When I was a little girl and lived with my grandmother I used to eat, but it was the sort of food you couldn't get your teeth into: a plateful of nasty soup with bits of potato and cabbage leaves and gristle floating about in it. At night I always dreamed of steaks."

"But I dream about you," said Giulio. "Last night I dreamed we were married. It was my birthday, you wanted to give me a present and asked me what I wanted, and I wanted to see you dressed in Eastern costume. You went into the room next door and came back dressed like that."

"What was it like? Like a dancing girl?"

"More or less: bra, wide transparent trousers, naked belly. And a veil on your face that left your eyes showing but your mouth . . ."

"Nothing doing, there," she said, laughing. "Right, I'll wear that costume. I like dressing up. At school I dressed up for several plays. I'd have liked to act more often, but the nuns said I was fat and never kept quiet."

"I'm glad to see you so gay, today."

"Yes," she replied. "Because this'll soon be over."

She said the words with a bitterness that chilled him.

"What will?"

"This watchfulness. Since you've been around I haven't been able to move, I can't take a step without them asking: where are you going, what are you doing? I said I was going to get the wash and Mama said at once: is Mr. Broggini going upstairs too? I said: why, can't he come? She said: yes, so long as you watch out for the Trumpeter. Then she told me Uncle Raffaele was going to call and if he wanted to say hello to me and she had to spend ages calling me he'd realize we were alone in the garden. So then I called him myself, we had a little chat, and now I'm free."

"This anxious uncle who never even comes to see his brother!" Giulio remarked viciously.

"What do you mean? He came one evening when we were all in bed."

"Why didn't you tell me?"

"Because I'd have had to tell you other things which you wouldn't have liked. He said that maybe you got someone to lend you the diamond, as we haven't seen it since. Then he said I'd got fatter. Papa said: she's well thank God. And he said: let's hope it's not thanks to somebody else."

Giulio said this was really going too far, and he would have to teach him a lesson. "That would be worse," said Ivana. "But I'm quite sure he sent that man the other evening, and the sergeant who came to your office as well. On the other hand, as he's my godfather . . ."

"What has that got to do with it?"

"Well, it has. He says that Italians have just one thing on the brain. And that things are going the way they are in Italy because, even when a man does think of something besides that, he's still thinking in the same sort of way: that is, trying to deceive his neighbor and get the best of him. Now, isn't that true? With you, ever since we met, it's always been the same. If we'd had more freedom, you know perfectly well what would have happened. And it would have happened just because I haven't had as much experience as you yet and I don't feel what you feel. But I've told you this because you're right."

"Ah. How am I right?"

"In saying we can take it or leave it. I am what I am, and if I don't suit you, we can be friends just the same. So, if we've got to try it out, let's start right away. If I've got to come to your place, I'll come, but I warn you what Uncle's like. You've got to take precautions. The worst I risk is getting my name in the papers: so many girls do nowadays, and it seems they get married right after these sexual assaults. But you're in danger of going to prison. As for Uncle, since I'm only seventeen he'd actually get a commendation. . . . You've promised to respect me; but you've got to be careful yourself, and I'll explain why, so that you can arrange things properly. . . . I grew up so fast that by the time I was nine men were already looking at me, and even the doctor they took me to said I'd better be married young because in our part of the country people like sex. I was a normal child but sometimes I was in a kind of fog and I didn't know what I was doing. Even now, my reason seems to get sort of paralyzed, as if I was in the sea, and being dragged along by the current. I'm telling you this because it might happen when I'm with you and you mustn't think I'm agreeing to what you're doing to me. I'm telling you for your own good, because, as he knows this defect of mine, Uncle's threatened to make me see a doctor sometime. And if you vanished, like that man of Aunt Giovanna's and so many others, then he'd take me to a doctor right away."

"But would you agree to such an uncivilized thing?" Giulio protested.

"Well, I wouldn't like it, of course, but what could I do? I wouldn't be the first. And anyway, it only lasts five minutes. . . . What's worse for a girl is that from the time she's quite little she can't be alone with a man for a minute without his thinking of the same old thing—everyone, from her relations to the slobbery old men who follow her in the street. In the south girls are never even left alone with their brothers. Papa says that's because they're real men down there. So, if you can't control yourself, there are two things you can do: either we don't see each other or else we hurry up the wedding, without all these trials and things. Mama says she didn't enjoy sex at first, but her confessor told her she must be patient, that what her husband asked was God's law; and then, when she got used to it, it was all right. Oh, dear!" she said, sitting down on the bottom step. "I've talked more today than I have since the day I was born."

Sitting on the step, in the short dress that bellied out around her like the petticoats peasant women wear when they bathe in the sea, she looked like a working-class girl. "It's true," Giulio said to himself. "A man can't think of anything else, and now the only people who think sex is at all important are people like the Scarapecchias, because they're the only ones who still have a sense of sin. We ought to try and strengthen religion, its practice, its outward signs, its symbols, everything." He didn't consider whether what he was suggesting to himself was right or wrong; on the contrary, he was thinking that he would soon get what he wanted and that money always gave him the chance of getting out of it. As he sat beside Ivana he began caressing the delicate nape of her neck, under the strong black hair. She was afraid her hair would come down, as it was precariously pinned up. "This hair business is another of Papa's manias. I'd like to have mine cut quite short, the way people have it nowadays, but he says a husband likes a woman with long hair and that if the man I marry asks him why he let me cut it, what can he say?"

Signora Adelina looked out, frowning: "Ivana, why haven't you brought the washing? It's nearly dark. Then you must come and help me in the kitchen. I'm sorry, Mr. Broggini. Love's all very fine but I can't manage everything, and I don't feel like climbing up and down all these stairs."

They crossed the garden and went up the stairs that led to the other apartments. Ivana said softly: "We must be quiet. If the Trumpeter hears us Mama'll have a fit."

The terrace was small and unattractive; but from up there the cupolas gleamed in the dusky dark red of twilight; and here and there, in thick clumps, they could still see the greenery of villas. "Come here," said Giulio, and she went over to him, her arms full. A smell of sun, of old-fashioned laundry. "It's a beautiful city," he said.

"I don't know," said Ivana. "I don't know any place but Rome and Catanzaro. I prefer Rome."

Touched by her ingenuousness, he put his arms round her waist.

"Darling," he said, "darling . . ." and ran his hands over her hips. He was sure now: she was not wearing the corset. Under the short dress she had nothing on. "Now, shall we begin?" he said.

"Up here?"

"There's no one around."

"Apart from the fact that Uncle's men now go around in

helicopters, it's too light. I'm ashamed." She hesitated a moment, then said: "Come."

Opposite the terrace, a long narrow passage led to the washroom. It was almost dark and, dazzled by the light outside, Giulio groped his way forward. Ivana led him: "Come on, there aren't any steps." They went into a small dark-gray room like a cave, where they could hear the sound of water gushing into the basins, dripping into the veined metal tanks.

"Clever girl," he said, drawing her to him. Under the loose, rumpled dress, her round body seemed firmer than ever. "Put that stuff down."

"Where? If it gets dirty and Mama has to wash it again, she'll kill me. On the edge of the basins it's all wet and the floor's as black as soot . . ." They stood hesitating, with that great clump of sweet-smelling laundry between them. Then she said: "Do you want to see me?"

"Oh yes, yes please, please . . ."

"Hold it then," she said, handing over the laundry.

She moved away a little, and went over to the side of the room, by the tanks; then she turned, as if Giulio were going to take a photograph. She was so fat in that shapeless dress that Giulio wondered if she was really not hiding an accidental pregnancy under it. ("Where, in some attic as a child, did I play doctor?")

He felt a cold, hasty curiosity, which might have been suggested by the presumed innocence of childhood. Recalling the language of those early days, he said: "Show me, show yourself."

She began taking off the dress, in stages: it was already halfway up her thighs, and would soon reach the groin. Giulio was unable to move because of the laundry he was clutching in his arms, which made him look sidelong at her, as if he were in the cinema and there was someone too tall in front of him. "Higher. Higher still," he said, twisting his mouth to avoid one of her father's shirts.

Against the gray metal of the tanks, in the gleam of light from the window, her glowing flesh gleamed white. In that big body—from the heavy breasts to the solid hips, to the round, slightly protuberant belly, to the strong legs—there was a majesty that invited contemplation. Giulio looked at the harmonious trunk without the desire that the image of Ivana naked had aroused in him on so many nights. It was as if she had unveiled, not herself, not a woman, but life itself.

"Have you finished?" Ivana asked, her voice trembling slightly.

"Wait. Please, wait." He never thought of approaching her, he could not have done so. He stood still, as if nailed to the floor.

"I'm stifling under here. That's enough."

Through the ceaseless gurgle of the water they heard footsteps coming up the stairs.

"It's Mama," said Ivana lowering her skirt. As she did so, her hairpins fell out and the hair fell around her shoulders. "My God! What shall we do?"

"Oh no," he said, stupidly, feebly trying to cheer her.

"It's either her or Papa," Ivana said desperately. "The Trumpeter can't get up these stairs." She took the laundry from him, they went out into the passage, and met signora Adelina head on.

"What were you doing in here? And why did you take off your corset, you dirty thing? I went to make your bed and found it under the pillow," she said, softly but violently. "Did you do it? Here, of all places . . . under the Trumpeter's very nose! Look at the state you're in!" she went on, indicating the hair that had tumbled round Ivana's face and the strap that had slipped off her shoulder. "Take that," she said, and smacked her cheek.

Giulio intervened to defend her: "No, signora, no, I assure you . . ."

"You keep quiet!" signora Adelina broke in. "It's not your fault, because everyone knows that man's a hunter. It's the woman who's got to be careful. But I thought that at least you'd have had a little consideration for that poor man. . . . Well, that's enough, come on."

Ivana and Giulio went ahead, their heads hanging guiltily. One of Ivana's cheeks was red and she was trying to arrange her long hair. They went down two flights and as they did so heard a chain being drawn cautiously on the floor below.

"What a lovely evening," said signora Adelina, in a slightly phony voice. "We really must come up more often and enjoy the fresh air, don't you think so, Mr. Broggini?"

He nodded, not understanding. Moving her lips, Ivana explained: "The Trumpeter."

In the crack of the door stood a bald old woman in a long skirt, holding a pair of binoculars in her right hand.

"Who is it? Signora Cesira?" asked signora Adelina, bending forward as if to flush out a child who was hiding. "Isn't that lucky? Now I can say good evening to you. . . . I went up to collect the wash with our two lovebirds. This is Ivana's fiancé, Mr. . . . Why, what lovely binoculars, signora Cesira! And what do you look at with them?"

The old woman looked up at the sky and raised the glasses as if replying: "The stars."

"What a good idea! That must be nice for you. . . . Well, good night," she said, and continued down the stairs, leaning on Giulio's arm, as in a wedding procession.

That evening Giulio didn't stay as long as he usually did when he had supper there. On the face of it, it was an evening like any other: Scarapecchia seemed better after his long afternoon sleep, and was going back to the office next day. He was in a good mood, slapped Giulio on the back and said: "Health's the main thing," in a pleased sort of way. Ivana had changed her dress and behaved as if nothing had happened. Signora Adelina complained that she was tired, but on other occasions this had not stopped her gushing over Giulio; now, for the first time, she quite noticeably neglected him. She suspected Giulio of what hadn't happened—though he was longing for it to happen, as soon as possible—and when Ivana prepared to go to the gate with him, she called her back and shut her in.

He had no wish to go home again; for a while he roamed round the Pincian wall, as if outside a hostile citadel. From one of the arches he looked at the street that until a couple of months before had been the scene of his evenings and adventures—a few streets, a few unvarying restaurants, where he read the same menu every evening, as he had done for the past twenty years.

At home he saw the light on in the kitchen. Considering his habits, Diodato could hardly be home yet—it was only a little after eleven. But Giulio found him in the kitchen, facing the window. When he heard him come in, Diodato turned.

"Already home? I'm glad I've found you here. Two single men never meet, even if they live under the same roof."

"Quite true, sir."

"Did you go out into the country today? It was such a beautiful day that I said to myself: 'Diodato's right. It must be wonderful getting out on his brand new Vespa.'"

"Yes, it's very nice," Diodato said, without enthusiasm. Then, seeing Giulio looking around for the whisky, he asked: "Would you like a drink, sir?"

"Yes, good idea, bring me a whisky on the terrace, I'll get a breath of air before going to bed."

The armchairs on the terrace were folded up, because he never went out on it. And yet the terrace had been one of the apartment's main attractions when he first looked at it. It must have been at a time when he was drawn to the simple life, but by now he couldn't remember. *The wind lifted her skirt on the terrace, she lifted her arms to hold her hair, everything was flying about.* The idea of the terrace must have been Daria's, because she was mad about the open air, mountains, outings with a rucksack and a picnic lunch. Another unbearable thing about her. He wondered how his father got on with her, certain, now, that it was Daria. He had introduced her to him himself, one evening when his father was passing through Rome. Giulio was bored at the prospect of their usual meal alone together in a restaurant, at having to keep saying: "I don't know, I haven't read it yet," and of hearing his father say how surprised he was that Giulio went around with people he called reactionaries or fascists, however well-known, sought-after and powerful they might be. He had asked Daria to help him get through the evening with his father; but the pair of them had talked entirely to each other, and Giulio, who was at first relieved, had finally felt left out. When he got into the car to take Daria home Giulio said, "Papa, shall I put up the top?" and his father had been almost offended. During the drive Daria continued to talk to his father—who seemed younger, with his hair blown about by the wind—and as she turned on her seat Giulio could see her legs. The only good thing about the evening would have been ending it together, but that was impossible. After saying goodbye to her, his father sat down beside Giulio again, smoothed his hair and remarked: "Nice, very nice indeed. What did you say she was called? Giacometti. Daria Giacometti." For some time afterward he asked Giulio whenever he came to Rome, "How's Giacometti?" in an affectionate tone. Giulio answered evasively, "Oh, working away," because by then it was all over.

As he poured out the whisky Diodato said: "Excuse me sir, your mother telephoned a while ago. She said she'd try later."

"Hell! What did you tell her?"

"Nothing, that you were still out, sir."

"Listen, when she calls again . . . But you'll be asleep."

"I'm not sleepy. I can wait up."

"Really? . . . Oh, thank you. Well, then, tell her I called from somewhere outside Rome, telling you I'd be away for three days. I'm doing it because I'm terribly busy and my mother'll want me to look up one of her chums." Giulio felt like chatting. "Did you go out to the country today?" he asked again.

"No, I didn't go anywhere."

"How was that?"

"I had some trouble with the Vespa, and had to leave it with the mechanic. . . . I'll go, because if the phone rings . . ."

Diodato seemed very much on edge. Maybe he was expecting a telephone call from his "nephew." His rather taciturn character made him seem self-controlled. ("Why did I have to explain about my mother? I'm always too friendly," Giulio reproached himself.) *Her round belly, her hips like an amphora, her soft, velvety skin.*

He had promised his mother to see what was happening, but had no news except Ettore's information, which might be wrong. *A white solid form, like Parian marble.* Whatever had happened, he must now go in search of his father: his mother had already telephoned him very early that morning, before he had time to prepare or invent something reassuring. "Do you know, I've just realized what's happened," she had said. "He's starting all over again. He's always doing it. Anywhere you like to think of. He'll always be a revolutionary commercial traveler, a merchant adventurer who isn't interested in money—in fact, who just spends it like water. But when his ideas have triumphed, the ideas he fought against come back and reassert themselves in some form or another. It's only a matter of time, and everything's back where it was. Then he starts up again somewhere else. You were right, you see: he must be in China or with the Vietcong. Here, at least, we knew who we were dealing with, but no one knows a thing about *them!* I can't remember a single one of those hiccuping little names of theirs. . . . To think that at his age, instead of staying quietly here at home, where we have everything for a pleasant old age, waiting quietly for death, he starts up again!" Giulio thought: "He's vanished."

He might have told her that she was idealizing her husband, who was not in China, let alone with the Vietcong, but in Via Sardegna with a woman. But he did nothing of the sort: he reminded her that his father never decided anything without her agreement. "That's true," she said. "That meant he could go off feeling easy." But she soon dropped the rancorous tone. "I feel so abandoned," she said. "What should I do?" He told her to let him think, because he meant to go to Via Sardegna and see his father; but he had done nothing, he had thought no more about it. *She had come to open the door, smiling, and then in the garden she had looked at him with a new, inexplicable expression and then she had said: "Come," and then: "Do you want to see me?" and she herself had gone over to the gray tanks and there she had turned, her eyes wide open, as if for an execution.*

Since he couldn't get out of it, he had to face up to the problem right away. He went and sat down at his desk, took a sheet of paper and began writing, hesitating between discretion, clarity—contempt, between the lines—and affection in spite of everything, the man-to-man understanding that couldn't go too far, considering they were father and son. The first draft he tore up, and the second. At last he wrote merely: *"Tell me what I've got to tell Mama,"* sealed the envelope and went into the kitchen.

Diodato was still at the window. He had put on his glasses and was staring at the sloping end of the street, was shading his eyes with his hand from the light of the lamp. He took off his glasses, cleaned them with a handkerchief, then put them on cautiously and started watching again.

Giulio wondered if Diodato had cleaned his glasses because they were wet with tears. He was about to withdraw. But there was such loneliness in the way he was waiting that he hadn't the heart to leave him.

"Diodato, would you please see that this letter gets off tomorrow?"

Without turning, Diodato answered: "Certainly, sir."

He blew his nose, trying to compose himself, then turned to Giulio and said: "I'll take it tomorrow."

Perhaps it was better to pretend not to notice, Giulio said to himself, and to go on talking about practical things: "Don't go upstairs with it, leave it with the porter. And then I want you to be careful about something else as well: when my mother calls this evening, or tomorrow, or at any other time, if she asks you for news of my father, you don't know anything. Do you understand? Whatever happens you must never mention this letter or give her this address. I'm not going to explain why—it's a complicated business."

"Everything's complicated," said Diodato, and two tears rolled down his cheeks onto his white jacket.

Giulio said to him: "Come here, sit down." He sat down himself, to put him at his ease, and said: "What's the matter, what is it?"

Diodato unfolded and refolded his handkerchief, tugging at its edges. "What do you suppose it is, sir?" he answered, without looking up. "Love."

Abnormality repelled Giulio, and very likely Diodato realized this, because he had never mentioned his own bent. Yet, since the sergeant's visit, Giulio had felt a secret bond between them, even if Diodato had no idea of it, just as he had no idea what the doll the porter's child now played with meant to Giulio.

"I know," he said. "Women are vile."

"Yes, and so are men," sighed Diodato.

"Of course, of course, so are we. Women seem to think we're made of stone."

Diodato turned, and raised his smooth, worn face, with its network of tiny red veins that gave color to the cheeks, toward Giulio.

"Not men," he said. "Boys . . . After all, sir, you know what I'm like . . . Love's always love. In fact," he went on, hanging his head and opening his eyes wide, as if to see the handkerchief he was obstinately tormenting, through his tears, "in fact, just because it's secret, just because it's something you can't confess, something other people don't understand, some-

220

thing they may get you for and lock you up for with such delight, such perversity . . . A perversity known only to people who are called normal. But we understand everything . . . it's love. And just because this sort of love is . . . how shall I put it?—heroic, desperate, when someone disappears, it's even meaner because he knows he's leaving you alone with it . . . with what's called this abnormality. Which isn't the least bit abnormal, anyway, because what about the Greeks? . . . No, it's not abnormal: it's different. But the pain of not seeing a person again, of not hearing him speak, even if he's only being mean to you . . . that's the same pain. The world becomes a desert. Do you know how I feel, sir? Just the way they show the first man landing on the moon, with no one and nothing around him, and the surface sinking under his feet. Forgive me for talking like this, sir, but when I saw you coming back I said to myself: I can't bear it any longer, I'll break down, because you can die from suffering like this, but at least there'll be one human being to say to me: 'Poor Diodato.' You've always been good to me," he said, and sounded moved. "You didn't make an excuse to dismiss me, as plenty of people would have done who had no complaints about my work or my honesty. . . . You understand. I'm not sure if you did before, when you were younger, but now . . ."

"Of course I understand, but why are you so desperate? Who were you waiting for at the window?"

"Him—Sergio. My nephew, that is. Well, that's what I called him, because of what people might say and out of respect for you as well. He's a fiend; everyone told me; you'll see he is. . . . I've done so much for him, done so many desperate things for him, and now I'm left like this—as you see me," he said, raising his arms. "Naked. He swore he loved me . . . oh, who knows . . . even now, yes, even now I believe he did, but he was always sulking because he used to say: 'Other people have got everything and I've got nothing.' Yet I never let him go without shoes or clothes or even those 'Dolce Vita' sweaters he always wore. He used to show me the airline posters of London and New York and grumble because I couldn't take him where people lived the way he wanted to, and he'd say: 'I could go away with a rich man who's asked me to, but I love you, and I'm staying with you'—he really meant it, you see—'but you haven't got a car and you haven't even managed to get a miserable Vespa to go and get a breath of air at Castel Gandolfo or Genzano.' One day he told me: 'Unless you get a Vespa, I'm not coming with you again.' And that was that! He simply vanished. Well, I searched for him, and sent messages telling him to call me. He'd call and say: 'Got the Vespa yet?' And when I said no, he'd hang up. A few days ago, I won't tell you how, but thanks to someone really good, I got one. Oh, the times we had, sir! . . . Because Sergio could be quite different if he wanted to: gay, and nice, and pleased with very little. He was really just a boy. . . . Yesterday he called and said: 'Lend me the Vespa because I've got to take my sister somewhere'—his sister has a job that involves getting around—and I said no, the Vespa was for the two of us. Maybe I was wrong," he said thoughtfully. "I ought to have let him have it, it's my own fault, but he didn't even press me, he just said: 'My sister can manage, meet you tomorrow at your place.' Today he turned up, gay as could be because that's what he was like, he'd ask for something and if he didn't get it he'd sometimes forget all about it. It was a lovely sunny day . . . He said: 'Well, where are we going? I'll let you choose,' and I chose Rocca di Papa. We got on the Vespa and he said: 'What's up? It won't start.' He tried, and tried again. . . . We got off, because he said he wanted to have a look, and he's a good mechanic. He poked about and looked at it and said: 'It can't be anything much, just a wire or something.' Then he said: 'Wait, we'll give it a shove.' He got on and said, 'push,' and I pushed, and he went off slowly, slowly down the slope, then he switched on the motor and streaked off like lightning—just vanished, and that's the last I've seen of him."

"He'll come back, he must have taken it to a mechanic," Giulio said encouragingly.

"That's what I hoped myself: at five o'clock I was still down in the hall. The porter laughed and said: 'Put salt on his tail, Diodato!'—you know how vulgar people like that are. . . Actually, sir, as he was moving off he made a gesture. My eye sight isn't too good and I thought, he's waving goodbye, but I knew he wasn't really: it was a filthy gesture that meant good-bye among other things. . . . I called his home and his sister answered. She said that Sergio had told her to tell me that I was a penniless nobody, that I needn't call again because in any case he was never coming back, and that as far as the Vespa was concerned I could go to the police."

"But the Vespa's in your name, you ought to go to . . ."

"Who to? The police?" Diodato shook his head. "Normal people can, but I can't. It's better not to attract attention."

"I'll see what I can do," said Giulio.

"No," said Diodato. "If it's a case of Sergio and the police, Sergio'll always win—because he's got so many friends, good electricians like himself, mechanics, house painters, and they always meet there at Porta Portese. And anyway I'll never go to the police. There's a law, even among those of us who are outside the law: if we steer clear of 'them' when things go well, we can't appeal to them when they don't. It's all a game—I've lost and I'm paying for it, paying bitterly, believe me, because Sergio wasn't really bad. . . . He was the way all men are when they want something . . . only that you can hold a woman with marriage and children and the law . . . but how can we hold these boys? They're leaves swept by the wind, they come and go and vanish and nothing's left but this suffering. Such suffering, sir . . ." he said, and covered his mouth with his damp handkerchief to stifle a moan of agony.

Giulio ran a hand over Diodato's arm without speaking, with kindly detachment. *A long narrow hall, a half-lit cave, a white body, a trunk showing the faint indentation at the waist, the opulent arms cut off by the dress held up on the head.* Disgust at the tears that streaked Diodato's face, disgust at suffering.

"Now I'm going to give you a whisky," said Giulio. "Wait now, it'll do you good." Diodato murmured, "Thank you," and Giulio went onto the terrace where he had left the bottle.

An August night, full of stars: occasionally, one of them drew away from the rest and rolled through the firmament. *White, and in the hollow of the armpit a dark shadow, a secret suddenly unveiled in the movement that had made him open wide his eyes.* As a boy, when he was in the country and saw a shooting star, he always made a wish and it was always the same one: to succeed. To succeed how, and at what? He didn't know, but even afterward, when a star fell, he always had to think it and to believe that the wish would come true.

He went back to the kitchen, poured some whisky into a glass and held it out to Diodato, saying gently: "Go to bed now. It's late."

Diodato took out his glasses and went over to the window again: "This is his time of day. It's now that I have some hope."

He wondered why Ivana had refused to tell him what she had been thinking, several evenings before, when she saw a falling star. "No," she had said decisively. "If I tell you, it's done with. It won't happen." "Tell me at least if it has anything to do with me," he said. "Well, yes, in a way it does," she answered, and that was all. "I must know what it was," Giulio said to himself, as he went into his bedroom.

There he found an envelope addressed by hand, and recognized Sylvia's handwriting. The envelope, which was very full, contained the gold cigarette lighter she had given him and he had forgotten on the bedside table, the last time. Since that night he had not been in touch with her. The note attached to it said merely: "To save you the trouble of coming to get it."

He was put out. He went over to the telephone and dialed. "Sylvia . . . no, Sylvia, this gesture isn't like you, it isn't the kind of thing you . . . If you take it like that I'll have to send back your letters tied up with pink ribbon, as if it was a broken engagement. . . . Oh come, aren't you ashamed of being so sulky, so middle class?" When he accused her of that, he could always annoy her, it was the most cutting thing he could say. "Let's forget what you've done. We'll cancel it out. Look, I'll tear up the note and throw it away," he would say if Sylvia replied; he would accuse her of being jealous—an attitude that was conventional, old-fashioned, ridiculous. *Her still face, her large round knees.* "You're wrong. I'm absolutely alone," he would say with a tinge of melancholy in his voice. "Do you know the truth? I'm going through a crisis. Because of money? I don't know. But I do know exactly when it started: May twenty-seventh. I remember it because I'd been to Amati's that evening about the deal. Then, quite unexpectedly, I had two hours' freedom. Two hours off the chain that had bound the hours of my day together for the past fifteen years. Suddenly I found myself free of appointments and meetings. Free of the telephone . . ." *Only the body, faceless, expressionless. Only a woman's body. I wanted to see her face and she hid it from me by turning away. The mouth, no good.*

For a long time he waited, while the telephone rang: maybe Sylvia was in the tub; or else his call was ringing through the empty rooms, shaking all that corpselike bric-à-brac—dried flowers, butterflies under glass, empty shells and animated, ghostly objects (a Barbary ape playing a violin, a box that recited an acrostic when you opened it), and the hands of a mobile—white hands, black hands, hands large and small—that twirled about as the air moved them.

Anyway, Sylvia wouldn't be very late, as she was bound to

think he would telephone. He imagined her coming into the house—a cigarette in her mouth, a scarf around her very long neck, and hanging down her back, her wrists clinking with bracelet charms. That clinking was a sign of her passing, of her existence. Each charm was an animal's head that symbolized a onetime lover. "When the affair's over I realized how much there was of the animal, in fact of a particular animal, in each one of them. I can't see them otherwise." In fact, she never named them: she said "the falcon," "the tortoise," "the squirrel." At the beginning of their affair Giulio had said to her: "I wish I knew what animal I'll be turned into." And in her usual amused and trilling voice she had answered softly: "I hope I'll never know."

The fact that she had sent that note showed that she still thought of him as human. He hoped he could still visit her home, where he had met so many important people who were now his clients. Women had always helped him and he believed that only strong men could be helped because they never disappointed their women, and because no one suspected that this help might fill their emptiness.

"Well," he went on, "I was free that evening. And I was pleased: Amati had signed at last (and my share of it would amount to a pretty fat check), and there was nothing to suggest trouble. I looked at the shop windows and at the people in the street, enjoying the fresh air and my state of unusual freedom: it was as it used to be when I was an adolescent, in streets made remote by the blackout, between the shadowy trees and ghosts of white houses. In those days I would wander about without an object or any money, and the darkness urged me on to follow women I would never have dared face in daylight." *A body with protuberant hips I could cling to, a trunk with deep roots that nothing could shake. A stony expression on her face, whose natural expression was one of severity and pain.* "When I tried to stop them, they stared at me, dismayed. As long as they looked at me that way, I could be brave—that is, as long as they were scared of me, as long as they expected anything at all from me, but always something evil, an attack, a theft, some irrational violence. My father used to say one shouldn't humiliate a woman by paying for love, and I would have liked to pay to humiliate her, but I had no money. . . . I had been tough with Amati, for his own good. Amati's neurotic, torn between his longing for money and a reluctant yen for honesty. In business you can't be too scrupulous: he wasn't, yet he wanted his victims to love him, to persuade him that he had a right to sacrifice them to himself. But the opposite happened: his victims shrieked and threatened and sent their wives and children along to entreat him. Then he'd offer them money: that is, he'd give back a bit of what he'd stolen, thus implicitly admitting he was guilty. Then he'd call me: 'Mr. Broggini, I've been a fool, get me out of it.' How could I? And anyway, why should I? That same evening, after signing, I said to him: 'It's too bad, a firm like this. When did you realize things weren't as they should be?' He answered: 'You realize these things when something that's been crumbling within you for ages suddenly—with a roar we hear too late—collapses, falls and crumbles. You try to escape and save yourself. No good: the exits are all blocked up. You stay under the shelter you've built yourself. You burrow in the ruins, dig till your hands are bleeding. . . . But you've got a date when it's got to be done—May twenty-seventh, say—and you're too late.' I can see him slumped at his desk, apparently talking to himself: 'Sometimes we see signs of it, but can't interpret them. I'd begun to stop relying on myself and to tell myself that I'd always been lucky. I regarded my firm as something that could exist on its own, and no longer as a part of me. Gradually you come to see that the firm's a bulwark you've raised between yourself and reality, in fact between yourself and your apparent reality. The firm's mechanism still works; it works so well that you're already cowed by its strength, and one fine day you find yourself defenseless before the creature you created but which no longer recognizes you.' Then he went on, stressing what he was saying: 'Then you commit your final idiocies. You lose because you want to confess, because you want to prove that you're still the same, still in a position to recover. And, at the same time, you use a special, nostalgic tone of voice when you refer to the past; you notice the weight of the loneliness that was previously your strength. You confide, maybe fall in love; you think that, if your firm no longer understands you, a woman does. In short, you let yourself be smeared by viscous humanity; and that's a sure sign you've slipped. Other people notice it because, for the first time, you're accessible. If you listen to those less fortunate than yourself, if you understand them, it means you consider defeat a possibility for you. It's a threat, a danger that touches you, lightly at first, and gradually grows inevitable. Then the phone rings as usual. Even this time, in a couple of hours, *it was foreseen*. Some men, sitting alone in their offices, hang up—all at the same time, you'd imagine—and the steel doors of the banks clang down like guillotines. The shareholders make some excuse to come and see you, to find out if you're still twitching, if there's the least sign of life in you. No, there's no need for the *coup de grace*, and off they go, reassured. I'd sooner say it's over and throw in the sponge.' "

Through the open windows, the stars came into the room. Giulio had got into bed and still kept dialing Sylvia's number: once he had lost hope of talking to her, all he would have left would be the dark journey into the womb of night. But Sylvia was still out: her friends were putting off the moment when they would be left alone. Someone always begged: "Not this evening, don't leave me this evening." And they kept trailing from one nightclub to another. "Or else she's gone to bed with some other man," he thought, annoyed. If this were so, it meant she no longer cared. So she would soon turn him into an animal. He wondered what animal. This was one thing he was calling so insistently to find out.

During their last weekend they had ended up at a country inn; in the farm nearby there were horses, goats, rabbits, and an enormous chicken run. Sylvia had rushed in with the slightly exaggerated air that embarrassed any man who was with her and gave her an excuse to move her hands, shake her hair, show off her slim, slightly too tall figure, and give her voice a candid, ironic tone. "I think the human species is still miles behind, in the scale of evolution," she said. "We've got logic, thought, and reason. But nothing you can compare with the horse's pride and nobility, or with the astonishment of the rabbit as it takes a leap, flapping through the air and dreaming it's got wings. We're still on the level of the chicken run. Once in a while, in a genius—Beethoven or Einstein, say—we get up to the dog. . . . But the strength of this country lies in the fact that its population consists of cocks and hens, people still trapped in the limitations laid down by biology. A world surrounded by drinking pans and feeders. . . . Have you ever noticed old couples in restaurants? Chest forward, beak always shut, pin-sharp eyes that never meet yours . . ." They were behind the chicken-run wire netting. The cock was strutting smugly, and when he passed them the hens scuttled off, as if he were really the boss. "I wish I knew what form you'll remember me in," Giulio said to Sylvia. "But I'm scared of guessing."

She flung her scarf round her neck. "Do you think I'll end up like Isadora Duncan?" she asked him gushingly. She used to come out with pointless remarks like that, to get her breath back after something had worried her. "I don't think I'll turn you into anything. In other words, there's still hope," she said. "But now I realize that men are all alike: they all hold out their arms to you, like tiny babies. . . . Light my cigarette. . . . Thanks. . . . Now guess: what animal? . . . The cock? Oh no . . . It's very, very hard to be normal, do you know that? I used to have lots of illusions; I'm afraid my next animal head will just be a man's." She laughed and pretended to cough so that she could take a pill out of her bag and swallow it even if it did her cough no good, so that she could say in her usual tone: "I adore animals."

There was no point in pressing her: the bell rang gloomily through Sylvia's empty flat, among the shifting hands swaying in the darkness. It was becoming a cry for help. "Why doesn't she answer?" Then he remembered that Sylvia slept with wax earplugs to stop noises from waking her; and later the pink, yellow, green and turquoise pills started working. "That must be why I dream in color," she said. "Do you dream in black and white?" Between sleeping pills and earplugs how could he reach her? And besides, why?

When he came in to wake Giulio in the morning, Diodato was not as solicitous as usual; he kept barging in and out and talking curtly, as if to show how busy he was.

"Time to get up: sir. . . . Here's the paper and your coffee, don't let it get cold. . . . I'm going out soon."

"Where are you going?"

"To take this letter to Via Sardegna. Then I'll buy a couple of steaks—got to keep up our strength."

He was so lively that Giulio asked: "Have you had any news?"

"No, he hasn't come, but it doesn't matter. He'll turn up at the end of the month, when he needs money. I'm very sorry I wasted your time last night. But now I've realized, as long as they want money, we've got the whip hand. All I've got to do is get used to something that so far has driven me crazy—the idea that Sergio came to me for money, not out of love. But once I've cleared that up, since I've got the money, I give the orders. . . . Look, it's a marvelous day," he said, raising the shutters.

Giulio drank his coffee and began to light a cigarette; he found himself holding the gold lighter Sylvia had given him. He had missed it, these past weeks. "What shall I do? Send it back to her? I must call her." He realized that if he didn't, their friendship was over. "But what's the point of keeping it going?" He looked at the lighter. "I like it, I'll keep it," and he lit it with a sense of liberation that redoubled the pleasure of the cigarette.

"The only thing is, you mustn't be off guard," Diodato continued, like a housewife chatting to herself. "You've got to settle how much you can give and that's that. You've got to stop suffering over what they say, the way they insult or even betray you," he said, bringing Giulio his dressing gown. I suffered all it was possible to suffer, last night. I'd told him we ought to set up house together, if it was only in one room—you can imagine how I'd have kept it . . . all to give him a shelter, a nest . . . but they're untamed creatures and they love the open air and the night, they hide under the bridges on the banks of the Tiber, in the sarcophagi of the Foro Romano and say: no matter how bad things are, you can see the pines of the Gianicolo from Regin Coeli. . . . Do you know, sir, these boys may have broken my heart, but they've certainly taught me plenty about life! I despise and curse Sergio, but he's brave and bold: every day is an adventure to him."

Diodato was right: anyone clearsighted could see that the man with money always had the whiphand over the man without it. Ivana was now his accomplice, and no longer part of her family. *Naked, inadequately covered by the skimpy green dress, a dress of leaves, flowing hair in two long swathes, cheeks red with shame from punishment more than guilt, she walked slightly bent: Eve thrown out of Eden.* Besides, there was no doubt now about what would finally happen because she had told him: "If you want me to come to your place, I'll come." That was why Uncle Raffaele kept such a strict watch on her. Diodato said cars were often nearby, moving or parked and apparently searching for someone. "They must be men who want to know if Sergio's still with me—dark, ugly-looking southerners, they seem to be."

But once he had settled this, he must go straight ahead, particularly because he lacked the adoring longings Diodato suffered from. When he went to Bulgheroni's to get the ring the salesman asked slyly, "Will it do?" as if he had known his plans from the first. Giulio shut the box and said: "It's fine."

Today's technique was corruption, he told himself as he went out into the street; yet corruption seemed to him more honest than a love that meant stealing, often aggravated by deception. "It's all buying and selling, in a case like this," he told Uncle Raffaele. "There's always one who comes out on top and you know better than I do that it's never the buyer." Whether he was deceiving Ivana, in spite of the huge sum he had spent on the ring, depended on the meaning traditionally attributed to the ring. But a ring like that, given almost secretly to a girl of humble origin, didn't, couldn't, mean what it was traditionally intended to.

Outside it was already very hot, although it was only half-past nine: heat, weariness, sweat showed in the faces of those he met, every one of whom looked disgusted with everything around him. Material longings appeared so clearly in everyone else that he made no effort to hide his own. Everyone's life, and women's lives in particular, was merely a commodity to be buckled on to someone else's. No good hesitating, as Amati had done, no use stopping to listen to a voice, or to a lament.

All the way Giulio felt he was walking under the eye of Uncle Raffaele, which followed him from a break in the clouds, as the eye of God the Father shoots down in a ray from the sky, in some paintings. "Really without your interest, without your

233

underlings' visits, I might have got bored. That was another mistake on your part: constant vigilance would have been all very well if you'd wanted to push me into committing a crime; but in my case I doubt whether crime is the end you have in mind. I'm a corruptor—right; but you must admit that, out of the many ways of corruption that are fashionable nowadays, mine's the healthiest, the oldest, and if nothing else, the most natural. It's a fault, I agree, if you consider what my parents and background were like. But, forgive me for saying so, don't you think there's something rather odd about choosing the career you did (and particularly about using it for your own purposes)? A career like any other: it's just that some people choose it and some don't. My attempts at corruption at least take place in a small circle—in fact, in a single field: women, sex. It's just another way of gratifying one's own unconscious impulses, a way that's justified, after all, by psychoanalysts and eminent writers. I don't punish anyone, I don't indulge my longing for power at other people's expense. Besides, you have your victims arrested, shut them up behind bars, with great locks, guarded by armed wardens. But mine end quite spontaneously," he concluded, seeing Angeletti come in.

"You sent for me?" Angeletti said politely.

"Yes," said Giulio. "Sit down." *Did she really take the initiative, take my hand and guide me? Then why didn't she even glance at me afterward? Her mother I can understand; but at least a gesture of understanding, a word, as I went by.* "What's this business about your holiday? Why won't you go?"

"I didn't say that. You're not used to staying here in August, and it's very hot this year."

"I've made up my mind—maybe I'll take a few days off in October." He had no idea why he said it, had nothing very precise in mind, but perhaps was afraid of being forced to set off on the famous cruise—that is, to escape. For this reason, too, he needed Angeletti in the office. "I always eat out of doors in the

234

evening, at the golf club, or else out on the terrace. It's very cool up there; in August you see stars by the million, and I have a feeling we may not enjoy them in peace for much longer. . . ." *I wish I knew what she was thinking when she saw the shooting star. She's got to tell me. She's got to.* "Besides, what's the use of your staying here when you never want to entertain the clients? Do you know all the dreary things I get involved in during the summer?"

But that year he had avoided plenty, apologizing, sending flowers instead, although just recently he had worked hard without the least enthusiasm, because a great many foreign clients preferred to come to Italy in summer, to combine business with culture, touristy religion, and picturesque slumming. This meant that Giulio sometimes had to go along as a guide. "And don't think it's always a matter of sending flowers; I may take a little advantage of their enthusiasm for Michaelangelo—or for Orvieto and spaghetti, which comes to exactly the same thing—but I also get the tail-end of their scorn for this city of thieves and pickpockets. And when things don't go well, which often happens—thanks to our fellow citizens' usual summer activities—I've got to listen to them telling me that their travel agents advised them not to bring jewels to Italy unless they were insured, not to lose sight of their suitcases at the station, not to let their wives carry travel documents or large sums of money in their handbags because the cyclists would snatch them, as well as their mink stoles . . ."

"I know, I know. I'm sorry."

"Sometimes, to get the husband back in a good mood, I'm forced to take them to dinner at a nightclub and to dance and even flirt with the most frightful hags, to make them forget the pickpockets or their suitcases, or anyway the overcharging and the ridiculous tips. . . . This has got to stop," he said. "I'm old and tired. You're young and you've got to do your share."

"It wouldn't be the same thing," said Angeletti. "In fact, we'd get the very opposite of what we're after."

"Why? When they turn up, they always ask for you."

"Because I'm the one who sees to the correspondence and I speak English a little better. But outside the office it'd be different. I'm not really liked. Besides, that's why you took me," he added, smiling. "Because I wasn't a rival to you in any way."

"Whereas I'm liked, do you mean?" Angeletti made a gesture that said: "Do you have to ask?" "But you don't like likable people. I remember you once saying: 'There's always something decadent in the liking we arouse.' "

"You've got a good memory," said Angeletti, smiling.

"That remark of yours left me slightly curious and slightly cross. Why decadent?" Angeletti hesitated. "Come on, tell me."

"I don't know if I can explain. . . . But I've noticed that the people we esteem, people who've really achieved anything or are actually famous in any field, are never really likable. They're respected, sought after—feared, maybe—but it's rare for anyone to find them likable. To be liked," he explained, with some embarrassment, "you've got to flatter people, put up with their mediocrity, not be annoyed by them. In other words, you've got to pretend to like them for the very qualities you despise. You must never judge them, never have unorthodox opinions, still less stand up for them when anyone else expresses his own."

"Is that all?"

"I think so," said Angeletti, laughing. "Oh, yes," he added, "you've got to laugh at their funny stories, which may be obscene, scatological, or just silly."

"Don't you think likeableness may be a gift, something that's beyond all that sort of thing? Couldn't it be warmth and humanity, spontaneous sharing . . . ?"

"Yes, of course, it may be. Sometimes it even depends on looks," Angeletti admitted. "But don't you think that warmth, humanity and sharing are also decadent? As a rule they express insecurity, the fear of being thrown out, scolded, excluded. To me they seem a way of asking constantly: 'Take me. Take me the way I am.' "

What was Andrea really like, anyway? Not bad looking, but hiding behind ambiguous silences that dampened other people's enthusiasm: his shyness, his low opinion of others, were so obvious that he froze any liking they might have felt. Besides, he was never your accomplice: you could never be really frank with him, because he showed no pity in his judgments. No, Giulio concluded, he wasn't the least bit likable, and it took a great deal of patience on his part to put up with him at all.

He decided to ignore what Andrea had said—in fact, he laughed at it. (His frank, friendly laugh was another asset he could count on to make people like him.) Once again, he must watch out for his own interests, and nothing else.

Until a few months earlier, Giulio had thought Andrea incapable of dealing with anything important. Yet he had sometimes wondered if this wasn't because he was trying to ignore the fact that Andrea was perfectly capable of taking over from him, indeed trying to avoid being shown that he could do so. But this was all in the past, when he had so wrongly tried to keep all authority to himself; now, it was a relief to realize that he could hand some of it over to Andrea. It must have been humiliating, he thought, for Andrea to work for a man who was likable but decadent: the offer he was about to make him, which would bind them more closely together, looked like a reward but was in fact revenge.

So, with his temples burning, he said: "Likable or not, I think we get on very well. Maybe it's the law of opposites . . ." Angeletti was about to agree but Giulio stopped him. "Oh drop it," he said, "and take off those dark glasses, because I've got to see into the eyes of the person I'm talking to. . . . I've been wanting to talk to you like this for a long time: at your age and with your experience, you shouldn't be standing in for someone else, even a man who hangs on to his own authority, like me . . ." He laughed again. "I'd like our firm to carry both our names: Broggini and Angeletti, what do you say to that?"

The telephone rang. "It's your father, sir."

"Put him on," Giulio replied, and then: "Hallo, Papa, at last . . ."

"Giulio, why didn't you come in when you left the letter? Maybe the portress didn't know . . ."

"Yes, that's it . . ."

"When are you coming? Tonight?"

"No, I've got something urgent on later this evening," and he winked at Andrea. "Would six o'clock do?"

"Fine. But it's still hot indoors at that hour . . ." ("An excuse, a pretext to avoid having me in his apartment.") "I tell you what, we'll go to Giardino del Lago. So long, then."

"Till then, Papa." He hung up. "Giardino del Lago . . . Only my father would think of such a place. Well, Andrea, as we were saying . . ."

But while he was talking to his father, Andrea had disappeared.

It was a difficult day—the talk with Andrea, the meeting with his father and not knowing how it would go. But before he parted from his father he would tell him that he was now the more left-wing of the two of them: he intended to hand half his firm over to Angeletti, and he was engaged to a working-class girl, or rather to a girl from the lower middle class, that unloved section of society no one wished to be saddled with; although, come to think of it, both classes got on perfectly well and even managed some shady business, like Scarapecchia.

It was all the harder as he was still befogged by recent memories—a skirt suddenly raised, a suggestive, promising voice, and afterward as if nothing had happened, a return to the hostile, months-old attitude—over two months old now—to the scathing tone, the defensive, repelling hand, which nevertheless foreshadowed secret pleasures he no longer wished even to imagine, since there was always the wondering and the sense of emptiness, after the joy of a meeting he had been longing for. Facing this emptiness was Scarapecchia, with his suspicions, and Giulio's own father, with all he had written, all the ideas that had put him in prison and now made him so unpopular; and both of them were defending Ivana from him—that is, from bright young professional men who thought they had a right to everything, even to taking advantage of a class their forebears had terrified, and of a penniless girl. Elpidio Broggini would line up proudly on Ivana's side. He could not defend himself by saying: "I've left her a ring worth ten million. The girls who undress in the world's most famous cabarets are delighted with a few thousand, so ten million's not bad."

This little house wasn't bad either, he thought as he went up the stairs. Then he saw his father, who leaped up them, two at a time, to catch up with him.

"Not up here, on the ground floor." The portress looked at him as if she was going to spit, and they hadn't even said hello.

They looked at each other as they went out into the small garden, shaded by the branches of the great cedar. "Nice here," he said. "Yes it's nice," his father answered. They were trying to find an excuse to start talking and yet deliberately kept putting it off. Finally his father said that there was someone there, guess who, and he nearly said: "Giacometti, eh?" But it was a big black cat that arched its back when it saw him. "Why do you do that? This is my son Giulio and the two of you ought to be friends." Then he explained that it belonged to the owner of the flat and was called Barberina, as it had been found behind the gates of Palazzo Barberini, yowling with hunger, and that since they first met they hadn't been parted, had they, Barberina?— and it was a bit like being young again, because since the days of Clytemnestra—you do remember Clytemnestra, don't you? of course you must, that tabby that looked like a tiger—there hadn't been a cat in the house, because of Mama's china. Giulio was wondering where all this talk about cats was leading, when his father vanished into a passage with a tiny icebox in it and from there asked: "Orange juice? Scotch?" A scotch, he replied, perfect. "It certainly won't be perfect because I forgot to buy soda" and then he realized that the two of them had never really talked together and that maybe his father was embarrassed by this stranger with whom he felt quite unfamiliar yet whom he had to treat familiarly, and that it wouldn't be easy to get at what was really happening.

The big room was quite modest, but had already taken on the character which his father, with his papers, his books and his presence, managed to give to any place he lived in. An unmistakable character. The only new thing about it was the wide bed: in the one he had in Milan, there was no room for his wife; and in any case, what on earth would she have done in it? Double beds disgusted Giulio. After a few years they were no longer used for lovemaking, merely as the scene of a kind of injection to produce children, and there was no need to sleep together for that.

When Giulio had been there half an hour they had still not said anything; his father had taken off his jacket—his lean figure still had the enviable style and elegance Giulio had never possessed—and they chatted like friends meeting after a long separation. They might have gone on like that all evening if it hadn't been for the business of Mama and China, and something undeniably odd in his father's appearance, maybe due to the atmosphere of Rome.

Suddenly and simply, without preamble, his father turned to him: "You asked me what you should say to Mama and I've been wondering about it myself ever since the day I was supposed to go off to Mexico and didn't, but I still don't know how to explain to her what's perfectly clear to me." ("Giacometti.")

"This kind of thing happens because in a marriage you peer at each other so closely that you know the details perfectly, but not the whole; on the other hand, it's not a case of a marriage that's failed, because if it was, I think it would be easy to write a letter, dragging out all the poison, all the recriminations kept silent for so many years. It hasn't failed, except insofar as all marriages are failures, except for those between people who've got to live together out of economy—which seems to me the only cast-iron argument for it—or else those rare marriages between people who miraculously manage to have tastes rather than character in common, so that each likes doing exactly the same things as the other. Or else when it's a case of some obscure, mysterious bond between them—like an English couple I know, who quite honestly I've always thought were brother and sister living abroad under a false name. . . . And yet you must know, at least you must have heard, of the sort of protective tenderness a man feels for a simple woman who really doesn't understand a thing, who may even be tiresome or actually unbearable, and it's lucky that there's this film of compassion to make you imagine there are all sorts of mysterious treasures hidden in her—wisdom and silent understanding, instead of stupidity . . . Mama," he said, but looking up met Giulio's eyes, which stopped him—although in fact his mother was tiresome and rather stupid.

". . . As I was saying, you couldn't call her entirely stupid, because women always know how long a spinach souffle has to stay in the oven and what to do in the case of births, deaths and illnesses, although in her case even this side of her was ruined at school, where these housewifely talents, which were the only kind it was worth encouraging in her, were neglected and actively discouraged, and so were a lot of others which, equally, she wasn't taught, as neither she nor her parents believed in them and neither, in particular, did her teachers."

And yet, his father went on, there was one thing about Mama he could never forget, and that was the way she'd put up with his political decisions; she'd never tried to dissuade him about them, in fact she was proud of having helped him to make them, although you couldn't say they'd involved her in any real sacrifice—apart from being separated from him—or that they'd put her life in danger. Indeed, she'd bought the best pieces in her collection at the very time he was in prison; as the black market was then growing, nobody had ready money and there were plenty of bargains to be had. As for courage, she'd never been asked to show it, and anyway it wasn't her fault if she didn't have great strength of mind. Giulio said she had amply proved she had by waiting for him when she was young and beautiful.

"No, that's not true. I think it's a mistake to consider what a person might have done and never did because he didn't want to, which means it wasn't any sacrifice, or because he had no chance of doing it, in which case it was unavoidable. Actually the time she spent waiting for me, and her mental suffering, though she didn't understand a thing about what was happening, were a source of interest and excitement. What I'm more grateful to her for is the way she looked after you, so that you could grow up quietly and do your school work; it mayn't have been the love between like-minded people" (which in our case didn't exist, Giulio thought), "but she never left you, even though it was Cecilia who really took care of you. Actually I don't think your mother could have brought you up or given you ideas—she was in too much of a state—but one thing she must have shown you, if nothing else, and that was just how silly a woman can be." Giulio nodded, persuaded. "Anyway, whatever happened, you can't deny that she did you a lot of good. By making you the center of her life (as you and I were never particularly able to communicate well, either through masculine reserve or through basic shyness), she pushed you into packing your bags and getting away. In other words, she freed you from the family, which was a tremendous advantage that freed you from complexes, and made you succeed in your career, which you wouldn't have done otherwise. And believe me, Giulio, that's something you should always be grateful to your mother for, now and in the future; besides, she's always been so attractive, with her pretty white hair and her little mauve hats, and the elegant way she dresses and, you must admit, has always dressed. No one could say she wasn't elegant, and in such a quiet way that she suggests all that's best in femininity. What saved you was your decision to get away—and besides, the more I see of Rome the more I'm convinced that it suits you—but what saved me was airplanes, because they simply terrify Mama, though she's never been up in one—in fact she gets quite ill at the thought. So the only time in my life that I could ever find myself was when I left for some congress or seminar, anyway a meeting of some sort, one of those gatherings that allow us to take action because once we're dead there'll be no one left with the courage to take it; without hurting anyone, they give people the idea that there's freedom in this country and that everyone can write and say what he likes. Well, I got into the way of extending these delightful parentheses in my life by secretly stealing the luxury of a further three or four days, which was when I came to the conclusions we've been talking about. Also, I tasted the pleasure of living alone—of course, as you say, I've always been able to retire to my study, in Milan or at Pallanza, but it was a supervised freedom: I was free for just as long as Mama didn't walk in and ask me what time I wanted dinner, tacitly reminding me that we had it at eight and that everyone was waiting for me; I'd say: in ten minutes, which was exactly like getting right up. The fact that you were waiting made me feel that my being alone was somehow monstrous and insulting. In those stolen days I liked going to a restaurant alone, not always turning up as one of a pair, like oil and vinegar bottles. I like living in a hotel where no one interrupts me in the middle of an important article—important to me, at any rate—to tell me the cook's given notice, and what a disaster it is, which of course it undeniably is, although there are other disasters in the world as well as cooks—worse disasters, at that—which you try and bother about but pretty well no one else here in Italy gives a damn about. You can always be sure these disasters will happen in the hardest places to reach, and those that most urgently need to be reached, as passions can be found there which Europeans are no longer capable of, and where I, as economic consultant, as a rule, feel I can still be useful because I'm dealing with young peoples, and young countries. Yet as soon as I get back to Milan or Pallanza, I feel death is close to me again." Giulio said that of course everyone was afraid of death.

"Oh no, that's not it, to me it's an unknown state and I have no imagination. I think of my biological end because I'm nothing, but I know you're not interested in these things, so I'm talking to you in a scrappy, hasty sort of way . . ."

"*Ad usum delphini,*" Giulio said smiling.

"That's quite true. But anyway, one day your mother, without realizing it, made me see my death in its entirety. You know I buy a great many books and am given a great many more, and that I've always carried round lists of books I want; you know I love looking through them, and arranging them in the library. Well, one evening I was opening a package of books that had just arrived, and Mama said: 'Don't you think that you ought to stop buying so many books, Elpidio? At your age, you won't have time to read those you've got and haven't yet read; I'm sure they'll last your lifetime. Now, take me: I'm not buying any more furs: those I've got must last me.' I pointed out that she still continued to buy china for her collection; but she said: 'What's that got to do with it, my dear? It takes only a minute to look at a piece of china, but to read a book the way you do, with your notes and scraps of paper, takes time, and then china keeps its value, but books are valuable only to the person who reads them. Really you've got too many and they'll be left over, in fact you'll have to decide where they're going to end up someday. I don't think Giulio wants them and you can't leave him all this rubbish; and if he marries, where would he find a girl who'd be prepared to put up with such dust traps, the way I have? . . . China and rosaries are things that last, Giulio and his children can always sell them; but maybe books won't even exist by then, people will study while they're asleep, and apparently you can get the whole of the *Divine Comedy* into some tiny space. . . .' I often hear her say, these days: 'Better throw this away, it'll be one less to bother Giulio with.' In other words, those books of mine are nothing but *commodities*, you see, commodities that ought to last me out. But I'd have put up with all that, although Mama's always spreading gloom around her, even on to other people. . . . But I don't know how it happened: we'd gone to Fiumicino in Conforti's car—he's a pupil of ours, a young man who always comes along on these occasions . . . and now that I think of it, maybe he could look after my library someday. . . . Anyway we were all very gay, you know the *Orsa Minore* crowd, how jolly and argumentative and lively and interested they are, although plenty of them can be bitter and cruel and make malevolent forecasts about our present affluence —oh, laugh away, dear boy, I've seen you laughing at us often enough. . . . Anyway, we got to talking about the congress, and what we must see was done at all costs, when we were called to get on to the plane." He rose and poured out a glass of water. "It was seven in the evening, the light was already shadowy and the plane that was to take us gleamed on the runway; and there we were, the same people who'd been going for years, to say the same things that were never followed up, but which it's important to say, which we've got to keep saying—what a waste, I thought—and when I looked ahead of me at the melancholy group of old men going to the plane, I realized that what people said about us was right: let them meet and rant and thunder and rebel, because they won't live long enough to read all the books on their shelves. Then, at the bottom of the airplane steps, I said to Treves: 'Look, I'm not feeling well, it's nothing serious, but I'll follow you on the next plane.' The others had already got on, with their beards, and gold-rimmed spectacles, and slightly down-at-the-heel shoes, and slightly shabby suits, all of them very serious, partly because some of them were ancient and going up the steps made them puff; wherever we went we were a group of old bores quite out of touch with reality. I went back and ate at a hotel, irritated by a crowd of women attending a convention and wearing orchid sprays and mink stoles; I looked rather glum in my dark suit among all those bright dresses. And so, I don't know how it happened, but I asked the porter if he knew anyone who'd rent me a quiet, cool room, and then . . ."

"But what am I to say to Mama?"

"Of course, what are you to say to Mama. . . . We've been together over forty years. She ought to understand without my explaining, but she doesn't and I don't think she will. Besides, I don't know if an outsider can ever understand our personal history. . . . Are you hot? Do you want to go out? Like to go to Giardino del Lago?" Giulio said he was quite happy where he was.

His father went on thoughtfully: "Who'd understand? People say we can't be happy because the world's wrong. On the contrary, it's no longer a question of right and wrong, and that's really not a paradox. . . . Of course, lots of people hate not having the right to flog their servants, get rid of their women, and make their children do exactly what they want. The pleasure people got from that kind of thing has faded since violence began to depersonalize us. Violence is now exercised at a mass level, at a collective level. For man in the singular it was a familiar, delicious delight, a kind of excretion of ill humors. Particularly since the idea of good flowered from the idea of evil—I mean, the one didn't exclude the other, at least as far as what you might call the mind's health was concerned. . . . But today violence needs no passion; as for evil, people wonder what it is, and what good is as well. But don't worry, there's always a need of it. Civilized living isn't the least bit likable. It's like us on *Orsa Minore:* we're holding a balance that lies in respecting other people's ideas, and if what we maintain was listened to as we'd listen to it, with nothing magical or sacred about it, who'd save us from ourselves? What man really fears is meeting himself; evil acts as a screen for him. And then I wonder: if this evil is so necessary, why can't I do your mother a small wrong by getting away from her into the solitude that's the only freedom I'm asking of her?" Giulio asked him if he was sure he was looking only for solitude when he came to Rome.

His father paused a moment, as if questioning himself, and then answered: "It's hard to say, you wouldn't want me to confide in you . . ."

"I only want you to tell me what I'm to tell Mama."

"Look, Giulio, will you tell me why I've got to give an account of myself to Mama, to this rather silly, let's face it, rather stupid woman. Why can't I vanish, why can't I? She's got enough money, and enough furs to last her, as I ought to have enough books, with those I've collected." He made a gesture, as if he would have liked to smash the back of his chair. "Why can't I be allowed this scrap of garden and this room at forty thousand a month? In the first few days I wrote dozens of letters to your mother, half true and half false, and it was so much easier and simpler and even kinder to be false. . . . How can a promise exchanged over forty years ago . . . ?"

"But why did you get married?"

"Maybe because I wanted to touch a pretty girl, a girl who was then very pretty indeed, in a garden at Pallanza. Because I wanted to have her and it was forbidden, I couldn't have her without marrying her; and because I was a gentleman and because I was lazy and because she was very rich and I wanted to spend my time studying; and because I wasn't the man I am today and must have been a fool, actually. Do you follow me? The world is moving inexorably toward the good that sweeps us away; otherwise I could leave her, but even the good—in the false idea we have of it—is boredom, and corruption. . . . Forgive me, maybe I'm boring you. Don't worry about what I've told you, remember it was just words. . . . Tell me, instead, how did you get my address?"

"Your address? Why, I saw you coming in here."

"Then why didn't you shout?"

"Because when I realized it was really you you'd already gone in. I rang you at the hotel, and then rang *Orsa Minore*, where they told me you hadn't gone to Mexico but were in Rome, no one knew where. So I sent a letter here, just on the offchance. Besides, you looked like a man going into a secret hideout."

"Oh, did I? And what did you think?"

"You know perfectly well, Papa, that you've always scolded me for it: I never think at all."

His father said that was an advantage, that they ought to work out how to stop people thinking, if they wanted to, by operating on them, instead of experimenting with methods to make them think better and faster, especially faster, starting at the age of two, when thinking isn't exactly the word for it, that it was all a great muddle, but that in the future people ought to think.

"What you people think."

"Oh no, that'll be superseded, as we're already superseded today, because we had a passionate political upbringing, and passion in politics is done with: it's dying in our periodicals, in the ideas that pervade them, in our faces that look like revolutionaries forty years out of date. The fact is that the spirit of revolt is dead in this country; all that's left is a few very young people rejecting a society steeped in the technological ideal of affluence; and, even supposing our society is technological—which it isn't—it's a spirit of revolt that's temporary and passionate, I'd say, and not yet political. Maybe it never will be, and maybe that's just as well. . . . For myself, I've only books left to me, or rather a few more years."

While he was talking he had taken Giulio to the door: the streetlamps were already lit. "Wait, I'll walk a little way with you," he said. He ran nimbly back to shut the apartment door and then they went out together. Giulio's father said that this time, in spite of its gay expansive air, Rome had failed to give him the sense of physical well-being it usually did, maybe because of the corruption you breathed in at every pore; but it wasn't so much the corruption that got him down—which was anyway too emphatic and overblown a word to describe it—as people's dreary determination to get down to brass tacks. "You know, when you meet one of these Romans in the street: 'Why are you in Rome, Broggini, what the hell's brought you here? You have no money worries, so what are you up to? Live and let live, that's what people are going to do whatever you and your discontented pals say.' "

They were walking along Via Po. Giulio thought he could see a woman's figure in the evening shadows, flesh yet untouched that time would devour, that the years would gradually dull; its splendor would continue to live in the jewel that had brought it. The hint, the foretaste, of its corruptibility lay in the timeless purity of the stone in the case Giulio was now squeezing in his hand.

They had passed the door of Amati's firm, and were just outside the bar where he had first met her. "Well then, Papa, what am I to say to Mama?" Giulio asked bewilderedly.

"Give me another evening," his father said. "Let me think. I'll call you, but why, why, why do I have to justify myself? Maybe it's because, as you say, I'm an idealist and you're a technician." They said goodbye, and then his father said: "What a lovely evening. It's so pleasant to have a few hours free. . . . It's easy. All you need do is steal them, do you know that, Giulio?" and he walked away; but Giulio was already turning toward that provocative, arrogant figure, a woman's body shaped by the light dress, drawing him on. He passed the window of a shoe shop, where rows of cruel pointed high-heeled shows seemed prepared to trample on him. He passed the butcher's and the red lumps of meat stood out against the marble slab. "Do you like meat, signorina? Do you like meat?" he kept saying, along the street: between plane trees, Ivana's body flashed naked in the bluish light of the old days in the blackout. He would marry her and then—not being an idealist, but a technician—he would get away from her.

It was the way it had been the first evening: Scarapecchia was not yet home and the two of them were sitting by the window. Ivana's mother was working at her sewing machine, wearing glasses, with something white on her knees. Before Ivana arrived she had given him coffee without stopping to chat, to show him that he had gone right back to the early days, in her opinion, the days when she didn't know or trust him. Yet, like a soul in purgatory gazing at paradise, he looked around, and the ring he had in his pocket, as well as his intention of marrying Ivana (though not very permanently), purified him, and made him feel near the end of his punishment. "Well, here we are at the finish line you fixed," he said cheerfully to Uncle Raffaele's portrait, "And, after the quarrels that have divided us, I must admit that if you hadn't forced me to be proper and well-behaved I'd have made the mistakes you foresaw and Ivana, being inexperienced, might have given in to me. I'd have taken quick advantage of her, as I have of any number of women I've possessed, through some undeserved luck of mine, and in a few days forgotten. Or else we'd have had an affair that would very likely have given me less than an experienced woman could provide. But now I'm overwhelmed with emotion because we're drawing near to the union of the flesh that is the object of life, for both man and woman. You may object that my love's physical, but even the Scriptures say that a married couple must be 'one flesh' and Ivana's not just been generously provided for by mother nature but, thanks to her family, has been brought up to be *merely* flesh. She's the statue of abundance itself, the epitome of sensual joy, which doesn't come, as people think it does, from skill in lovemaking, but from the chance that one partner may allow the other to experience the most delicate techniques in lovemaking.

In spite of his silent conversation with Uncle Raffaele, he couldn't bear the silence of Ivana's mother. "Don't you like me any more, signora Adelina?" he said. "What's happened? On the very day I've brought the ring along and we're going to fix the date of the wedding, and I'm the happiest of men, you're sulking because of something I'm longing to do but haven't ever done at all." Signora Adelina, with her threaded needle in midair, leaned forward to peer at him over her glasses. "Do you suppose that after you'd told me confidentially about Ivana's fears, that I'd have dared to try anything that would compromise our whole future? I must confess I didn't expect this from you."

Signora Adelina said that youth was youth, and some things were natural, but Giulio shook his head: "If I found myself in an empty house alone with Ivana as God made her, if you'll excuse my saying it, I'd never dare to take advantage of her. I give you my word." At that moment he spoke with the voice of truth itself, because if the husband failed to consummate a marriage it was annulled, *ipso facto*; indeed, he was going to consult an expert on canon law about it.

Later, beside the window, he repeated the same thing to Ivana: "Don't be afraid to come to my house. I swear I won't do anything to you."

"Then why do you want me to come?"

"To get more friendly. As far as the rest's concerned, now that we're close to our marriage, I want to wait, because I'm longing for you in your white dress and I want to make you mine in the same dress." Dressed in white, with a wreath of orange blossom in her hair, and a bouquet in her hand, like the figure he had stared at in the shop window every evening, until they wounded him by taking it away.

"Do I have to go away dressed like that? Aren't we going on a honeymoon?"

"We'll go wherever you like, you have only to choose. But nowadays people generally spend the first night of their marriage in their own home, or rather in an apartment loaned by a friend or relation, or more often by the parents. Anyway, I thought of this house as our first . . ." he said turning to Scarapecchia, who had just come in while he was speaking.

"What do you mean, Mr. Broggini? Maybe if it'd been the one we lived in before, in Via Emanuele Filiberto . . . It was so sunny."

"Why wouldn't this do?" said Giulio, indicating the divan.

"Of course, we'd take off the cellophane," said Ivana's mother.

"I'd send a florist who specializes in wedding arrangements to fill the apartment with white flowers. We could bring a big carpet as well."

"We've always wanted one, but . . ." sighed signora Adelina.

"Which we'd leave afterward, to remind you that we'd stayed here," said Giulio. Then, turning to Ivana, he said softly: "Here, if you don't object, you could keep on your wedding dress. I feel it's a husband's right to remove it."

"If you like. Everything's all right, as far as I'm concerned."

"In fact," he said, encouraged by her docility, "I'd like you to stay in that dress even while we're making love." She looked at him, surprised. "A dress with a full skirt and a bodice you can open a long way down . . ."

"And what about the corset? If I don't take off the dress, how can I manage?"

"Is it hard?"

"Well, when it's hot it takes two people."

"I don't think that'll be very hard," said Giulio. "I want to see you come into this room wearing your dress and veil. But I'll take the veil off last of all, after the dress. Also because I'd like to take a few photographs to keep as our loveliest souvenirs."

"And where will you take me afterward? I'd love to go to Capri. Or else Venice."

Giulio was terrified. Capri and Venice in October were full of his friends. "Those places are so hackneyed. We'll go abroad. To Scotland, to Ireland."

"It's always raining there. Paris, then."

"Good idea! In fact, how about this," he said to Scarapecchia. "Suppose we got married in Paris? That way, you and signora Adelina could have a nice trip," he suggested, thinking of the advantages of marrying abroad.

"In Paris? Would we get married in French?" said Ivana.

"Would it count in Paris?" signora Adelina asked doubtfully. "Of course!"

Scarapecchia was tempted, but his wife was adamant. "No, not outside Rome, because of the neighbors. They'd be quite capable of saying they hadn't got married."

"In Paris do they believe in God?" asked Ivana.

"Of course. And do you?"

255

"What a question to ask! Of course I do. I'm even a Child of Mary."

"Now that we're on the subject," said Scarapecchia. "Are you a believer?"

"I am. I practice devoutly and want my wife to as well," said Giulio. "In fact, I believe that a priest should be a married couple's best friend." ("And quite apart from that, he's an incontrovertible witness who heard the husband's most intimate confidences at a 'nonsuspect time.' 'It must be the parent's house that inhibits me, or the thought of hurting my wife, or the fear that children will be born from our lovemaking. I don't know what it is, Father, but for the first time in my life . . .' ")

Scarapecchia said: "Well, now, when are you going to give your bride the ring?"

Ivana was standing by the bed. Giulio went over to her, opened the case, and said: "Give me your hand." There was a faint excitement in the air. "Say what you like, moments like these are solemn," her father said as Giulio, staring at Ivana, put the ring on her finger.

Ivana bent her head. Heightened by its setting, the stone didn't look the same as it had appeared in the car. She said, "Oh . . ." disconcerted, then laughed loudly, her eyes snapping with joy.

That evening, when she went to the gate with him, Ivana promised to come to his apartment on Saturday afternoon. She promised it quite naturally, without false modesty. But when Giulio asked her for a kiss she seemed annoyed: "Don't insist. I respect your ideas, and this is a kind of wish of mine that you ought to respect." On the other hand, she was generous in allowing him to squeeze and caress her. "But how can you manage it on Saturday, when you don't go to school?" Giulio asked.

"I'll say I'm going with a girl to a shop that sells wedding dresses," she replied, adding that she thus hoped to throw off the policeman who was trailing her. "The shop's got a back door: I'll come out of it and take a taxi to your place." Giulio knew by

257

now that Ivana either didn't make promises or, if she did, kept them. So he was in a state of excitement anyone could have noticed. He told himself that Diodato was right in saying that the man with money was master, and was delighted with his idea of spending his wedding night at the Scarapecchias'.

Next day he told signora Adelina that he thought of staying three or four nights, so that Ivana should feel at ease in her own home, particularly since he had promised himself again that he would not consummate the marriage on the wedding night, but would wait until, after a few days together, Ivana herself desired what she now feared. What he really wanted to avoid was that Ivana should confide in her mother, and that signora Adelina, alarmed at the fact that the marriage had not been consummated, would urge Ivana to hasten things herself. He was also going to telephone Daria about the chances of an annulment if the husband should happen to wreck the plan with his own lack of control. He had failed in his attempt to have the wedding abroad, and had now thought up something else. Trying to sound indifferent, he asked Ivana: "Do you like children?"

"Why?"

"It's the sort of thing engaged couples ought to discuss, don't you think? I'm not keen and if we could agree not to have any, I'd prefer it."

"Why?"

"Because childbearing ruins a woman, especially when she's not exactly slim to start with. Her breasts are spoiled. It would be a terrible shame, with a body like yours. Don't you agree?"

"Well, plenty of actresses have babies and look just the same as they did before."

"Besides, when you've got children you can't get around, you can't travel. If we don't have any, we could often go on pleasant little trips, by plane."

"I'm scared of airplanes."

"Aren't you scared of children?" Ivana looked at him uncomprehendingly. "Aren't you afraid of having them, of giving birth?"

Ivana shrugged. "They say it's natural, and that when you see the baby you forget everything."

"That's rubbish. Even today women die in childbirth."

"Only if they have very bad luck."

"Well then, do you want them?"

"Where do I come into it? If they don't come, they don't, and if they do, I'll have them."

So, there was nothing doing there. No plan, no trick like that could shake the Scarapecchia convictions; every machination of his was wrecked on their spongy common sense and on their daughter's indifference.

His head was really in the clouds these days. He had actually told his mother to go to the police and ask them to search. "What do you mean, go to the police? What would your father say when he got back?" she said.

Then there was Angeletti, who was about to leave on holiday. "It was you who wanted me to go. I could have put off going. I could even have given up the idea. You've contradicted every suggestion I've made," he reminded Giulio. "Anyway, I owe you an answer. The other day I left the room out of tact, as you were talking to your father, and also because your offer made me feel uneasy."

"Why? You've been in this office several years. You'd simply go on doing what you've always done."

"But it isn't as simple as that. There's only seven years difference in our ages, but we've had a completely different education; yours is what you might call personal, whereas I was educated in a group. I was brought up to be the perfect anonymous cog in the neat, efficient organization. You, who began so early and are now on the level of those ten years older than you are" ("Thanks to Mama," Giulio said to himself), "work the way my father did as a doctor. You've got the personality of a leader."

"Which means . . ."

"Try and see that I don't mean to criticize. You people are centralizers, and we try to be operators. People like me are what you might call interchangeable: with a few days' experience any one of my colleagues could take over from me. Whereas not one of your contemporaries in the same profession could take your place. You people think as individuals—that's why you can compete. The people you help are in the hands of a friend; whereas those who trust themselves to people like me have merely the services of an organization in which it's pointless to establish personal contacts. . . . When we met I liked you."

"I never noticed."

"I came to you because I liked you or, if you prefer it, through the cult of personality, perhaps because of a narcissistic instinct in me. However it was, this meant leaving the group I belonged to, at Olivotti's. There, the old and the new in the system overlap—I was telling you about it a while ago—so that even in its overall plan the team spirit can coexist with the remnants of individualism and even a pinch of the magical and the messianic. In other words, the system's rigid, but the individual isn't alienated within it. I fled to you for reasons of prestige, very likely, or because of some upsurge of futility, or behaviorist curiosity. Yes, I've even worked out your way of dealing with business matters, which are often settled over lunch or else—forgive me, we're all in the same boat—through some kind of bribe, large or small. I wanted to sit behind a fine Empire desk like this one, in a well-furnished office in the center of Rome, rather than in a little steel and Plexiglas cell. But that was impossible unless I got into cahoots, and became friendly, with people I hated being involved with: this was because of my education much more than my character. The only thing I had left was to improve my languages; in industry nowadays, your career depends largely on whether you're able to read specialized foreign publications faster than anyone else."

Giulio was annoyed by what Andrea had said.

"OK, let's get this straight: you don't accept, then?"

"I can't."

"Right, then, nothing doing. We'll talk it over another time. I'm rushed, right now."

"But I wanted to tell you that—when it's convenient to you, of course—I'll be leaving you."

"Are you setting up on your own? You could take me on as your assistant. I'm an adaptable cuss, as you know. . . . What are you going to do?"

"I don't know, yet. I might go into one of the big corporations we were meant for, ever since university. Maybe to Spell, or Asso, or Monte Catena. Not back to Olivotti, at any rate, for the same reason that I'm leaving you. But I'll always be one of them: you carry the mark all your life, like a tattoo."

Giulio burst out laughing. "Do you suppose there isn't patronage and corruption and string-pulling in the big corporations?"

"Yes, but at top level. I'm not talking about the big executives—they're cogs like us, only bigger, who follow the party line, which is a pity. In these organizations corruption's at the level of the top state contracts. In other words, it's not we who've got to take the old hags dancing. It's the managing director or the company secretary. They're all tied up in it together—ministers, diplomats, churchmen. They're the ones who've got to wear Texan or Russian hats or a Tahitian garland of flowers; but we, further down, can keep our dignity in an anonymous dark gray suit we can wear anywhere. Our job's to elaborate, to do our homework, to plan, to keep up to date; we've also got to travel and to criticize, and always keep our passions in check. Imperturbability's our ideal, and the Anglo-Saxons our model."

Andrea wasn't likable; no, you couldn't say he was. But he was almost handsome; in fact, with his crew-cut hair and careful gestures, he was handsome in a dry sort of way. Had he been just a few inches taller he would have been perfect; but his determined expression and impeccable background suggested it was only a matter of time before he grew.

Andrea then said he was off on holiday next day, and said goodbye. Giulio went over to the window. From there he looked down on his exit from the street door, an insect mingling with other insects on the pavement. How unpleasant men were! That was one of the reasons why he had never understood his father, who had always lived in a masculine society—politics, journalism, even prison. But quite apart from the old madmen on *Orsa Minore,* and others like them, there was something that really repelled him about the very basis of a man. Women might be crazy, but he felt they were better.

One evening, while Ivana and her mother were cleaning the table, Scarapecchia had confided in him: "Remember, it's women you should live among. Men are for working and going to the café with . . . I must admit that when Adelina had her baby and I heard it was a girl, I was sorry. Partly because when you say 'a girl' other men laugh at you, as if you'd dropped a brick. Not in the least! The only man who lives really well is the man who lives among women: they look after him and spoil him, and accept the supremacy no other man's ever going to. Those old Romans and Egyptians, they knew how to enjoy life. . . . You've seen them on the films, haven't you? Every one of them's got two or three women around him, fanning him, pouring out his wine . . . Apart from women, who gives a damn about our daily struggle to survive, to carry on until the day of our death?" and he gave a small laugh: "Life's a fine old balls-up, and even if things go well, the earth's always shaking under your feet, and the only comfort in it comes from women. . . . You mustn't ever discuss things with them: you wear the trousers and that's enough. But what about pity, where does that come into it? The spaniel eyes they welcome you home with . . . and then nowadays they go out to work, as well. I'm not modern, but I think there's no point in stopping them if they want to, especially as they always bring home their wages. The great thing is to get them home in time to do the cooking—I'm very keen on my food. Why do you think men are so jealous of their wives? Honor, feeling? Don't you believe it, there's more to it than that. Any man who sees another creeping up to his wife thinks: 'Hey! I'm nicely settled—do you think I'm going to let you take her away? Nothing doing, nothing doing!'"

All Scarapecchia's haughtiness and pomposity, which were trying to impress on everyone that he was a man of education, were a front he abandoned as soon as he came into the house and took off his jacket, and his thick peasant's neck appeared above his unbuttoned shirt. He could let go completely, eat with his fingers, belch, say whatever came into his head. Giulio's father had the courage of his convictions, but men like Scarapecchia— who had no precise ideas and belonged to no party, but were open to everything, accepted everything, let things slide and never expected you to be strong or consistent, who were good for a laugh and a chat—were much more likable.

He ought to say frankly: "I'm marrying signorina Scarapecchia." I take her as she is, with her pink dresses, her hairdos, the way she speaks. And even if she never opened her mouth everyone would wonder: Where did he find her? What could he see in such a podge? All the same, I married her, married her because she's good in bed. How disgusting! they'd say. You could admit to marrying out of self-interest, social snobbery or calculation—the sort of marriage Angeletti would make—but you couldn't say: I'm marrying for sex, for the satisfaction of my senses. He couldn't present her to his parents, to his friends, to anyone. Even Diodato, though he would understand and pity him, would disapprove.

Finally he thought of a solution: he would marry her and keep her well hidden, in the country. Come out with me, be seen with me—never. Women like Ivana were quite used to being beaten without a thought of going to the police. A fine house and garden, the occasional car ride, and, to prevent her feeling lonely, a small apartment in the villa for signora Adelina and her husband. He would arrive home tired, in time for supper, then undress and unbutton as Scarapecchia did. "Come and do your duty, now!" he'd say. Ivana was surprisingly docile.

That very evening, as soon as he saw them he said: "There's a fine villa for sale, a hundred kilometers from Rome. In a big garden, in fact a park, with magnolia trees coming right up to the windows." (He was describing the family villa at Pallanza.) There he would prepare their bedroom, a room furnished solely for love, with a large bed, carpets, curtains, mirrors . . . Ivana was afraid, but marriage was marriage, and must be consummated; both the law and the sacrament said so and her confessor would tell her she must obey her husband. On his side would be the powers, the thrones and dominations. ("I've got to consummate it, father, I've got to very often . . .")

"Well, Ivana, shall I buy it? We'll go and live there when we're married."

"I won't," she said decisively. "I like the city. I like the lit streets, the shop windows, and the shops full of perfumes and materials and things."

"You could come in whenever you liked. I'd buy you a car.

Wouldn't you like to drive a car? Red, of course," he added with a smile. "Or else I could send you with a chauffeur."

"No," Ivana repeated. "The country makes me feel gloomy. Barking dogs, owls . . . do you want me to go crazy?"

To soothe her he took her in his arms and caressed her. "There, there," he said, thinking: "Once we're married she'll have to do what I say." He looked at the diamond she was wearing. "Do you think I gave it to you for nothing? You've got to earn it, my girl, you've got to serve me exactly as I say. Sit on this chair now, naked. Now get into bed. Now wake up and please me. And a baby every nine months. Live in town? What the hell for?" and he'd laugh like Scarapecchia. I'll take Scarapecchia along with me as well—I'll hire him: I really like him, he amuses me. Yet the only person who could make Ivana obey was Uncle Raffaele. Why? he wondered, slightly muzzy with the Montefiascone wine, while Ivana continued eating.

"Eat well, my love, eat well," said her father. "Mr. Broggini's a lucky man to be getting such a darling. The trouble we've had to keep her this long—you can't imagine! We've even had to give up going on holiday at Catanzano because the boys used to climb up on to the balcony, and we'd find them hanging round the house like burglars. Isn't that true, Ivana?" She nodded, her mouth full. "But you've got to look after her, you know. Don't get any thinner, will you, my love? Know what I'm going to do? I'm going to take your measurements and you'll have to answer to me if . . ."

"Shut up, Papa," said Ivana, wiping her lips.

"Shut up? After all I've done for you—shut up?" He turned to Giulio. "Medicines, food, school, clothes, and then—when her mother's decided what she needs—her trousseau. A lovely girl like Ivana has just got to marry young—it's her duty. So we began with the bed."

"Oh, what does it all matter?" said signora Adelina. "That's all over now."

"It's not over, it's still going on, inside here," said her husband, thumping his chest. "A dozen of everything, that's the minimum she can decently marry with . . ."

"I don't care about the trousseau," said Giulio.

"It's ready, anyway," said Scarapecchia. "It's in your bedroom, isn't it, Ivana?" Ivana kept nodding as if they were talking about someone else, while her father continued: "In fact, it might be wiser to take it out of this house and keep it at your place. You never know what those . . ."

"Now look," said Giulio, resolutely. "I've got a right to know what this threat is that's been hanging over you from the very first day . . ."

"Nonsense, nonsense!" Scarapecchia broke in. "What an idea! You just concentrate on Ivana and enjoy your happiness. You're going to get married and then go away on your honeymoon. . . . Will you be away long?"

"I don't know. I was thinking of a long cruise to the East." (He was thinking: "In some port I'll tell her I'm landing for a quick look around, and never go back—just stay on and get lost there. But what about the office, what about my money? If only that idiot Andrea would stay on. . . . No, we'd better leave the ship together: 'like a look around, darling?' And then I'd lose her in the street, in one of those anthill ports of the East. . . . But then when I got back on board they'd all say: 'What! Aren't you going to look for your wife?' So that'd be hopeless. Well, it would have to be on deck, then: 'Look at the stars, Ivana! Look at that shooting star! And while she was looking, shove her overboard. Not a soul would notice, I'd pretend to be snoozing in the deckchair, man overboard, everybody's run, I'd get up too, who is it, poor fellow, his wife. Tragic death of bride on her honeymoon! Black tie. Then back in Rome: 'Of course, you never met her, did you, Ivy?' . . . A silver frame passed around, among friends, with the photograph of a swan-necked blonde in it.)

"Two or three months on a cruise. Would you like that?"

Ivana was silent, and so was her mother. It was Scarapecchia who explained. "Ivana can't even look at a rowboat without throwing up. But anyway, take your time, take as long as you like. It means that when you get back. . . . Well, let's not think about that. Your old papa may not be here when you get back," Scarapecchia said in a broken voice, and continued, red-faced and tearful: "But remember, it wasn't God or your mother but I, Rosario Scarapecchia, who bought you your happiness. And you know the price I paid for it!"

Ivana rose, slowly as ever, and went over and stood in front of her father, glaring grimly at him. "Shut up, Papa, do you hear?" she said harshly. "Shut up." Her mother was holding the empty wine-bottle up against the light and shaking her head.

Giulio went over to her: "You might at least explain . . ."

Ivana stared at him, trembling with rage. "Why? This is my family. It's our business. In fact, will you do something? Will you just get out?"

At the door Giulio said: "Tomorrow?"

"All right, tomorrow," she answered, impatiently.

Signora Adelina telephoned him at the office next morning. "Mr. Broggini, it's Adelina," she said, like an elderly servant. "You knew who I was, didn't you?"

"Oh yes, of course. How's Mr. Scarapecchia?"

"So-so. But we'd like to talk with you, we'd like to ask your advice. . . . Are you coming this evening?"

"Of course, why not?"

"I don't know, Ivana was so odd . . . I just can't tell what she's thinking. Right, then, we'll see you about an hour earlier than usual. Thank you, thank you very much."

Signora Adelina's uncertainty alarmed him. He'd better hurry things up and marry Ivana. The hesitation in her mother's voice had made him realize that it wasn't the present that mattered—

at least not merely the present: he'd simply had to have Ivana bound to him, unconditionally: "One flesh," as he'd heard it put in wedding sermons.

At once he rang Daria. They told him she was in conference, and that he could try again at one o'clock. Whenever he got in touch with her he felt the same dull irritation. Refusing to listen to him was sheer affectation. "Maybe women have to do that sort of thing to pretend they're really serious," he thought. Well, he couldn't wait: he had to make sure right away that Ivana wouldn't be "odd" any longer. After all, it was Friday; she was to come to his place next day. But he was prepared to give this up, prepared to wait for the wedding, the altar, the white dress. "Everything, if I can still see her."

Suddenly he wondered if the request for advice was an excuse. Were the Scarapecchias going to say, "It's over"? Polite regrets, declarations of mutual esteem, then the gate would clang behind him and he would be left in Via Delle Alpi, completely alone. Sometimes when he went out he stopped to look up at the sky and stars, remembering the starry landscapes of his childhood: all that he now meant by success was success in having Ivana.

If Daria couldn't be found, he must consult another lawyer. Or rather a fortuneteller or a witch, someone who'd look at his case objectively. Maybe he ought to write to the advice column of a newspaper. He'd always wondered what sort of people wrote in. People like him, maybe: I'm a lawyer, aged forty. How dreary to have lived this long and define himself so.

Soon afterward, Daria telephoned. "Giulio! At last."

"God knows how often I've called you. You're always on holiday or else working."

"What else is there?"

"Well, there's love."

Daria laughed. "Oh, I find time for that, as well."

"Good." (It was still there. What could it be—infatuation,

physical attraction, intellectual affinity?) "But I'm on the same tack too. Still calling about the same old thing."

"That nullity business for a friend of yours?"

"Well, it's a marriage that's got to take place, but that's going to take place only if it can be annulled afterwards."

"I don't understand. Explain," said Daria, sounding baffled.

"Well, what he must know, urgently, is what's got to be done beforehand if he's to get an annulment afterward."

"Why's he marrying her? Is there a baby on the way?"

"No. In fact it seems they've never been to bed together."

"Well, then, what's he afraid of?"

"Afraid of? Nothing. He wants to go into it and then get free."

"But why?"

"Just because. To get over his longings."

"Expensive longings. Is he rich, at least?"

"Not badly off."

"And in love?"

"Oh yes. Or maybe not. He's attracted by her."

"I see. But I'm afraid that's not true either. If he was attracted by her, why does he want to get rid of her? What's this physical passion based on?"

"God knows, it's a mystery," said Giulio, as she had said to him years before.

Clearly she didn't remember, though, because she answered in her hateful, pedantic voice: "Listen, Giulio, if this chum of yours isn't a fetishist, he's a fool."

"You're right," said Giulio, and laughed.

"In any case, the reasons for annulment never change: non-consummation, forced agreement, both parties' decision to have no children, the husband's impotence . . . I think impotence would be the best bet in this case."

"Good God, no. He's a big womanizer."

"That doesn't mean a thing. Quite the opposite. . . . But

honestly, do you think this is the sort of thing we ought to be talking about on the phone? Couldn't you come to my office this evening?"

"I'm busy tonight. How about tomorrow?"

"No good. I don't know why, but you always call me up when I'm just taking off."

"Are you leaving this evening?"

"No, tomorrow. But meantime I'm tied up at a meeting. Is it urgent?"

"Very. Can't you put it off?"

"Some things you can't."

"Such as?"

"Such as holidays," said Daria, laughing.

"I don't think much of holidays in August."

"Nor do I, but I had no choice."

"Where are you going?"

There was a moment's hesitation at the other end of the line. ("They're not leaving, they're lying low, she's going to live with him, she'll vanish, he'll vanish, it's their specialty.") "Are you going to Sardinia?" he asked, and whether he sounded more malignant or mischievous he couldn't tell.

"How did you know?" said Daria, amazed.

"I know everything."

"Absolutely everything?"

"Yes. I even know who's involved."

Daria burst out laughing, frankly.

"Then why didn't you tell him? We'd have avoided so many embarrassments if you had. . . . When did you find out?"

"A few days ago."

"Is that all? Then you weren't very perceptive or well informed, or else we've been terribly clever."

Terribly clever. Clever to the very end. He with his talk of cats and airplanes, and books and death. "Why? How long has it been going on?"

"Well, let's say since then."

"Right afterward?"

"If I've got to be truthful: during. During, for a few hours."

"Then it was because of him?"

"Because of him and other things. Do you mind?"

"Why should I?"

"You never know."

"Do you think I'd be stuffy about that sort of thing?"

"No, but . . ."

"Well, anyway, may I congratulate him today?"

"No, wait. Wait for him to talk to you about it. You know what he's like . . ."

Quite honestly, he didn't. Or rather, he knew just enough to strengthen his idea that parents and children could never communicate, except through conventional images, like middle-aged womanizer, or moralizing moralist. It had lasted "since then," Daria said: that is, since his father used to ask him: "How's Giacometti?" He came to Rome on her account, obviously; in fact, he'd never been so often before.

But during those visits—and during this present secret visit— he had come to know his father better than he had when they spent years in the same house. Actually this knowledge was based on a few words they had exchanged, in which both of them had found truth—words that at home would have been submerged by others, casually spoken. The same thing happened to him with women; each one left him the memory of a few sentences, because they contained something hurtful. Like Harriet, an American who had come to Rome specially to see him. He was terribly busy at the time, and told her he was sorry he had to neglect her for his work. "No, for the telephone," she said. Giulio laughed and then realized it was true: all he did in the office was telephone, while she waited for him. She tried to persuade him to marry her and go to the States and live in the country: "Otherwise, you'll just turn into a telephone." Giulio said that in the old days you had to cross the whole city for a meeting, or to talk to a client: calling saved time, if nothing else. "But you lose the warmth of a person's expression, and of the human presence," said Harriet. "You lose the warmth of the flesh." This, Ivana had restored to him. They hardly ever spoke on the telephone; she couldn't express herself in words. ("Yes, signorina, put him through . . . Hi, Toto, how's things? Well, here's the latest . . .") His father also seemed unable to use the telephone, maybe because he always called from a public phone. "Giulio, come and join me. I'm here, at Giardino del Lago." "What an idea! Are you chasing the governesses?" "Who? I can't hear a thing." "The governesses." "Governesses? What governesses?" "Oh, never mind, I'll be along." His father had said he loved Giardino del Lago because there weren't any cars there and it was well fenced in. "I feel comfortable in a fairly small space, you know, where I can collect my thoughts. In my study I read and work and quite honestly I enjoy arranging the books and sharpening pencils. I love the smell of paper and rubber and ink. They say that if it's to be at its best a tool can be used only for the object it was conceived for. Obviously I've got just one object: meditation." Then he asked Giulio how his work was going. "Oh, it's doing fine," said Giulio, pleased to be able to say so, partly because his father had never made money. "I've been made consultant to Baldi's." "Good God! . . . They're all fascists there." "So's everyone, Papa . . ." "That's quite true. Before, they were just party members. . . . But weren't you acting against them when we last met? For that fellow Amati? A nice man, I remember, we went to his place and listened to some records . . ." "Yes, he was nice." "What do you mean, was? Is he dead?" "No, he's gone bankrupt." "And you've gone over to the enemy? I hardly think that's quite . . ." "Oh, come on, Papa, you always see things in such an old-fashioned way. In any case, it was after Amati's bankruptcy." Actually, it wasn't, but his father and Daria had behaved exactly the same toward him.

("Get me Zurich, signorina, the usual number. And ask for Geneva.") According to Daria, there wasn't much chance of getting an annulment. If he wanted to be free, he must use her for his pleasure but leave her a virgin. How long could he resist the temptation? Better marry her and then, when he was satisfied, leave her. No one could force him to stay with her.

He realized he had overlooked the simplest solution: he was so used to looking for ways of avoiding the law that he hadn't thought of using what the law allowed: separation by mutual consent. He was prepared to say it was entirely his fault and to pay for it. Ivana could go back to her parents and he might even visit her occasionally: she was religious, and her priest would advise her to see him and to agree to whatever he asked in the hope that he might return to her. ("Do you want to finish that letter you were dictating, sir?" "Right, we may as well.")

He was stunned by the simplicity of this solution, and wondered why he had bothered about an annulment when all he need do was leave her: there was no point in a legal separation, even.

He realized he had been considering an annulment because the marriage couldn't take place, even in secret. If Ivana actually lived with him she'd lose all her enchantment: she had to remain a part of his fantasies, like the women he used to follow as a boy, in the district where he now met her. In those days his family lived in Via Allegri, off Via Po. In the evening the trams and buses in Piazza Fiume, and along Via Bergamo and Via Nizza, poured out a great stream of women from offices and shops, all heading for the big ugly blocks of apartments in Via Alessandria and Piazza Principe di Napoli, which still stank of the market held there in the mornings. The woman who had slapped him lived there, and he had wandered about the neighborhood for a long time afterward, hoping to run into her and persuade her to come to him, after which he would pull off her underclothes and thrash her mercilessly, to get his revenge. She was the only one who had ever refused him; something about him never failed to make these women accept him, the fact that it was wholly secret. He never knew their names, never wanted to know them; he would hear them panting—What are you doing? Are you mad? —and, in the ecstasy of the senses, they were a pair of delighted strangers, not murmuring silly love talk nor, at the height of their pleasure, having to pretend anything at all. A tall handsome boy like Giulio was a bonus in these women's lives: they turned to fend him off but when they saw him they softened and wondered how, tired and shabby as they were, they could have caught his eye. There must have been something of the girl they had once been still left in their faces. But Giulio cared nothing for their faces: he was enchanted by their bodies, by the Roman women's strong hips and lazy, disdainful walk. He wondered whether now, as wives and mothers, as model, pious housewives, they still remembered the wild boy who had followed them up the dark staircase one evening, and overwhelmed them. Maybe he still lingered in their memories, maybe he was mentioned in confession, transformed into a rapist who had forced them to surrender.

Andrea came in, ready to leave, in an open-necked blue shirt and a light suit: he looked much younger than usual, but of course he was only thirty-three. Giulio said: "It's been a ghastly day."

"On the phone since nine, then the mail. You just can't stand it, in this heat," said his secretary, and left them on their own.

"I wonder what you must have thought," Andrea said to him. (He'd thought of Ivana, of the meetings ahead of him, until their wedding. "Suppose we made it October the fourth? The feast of St. Francis, the Italians' saint," said Scarapecchia, and Giulio said quickly: "Then let's get married in Assisi. That would be a splendid idea, because I don't think I'll tell my father. He's got a very bad heart." Ivana's mother had agreed. "Lots of people get married in Assisi and then they come back with their wedding photos.") "Listen, Giulio," Andrea went on: "I want to explain why I didn't tell you right away. Maybe you think I've been false and hypocritical all these years . . ."

"No, of course not, it's the fate of despots; if they're not killed they're abandoned and betrayed. . . . When do you want to leave me?"

"No, I was talking of the other thing . . ."

"What thing?"

"Why, hasn't Daria ever told you about me?"

"No."

"She called up and said that . . ."

(The telephone rang: "Geneva, sir.") Giulio put his hand over the mouthpiece. "She must have forgotten. Wait." ("*Cher confrère, je suis heureux de vous dire . . .*") Andrea waited, but the conversation went on and on, and he made a sign with his hand and left. When he had finished speaking, Giulio said to the girl on the switchboard: "Send Mr. Angeletti in." "He's gone, sir. He left a message to say goodbye. He couldn't stay any longer, else he'd have missed his plane." "Oh well, I hope he enjoys it. . . . Now, no more calls, signorina. Say I'm out, say I'm dead . . ." He hung up and put his head in his hands: everlastingly talking and talking, just an old, over-used telephone. Who had said it? Oh, of course, it was Harriet. He needed Ivana, she was the only living thing in his life. Why had she been so odd? Uncle Raffaele must have been interfering again: and besides, he was certain he'd been followed, the first evening. A rickety white 600 was parked in Via Delle Alpi, the only one in the empty street. Two men, as always. He'd never seen their faces, but knew their fast, bad-tempered way of driving. ("I beg you, Dr. Scarapecchia, what more can I do? The ring, the wedding, Assisi . . . Forgive my arrogance, my evil thoughts . . .") The telephone rang again: "Look, signorina, didn't you hear what I said? I told you—"

"It's your father, sir."

Maybe he wanted to explain, maybe he wanted to tell Giulio that it was Daria who had made him change his mind over all sorts of things, that it was a unique case of spiritual affinity—or of smashing legs, Papa?—but he'd refuse to listen. What about Mama, he'd keep saying. "All right, put him on," he said resignedly.

There was a terrible row near the telephone, as usual, and his father had to shout: "Hello, Giulio! Listen, last night I thought it all out—I even wrote a piece . . . I wanted to tell you that evil doesn't bring happiness. I was wrong, it's sin. Do you hear me? Sin."

"Yes, I can hear you."

"Anyway, read it in my piece in *Orsa,* next week."

"Right, I will."

"And then I wanted to tell you I'm leaving."

"Would you like me to take you to the airport?"

"No thanks, I'm going by train, and I'm at the station already. . . . Hello, Giulio, do you follow me? I've plumped for sin and *coute que coute,* I'm taking her with me. You know who, don't you?" There was a giggle on the other end and the sound of a train drawing in. "Barberina! . . . She's here in the basket beside me, and she says goodbye. . . . So long, Giulio. Come and see us soon, won't you? I've really got to think seriously what I'm going to tell your mother. Can you imagine what she'll say when she sees me turning up with a cat?" They laughed, then his father said, "So long, or I'll miss the train," and he imagined him running along under the platform roof, carrying the basket.

That evening, when she opened the door, signora Adelina told him her husband was in but didn't dare to show himself because there were some things he was ashamed of telling his future son-in-law. " 'What a family he'll think he's marrying into,' he said. I told him that everyone at Catanzaro knew our family and that it wasn't because of this money that . . ."

"How much?" Giulio interrupted her, regretting he had not brought his checkbook.

"Well, I don't know how much exactly. I've got it all down in a notebook but it's not money we want from you, what an idea! It's your advice we want, while there's still time. You know what it's like once you get in the papers; people are jealous of anyone with a car or a bit of cash or a bit more brains than the rest of them, and they're dying to discover he's been a thief all along. Not that we've ever thought of stealing, of course . . ."

Signora Adelina was the same as ever, slightly more hesitant, slightly more tired-looking, that was all. But Scarapecchia, when he turned up, was nothing like the brisk swaggerer who had received him the first evening.

"What do you think you're doing?" said his wife reproachfully. "Go back to bed, I'll talk to Mr. Broggini."

"I want to tell him something first. I want to tell him it wasn't my fault, that I wasn't the one who took the money. It was you."

"Me? Where do I come into it? What else could I have done? They put the money there, on that table, I told them and told them there was nothing doing and they'd have to take it back, but they left it there, right here," and she banged her hand on the table.

"It's your fault, you shouldn't have left it there in full view, you should have picked it up, put it in your pocket, thrown it away and burned it . . . Anything. But no—you made those little heaps of it: 'This would have paid the grocer, what a shame! This would have paid the insurance, this would have covered the four installments on the telly we're behind with, and then there's the butcher, who's threatening legal action, and your watch at the pawnshop, if we're still in time to redeem it' . . . Is that true, or isn't it?" Giulio thought they might as well tell him how much it came to without all this fuss. Maybe it was over three hundred thousand, maybe a million, he was thinking. Scarapecchia continued: "There's something I want to say, Mr. Broggini, and I'd like you to spread it around—I don't know how, but anyway, everyone ought to know the sort of life a man leads when he's spent his wages. People are made on publishing balance sheets, these days, so let's have a look at the balance sheet of a family in which the wage-earner's a clerk. Four or five items: rent, food, clothes, entertainment. Right.

And when that's done with, the rest is pocket money, they say. I like that! People who tell you so ought to be put away for lying. They talk about the affluent society; they say we've all got washing machines and record players and TV. But we don't get them free from the government, you know, any more than a couple gets its furniture free as a wedding present. I tell you, what rules the lives of people like me is credit, the never-never. It's both good and bad; on the one hand, it means hope and help, and on the other, when the date for paying comes up on the calendar, it means terror. Then there's another thing: the minute you get home from work you hear nothing but trouble—this has broken down and that's come apart. I tell you, if there's a day when something hasn't gone wrong, by some miracle, you're practically scared and wonder, what's up? Anyway, what I mean to say is that in a man's life—even if he's only a clerk—there's always something out of the ordinary: a wedding, a birthday, a death, presents. In other words, when his wages come into the house they're already spent. How long does the money last, Adelina? An hour? A couple of hours? Time enough to touch it and persuade yourself it's really cash, not just bills and loans and pawn tickets and things the shopkeeper signs. Just for a moment you've got ready cash, actual money in your hand: as a rule it's a will-o'-the-wisp, but just for a second you've got it. Then it vanishes again, but you go on hoping it'll come back, that there'll be another miracle. Those famous trick balance sheets never use the words 'bingo' or 'lottery' or 'the pools,' but when a guy's fished out of the river or hangs himself in the toilet they always find some old try-out of his in his pocket, a lottery ticket or something. And I'm not talking about actual longings, because you just can't hope to satisfy them—you've got to clamp down on them, they're nonsense, unthinkable—a tie, say, or else something quite unnecessary, an hourglass, which is something I've been wanting for years, with pink sand running through— or else a woman might want a dress or a pair of shiny earrings

. . . No good. Apart from a season ticket for the bus, all we've got in our pockets is enough for coffee and rolls. I've heard them in the co-op bar saying: 'Look at the clerks, they can't even afford a roll.' And so . . ."

"Don't get so excited, you'll feel worse."

"Can you imgaine what it means to a man like me to see a package of clean, brand-new notes there on the table? That's why I said Adelina shouldn't have done it to me. She shouldn't have said, 'Don't touch it,' because of course those creeps would be back at the door—oh, you don't know what those debt collectors are like when they use all those legal terms—sequestration of goods, dismissal, eviction . . . I'd like to say: 'Well, my dear minister, and what would you have done, in my place? Of course, we know perfectly well what you'd have done; you'd have done what everyone does.' We see it, we read about it, but you can't touch old so-and-so, you can't get at old such-and-such, because of the party, and the state, and industry and the rest of it. So why Scarapecchia? Because he's a clerk, and who gives a damn for clerks? Who cares if they catch Scarapecchia? One fine day two guys come and carry him off. The Trumpeter sees and tells everyone in a couple of hours, but who cares? A house like this doesn't count, doesn't exist, except in the tax registers." Scarapecchia walked up and down, wiping the sweat off with his handkerchief. "Especially as they thought I could easily ask favors from Raffaele. But how could we?"

"A fat lot of help that would've been, considering what he's like," said signora Adelina.

"But the money they'd left wasn't here any longer, so I said: 'Don't worry, I'll see about what you want.' Unfortunately, I was successful. Sometimes, quite by chance, things go right without your raising a finger, and then everyone's bursting with thanks and gratitude. In a few hours everyone had changed toward me, even the office boys. I was given the key to the elevator and the toilet . . ." He hung his head gloomily. "And I thought what a sweat it was to keep working and how easy it was to give a nudge or a wink that meant: 'Don't worry, I'll see about it.' Nothing more. But people know they've got to oil the wheels, so they oil away to keep things turning—guys they've put up for jobs, licenses and permissions and things. So the whole farce went on. Of course, I should have said I wasn't playing ball, right from the start. But when people think you're in with a powerful fellow, they don't let you say a word, they put the money in your hand, not vulgarly, the way those guys did, but quite nicely and tactfully. They say: 'Do you like Swiss cigarettes? I've brought you a pack, a rather special one. Smoke them quietly at home.' A pack that's properly sealed and inside it, instead of cigarettes . . ."

"Dangerous, though," said Giulio. "You might hand them to someone else and . . ."

"No, they give you a special look. Everything's done with glances and gestures, so that you can truthfully say you haven't said a thing or offered them a thing. All I'd do was say, very casually: 'When we were kids, my brother Raffaele and I . . .' Nothing from the present, even, nothing indiscreet, just old reminiscences, you know. Then they say: 'Really? Are you Raffaele Scarapecchia's brother?' I'd say: 'Yes, why?' After that there wasn't any need to say anything. The guy would say, 'How much?' by rubbing his thumb against his first finger—it might even be a tick of his, mightn't it? Oh, the money you can make in this country, with a gesture or two! Finally there's a real love relationship between you and the one who's giving you the money, a physical relationship, the way there is with a woman. But you're the woman, this time, and the guy who's giving you the money gives you much more joy than a woman does—hers, after all, only lasts a couple of minutes. What was it they wanted from me? Dishonesty. Well, I was dishonest. And now they're going to denounce me. But if I'd done what they wanted me to, it'd have been: 'Splendid, Rosario, you're a marvel!' ''

"And how did it end?"

"Just as you might expect, when they realized that Raffaele Scarapecchia wasn't . . ."

"Wasn't in touch with anything, knew nothing, promised nothing, and so would do nothing," signora Adelina put in quickly. "They came here and said: 'Hand over the money or we'll denounce you as a con man.'"

Ivana had unlocked the front door, and now came in; from the doorway she was staring suspiciously at them. "What are you up to? Why are you here?" she asked Giulio; then she went over to her mother. "What have you told him?" she said threateningly. "What have you asked him for?"

"Nothing," said her father. "I've never asked anyone for anything. All I told those men was: 'My daughter's getting married, don't ruin me before that happens.' If it gets into the papers, what'll this young man and his parents think of me? They don't know a thing. Don't ruin this special, happy event in a wretched man's life. And so . . ."

"And so we must get the whole thing settled," said Giulio. "I'll see to it. I think there are others far guiltier than you."

"It's not as simple as that," said Scarapecchia doubtfully.

A great silence hung over the city, because no one was left in Rome. On the wings of more loans and overdrafts, hastily signed for, or with another bundle left at the pawnshop, every clerk and laborer had vanished. The streets were empty, the petunias still smelled sweetly—a smell of sugar and face powder, and women as they used to be.

They were in the garden. Giulio had said, "Let's go into the street a minute," but Ivana had refused. That evening, Giulio felt he could do anything and no one in the house would worry: indeed, the way signora Adelina smoothed Ivana's dress, as if smoothing down a bed, and said, "Go out for a breath of air," meant "This is all we have to pay you with." And it was something very beautiful, the sweetest thing of all. Giulio now realized that there was nothing else; but what was left was the best thing God made or the earth had sprouted—did it matter how? The main thing was it existed.

So, though conscious of his new rights, he was reluctant to press them that evening, like a man who digests a meal slowly, after suffering from hunger, because the certainty that he can eat whatever he wants is more comforting than the food itself. "You should have told me about these things right away," he told Ivana. "Your father would have been spared a lot of worry."

"You're a good man," said Ivana. "But it won't help you a bit in life."

"Aren't you good?"

"Me? I should say not. I've lived long enough to know that when you want to get rid of someone you say: 'He's good.' "

"And what about uncle, isn't he good?" asked Giulio.

"Do you think he'd have got where he is if he was? You've got to be tough in a job like his."

"You prefer tough men, don't you? Be honest."

Ivana shrugged. "It's not a matter of what I prefer. Everyone's the way he is, and it's a waste of time trying to get him to change."

Giulio pulled her up against him and asked: "Do you like it?"

"No. Maybe I'm too young. Mama says that when I've had a baby it'll be different."

He told her there was no need for her to like it, that what touched the husband in particular was the proof of love his wife gave him in putting up with it; that they would get along splendidly with this most important part of their marriage, and he hadn't the slightest doubt that it would be perfect. He felt heartened; in the early days, when he had first known Ivana, he had been afraid that Scarapecchia was incorruptible, like his father, although for different reasons—for fear of being caught,

286

as all humble people feared to be, for fear of the Trumpeter, maybe, or even of Hell. Incorruptibility seemed to him monstrous—a monstrous form of narcissism. But now he knew that Scarapecchia wasn't incorruptible, and his own view of life had been reassuringly proved true. Everything could be bought; once again, it had been a matter of technical skill, and he had been skillful right from the start. After all, you might ask a man or even a woman, "How much?" but you couldn't ask a father how much he wanted for his daughter. Giulio's precautions had all been necessary, and with a little money and a little patience, he had bought up the whole family. He was now thinking of a long, hot honeymoon; they might follow the summer to Tunis or Morocco, and rent one of those bungalows where the servants were young boys who glided away like lizards. "Walk about naked, no one'll see you," he would tell Ivana. "But watch out, there are lots of cactus thorns around and you'd better wear shoes." She always obeyed, which made him realize how much better was the silent devotion imposed by the church than any agreement based on reason. Women must be kept in ignorance, so that they would always think the man was right and always remain desirable; and they must be kept dependent, to keep them from longing for something extraordinary, which might be culture or even protest. Even his father had submitted in the end and admitted that the only work that mattered was one's own personal activity and that the only really authentic activity for a man was to empty all his strength into the womb of a young woman with strong, heavy hips.

It took a doctor's particular brand of cynicism to think, as Ugo did, that children pushed a man from the center of the stage. Perhaps Ugo was embittered by the suspicion that his children weren't in fact his (it was rumored that his wife had betrayed him); a man could have no greater satisfaction than the sight of his wife's womb swelling. As Scarapecchia had told him, in fact. "I was pleased with what you answered, when I asked if you wanted children," he told Ivana. "I was testing you, you see, when I said you might die having a baby. That's how it should be. A woman should lie and let her husband pour all his fantasies into her, as the earth lies waiting for the seed. There's nothing I won't give you, I'll work like a black for it. Before, I used to wonder, 'What's the object?' but now you're the object, my darling, my doll, my lovely wife I'll be taking to San Francesco on October fourth to put the ring on her finger. And a couple of hours after we're alone, there'll be something in this sweet womb of yours, my darling, and when it's popped out I'll give you a bit of time to rest and then—wham!—another one. You do agree don't you?" Ivana shrugged, as if to say: "If that's what you want." What a wife, thought Giulio, what a wife to have found! "I'll give you a beautiful dressing gown with pink swansdown and slippers to match, and money to go to the shops and buy all the scents and things you want." When they came back from their honeymoon he could tell her he had sold his penthouse to build a house on the Appian Way or the Cassian, and for the time being he would go to a hotel and Ivana could stay with her mother because, in cases of pregnancy and childbirth, daughters always liked to be with their mothers. It wouldn't be hard to get a friend who was a doctor—Ugo, say—to tell her she must stay at home and be well looked after, otherwise she'd lose the baby. As for Scarapecchia, he'd find him a job in a big firm; a man who could make money out of nods and winks was no fool, and you might as well hang on to him. The only nuisance in the family was his own father, but even he now seemed to be going the right way.

"Tomorrow's August the tenth, the feast of St. Lawrence," said Ivana, looking up at the sky. "There are lots of shooting stars and if you see one and you're in time to make a wish, it's sure to come true."

"What will you wish?"

"I'll wish that our meeting tomorrow will go well, because our whole future depends on it."

Giulio said he had nothing to wish from the stars: he was the happiest man on earth. A long time had passed since they met and he had been through a great deal, yet, even though their engagement had been the old-fashioned, respectable sort, he'd been faithful to her throughout it. "Except on the evening your father threw me out and said I was an imposter: that night I went to an old mistress of mine, and made love to her because I was so angry. Do you mind?" Ivana made a face but said that all men went elsewhere if they were going to respect their fiancées. Giulio was tired and full of visionary longings. The image of Ivana as a slave to do his bidding was superseded by the image of Ivana as wife and queen, waiting in the darkness of the bedroom. So he said he must go and sleep: they must keep their strength up for tomorrow, which was to be a great day for them both.

He was standing on a step below Ivana, and when he took her in his arms he laid his head on her breast and stayed there for a moment, glorying in the scent of her skin. Ivana went to the gate with him.

"Giulio . . ." she suddenly called, and put her arms round his neck, held out her lips and for the first time asked him to kiss her. Giulio sank, lost, into her warm, full mouth. At last she drew away, as if regretting it, ran her hand over her face, and, gazing at him long and sadly, said: "Ciao." Then, hanging her head, she went back to the steps.

Giulio stood watching her until she shut the door, then stood in the street, feeling he was being borne along on a great cloud. At last he set off along Via Delle Alpi, driving his car with the virile enthusiasm that Scarapecchia claimed no one who had grown up since the fall of fascism had ever possessed.

He lived through the hours between then and Ivana's visit in a daze. On Saturday morning, in the office, his mind was a blank. Before going home he went to innumerable flower shops looking for white flowers, and found only heavy-scented lilies, roses and jasmine; luckily, he could leave the windows open. Since he had confided in Giulio, Diodato had become unbearable: that day, as he helped him arrange the flowers, he said that Sergio wasn't really bad at heart, because he loved nature and always picked daisies when they went out into the country. When Giulio told him he must leave the apartment at half-past four and not come back till nine, Diodato begged to be allowed to stay in his bedroom in the dark, beside the telephone: on Saturday Sergio always needed money and would very likely call, he said. But when it was time for him to go, Giulio sent him off, unwillingly, down the back stairs.

Giulio was appallingly nervous. He kept peering out of the window hoping to see Ivana. A taxi drew up, and two expensively dressed girls got out; then another girl in red trousers and boots got out of a sports car. This was lucky, he felt, because it would confuse anyone who might be watching. A policeman had been roaming about there for some minutes, staring insistently at the street door; but Giulio was sure it was just a coincidence, especially as the man didn't look like the one who was generally on duty; in fact, when he looked out again he could see no sign of him. When the doorbell rang, Giulio was feeling slightly sick with excitement and his head was starting to spin.

It was Ivana, followed by the porter. "Listen, Giulio," she said. "I've got no money and I asked the porter to pay the taxi, but he hasn't got any change. Will you give him a thousand lire, please?" Giulio rummaged in his pocket and found five thousand. "Keep the change, Ernesto," he told the porter, and followed him out onto the landing. "If anyone asks you where this young lady's gone, say . . ."

"She's on the floor below—at a charity do," said Ernesto, with a wink.

Ivana was on the terrace, perfectly composed and gazing about her. But Giulio—because of the time he had been waiting, or because the porter's presence had stopped him taking her in his arms right away—was now wishing she hadn't come. He had no idea what to say to her; in fact he scarcely recognized her. What an idea, he said to himself, thinking how much more suitable somewhere anonymous would have been, a hotel or even his office, because the meeting he was planning was so out of the ordinary that it completely failed to fit into the framework of everyday life. He tried, of course, to hide his embarrassment.

"Well, do you like the place?" he asked.

"The terrace is lovely and I don't mind the apartment," said

Ivana. "But there are too many ornaments, too much clutter. What a time it must take to dust!"

Giulio laughed and confessed that this had never occurred to him. In those tiny, low-ceilinged rooms, Ivana looked fatter; and he noticed the striking contrast between her way of dressing and the apartment's decor. In her own home, he had grown used to her sometimes vulgar way of speaking, but in his, where he had never heard such a voice, her lower-middle-class Roman accent grated on him with the first word she spoke.

"Sit down for a minute," he said, "while I bring you a cold drink."

Ivana followed him, curiously.

It was too hot, and a blinding white light was reflected from the houses opposite. Giulio felt he had arranged their meeting at the wrong time of day; but in fact he had had no choice. The kitchen was cooler: it was decorated in an English, publike style, with expensive wood paneling on the walls; it had been featured in several design magazines.

"What a hideous kitchen!" Ivana exclaimed. "Is your servant a foreigner?" Giulio told her that Diodato came from Orte. "Then why are all the containers labeled in English?" Still laughing, Giulio gave her some orange juice, but somehow he couldn't relax.

"In other words, you just don't like this place. . . . Right, we'll get another."

"It's not so much ugly as uncomfortable," said Ivana. "And why do you have all these pictures of ships? Did you ever have a naval officer in the family?"

"No," said Giulio. "It's just a subject that suits a man's house."

"Oh, really? I didn't know."

In his bedroom, the theme was hunting. Giulio felt sure Ivana would dislike it, and although he was tired of it himself he felt irritated at the thought of what she would say. "Now for some more clinkers," he said to himself, when she was standing in front of an Empire chest of drawers, the finest piece of furniture in the place. "Now this is a real piece of furniture," she said. "The rest—forgive me, won't you?—looks like a shop window full of Christmas presents."

Giulio had to admit that people like Ivana, however ignorant, had their own wisdom and their own intuition, and that she was no fool; but he felt an unbridgeable gap between them and suddenly felt a great longing for the garden in Via Delle Alpi— for that old-fashioned, countrified atmosphere, irrevocably lost almost everywhere else. There was no point in considering a change of apartment: what would the Scarapecchias do in any he had chosen? Yet he wished they could enjoy it: signora Adelina in the pub, and Scarapecchia in the bed, all gleaming brass hunting horns. Giulio closed the shutters and switched on the desk lamp. The half-light was cozier, and he felt more cheerful.

"Look, I didn't jump on you like a brute the minute you came in, did I?" he said, gently. "But take your clothes off, you'll be much cooler. Are you wearing the corset?"

"I always do," she said. "It's torture, in this heat." She sighed, and sat down on the edge of the armchair. "Particularly since I'm pregnant. It's a nuisance, although I'm only in the second month."

Giulio thought he hadn't understood her properly. "I'm sorry, what did you say?"

"I said this corset is a nuisance, because I'm pregnant, I'm two months pregnant."

"You're joking, aren't you?"

"No, I'm quite serious."

"Oh, splendid, really splendid!" he said, rage and astonishment spreading through him, and taking over his earlier mood of slack embarrassment. "And who, may I ask, is responsible?"

"What do you mean, who's responsible?" Ivana repeated, taking a handkerchief out of her bag to wipe her face. "You."

"Me?" said Giulio, ashen with fury. "Oh really, this is too . . ."

"Listen, Giulio," Ivana said angrily. "If you don't like it, that's another matter, but I'm not having you asking me who's responsible. Who else could be? I've never seen anyone else. When I get to school my teacher calls Mama and says, 'Ivana's arrived,' and at the end of the day she says, 'Ivana's leaving' . . . I can't take a step on my own. I'm sure Uncle Raffaele knows the exact hours and minutes I've spent alone with you, that evening in the car, and here today. I didn't mean to tell you, but there's a policeman on duty down at the front door. And you ask me who's responsible! That's really a bit much, don't you agree?"

"Let's see," he said, trying to calm down again. Maybe she's so naïve that she doesn't know how babies come, he thought. His mother always told a story about a maid who was sure she was expecting a child after a man had kissed her, since virtuous girls in her day were told that this was how babies were made: the husband kissed the wife, and nine months later the baby was born. "Come here, my darling," he said, softening. "I'm quite sure you don't know what you're saying. Do you know what's needed to make a woman expect a child, and what are the signs that show it?"

"Giulio, do you think I'm an idiot?" said Ivana. "Do you really think I don't know? I'm two months gone all right, but because I wanted to be sure before telling you, I've had an analysis done at the laboratory, you know, the test they do on a rabbit. Here, look," and she held out a sheet of paper. On it was written: "Signora Ivana Scarapecchia Broggini. Pregnancy test. Biological reaction: positive."

"Listen, Ivana, what game are we playing?" Giulio said, jumping up. "I can't believe you're so two-faced. Now tell me, when do you say it can have happened?"

"I don't know," she answered candidly. "I get sort of dizzy

spells—I warned you, and the doctor's even given me a certificate to say so. I've wondered myself. Now think, think hard, and calculate the time. I think it must have happened when the co-op men came and Mama shut us up in the cupboard."

"What are you talking about? We can't have been there more than ten minutes . . ." Ivana made a gesture, as if to say that was quite long enough. "Don't think I'm going to fall into this trap of yours."

"It must have happened, there, though," said Ivana obstinately. "And I'll tell you why. This amnesia, which is what it's called, came on after a shock I had as a child—they've actually put that on the certificate. I was in the house of a relation of ours whose husband was the sort of man who was always making jokes. It was summer, very hot like it is today. We were playing some game, I don't remember what, and he said I'd won and that as a prize he'd show me something very nice but first I must let him tie me to a chair with a strap, like a seat-belt in an airplane. I said yes, and he said, 'Look out now—one, two three!' and a thing that made me laugh and laugh popped out of his trousers. But his face had changed: it was all red, his eyes were bulging, his mouth hung open and he looked like a clown. It wasn't the thing that made me scream, but his red face and his sort of rattly voice. That's why I get those dizzy spells I told you about. Before, whenever I saw a man, I used to tell him I didn't want to see his thing. Now, if you really want the truth, that evening in the cupboard your face was like that, and you were panting and hideous. I turned away to avoid seeing you, and then I had this amnesia. You could have done whatever you liked, that's all I can remember."

"Nothing happened. Anyway, why haven't you told me all this before? Not that I believe a word of it."

"Because, apart from the way you behaved when we first met, I thought you were decent. Then I got to know you from all sorts of things you said, thinking I didn't understand; and the very fact that I'm here shows what your intentions are, though you've got Papa just eating out of your hand. You know that we're not properly engaged. You've never told anyone about it, you've never taken me out, you've never taken me to your office or brought me here. That proves it. And why were we supposed to get married in Paris, and then at Assisi? And yesterday evening you told Mama that we'd just have the religious ceremony but the civil ceremony and a big reception would come later, when your parents could come. All those things—I don't need to remind you. I may have these blackouts, but I'm no fool. Papa and Mama are as they are—because they've suffered on my account, and because of that nasty man—but luckily we've got Uncle Raffaele. I don't know where it happened. The evening we stopped in that lonely spot by the river I actually thought you might kill me, like you read about in the papers, so that you'd get the ring back. . . . And there's no point in playing dumb: the man with the thing got away with it because Papa and Mama never breathed a word, because they thought that if anyone found out I'd be ruined, from childhood. But that's not going to help you, because I'm grown up now and there's Uncle Raffaele as well."

The house telephone, which connected with the porter, rang. Giulio hesitated, and let it ring. Then he went over and answered it. "Excuse me, sir," said Ernesto, "but there's a cop who's been at the door for some time. He came in and asked me—confidentially—if I'd seen a girl dressed in white coming in. I said all sorts of girls have come in today. He said she was very young, seventeen, and must have gone up to the top floor. I said, oh, and told him to stay where he was because if she'd come in I'd have seen her go out. Forgive me if I'm poking my nose in, sir, but if the young lady goes down the back stairs she'll come out in front of the garage and no one'll see her."

Giulio thanked him, said he would ring back and turned to Ivana.

296

"There's a policeman downstairs looking for you, who knows you're seventeen. I see it all now: you're in league with this uncle of yours; maybe you're pregnant by him and trying to find someone to pin it on. But if you thought of me, you've come to the wrong man," and he gave a shrill, sardonic laugh as he marched up and down in front of Ivana, who was giving nothing away. "Look at the proof of my good faith—white flowers. White," he repeated, sneeringly.

"Flowers don't prove a thing. What proves it is the lab test, the porter who came up with me, Mama finding you in the laundry room, the neighbors who've seen us alone in the garden, and Uncle Raffaele's men. You must see that—it's your doing, after all. . . . Would you defend a man like yourself against a minor who had all these proofs? A *handicapped* minor, the certificate calls me, because of my amnesia."

"A gang. I've fallen into the hands of a gang," said Giulio, staring into space. "And, like a fool, I'd already written out a check for your father . . ."

"Yes, and if we were a gang I'd come and tell you these things today, of all days, I suppose . . . If we were, I'd have waited till you'd handed over the check, wouldn't I?"

She was right. She was always right, because, since he had heard her lying so readily, he had begun to desire her again.

"Don't your parents know, then? Aren't you in cahoots with them?"

Ivana raised her chin. "No," she said.

"But you must have told them you're pregnant. . . . Not even that?" He had a moment's satisfaction. "I'm going to tell them right away. I'll tell them it wasn't me, that it must have been some other man, some stranger . . ."

"My God, you're innocent! Someone they don't even know—who might be married, or penniless—do you think they'd believe you? They'd be the first to say it was you."

"Suppose I went to see your uncle at the Viminale instead, and told him everything? I wonder what he'd have to say."

"Like to try?" said Ivana provokingly. "That'd satisfy your curiosity right away. I'll call him up and tell him I've come to your place to tell you I'm pregnant and you can say it's not your fault and you know nothing about it. That's it, isn't it?"

"Of course it is."

"Right." She rose from the armchair, with an effort because of her corset and her narrow skirt, showing her full thighs pressing against the stockings. She went over to the telephone, dialed a number and waited. "Is this the Ministry? Dr. Scarapecchia . . . It's his niece." She looked up at Giulio and they stared at each other, both frightened. "I'm mad," Giulio said to himself, took the receiver from her and put it down.

"There's no point in telephoning, you're right: you're a minor, there are too many witnesses, the child is mine. So . . ." Ivana was staring at him, not knowing what to expect from this sudden change. "I'll make amends: I'll atone for what I've done and marry you as you are. Will that do? I've made up my mind and we won't mention it again. But now undress and get into bed."

He took off the bedspread, uncovering the fine embroidered sheets which Diodato, had hurriedly put on the bed while Giulio tidied up the records in his study. He had seen Diodato running his hand over the cool, well-ironed linen, and had a foretaste of its pleasant coolness on his skin.

"That's what you wanted, isn't it?" he went on. "You wanted me to marry you when you were pregnant by some other man, so that I'd give my name to the child, fathered by this uncle of yours, the policeman . . . Right, then. I'm a cynic. I don't give a damn. . . . God knows how many legitimate kids there are around who aren't their father's kids at all, but the children of amnesia. . . . It's all the same to me. I'll marry you, I'll accept the child. But now let's get into bed. Besides, it's not the first time," he said sarcastically. "It's happened already, you know—in the cupboard, in the laundry room . . ."

"No," said Ivana. "The main thing is, I just don't want to marry you. I'd always say no even in church or in court. No. Haven't you understood?" She stood staring at him, her neck stuck slightly forward, her eyes dark with hatred. "I'm not marrying you, and I'm not going to bed with you. I never will."

"If you don't want to marry me, why do you come telling me the child's mine? What do you want from me? You're mad."

"I'm not mad. I know it isn't yours. We both know, but what does that mean? I've only got to say the word and that makes it yours," she said, with a vulgar bray of laughter. "You followed me home. Who asked you to? I'd told you to get away. I was sick of your trailing after me. But no, you had to introduce yourself. You came on your own. Do you suppose you'd have been welcomed the way you were if you hadn't seemed a gentleman? If you'd been the grocery boy or the butcher's boy, say? You should have tried it then. . . . I said: I don't want him. I'm seventeen. But it was no good. They'd been waiting for you ever since I was born. Debts and disasters—why do you think we were up to our necks in them? To buy me clothes and shoes, to fatten me up . . . oh, no, no, no—I don't want to marry you."

"What do you want, then?"

She stared at him for a moment, and said: "Money."

In the corners and along the edges of the mattress, and under the pillow, the sheets were still cool, but he no longer knew where to turn for relief. It wasn't the vigorous, burning heat of a Roman August, nor the buzzing heat of the cicada-filled pinewoods. The air was heavy and damp, and in the houses, with their closed windows, silent white shadows glimmered on the terraces, hung over the balconies.

Giulio had flung all the windows open, but it was no use. It was useless lying out on the terrace, which faced south and still held the midday heat in its tiles. The flowers were already drooping, and gave out a scent even more revolting than the heat. Giulio couldn't summon up the energy to take them out of the room and throw them away. He had tried everything—a shower, some ice; and from a bottle on the floor beside the bed he kept pouring cologne on his hair and neck, for momentary relief. He was fighting the heat with an obstinacy that stopped him from bursting out into some wild revenge, some violent action that would only make him look ridiculous.

Lying flat on his stomach without a pillow, he shut his eyes, concentrating on his longing to draw a black veil between the day gone by and the day soon coming. It was light already, and he ought to close the shutters. And what's more, tomorrow's Sunday, he thought. Trying to fall asleep, he thought of running water and flocks of sheep, but the heat became more unbearable and kept him awake by buzzing in his ears like a hornet. Why get up? What was the point? He must go back to where he had left off. "What was I doing the Sunday before I met her?" A trip out of town, perhaps, or else nothing in particular; he used to curse the public holidays on which he trailed round with Sylvia and ended up at the movies, standing, with his overcoat slung over his arm. "I wonder if Uncle Raffaele goes to the office tomorrow." He must insist that he had written what was dictated to him, with threats. "With a gun, or knife? By a girl of seventeen . . . Oh come, sir, come . . . In cases like these, if all they want is money you're pretty lucky."

There were two French windows in the walls on either side of his bed, but he could never open them because the wind made a draft through the room. That evening, though, there wasn't a breath of air. Yet, when the veil of daytime mists had lifted, he saw the sky, the infinite stars of the galaxies and gleams of light flashing through space: mad meteors hurled about, shooting stars on the feast of St. Lawrence. Here and there a touch of bright red, like a poppy: these were stars roaring down to earth, the sound of them ever nearer, more persistent and precise. "These reactors are shaking up everything," Giulio thought. "Even this feast day is over and done with." "What will you wish if you see a falling star?" he had asked her. "I'll wish that tomorrow will go well," she had replied. It had gone well: she had acted without wandering off into chatter, without compassion, and with pitiless, childish insolence. Could she be the leader of a gang of juvenile delinquents? The letter, the check and: "Now send for a taxi." The only man who'd treated her as she deserved was the one who'd tied her to a chair when she was a child. He should have done the same: tied her wrists to the back of the bed and shown her everything, everything. "Taxi my eye," he said, and tried to pull off her dress. She was completely enclosed in the corset, as in a shell. It was the corset that made him lose his head: it was a joke, a way of castrating him. "You whore!" he said, and slapped her, then slapped her again: the rage and disgust, the sense of helplessness expressed in that word and action must have painted on his face everything she loathed about a man. "Whore," he repeated, dribbling with rage. Silently, she let the word wash over her before she replied: "Do you know what Papa always says? That there wouldn't be a single whore in the world if there weren't the swine to buy her." She went up to him, as if she was going to attack him: "Why didn't you say it the first day? Why didn't you have the guts to say it? Especially since we were used to taking money. This," she said, indicating the ring, "isn't a present. I earned it. But you wanted playacting as well, as part of the price. You wanted us all to act. And so we have. Papa and Mama were afraid that at some point the curtain would go down and the play would be over. Papa used to say, 'It's a bad sign, the way he's never taken me out in his car,' but not nastily at all. He's in love with you. They're both in love with you."

It was true, as Scarapecchia had said, that there was a kind of love between giver and taker. Between the Scarapecchias and himself—Mr. Broggini, Ivana's fiancé, my daughter's husband, my son-in-law—there was practically a blood relationship. It was like having bought, not just a woman, but a whole family, a class. Later, it might have turned into love, the only love he was capable of. Why not? Besides, now that he had paid—by signing the letter and handing over the check—he didn't want to lose her. He had dashed after her but she had threatened him, saying: "Stop, or I'll scream!" The policeman was still walking up and down, like a sentinel. "And what about that fellow? It was you who warned him, wasn't it?" "Me?" said Ivana. "What have I got to do with it? Uncle Raffaele gets loads of anonymous letters." "Uncle Raffaele! I wish I knew why I've got to make amends for what he's done to you." "What a filthy mind you've got. You say you want to marry me. I say that—after what's happened—I don't want to. You think you're strong because you've got money. Then you shouldn't have fallen for me. One thing or the other, you've lost and you've got to pay for it!"

The heat was unnatural. Something new, some meteorological phenomenon was on its way. Maybe a star had escaped the astronomers' calculations and was silently approaching the earth, like a ball on the green baize of a billiard table. Shall we survive? His father had said: "There's a danger, after the age of forty: you feel tempted to let go, to give up, because you realize you're no longer cruising quietly around in a sheltered bay but that, in the second half of your life, you're out in the open sea and all sorts of things aren't any use to you there—you've just got to steer. That's when things happen to you. . . . Think: suppose you could find some little port, any sort of refuge, in case the boat couldn't manage it? . . . But of course, you're nearly forty yourself. . . . It seems like yesterday you were the funniest little thing—tiny babies aren't ever exactly pretty, are they?—a sort of pink blob. And at Milan three weeks ago Mama said to me: 'Do you know Giulio will be forty at the end of August?' But you'll manage, you're strong," he said, pressing Giulio's arm. At Giardino del Lago, in the shade of the ilexes, the grass grew thick and gleaming. "Anyway, you hang on as long as the flesh does. We're like mushrooms. Everything with roots in the ground can't grow tall—how high's a tree? A tree like this—would it be thirty feet? Anyway, even if you take the tallest—tropical palms, say—for all their efforts they aren't more than a few yards above ground. And as for man! You and I are lucky to be the height we are . . . Mushrooms, that's what. And yet these dwarfs do so much evil, and a tree's so fine. We're the cancer of the earth, the cells that have run wild."

Ivana's flesh was radiantly young, and she was now giving the orders: "Write the letter, and sign it." "Would you care to dictate it?" he asked ironically. "No, you know I'm not much good with a pen." And so at last he wrote the letter he had so often begun in his mind: "Dear Mr. Scarapecchia, An overruling motive—as family motives always are—impels me to break the promise that links me to Ivana and, just as spontaneously, to you and to your wife. The fault, if what is imposed on me can be called a fault, is all on my side. I should like Ivana to keep as a souvenir of me" ("You must put in the word 'present,'" said Ivana who was reading over his shoulder.) *the engagement ring I give her as a present and which,*" etc. etc. He signed, and then sealed the envelope. "Here it is. Is there anything more you want?" "Yes, I want some money." "How much?" "A million." He had given her a check made out to "Bearer," as she had told him to. Uncle Raffaele had certainly coached her well. "Are you going to tell them tonight?" "No, I'll let them have the letter tomorrow." He called for the taxi, and when he went to the door with her, Giulio was not yet suffering. "How do you get out of here, I just can't see . . ." Suddenly the thought struck him that perhaps Ivana was a pathological liar who had invented the whole thing to get money. He laid his hand on the doorknob. "But does he know?" "Know what?" "That it was me." "What do you mean? Of course he knows it, he knew it from the first minute, when I was calling in that bar. It was him I was talking to. I said: 'There's a man here, looking at me.'" "And does he know the rest?" She nodded. "And doesn't he mind?" "No, all he said was: 'Hell, it's always guys like that who've got Ferraris.'" Then Ivana left, he saw the taxi from the window and in it something white that moved as if she were talking to the driver. When the taxi had vanished, Giulio's rage overwhelmed him. He went to look out again: the policeman had gone. Everything was over in less than two hours. He had an empty evening ahead of him. In spite of the heat he shut the shutters and lay down on the bed.

He went out onto the terrace—silence, space, heat. But there was something new, something approaching, those red dots glittering in the night, that tingling feeling. So it must have been at Hiroshima, a few seconds before the explosion. *Giulio Broggini, a lawyer, went out onto the terrace, and had a feeling there was something abnormal in the air, apart from the oppressive heat. Signorina Ivana Scarapecchia was in a taxi: she said that, being shortsighted, she had noticed nothing.* Apart from the letter, the check and the diamond she wore on her finger, she had taken something more valuable with her—the girl in Via Alessandria, and the first woman he had had, in a street behind Piazza Crati. The night, without ghosts, was a huge black screen on which nothing was reflected but a woman's body, the arms raised in self-defense.

He was certain something was happening, and wondered if he should telephone the hospital or else a doctor. He felt suffocated, ill, panic-stricken in the still, soundless air. "Never stay in Rome during August," Sylvia had said the last time they met. "If anything happened, what would you do, where would you go, who would you try and find? Not a soul around. Nothing but *the friendly voice.* You know, that woman who answers the phone for callers who are thinking of suicide. I wonder who it is? A psychoanalyst? A priest?" Giulio had said that if he ever called he would rather have it be a pretty girl. "It must be a record," Sylvia said, and they laughed. Then she went on: "This ghostly life . . . Records answering you on the telephone, records talking to you on the radio. Anyone living alone and not leaving the house could carry on like that for quite a while, and one day he'd go out and find empty streets, closed shutters, closed windows, everything shut—just as it is on an ordinary mid-August Sunday—and then realize he was left alone, the last man on earth."

Later, the telephone rang. "It's Ivana," he said to himself. "Why, Giulio, didn't you realize it was all a joke? Silly as ever! Come on over. Papa's bought a melon." Where was the telephone? He heard the bell ringing in the darkness and couldn't find the instrument. It was still on the floor where Ivana had laid it. The short twisted wire made him kneel. "Hello, hello." (A man's voice. His heart thudded.) "Please, could I speak to signor Diodato?" "He's not in." "Oh, isn't he back yet?" "If you want to leave a message . . ." "Thank you. Please just tell him that Picuti rang."

It was Monday morning in the office, the mid-August holiday week. In the piazzas, the fountains were no longer surrounded by parked cars; Giulio had been able to park outside his office. The thought of Monday was something he had clung to, as he suffered throughout that Sunday.

"Aren't you going away, sir?"

"How can I, with all I've got to do here?" he said, making the staff feel guilty for going away themselves.

"If you like, I can stay on. I don't particularly like this holiday," said the elderly woman on the switchboard. "To me, public holidays are just like any other day."

"You're quite right," Giulio said delightedly. "It's crazy to go dashing around on them."

"Yes," said the woman, a little uncertainly. "But when you start giving them up, you gradually give up everything."

He could, in fact, have stayed away from the office. He couldn't telephone anyone: recorded voices replied, saying the subscriber was away. One of his friends had made a record: "We're at the sea and this is our address . . . Come and see us." Before, Giulio would have thought it an amusing invitation and would have set off, taking some bottles along as a present.

The sirocco had been blowing for the past three days. Giulio trailed around exhaustedly, dragging his feet, paying no attention to his clothes. His warm attractive voice, which usually cheered everyone in the office, had grown benevolently weary.

"You can't go on without taking at least a day's rest," he told the switchboard woman, as she handed him a cup of coffee.

She sighed and told him he was pale. Then she looked up at the gray, sultry sky. "If only it would rain . . ."

It didn't rain. On Tuesday his secretary came in to say goodbye, fresh from the hairdresser and wearing a sundress. "Yes, there's a group of us, all gay, amusing people. Goodbye then, see you in a month, sir."

The office boy sat opposite the switchboard woman, who was knitting, and said: "The great thing is to get off early. At first, of course, you go at a snail's pace, but suddenly the traffic starts flowing and you really get going."

Nobody telephoned. Giulio had tried to contact Ugo, but he was at Riccione until the end of the month. Besides, he wasn't sure that he really wanted to see him. It wasn't that he was ashamed of having given himself away when he was feeling low, but that the worst thing about love is that it drags you out of a routine you've followed for years—friends, work, habits—without ever stopping to think, without judging the friends you've made quite haphazardly, through inertia. Then, when the love affair's over and you have to start again from scratch, you realize

308

there isn't anyone—or hardly anyone—worth the trouble of starting from scratch for.

He was always sleepy, that was something, and it meant he could shorten the days. On the Tuesday after lunch he slept until late, and when he awoke wondered whether to go into the office. Out of a sense of duty toward the switchboard woman, he decided he would. "I had a meeting that went on and on," he said as he arrived. "Is there any mail?"

"Nothing. But, signorina"—and she looked at her note pad—"Scarapecchia telephoned twice."

Giulio turned to go into his office, to avoid signora Tilde seeing his face. "And what did she say?"

"She asked if you'd be coming in later. I said I thought you would, because you hadn't said you wouldn't."

"Did she say she'd call again?"

"No, that was all she said."

Signora Tilde opened the shutters. "I left them closed to keep out the heat." He took some papers from the drawer and pretended to look carefully at them. ("He'll be back," Diodato had said. "And if he comes back after something like this, I'll be in charge. Do you know what I've done, sir? I've taken my wages and got a whole lot of envelopes ready. Each time he comes, I'll give him one. Before, he used to yell at me, but he won't any more.") He must do what Diodato did; when a girl called him up and said, 'A friend of yours gave me this number,' he did it. Ivana wouldn't have minded if he'd done it right from the start, if, instead of sticking to old-fashioned gallantry, he had simply asked: 'How much?' But perhaps, as Ivana had said, he was ready to pay more for the privilege of playacting.

"And now," he said, addressing Uncle Raffaele, "I'd like to know what a man should do when he's offered everything to a woman, even offered to marry her and take on another man's child. I'd really like to meet you face to face and see if you still dare to repeat all those cast-iron clichés of yours, all that nonsense that has nothing to do with reality. I hope you won't tell me it's all my own fault that I'm this way, or that we all know now that our character's formed in the very early years of our life. So the law, in whose name you try to punish, is nothing but an abuse of power, because it deals with man as he is on paper, a convention that takes no account of what he really is or of how unlikely he is to change. You may say that after twenty years in jail men come out quiet and meek and so different that some of them take to making cork boats or doing embroidery. But you don't realize that after twenty years a man's instincts have gone to sleep, and he's like a castrated cat who's given up howling on the roof. I'll come and talk to you, even if you won't answer." The Viminale and its great passages once again, but even when he saw the door of the police chief's office in front of him he couldn't go in; he had cotton-wool legs that caved in under him, the way they do in dreams. After only two days he no longer saw Uncle Raffaele's portrait quite clearly. "We're poisonous toadstools, plants that can rise no higher off the ground than their species allows them to; and, judging from your top half, you can't be very tall. You want to segregate the sexes because you've got a sense of sin rather than a feeling for nature. Otherwise, tell me why your niece . . ."

Ivana was not going to telephone again. In half an hour the office would be shut. Already they are waiting for him to say: "Let's go home." After all, it was the afternoon of August 14, the eve of a public holiday. But he lingered on, hoping to find out what that kiss at the gate had meant, and the way she had looked at him.

The telephone rang: "That young lady's here." "Put her on." "No, she's here. Shall I bring her in?" No time to recover himself before Ivana was at the door. She came in, walking wearily as usual on her high heels, her head poking forward a little. Giulio went up to her and said: "How are you?" naturally enough, and sat her down on the far side of the desk.

"Isn't it hot?" she said, fanning herself with her hand. "It's the sirocco. It'll rain. It always rains in mid-August." He let her talk, looking at her plump young arms, at her puffy, always slightly open mouth. "I was afraid you wouldn't want to see me," she said.

"Why?"

"Well, you know . . ."

"And how's Papa and signora Adelina?"

"All right. They took it well. Papa said that when he'd made inquiries about you and found out who you were he was sure it'd end like this. That when something nice happened to a man like him he was always suspicious. Mama said, 'There's something fishy about all this. You must know some more . . .' and stared and stared at me. I said: 'Are you being funny?' Oh, I'm sorry, you're probably busy and here I am, taking up your time. I just came in for a minute, you see, to tell you it wasn't true."

Breathless, Giulio waited to hear what wasn't true.

"It's not true that I'm pregnant. I wanted to tell you because no one gets anywhere with me in that sort of way. Not even Gigino. I had the analysis report because Gigino's sister, who's expecting a baby, gave me the bottle and I took it to the lab with my own name on it, and so they gave me that paper."

"But why invent all this?"

"Suppose you'd said: 'Call a doctor'? Or else: 'Give me back the ring'? Besides, we'd been to see a priest with that paper, and apparently he'll marry us without telling our parents; otherwise we'd have to get their consent."

"But then why did you accept me, if you preferred this gentleman?"

"Gigino? Gigino's no gentleman. He's the grocer's son. It's not that I prefer him. Gigino's Gigino. We grew up together. He'll be eighteen in six—no, seven days. When you first came I didn't want you to, but Mama told me: 'You can't possibly not like him when you like that good-for-nothing . . .' I explained to her that you were too grown-up, that when you talked to Papa I didn't understand a word."

"You're right," Giulio said. "To you, I'm an old man."

"Well, you did seem old. But later I realized you weren't all that old, it was just the way you dressed and the way you talked so much. The two of us often go to Colle Oppio or Villa Sciarra. They don't know that, at home. We go on a Vespa, with a transistor, and sit around, or else read comics. We're not sentimental. You sentimentalists have had it. Gigino said: 'You say yes, then get out of it and we'll be all set.' "

"Did Mama know about Gigino?"

"Oh, yes. He used to come occasionally to bring the vegetables, and when he phoned, Mama was nice to him because she was scared I'd spoil the whole thing. It depends how you look at things. Take Papa, now: He was so thrilled when he found the money for the co-op men in with your letter . . . Yes, I'd put the money in with your letter, that's what was supposed to pay the doctor; it was nine hundred and thirty he owed but I made it a round figure. Papa was thrilled, but afterward he banged his head with his fist and said you weren't coming again because he'd talked to you about the money. He said: 'I've ruined my daughter's future.' You know Papa, the way he goes in for play-acting . . . So I said: 'Well, send the money back,' but he said no, because if he didn't pay up, he'd find his name in the papers. . . . Papa's always worrying about where money comes from. That shows he's old. Everyone gets into the papers nowadays. People even try to do things that will attract attention so they'll be written about. Yet one evening he actually said: 'I'm going to shoot myself.' " Ivana shook her head: "Gigino always says: 'What can you expect, when your father doesn't know his onions?' It's a handicap we've both got, because his father's the same, he doesn't know the first thing about buying wholesale and all that stuff. And either he'll have to shut up shop someday, or else they'll take it away from him."

Giulio listened, telling himself that there was no reason to suffer: this sort of thing happened to everyone, and he'd been lucky so far to have kept out of trouble over work or women. But gradually, as she went on speaking, the pain became unbearable.

"Papa and Mama are like that: neither fish, flesh nor fowl. I hate them because when I was little they kept saying: cover yourself, you ought to be ashamed, everything was shame and filth. And then I realized they depended entirely on that shame and filth to get themselves nicely settled. . . . We at least know what we want. We want money. Gigino used to tell me: 'We'll never get another chance like this.' "

"Oh, really?" said Giulio, pretending to be amused. ("Suppose I kill her? Suppose I grab her by the neck and bang her head against the wall?")

"We thought of everything. He thought of stealing your Ferrari, but how can you sell a car like that? We thought of taking the keys of your apartment and robbing it when you weren't there. We've read so many books, so many comics . . . But it was no good. It always ended up with our having to kill you. When you bought the ring I was so thrilled because it meant we could fix ourselves up without hurting you."

"What did you care?" said Giulio.

"Well," she said, "that's something else."

"If I'd known how I was bothering you . . ."

"It wasn't a question of bothering me. You see, with Gigino, when we do certain things it lasts five minutes and then we forget them. We get on the Vespa, and go flying off. . . . I can't help laughing at him—he's so skinny, and he's got a tuft of hair sticking up like a rooster. . . . People say all sorts of things about young people nowadays, but it's you old people who think of nothing but that. In your case, it's a fixation. . . . Why did you have to look like that, and make those faces? But gradually, just because it was so old-fashioned, I got to like it. Sometimes I

313

actually decided I'd marry you. And do you know why? Guess. You won't be hurt if I tell you the truth, will you?"

"I know it: you'd have done it because I've got money."

"No, you're wrong. I was sorry for you, because if you weren't married, at your age, it meant you didn't like women. So I thought: 'If I leave him, I wonder how he'll end up.' I even told Gigino and he said: 'Well, marry him, then.' I said: 'There now, you see what you're like? How does marriage come into it? I just said he was alone. Maybe he could come and see us sometimes.' But he said we were just kids and so were our friends, and besides, you'd want to keep touching me, the way you do now. So it was no good. But on Saturday evening it felt so empty at home! Mama kept saying: 'What's up? Why hasn't he come?' I felt so wretched that I turned on her and said you weren't coming again because they'd talked to you about money. . . . And the garden's so gloomy, I can't bear to look at it. Mama's always grumbling that a woman's got to divide herself into four. As far as I'm concerned, I could do with being split into two, half for each of you." She laughed, and there was a trace of her father's vulgarity in her laughter, as well as something perverse. "But how could I be? It wouldn't look right. So we can't meet again."

Giulio thought that, in any case, he had something to help him: the fact that he didn't know where good or evil lay, the fact that he had never tried to find out, the fact that he really was a mushroom, a plant, a tree not far above the ground.

"Well," said Ivana, "I just wanted to tell you this, and now I must go, or else . . ."

"Else Uncle Raffaele . . ." said Giulio, laughing.

"Ah, I knew there was something else I had to tell you. . . . Uncle Raffaele's dead."

"Dead!" said Giulio. "When?"

"Oh, years ago. After the war . . . It was Mama's idea. One day she read in the paper that Raffaele Scarapecchia was a big

noise and she said: 'Rosario, this is going to make our fortune.'
Papa said: 'Why? He's no relation.' And Mama said it didn't
matter, on the contrary, if he'd been a relation there'd have been
nothing to hope for, as there never was from relations: we could
say he was, that was what mattered. Papa said: 'Suppose he finds
out?' Mama said: 'How could he find out about people like us?
Besides, wasn't your brother called Raffaele? And wasn't he a
policeman? Well, then . . .' It was she who told those men from
the co-op . . . Then, when you came, Papa didn't want her to
tell you, he said we'd had trouble enough over her bright idea,
but she begged him: 'For the last time. For your daughter's sake.
A man like that won't marry her unless he's afraid . . .' Oh, she
nagged him so!"

"But when you telephoned the Ministry . . ."

"I thought, would a southerner be in his office at five o'clock
on Saturday, August the tenth? But they told me to wait."

"Were you scared?"

"No, I thought you'd be scared and tell me to drop it. After
what you knew about Aunt Giovanna . . ."

"Oh, of course, there was Aunt Giovanna . . ."

"No, that part's true. She was a sister of Papa and Uncle
Raffaele, the man in the picture. You know, truth and lies are so
jumbled up . . ."

"I'm sorry you've had to put on all this playacting for me."

"No, we're quite used to it. How could we have managed, if
not? Mama always says: 'You've got to be prepared to do anything.' And they enjoy it. If they didn't have this playacting,
what would they have?"

"You acted beautifully—at least toward me."

She smiled: "I told you I used to act in plays at the convent
. . . and besides, I grew quite fond of my part. I felt I really
was an old-fashioned girl. Even our engagement seemed real to
me: all you have to do is convince yourself, you know. And
weren't you acting, too, to get me to bed?"

They were at the door. "Listen, Giulio," she said. "Maybe you understand why I never wanted you to kiss me, because of Gigino. But that evening at the gate, it wasn't because you'd promised the money to Papa. The money had nothing to do with it. You did understand, didn't you?"

Giulio looked at her. She was lovely, very lovely. He took her in his arms and pressed her to him. "Yes, I did understand . . ." He drew away. "Go, you'd better go now."

"Gigino's downstairs. If you want to see him, look out of the window. But you know him . . . he's the policeman who was standing outside in the street last Saturday. That really was tough, much harder than selling the ring . . . getting the uniform, I mean . . . A friend of his, one who always plays an Ethiopian slave at Caracalla in the summer, gave him an address. . . . Did you see how funny he looked? It was his idea. He said: 'If I don't stand there and can't come up when I want to, I won't let you go up.'"

Giulio opened the door: he had to send her away and could no longer control his voice. They crossed the hall. "This way, please, signorina, I'll show you out." Ivana glanced at signora Tilde and the office boy. On the landing Giulio rang for the elevator.

"Well, goodbye, Giulio, and good luck. . . . Oh dear, I'm really sorry . . . but it didn't cost you more than a little money, did it? Nothing more?"

"Of course. That's all."

"If you look out you'll see the car we've bought," she said, getting into the elevator. Then turning, she added, pleased and smiling: "It's red."

About the Author

Alba de Céspedes is one of Italy's most popular
novelists. Her books have also met with wide success
in several European, Scandinavian and Latin American
countries as well as in England, Greece, Yugoslavia
and Czechoslovakia. A number of her stories have
been dramatized for theatrical, television, radio and
other productions which have appeared in Italy, France,
Canada and Japan. A dramatization of La Bambolona,
produced in Italy, was released last year.

Alba de Céspedes, a Roman-born Italian writer,
has close connections with Cuba. Her grandfather,
a celebrated Cuban patriot, was the first president
of the Cuban Republic. She is married to an Italian
diplomat and currently divides her time between
Paris, Rome and Taormina.

Cespedes, Alba de
La bambolona.

2-71